EIGHT YEARS OF FEBRUARY

ELIZABETH GARLAND

ZZYYZX PUBLISHING

Eight Years of February / Elizabeth Garland - 1st ed.

Library of Congress Control Number: 2020917448

Ebook ISBN 978-0-9600923-7-6

Paperback ISBN 978-0-9600923-6-9

For my grandchildren, Cordy, Kymbal, Sedona and Vivianne. - native Minnesotans all.

A lot happened after Little House on the Prairie...

EIGHT YEARS OF FEBRUARY

A Novel by Elizabeth Garland

PART I

THE FARM

1

St. Paul, Minnesota 1996

"Take care of your teeth."

Not the most auspicious last words ever uttered but not without merit, either. After all, someone who had lived ninety-five plus years and still had all his teeth might be worth listening to on the subject. I filed the words away as simply the output of fading synapses...a brain easing itself out of existence. And then, I couldn't stop thinking about those words or the man who had said them.

I hadn't known him long, not really. He was almost ninety-one when I met him. His middle-aged son would bring me by to chat with him as we sat and waited for his coffee to perk or the TV dinner to heat in the microwave that sat on a rickety table in the drab little bungalow's kitchen. Dwight, my gentleman caller in those days, dutifully tended to his dad's needs after his mother's stroke had confined her to a nursing home over by Lake Phalen. After a late afternoon "supper" of a frozen Banquet dinner and a cup of weak coffee, Dwight would take his father out to the home for his daily visit. In the four years Dolores was confined there, Raymond only missed sitting with her on the days of major blizzards or treacherous ice storms. When he couldn't make it, Dolores hardly noticed, but Raymond would be overcome with guilt for abandoning his sweetheart. It was poignant and sad to behold his pain and also a bit ironic. Dolores was sixteen years younger than Ray but, like Jack Sprat, he could eat no fat and she could eat no lean. Her cholesterol was sky high and had plugged up the blood supply to her brain. Toward the end of her fourth year at the home, Dolores heaved herself out of bed in the middle of the night to confront her roommate about a hairbrush that Dolores just knew had been pilfered from her drawer. In doing so, she tripped on her slippers and tumbled to the floor, hitting her head on the corner of the bed frame. The last thing she saw in the dim light of the call button hanging down by the side of the mattress was the damned hairbrush lying under her bed. Her concluding thought was that being hateful never had worked out for her and now it would be her final undoing.

In our chats around the forlorn kitchen table, sipping instant coffee and snacking on saltine crackers, Raymond Saxby told me that until he met Dolores, he had given up on the idea that the perfect girl would ever come his way and if she did, that she would have any interest in him. He said he had never had much luck with girls; to his mind, he'd never had much luck with anything at all. He supposed he started out with a strike against him when he was born on Friday, April 13, 1900. At the age of four, he broke his mother's hand mirror, and the licking he got for that only validated what everyone said about bad luck. The streak continued from there, following Ray through most of his adult years. When he had seen Dolores standing in the Como Park Conservatory admiring the winter roses, he knew his luck would finally change.

Hastings, Minnesota 1907

The Saxby farm was about a mile outside of the town of Hastings,

Minnesota. The settlement had the advantage of sitting on the Mississippi River, close to its confluence with the St. Croix. The town itself had prospered since the mid-1800s, when the Hastings and Dakota Railroad was built, allowing area farmers to transport their commodities north by both river and rail to St. Paul, Minneapolis, and the world beyond. Other rail lines connected Hastings with the bustling town of Stillwater on the St. Croix River, a major hub for the Minnesota logging industry. Earl Saxby, Ray's grandfather, had come to the Hastings area from Pennsylvania in 1870 as a labor recruit on the H and D Railroad. The railroad had the grand plan of extending the line all the way west to the Pacific Ocean. Earl figured he'd work his way out to Seattle with the construction crew, but the H and D never made it that far west and Earl Saxby never made it past Hastings. At a Fourth of July Parade in 1871, Earl met Lillian Anderson. Earl was a rangy young man with a shock of dark brown hair and eyes the color of fine whiskey. When he laid those whiskey eyes on Lillian, he had enough experience to know that he had happened upon the real reason that the state of Minnesota had beckoned him.

She was a flaxen-haired waif of seventeen when he spotted her, waving a flag and giggling with a group of other young women. By the time the fireworks lit up the summer sky that night, Earl and Lillian knew that fate had intervened to weave their lives together. By Christmas, they were married. When Lillian's widower father died unexpectedly while singing a hymn during the Easter church service the following spring, Earl took over the farm, a modest spread of 160 acres within walking distance to town.

Farming had never been of interest to Earl Saxby. His family had been laborers and carpenters. On the rare occasions when he did think about the possibility of working a farm, he never had enough money to consider owning land, and tenant farming had no appeal for him. Having 160 acres fall into his lap, days before his twenty-fifth birthday, changed his perspective on agrarian life; he would learn what he needed to build a life for himself and Lillian, who was expecting their child in the fall. He consulted Lillian's uncles and cousins about crops and husbandry. In return, Earl helped them with carpentry chores.

Most of all, he listened to Lillian, who had a mind so full of facts on the subject of rural life that she was a walking Farmers' Almanac. He marveled at how such a tiny, young girl could know so much about crop rotation or the dehorning of cattle. He watched as she poured cottonseed oil into the ears of livestock to drive out the ticks, and he learned from her how to put a twitch on a horse's lip to subdue it when it needed treatment for founder. She walked him through puncturing a sheep in the gut to relieve it from bloat. She showed him how to slam a board between two warring hogs and talked him through pulling a calf from its mother with a rope and a pulley. He supposed she had learned all this out of necessity when her older brother died at fifteen, leaving her alone with her father to manage the farm.

The farm was laid out in grids of corn, barley and alfalfa, with a modest white frame house in the middle. The house itself was small; the kitchen, parlor and good-sized bedroom occupied the main level. Up a narrow wooden staircase was a small bedroom, with a sewing alcove tucked under a sloped ceiling. Lillian's father had built it himself with the help of his brothers and a few godly men from his church. The house had no ornamentation, but like a plain woman with a strong body and a keen mind, it made up for its lack of beauty with comfort and convenience. While the number of rooms were limited, they were each spacious. The kitchen had room for a large table and a black iron stove that always had a kettle warming for coffee. Its whitewashed walls were lined with shelves for tins and boxes, and a pine cabinet with a porcelain top and a flour bin made it the perfect place to prepare baked goods and cold meals. The parlor had large windows that looked out onto the fields. One year the view might be barley or alfalfa waving in the breeze; other times, the silky tops of tall corn stalks would limit the horizon from the windows as late summer closed in on fall. Earl's favorite structure was the barn: fifty feet long and thirty feet wide, sided in twelve-inch planks and painted a dull red. Earl never tired of standing in its center and taking in the smell of sweet hay and horse hide. When his son Everett came along, Earl built the boy a cradle from some old flooring lumber he found in the loft of the barn. This was the boy's "barn-bed." Earl brought the baby out to sit with him every afternoon while Lillian prepared supper in the house. The baby boy would lay in his rustic cradle and look up into the air above him to see motes of straw dance before his eyes. Earl had never been happier in his life than when he watched his boy reach out to try to capture bits of the farm in his tiny hands. When Everett grew and married the town beauty, Leona Bright, Earl dragged out the old barn-bed for his grandson, Leon, and then later for Raymond, who managed to fall out of it while reaching for a passing cat on his first birthday. That mishap left the baby with a gash on the back of his head where, from then on, the hair never did grow right. One thing or another always seemed to go wrong for little Raymond Saxby.

Leona Bright, her mother and older sister had come to Minnesota from Illinois to live with relatives after an accident left Leona's mother a widow. They lived in a boarding house owned by Leona's Aunt Mabel, who welcomed the women not so much out of familial love as for the domestic labor they could provide. Leona's mother and aunt were constantly bickering, just as they had when they were girls living with their parents back in Illinois. Never a day went by that Leona's Aunt Mabel didn't point out to her mother how destitute they would be if she hadn't saved them with her offer to let them live in a single room in the boarding house. Leona longed for the day when she could escape the shrill arguing of four females who each harbored long-standing resentments and wounded pride. Her opportunity came when she discovered that she was carrying Everett Saxby's child. A hurry-up wedding was worth the humiliation to Leona if it meant leaving the chaos of the boarding house behind.

By 1907, Leona and Everett were the sole managers of the Saxby farm. Granddaddy Earl had died of lung disease a few years earlier, and Lillian used a small inheritance from her own family to move into town, leaving the farm to her oldest son and his wife. Unlike Earl's early days of farming, Everett had started his life in a barn and knew all he needed to keep the operation running smoothly. If something unforeseen popped up, he had his indomitable mother to advise him. At fifty-three, Lillian was spry and wiry, with a crown of gold and silver-streaked hair bunched up into a tidy bun that topped a head filled with an encyclopedia of agronomic information.

Leona found farm life with Everett to her liking. She enjoyed the long days of hard work, knowing that she was working for an existence of her own making. She enjoyed her nights tucked into bed beside Everett even more. She had never set sight on such a dash-fire man; she didn't see him so much as she felt him in her belly when she gazed upon his form. His broad shoulders and narrow waist were carried about on fine, muscled legs that propelled him with a natural swagger. When she and Everett married in 1893, he had a full head of sandy hair. His hazel eyes looked as if the amber of Earl's and the blue of Lillian's had been poured together to give him his own unique ocular color. It nearly killed Leona with desire when he winked his approval of her daily doings around the farm. The one misgiving she had about a Minnesota summer was that she had to wait so long for the days to end before she could fall into bed with Everett. Their son, Leon, arrived in 1894, about seven months after their wedding. The ladies at church busied themselves counting months on their fingers, but Leona never let their disapproval diminish the joy she felt from bearing Everett's child.

It took six more years for Raymond to arrive. Several more children had dribbled away from Leona's body during those long years, so Raymond was a gift that defied his Friday the thirteenth birth date. Everett nicknamed him Lucky, but the name didn't stick. Raymond had no luck with luck. The boy had the jagged, hairless scar on his head from his fall as an infant. When he was five, he tumbled from the back of the wagon while rough-housing with his brother and knocked out his two front teeth. He seemed unable to write a single letter of the alphabet without spinning it backwards, turning his name into a hieroglyphic scratched on paper with a pencil. He was constantly losing his meager possessions, and the one time he had gotten to eat ice cream, something he had begged his mother to try, he promptly vomited it on the church lawn and the minister's shoes. His brother Leon had taken to calling Raymond the luckless runt. Some version of that moniker stuck to Ray all through his boyhood.

Leona would often take her two tow-headed boys into Hasting with her when she needed to fetch groceries that couldn't be produced on the farm. Everett made her a little trolley with parts from an old perambulator he had found discarded in the basement of his mother's cottage. With it, she could haul a sizable amount of goods home from town with little effort. What she couldn't fit in the trolley, she had Leon and Ray carry for her. On one such day, she told the boys that she had to stop in to see Dr. Becker before she did the shopping and that they could amuse themselves for an hour or so while she kept this appointment and picked up supplies. She warned them to stay out of trouble. Excited by this rare interlude of freedom, Ray and his older brother worked their way down to the banks of the Mississippi River to try out a pole Leon had fashioned from a discarded curtain rod and some waxed twine. A bent nail at the end of the twine served as a hook. While Leon practiced whipping the line out into the eddy swirling by the bank, young Ray sat on a rock at the river's edge and worked off his new shoe, which was really an old shoe that had been well-worn by Leon. For the entire hike down to the river something in that damned shoe had been eating into the soft flesh right under his big toe. As Ray pulled off the shoe, he was distracted by the sight of a wagon drawn by two rambunctious bays making its way down the spiral bridge that joined Hastings with whatever was on the other side. Ray had never been there--the other side. When one of the bays reared its head and made a fuss, a startled Ray lost his grip on the shoe and had to watch as it plopped into the river and began its journey to the Gulf of Mexico.

"Jesus Christ, Ray! You better get that or Ma's going to kill you!"

Leon was always giving Ray advice.

Ray teared up, as a seven-year-old does, and began to consider his options for retrieving his shoe. He grabbed a long branch he found laying on the shore and ran down-river to head off the now sinking oxford. Climbing onto a rock that hung out just a bit over the river, the boy reached with the branch as far as he could, hoping to snag his wayward footwear. Next thing he knew, he too, was headed south on the river's current and would have been in Lake Pepin before he knew it if Leon hadn't screamed for help. The man in the wagon had seen what was happening to Raymond; he'd stopped his horses on the bridge and went running for the boys, all the while swinging a heavy rope over his head. The man let the one end of the rope fly out to just beyond where Ray was flailing in the water, clutching the branch to stay afloat. Despite the current, the boy managed to grab the rope and get himself pulled to safety.

Ray considered getting saved a pretty lucky thing. Still, all in all, it was a typically lousy day. His clothes were wet and smelly, his shoe was gone, his brother was still laughing at him, and his mother had tanned his hide for just about everything that happened that day. Then she'd kissed him for not being dead.

"Leon!" Leona shouted. "I should tan you, too, for not keeping an eye on your little brother. That child could have drowned. I can't let you boys out of my sight for the five minutes it takes to buy some flour without you getting yourselves into trouble. You're old enough to know better, Leon," his mother told him. It was a phrase he heard often in those days. She said this to Leon while she rummaged through the old trunk in the room the boys shared. Ray had been left down in the kitchen, scrubbing potatoes for penance. "I could have sworn there was more old shoes in here." Leona tossed blankets and sweaters onto the worn pine floor. Rooting through the ancient refuse, she pulled on something hard and leather at the bottom of the trunk. With a mighty yank, a pair of old boots broke free from the tangle of junk, sending Leona about to the floor herself.

"Land's sake. Here they are!" She hoisted the battered boots by their laces in a show of victory.

"Those won't fit him, Ma." Leon was half hiding behind his bed, hoping his mother would agree with him that those boots didn't even bear considering for his brother.

She held the boots to the light of the window. "Well, these will have to do for now," she said. "There's no money for extras until after the next harvest." When she turned the second boot over in her small, rough hands, she saw what had Leon so worried. "Oh, for Christ's sake, Leon! What have you gone and done to these boots?"

"I done nothin', Ma." Leon knew his mother would see right

through the empty protest, just as she could see right through the side of the boot where Leon had cut out a big chunk of leather to use for making a really fine slingshot.

"You brainless little guttersnipe," his mother said to him in that sad, disappointed voice that always made him feel full of shame.

"Ma! I swear I didn't do it," cried Leon, knowing the lie would get him nothing but more trouble.

"This family has to scrimp and save for everything we've got and we don't got money for shoes right now, even used-up ones like these." Leona threw the old boots back into the trunk. They landed with a thud that was almost as loud as the heartbeat in Leon's ears. "Go get the knife you used on these, boy."

Leon swallowed hard and went to the glove box he kept under his side of the bed. He pulled the box out and gently lifted it to the top of the mattress. Inside was his prized possession, a hand-me-down Barlow knife from his Granddaddy Earl.

"See there, Leon. If you hadn't been the one to cut up them boots, you would have said, "What knife?" Leona had used her exceptional interrogation skills to trip him up. She was a master at that. "Get it out of the box," she directed. Leon complied. He reluctantly offered the bone-handled beauty to his mother.

"I'm not the one who's going to use it, son." Leona shook her head just slightly in that "look what you've made me do" sort of way. "Take that knife out to the apple tree and cut me off a switch to use on your backside," she ordered. "Then meet me on the porch, you hear?"

This brought a new kind of fear to Leon. He had never been asked to participate in his own punishment before, and he wasn't sure if it was a good thing or a bad thing.

The boy slowly made his way down the stairs and through the kitchen, where little Raymond kept his head down and smirked to himself at his brother's predicament. Leon slammed the door behind him. He cautiously approached the old tree, one that produced just enough misshapen green apples each year to make about two and a half pies, and searched for a switch that might cause him the least possible damage. He selected a thin, pliable length that looked like it would inflict minimal pain. By now, his mother had come out to the porch and was standing with her hands on her hips and the look in her eye that she might have if she were supervising a chain gang.

"Oh, for God's sake. You call that a proper switch?" Leona said these words with a measured calm that sounded sinister to Leon. He was accustomed to his mother's "more bark than bite" routine, and this new approach had him off kilter. "Throw that worthless, puny little thing down and try again." His mother never raised her voice or changed her expression of stony control as she rejected his first branch.

Leon, who prided himself on never crying like his sniveling little brother, felt the unmistakable sting of salty tears forming in his eyes, mostly the left one, and he ran the back of his wrist over his left eye like he had something in it to keep the tear from running down his cheek. He was pretty sure his mother knew what he was doing, but he steeled himself to staunch the tears so she at least wouldn't have the satisfaction of making him cry like a baby.

"Go ahead. Get me one that's going to work." She motioned Leon back to the tree. This time he cut off a switch about the diameter of a small wooden spoon handle, and he made sure it was green enough to have a little give but dry enough that it wouldn't whip too much and make matters worse. He made his way to the porch and handed his mother the switch. She looked it up and down and swung it through the air a time or two. It sang a high, bright note as it slashed the summer sky. She brought it up over her head, then whacked it down full-force onto the porch railing like she was beating a dirty rug, causing the stick to splinter in her hands. She threw it down in disgust.

"Again. Not good enough, Leon."

At this point, Leon could no longer fight the storm of tears that was beginning to overwhelm his eyes. They dribbled down his face, and he felt his tongue instinctively suck them from the vertical furrow right below his nose. They tasted of the bitter salt of shame, more for the fact that he was crying than for the crime of boot mutilation. Leona sauntered off the porch and came to stand under the tree. She silently motioned for Leon to hand over the knife, and she set about cutting a fine, green limb off the tree, stripping it of feeder branches as she worked. When she finished her whittling, she held a stick about three feet long and as thick as a fireplace poker. She ran her hands up and down the shaft and nodded to herself to validate its perfection.

"Now this is a proper switch, Leon." She closed the knife and handed it back to her son, who was unable to see what she was talking about through his blurred vision. He burned with humiliation, his face red and snotty from blubbering. He hung his head in resignation and steadied himself for the pain to come.

"Go on in and clean up," Ma ordered Leon. The boy looked up to see his mother lean the stick against the porch steps and head into the kitchen. Leon couldn't believe his eyes, or his ears. He realized now that his mother had no intention of physically punishing him with that damned switch. Her goal the entire time had been to bring him to his knees with the psychological manipulation of a practiced inquisitor. She had won this round, but Leon swore to himself that he wouldn't fall for such an evil trick again. With a hard stare and a face full of runny mucus, Leon marched into the house after his mother. Behind her back, he reached out and cuffed Ray upside the head for being the actual cause of this mess in the first place. Raymond wisely stifled any inclination to yell at his brother. The look in Leon's eyes said it all.

* * *

Little Raymond's luck wasn't all bad, depending on how you looked at it. He still had one shoe and the intact boot from the trunk just happened to be a shoe for the other foot. He supposed that was a break, of sorts. The bad luck part was that he now had to wear the mismatched, missized footwear all that fall and winter. He knew before he set foot in school at the start of the fall term that it would not go well for him, but he had underestimated the derision of his classmates. He was called poor, gimpy, slew-footed, hobo, lame, club-footed---you name it. When Christmas came, they called him Tiny Tim. Only the "poor" designation was accurate. Given shoes that fit, or even bare-footed, Ray could run like greased lightning. But now his gait was all off. He had to raise his right leg higher off the ground when he ran to keep himself from tripping over the two inches of extra length in the boot. He stuffed an old rag into the front toe space to fill in the void, but that had very little effect on his overall ability to walk like a normal person. All that school year, Ray languished on the sidelines at recess because no one wanted the club-footed gimp on their team.

The child didn't fare much better at home. Since the "switch incident," his brother had acted a little different in a way that troubled Ray. Leon seemed to hold his little brother responsible for every difficult moment of his life. If Leon failed an arithmetic test, it was because Ray had distracted him when he tried to study. If Leon tracked mud into the house, it was because Ray had thrown his ball into the muck. If Leon got caught stealing candy from the mercantile, it was because Ray had begged him to do it. Raymond couldn't understand how he could be causing his brother so much grief when his brother had barely spoken to him since that late August day. And he knew for a fact that he had never asked his brother to steal for him. That was an outright lie. The young boy accepted that lying was necessary from time to time, just for survival, but his brother was now more committed to lying than telling the truth.

"Why do you lie all the time?" Ray asked his brother. They were walking home from school on a dark November afternoon. The gray sky was spitting tiny shards of ice into their faces as they leaned into the wind. It would likely snow by morning, bringing on the long, brutal winter that always visited Minnesota early and stayed too long.

"Because I hate the truth," replied Leon. Ray was surprised that his brother had bothered to answer him. He'd thought it was a rhetorical question when he'd asked it--just a thought that had been in his mind and had slipped out of his mouth with the steam of his breath. He reckoned that the truth wasn't always pleasant, but he couldn't understand hating it.

A sharp gust of ice-flecked air blew the scarf away from Ray's face. His ears were numb and he knew that they would sting like hell when they thawed in the house once he and Leon made it home. With his hands in bulky mittens, the child did his best to pull the scarf back into place. Leon looked down at his brother and shook his head. "You're such a worthless little runt," remarked Leon. To Ray's surprise, his brother stopped by his side and considered the young-ster's chapped face and bone white ears. Leon brought his own right mitten to his mouth and pulled it off his hand with his teeth. He stuffed it under his opposite arm pit, then did the same with the other chopper.

"Come here, kid."

Ray stood silently in front of his brother as Leon worked the old muffler back around his head and ears. Leon fumbled a bit himself, trying to keep his own mittens from falling out from where they were clamped against his sides.

"Jesus, Ray. This thing is as disgusting as you are. It's full of crusty, old, frozen spit--and snot, too, I think."

Leon's face registered a degree of distaste for the task, but he helped his brother all the same. For the first time in months, Ray felt a warmth from within. A tiny spark of happiness deep inside started to light that dark place in his heart where he'd been sure his brother's love would never be seen again. He could get by with frozen ears as long as he could use them to listen to his brother after all the months of silence and dismissal.

"That better?" asked Leon. Raymond gave Leon a smile he couldn't see with the scarf wrapped over his mouth, but Leon could tell the younger boy was smiling from the crinkle around his eyes. Ray nodded his answer.

The boys walked on companionably, Leon a couple of steps in the lead but close enough for Ray to feel that he wasn't being left behind. "Hey, Leon," the boy called to his brother's back.

"What?" Leon kept walking ahead. The bitter sleet was coming harder now and at an angle that nearly paralleled the ground. The wind was sharp and fierce, pushing big, dark clouds over the dried stubble of the cornfields and making each step a hardship. Ray was thankful for the wad of wool he'd scalped from the hindquarter of an old ewe and had stuffed into the front of that sorrowful boot on his right foot. Those toes were much more insulated than the ones in his real shoe. He was pretty sure he wouldn't lose those toes to frostbite.

And since it was just a small patch he'd sheared out, he wasn't worried about the old ewe, either. Ray tried again.

"Leon. Can I ask you something?"

"What is it, runt?" The older boy slowed his pace, allowing Ray to catch up to him. Fat drops of frozen rain were beating down on the top of Leon's canvas jacket, sounding for all the world like box elder bugs banging into a closed window. Leon puffed into his mitten-covered hands and applied the warmth to his own ears where the flaps of his cap were flying away from his head in the wind.

"So, what'd you want to ask me?" Leon was growing impatient with any conversation that was keeping him from getting out of this cold. He was tempted to ignore his brother and race ahead to the shelter of the house, but something about Ray's voice rooted him to his place. If he died of pneumonia, it would be his brother's fault.

Raymond had been thinking about his question while they walked along. He wanted an answer so he could figure out in his mind how he could stay on Leon's good side. If lying was what kept Leon going, then he needed the rationale for why his brother had adopted such a strategy.

"I want to know why you said you hate the truth? Truth is supposed to be the best thing ever, and I'm sort of worried that you're going to go to hell because you lie so much now." There. He had said it. He was prepared to have Leon smack him on his icy head for calling him out as a liar, but Leon surprised him again by throwing his arm around his shoulders and pulling him along.

"This is how it is, Ray. Everybody lies all the time. Me, I got to lie to myself to get through each and every day. I got to tell myself that we're not really poor when I know damned well that we are and likely always will be. I got to tell myself that I'm going to get out of this lousy, nowhere town someday when that's probably not going to happen, either. The truth that you and me live is just plain ugly, and if I can lie my way out of it, then that's what I aim to do. I'm going to lie my way to something better."

Raymond had never thought that their lives were quite so desperate that they should be discarded in favor of some half-baked, make-believe existence. And that still didn't explain some of the more specific lies Leon told, such as the one about the stolen candy. Why did Leon have to include him in his philosophical pursuits?

"Ma says we can pray for a better life. That God and Jesus will help us." Ray thought that this must be true since his Sunday school teacher, his grandma and pretty much every adult he knew seemed to back up what his mother always said about praying.

"Well then, why doesn't Jesus or his Old Man bother to answer those prayers? I think God is just another big lie, like Santa Claus." Leon realized too late that he had spilled the beans to his brother who, even now, when it was still November, had been writing and rewriting letters to Santa Claus. Sometimes, Leon forgot that the boy was only seven.

"Well, not like Santa Claus," Leon corrected. "Santa Claus is probably real. I mean, all the presents sort of prove it." Leon hoped he had shut down any doubt in Ray's mind. Every kid should get the Santa myth for at least as long as he was missing his front teeth. He wasn't going to get into the tooth fairy thing right now.

"Yeah," said Ray. "Santa is real, for sure. But why did you lie about me and the candy? I never asked you to steal anything for me. Besides, aren't you scared about going to hell?"

"I had to lie about the candy because I got caught. Nobody's going to get over-mad at me if they think I'm just trying to be kind to my little brother," Leon reasoned. "And hell is probably just another made up thing, like God. Just a way to scare people into doing stuff and keeping them in line."

Raymond considered this, and he could see the wisdom in Leon's words, if maybe not the God and hell part. People do tend to go a little easier on you if they think you're just being nice, even if it causes a problem. When Ray was still almost a baby, he had gone out to the chicken coop and scattered marbles in the pen, pretending he was giving the chickens a tasty treat. His father had come in from feeding the stock the next morning, holding a dead chicken by its feet. He said that three of the chickens had keeled over dead during the night and when he cut this one open to investigate the cause, he found a nice, fat cat's eye marble choking up its craw. Ray had cried and spurt out that he had only been trying to feed them. He didn't want to kill them. He loved the chickens, even the rooster. Nothing bad had happened to him for that confession because, as his father said, he'd been trying to help.

"OK, Leon. That makes some sense, I guess. But next time, you ought to at least give me some of the candy. I deserve something for not ratting on you and that way, you would only be lying half as much."

Leon laughed out loud at his brother's logic. He supposed the little guy wasn't such a pain in the ass after all.

When the boys finally slogged home, it was almost dark. Dark comes early to the autumn sky somewhere as far north as Minnesota, but on this particular afternoon it was the heavy rain clouds that meant that the oil lamps were burning when the boys walked in the door. Both their mother and father were sitting at the farm table that took up so much of the kitchen. They were each sipping from a cup of coffee, and Raymond figured his father was inside at this time of day because of the weather. Either that, or someone important had died. His father didn't usually wander in until suppertime, but he had come in early when they'd lost Granddaddy Earl.

"Hello, boys. Bet you're glad to be in out of that rain." This was unusually chatty for their father, so both Ray and Leon shared a quick meeting of their eyes, signaling "oh, oh" without saying it.

Leona got up and went to the stove to stir the steaming kettle sitting over a low flame. She lifted the pot away and carefully poured two mugs of brown liquid. The smell wafting from the metal mugs was rich and sweet. "Here you go, boys. This should warm you up after that long walk home in the cold." She placed an aromatic mug of hot chocolate in front of each child. Ray appreciated that they were getting such a treat on a regular day, but it only confirmed his suspicions...something bad was going to happen. Mounting anxiety made him forget about the throb in his thawing ears. Leon accepted his mug with a skeptical glance at his brother.

"Thanks, Ma," said Leon.

"Yeah. Thanks." Ray thought he should follow his brother's lead in this situation.

"Boys. Your Pa and I want to tell you some exciting news."

"I must be wrong," thought Raymond. "Maybe it's not bad news at all. Bad news isn't usually exciting." Everett just nodded along as Leona smiled brightly at her sons.

"We're going to have a new member in our family soon," said their mother.

Leona darted a conspiratorial glance at Everett. Her brown eyes sparkled at him, and he rewarded her with a signature wink. He couldn't help thinking what a lucky man he was to have such a woman in his life. Now past thirty, Leona was still a startling beauty. Her long dark hair framed a perfect oval face with full lips and high cheekbones. Only the soft lines around her mouth and eyes bore any hint of the hard life she had led since she turned nineteen and joined her star with Everett Saxby. She focused her open smile on her sons to invite them in on the secret. Leon stiffened in his seat and kept his eyes glued to the steam rising from his mug.

Raymond looked confused. "When was this person coming and where was this person going to sleep?" he questioned in his head.

"When?" asked Ray.

"Who is a better question," put in Leon.

"Boys, your Ma and I are having a baby in the spring. Right about planting time so we're gonna need your help a bit more around here," said their father. "Your ma will need to take it easy now and then for the next few months."

Leon erupted. "You call that exciting news?" He angrily pushed his mug back to the center of the table and got to his feet. "That's about the stupidest thing I've ever heard of. You and Ma are too old to have another kid. This is just plain sickening."

Leon was clearly not happy about this new brother or sister. He had just now gotten used to the one he had.

"Well," said his mother, "it seems God has different ideas for our family than you do, Leon."

"Is this really true?" asked Raymond. Both his parents just nodded and smiled like idiots.

Leon turned to Ray and held his arms out from his sides in an expansive gesture. "See what I mean about the truth? And about God, too, for that matter?" Leon cried to his brother. With that as his parting remark, Leon stormed up the stairs. All Raymond could think about in that moment was whether or not Leon would get mad if he finished the hot chocolate he had shoved away.

"I'm not going to let a thirteen-year-old kid act that way in this house," said Everett to Leona. He too had gotten to his feet and was actively working to pull his heavy leather belt from his work trousers. He wasn't subtle in his punishments. When he got out his belt, he always used it.

"Oh, let him be for a bit," said Leona. "He needs some time to think things over, is all. He'll come around. You'll see." Everett gave Leona a hug around her shoulders and kissed her lightly on top of her head.

Ray didn't like seeing his parents express physical affection, but it was also reassuring. He reasoned that at least they weren't likely to fight right then and Leon was safe for the moment, too. The idea of someone else besides him and Leon taking up room here in this little house was too much for Raymond to contemplate so he went back to thoughts of hot chocolate and slowly worked Leon's mug over to the mat in front of him.

* * *

Leon never did come around as Leona had predicted he would. The more his mother's belly grew, the more distant from his family Leon became. It was almost as if the hideous, pregnant bulge was physically pushing Leon out the door. Many afternoons, Ray walked home from school alone because Leon had taken to skipping class to smoke cigarettes and play cards with the old men at the feed store. Leon was apparently welcome there because they didn't have candy to steal, and they liked that he could run errands for them in the cold before sweeping up spilled seed at the end of the day. Mr. Hanson paid Leon in smokes, and lately Leon seemed to prefer those to sweets.

"Soon as you turn fourteen, boy, you can work here for a wage," Mr. Hanson told Leon.

"That's great, Mr. Hanson. I won't let you down, I promise." Leon was happy to hear that he could start getting some of his own money. That would help him prove to his parents that he was ready to get on with his own life. He didn't want to be around when that new kid got here. The very thought of his parents doing stuff to get a baby on his mother made Leon's skin crawl. The guys his age had snickered when his mother came by school one day to drop off his lunchbox. He had stupidly forgotten it on the kitchen table. Her belly told anyone with eyes what she'd been doing. He couldn't stand it that the fellas were thinking about his own mother that way...he couldn't stand himself for thinking about his own mother that way. But, try as he might, Leon found that more and more of his waking thoughts involved some sort of sex. As did his sleeping thoughts. Walking by a pretty girl could set his mind off on an hour's long reverie on what was hidden under her dress and how it might feel to touch her skin or see her breasts. He had been so troubled by the physical reaction his body produced in these moments that he no longer felt comfortable at school, where he had to cover his crotch with his books so he didn't appear obscene. It was simply much less stressful to be around the old guys at the feed store. They talked about sex all the time, but hearing the words come from their ancient mouths didn't encourage his body to react the way an actual girl did.

Raymond, too, had conflicted feelings about the baby that was coming and the disruption the announcement had caused in his family. He was particularly bothered by the timing of the whole thing. On the very day when he thought that he would get back into Leon's good graces, this baby news had happened, pitching Leon back into an emotional exile of minimal communication with anyone in the household, including Ray. It made him sad to think about his big brother being so upset that he couldn't even talk about it. And, he worried that Leon's view of religious matters would land him in hell. Despite what Leon had told him about God and hell being made up by people to scare other people into doing their bidding, Raymond still thought that there must be some truth to the stories or why else would there be so many churches everywhere? On the other hand, the more Leon pulled away from their mother, the more she lavished her love on Raymond. He reasoned that he might as well enjoy this unique happenstance because once that baby showed up, he was sure he would return to his status as a second-class citizen.

When May 1, 1908, rolled around, Leon was still sleeping in the full-sized bed he had shared with Ray for so many years. Having a small wage from the feed store didn't turn out to be enough money to propel Leon into financially independent manhood. Not only was Leon still under the roof of his parents' home, he now shared it with Amelia May Saxby, who had arrived that very morning, right before dawn.

Everett had awakened the boys early that day to tell them that they had a baby sister. Of course, the boys weren't surprised because Leona had started moaning the night before and acting like a milk cow right before it drops a calf. When their grandmother arrived early that night with a basket of towels and rolled up her sleeves before heading into their parents' room, the boys knew that life as they knew it would soon come to an end.

"Get up, Leon," ordered Everett. "I need help with the milking this morning. I'm getting a late start on account of the baby and those cows will be ripe and ready."

Leon knew that cows who were overfilled were the hardest to milk. They couldn't wait for the relief and yet whenever you touched their swollen bags, they lashed out with their hind legs, making it hard for a person to get settled in close enough to the udders to latch on properly. It was going to be a long morning for Leon. He grabbed his overalls and a beat-up chamois shirt. It was spring but still damp and chilly most mornings, so he wore an old jacket that had been his Granddaddy Earl's out to the barn. He let the oversized sleeves fall down to cover his fingers to keep them warm. Cold hands on an agitated cow were never a good thing.

Leon ran his hands along the spine of the Guernsey cow, Lovely Lydia, who wasn't necessarily more attractive than any of the other cows, but she did have a compliant disposition. Leon supposed that's how she came to be considered lovely. He led her to the stanchion and secured her to the post. It couldn't hurt to start with the least ornery creature in the barn. He pulled up the stool and placed the galvanized bucket under the cow's bag. He wiped her udders clean with a damp rag he had stuffed in his pocket to keep it warm.

"Now then, Lovely. Let's get you going here." Leon spoke softly to the cow and blew on his hands before wrapping his fingers around her two left udders. His hands were instantly welcomed by the distended teats and he began to rhythmically expel the milk into the bucket between his knees. As usual, Leon's thoughts rambled to places where they shouldn't. As he massaged the milk from the docile cow, he couldn't help but think about the fact that his mother would be making milk for that baby. He honestly hated himself for thinking about his mother's breasts, but he couldn't banish the troubling thoughts and his fixation made him feel uneasy touching the cow...as if he were doing something forbidden. He hoped this phase of thinking wouldn't last long.

By the time father and son had finished the milking, gathering the eggs and throwing some hay to the other stock, it was well past breakfast time. They made their way back to the kitchen door and kicked their boots against the stoop to clear the mud and cow dung from the soles of their galoshes before they entered the quiet house. Leon and Everett had expected to see Grandma bustling around the kitchen, bringing them big mugs of coffee to perk them up. Leon had graduated to coffee since his time spent at the feed store. He told Ray it went good with cigarettes and focused his mind. Instead, there was Raymond, sitting by the stove and rocking his new sister back and forth. Leon couldn't believe what a patsy his brother was. Nor could he believe how little and vulnerable the baby looked, swaddled in clean flour sacks and sucking on its own thumb.

"Where's Grandma?" asked Everett.

"She's in the sewing nook. She said she had to sleep. That's she too old to stay up all night anymore," replied Raymond. He motioned his head toward the oven door. "She left you and Leon some hotcakes and bacon in there...and Grandma says there's coffee in the pot on top. You just need to heat it up some."

As usual, Leon didn't bother to reply to his brother. He finished pumping water over his hands, wiped them dry on his dirty overalls and went directly to the oven for his plate. He sat the plate down on the table, then returned to the stove to pour himself a mug of reheated coffee. Ray continued rocking his tiny bundle as he watched his father and brother gather their breakfast food. The boy observed that his brother still had a sweet tooth because he'd put about four spoonfuls of sugar into the mug before he cooled it with a generous helping of cream. Fresh cream was one of the best things about the milk cows, thought Raymond. He pitied people who didn't have their very own cows.

Everett looked over at Raymond and Baby Amelia, who was starting to fuss and wiggle in her brother's arms. The small boy tried rocking faster, but this just seemed to rile the infant into a state of discontent. The baby started squeaking and scrunching up her little red face.

"How's your ma doing, boy?" asked Everett .

"I don't know, Pa. Grandma told me to mind the baby for a while so that's what I been trying to do," he replied. The fact that his mother wasn't screaming anymore must be a good sign, he thought. That probably meant that she was okay.

Everett finished his food and rose from his chair. "Clean up for me, Leon," he said.

"Grandma will do it," Ray advised his father. "She said leave it all for her to do later."

"No. Grandma is already doing more than her share just by being here. Leon can help out in the kitchen this once," his father told him.

Leon looked around the kitchen. A thick sheen of congealing bacon fat covered the old iron skillet; globs of syrup and grease coated the tin plates. He was thinking he'd be lucky if he had to do women's work only once. He could see that his near future might involve an apron and a broom and that added to the ever-present humiliation this baby situation had caused him. He swore to himself that he would get out of this place as soon as he could reasonably manage on his own. For now, he only nodded to his father and kept his head down. When Everett left the kitchen, Leon planned to call Brownie in to lick everything clean.

Everett walked over to where Ray was jostling the baby in his lap;

he smiled down at his two younger children and held out his callused hands to take the infant. Raymond was ready to relinquish the baby. He marveled that someone so small could actually make his arms go numb when she felt absolutely weightless. Everett scooped the baby girl from Ray and gave her a gentle kiss on her downy head.

"Alright, Amelia May. Let's go see if your ma is ready to feed you." Everett cooed to the baby as if she could understand every word he said. He carried the baby into the room where Leona lay in a post-partum slumber and closed the door behind him. Raymond stood up and shook his arms to bring the feeling back to his fingers.

Leon silently watched his father leave with the baby. He sipped his coffee and thought about the baby's mouth trying to find the nipple on his mother's engorged breast. He was shamed by his thoughts and wished for a way to scrub them from his mind.

It turned out that Raymond was the one who ended up doing women's work. He guessed that Leon had been right when he declared that his parents were too old to have another child. He knew kids who had grandmothers who were about as old as his mother and here she was with this crying baby who needed constant atten-tion. He hoped he hadn't been such a burden to her when he was small. Raymond thought a lot about ages that summer, mostly as he peeled potatoes and washed the dishes for his ailing mother. He worried that his parents were getting so old that they could die soon. And his grandma looked older every time he saw her, which was often in the months following the birth of Amelia May. His mother seemed to be in some sort of slump, probably from being thirty-two, thought the boy. Before the baby came, his mother had been a whirl-wind of arms and legs--scrubbing the floors, hanging the laundry, rendering the lard or canning the bushel upon bushel of fruits and vegetables produced on the farm in a typical summer. Now, she seemed as limp as a dead rabbit and, like the rabbit, the life had gone out of her eyes. Everett himself appeared to dim a notch every time he looked at his formerly vigorous wife. Only little Amelia May, who he called his May Day Bouquet, consistently brought a smile to Everett's furrowed face. Like a pair of denim trousers washed every

Wednesday, the fabric of their family faded and frayed as the weeks went on.

* * *

In the summer of 1908, Leon was fourteen and about an inch taller than his father. Consequently, he was commandeered more and more to help out in the fields. This meant that his earned wages from the feed store were dwindling and so was his supply of cigarettes. Leon seemed more antsy than usual, and when Ray asked him about it, he told his brother that it was because he needed his smokes. He was cutting his tobacco with chicory leaves before he wrapped it in a paper sleeve but chicory didn't work like tobacco, Leon said. The younger boy had no idea why this should make any difference in how Leon acted but decided that Leon had his reasons and he let it go. Ray rarely understood why Leon acted the way he did. He only knew that the more pimples popped out on Leon's face, the stranger his actions seemed to become.

Raymond, too, kept waiting for things to get back to normal, but that never seemed to happen. He eventually gave up caring that Leon and the other boys called him Raylene whenever they saw him hanging up the ragged sheets on the line or, worse yet, the stained diapers that he had to wash almost daily. Being a farm boy, he'd been around a lot of different kinds of excrement in his day, but a dirty diaper was its own special, disgusting mess. The smell and squishy texture reminded him of fresh dog dirt, and he had to scrape the smashed feces off the cloths with a stick. He dumped the goo in the outhouse hole before he washed the muslin by hand in the metal tub. He could hardly stand to touch himself with his own hands when he finished doing a batch. Only the sweet, sad smile and gentle "thank you" from his mother made up for such an onerous task.

The little boy would have done anything to make his mother smile that summer. He was dismayed that his mother was a shell of hollow sadness. He acknowledged in his mind that his family was folding in on itself little by little every day, and he started to look forward to the beginning of school, a few short weeks away. Raymond had never looked forward to school before. He usually relished the long, humid days of summer, interrupted by predictable intervals of violent rainstorms and trips to the cellar to shelter from an angry sky that threatened tornadoes. At those times, he felt a certain excitement by the possibility of danger and the change in routine. Afternoons in the cellar were dark and cool. The family would light a lantern, eat canned peaches and play cards until the danger passed. Those had been among Raymond's favorite days. Now, a subtle danger seemed to haunt the farm even under a blazing sun, making the upcoming school term a welcome escape for the worried boy.

"Ray. Hand me that ax and grab a hat. You're going to help me and your brother today." Everett took the ax from the youngster and finished chopping the kindling in about two seconds flat. The boy had been whacking away for twenty minutes with only a piddly pile of wood to show for his efforts. That was another of Ray's jobs that summer...keeping the stove going. His mother had enough strength to boil water on its burners, but chopping kindling for it was beyond her current abilities.

"Who's going to watch over Ma?" Ray asked.

"Grandma will be here shortly. She's coming over to help with putting up the preserves. She just needs to stop in town to pick up some more jars," his father told him. This was good news for Raymond. It meant that he could go back to being a boy for a few hours and Ma and Amelia would get some special care.

"What are we going to do?" Ray asked his father. He was excited to join the ranks of the men after the months of being a "housewife"-- Leon's slur for his domestic servitude.

"We're going to get started mining the rocks from that fallow field at the east end of the property. Get it ready for next year's planting," Everett told him. Upon hearing this, Raymond was a little less enthusiastic about joining the men, but he dutifully retrieved his straw hat from the chair on the back porch and followed his father out to the barn. Leon was hitching King and Queenie to the old flatbed wagon as he puffed away on one of his hand-rolled disappointments. He wore only his overalls and Raymond could see that Leon was not only taller than their father, he also had some sizable muscles that flexed through his naked shoulders as he worked. Leon was more man than boy. At least in his body. Ray was pretty sure Leon's mind wasn't quite so developed yet.

Everett tossed a pair of too big gloves at his younger son. "Take these with you, boy. You're going to need them." Raymond stuffed the gloves in his back pockets and walked over to open the barn doors wide enough to allow the horses and wagon to pull out. Everett hopped up next to Leon, who took the reins and clicked his teeth to get the horses going.

"Close it back up, boy," Pa told Raymond. "Keep the dogs away from the sheep."

A few ewes and their sturdy lambs were bedded down in a pen at the back of the barn. Normally, they would be outside like the rest of the stock in the summer, but marauding dogs, mostly dumped as strays, had ripped the throats out of some of the sheep only the week before. Raymond had found them when he went to play with the lambs. He loved the way the lambs would bounce forward on their tiny hooves, eyes down, and smack their heads into his outstretched hand. Ray thought that he had progressed beyond crying--his little sister and his mother did enough of that for the whole family--but when he saw the bloodied carcasses of the old ewe and her twin lambs, he burst out in tears. Though the hank of fleece had grown back in, Ray knew that this was the old girl who had saved his miserable toes. For reasons unknown to Raymond, the ewe had always been called Sow Bug. Now she and her little babies were gone.

Everett and Leon sat out for several nights, waiting for the pack to return. On the fourth night, right as Raymond had settled down to sleep, he heard a series of dual blasts from out back of the barn. About a half hour later, his father and Leon came in. Ray raced down the stairs when he heard their footsteps to find out if they'd gotten the mangy outlaws.

"Did you get 'em, Pa?" asked Raymond. He liked most dogs, but he wanted vengeance for those innocent animals that had been slaughtered.

"We knocked two of 'em down dead and the others will be licking buckshot out of their asses for a week." Leon had a crazed look in his eyes and a sly smile to go with it as he recounted the successful stake-out mission to eliminate the dogs.

"One of the dogs we got looked to be Mr. Padgett's cur," Leon continued. "He must of took up running with the pack. Remember, Pa?" Leon asked his father. "Remember when you said months ago that dog was no good and needed to be shot?"

"I remember, son," said Everett. Everett Saxby didn't relish telling Warren Padgett that he'd had to kill his no-good dog, but he knew Padgett would understand. It was an unwritten rule that a farmer had the right to protect his livestock. Padgett would have done the same if it had been the Saxby dog. Then again, the Saxby fox terrier wasn't much of a threat so he doubted he would ever be in Padgett's shoes. Since that night, they had kept the ewes and their lambs penned up in the barn. They didn't worry about Rolando, the big ram. He was famous for killing anything that came near him with a single butt of his cement block head.

The bottom half of the barn doors closed, Raymond scrambled after the wagon. When he made it alongside, Everett reached down and yanked the boy up onto the running board. Raymond climbed over the rail and settled next to the pry bars and shovels lying in the bed. He steadied himself for the bumpy ride to the rock-strewn field. It seemed to him that they had worked on this field already. Well, maybe not Raymond himself because he had been little then, but he was sure his father and Leon had cleared this land once before.

"Didn't you and Leon get the rocks out of that field a while ago?" Ray asked his father.

"That's right, boy," said Everett.

"Then how did the rocks get back in there?" Raymond was puzzled.

"You think the rocks just up and rolled themselves back to the field, Ray? Sometimes, you're just plain stupid," Leon told his brother.

"That's enough now, Leon. Your brother asked a logical question."

Everett turned to face his younger son. "I wish we could just clear a field one time and be done with it," he said to his child, "but it doesn't work that way. The wind, the rain, and the plowing uncover new rocks all the time. We usually have to clear them out every now and then so we don't break the blades on our equipment."

He thought his father offered a solid explanation but it also made him wonder how soon he was going to have to do this job again. Not for a while he hoped. He preferred picking corn to picking rocks. Most of the problem rocks were still too heavy for him to toss up onto the wagon, and he was sure Leon would be happy to point out just how worthless and runty he was if he needed to ask for help.

It was a swampy, hot day, typical in the Minnesota summer. By the time they reached the field, both Raymond and Everett were drenched in sweat, their shirts clinging to their torsos. Leon had made the right decision to go shirtless, though his perspiration was attracting mosquitos to his pink shoulders and he swatted left and right to drive them away. The horses stood swishing their tails for the same purpose. Occasionally, one or the other would snort and twitch its head, and Raymond knew it must have been bitten. Grandma had always warned the boys to rub some mud on their bodies to protect them from the sun and the bugs, so that's what they did. They were likely a sorry sight, but being blond and fair, both boys were susceptible to sunburn. Everett never seemed to be bothered by the sun or the pests. He simply stripped off his shirt and started working.

It took them until noon to finish the first acre. The wagon had been filled several times, and the unloading was only a little less grueling than the loading. They used the rocks to line a shallow gorge where water ran and eroded the field in a storm. When they tossed the last stone down, Everett told them to take a break.

"Pa?" Leon asked. "Did you bring any food or are we going back in?"

"Look under my shirt. There's a tin there with some sandwiches in it," Everett told him.

Leon pulled the twill shirt aside and brought out the tin box. Inside were six ham sandwiches wrapped in a towel and three apples from the tree by the porch. Before the baby came, there would have been fat slices of cake or pie to finish the meal, but Leona no longer baked. Though his grandmother had been coming over at least once a week to make the occasional supper and help Raymond keep up the house, she rarely had time to bake extras.

Leon handed Ray a sandwich and an apple, then passed him a canning jar full of tea to wash it down. All three Saxby men sat with their legs dangling over the back of the wagon and ate without saying a word. Sitting there in the sun, Raymond felt a quiet closeness with his father and brother. He had missed being part of their world in the aftermath of Amelia's birth. He didn't blame Amelia May for making his mother so sick, but he did wish that he could have his mother back the way she had been. He began to think that Leon was a lot smarter than he'd thought. After all, Leon had predicted that a new baby would not be a good thing. If Leon had been right about that, maybe he was right about other things as well.

By mid-afternoon Everett and the boys had cleared three acres. The first acre had been much rockier than the rest of the patch they worked on that day, so the next two acres went faster. They were tossing the rocks from their last load into the ditch when they thought they heard a cry. The clang and thud of rocks hitting each other, or the soft soil, muffled other sounds around them.

"Hold up a minute, boys," Pa told them. "I hear something."

"Me, too," agreed Ray.

All three stopped what they were doing and listened. They could hear birds chirping, the rasp of grasshoppers grinding their legs together, and the sounds of the horses chewing on weeds and dropping turds to the ground. For a brief time, that was all they heard and then it came--the high wail of a woman in distress. When they looked into the distance toward the sound, they could faintly make out Grandma batting aside cornstalks and heading their way. Hugged to her chest was little Amelia May. Everett took off running toward his mother and the infant girl she carried tightly against her body. Grandma Saxby swung her free arm in a frantic wave so that Everett could find her in the head-high corn. The old woman stumbled over her running feet and caught herself on her knees, hoping to protect the baby from the fall. By the time she struggled up from the dirt, Everett was by her side, helping her to stand. His mother's dress was covered with blood. When Everett saw the stains, his heart dropped into his bowels.

"Mother, what the hell is going on? Are you OK? Is Amelia OK?" He took the crying baby from her grasp and peeled back the swaddling to be sure the child was uninjured. She had blood on her precious little hands.

"Oh no," Everett prayed. "Let her be safe. Let my sweet baby girl be unharmed."

"Me and the baby are fine, Ev," Lillian told him. "But Leona's had some sort of conniption fit. The girl took your razor to her arms. I found her that way when I came up from stocking the cellar. She was sitting in the rocker with the baby on the floor next to her, rocking and crying and bleeding all over the damned place."

Alarm shot through Everett. Would Leona have finished the job by the time they got back to the house? "Christ, Mama. You didn't leave her alone, did you?"

The boys quickly maneuvered the wagon over to where the adults were standing. They'd never seen their father look so stricken. His tanned face was white with shock, and tears moistened his eyes. Seeing his distress made them fear for the worst. Ray fought to keep the sandwich he'd eaten at noon from inching its way back up his throat. Leon's eyes were glued to the blood on his grandmother's dress.

Everett put his hand on his mother's face to direct her eyes to his. "Did you just leave her alone there?" he asked again, his own anxiety causing his voice to crack.

Lillian nodded her head yes, but that wasn't the whole story. She tried to explain. "Leona is alone right now, yes. But she can't get in any more trouble."

This statement terrified Everett. Was she dead? Was that why she couldn't do any more harm?

"What do you mean, Mama? Tell me," he demanded.

"I bandaged her arms and tied her to the bed, but not before getting some whiskey down her throat. I sincerely didn't know what else to do. And I sure didn't want to leave the baby there with her."

Everett Saxby sprang into action. He hopped up onto the bed of the wagon and tossed the few remaining rocks to the ground, clearing some space for the riders. "Come on, boys. We gotta get back right now. Here, Ray. You hold Amelia May and don't let her get banged around back there."

Everett handed the baby to Raymond. He hugged her close and cooed to soothe her as best he could. He was comforted by the feel of her warm little body next to his. Once Lillian was settled, Leon swatted the reins against the horses' backsides to start them for home. He needn't have bothered. King and Queenie were barn sour and had been itching to get back to their stalls all afternoon. They headed in the right direction without any prompting at all.

2

For as long as he lived, Raymond never forgot the trauma of that day. When the family returned to the house from the fields, Ray had been sent directly upstairs and told to tend to his crying sister. Amelia May was about fourteen weeks old; she was no longer a squished little thing with a bald head and wandering eyes. She looked you full in the face now, and she appeared to Raymond to have some idea of life going on around her. She was also hungry. He put the baby girl in the center of his bed and considered how best to clean her up. She needed the blood washed from her hands and her soggy diaper had soaked through her gown. The boy was overwhelmed by fear for his mother, but he also recognized that caring for the baby was one thing he could do to help her. He wasn't exactly sure how he was going to do that without breaching the sanctity of his parents' room, where his father and grandmother were hovering over his mother's prostrate figure. Leon had been sent to fetch Doctor Becker; his office was about a mile away on Second Street in downtown Hastings. Everett had told Leon to get the doctor quick and to tell him that it was a life and death emergency.

The worried boy piled pillows and blankets along the perimeter of the bed. He knew he needed to leave the baby alone for a few minutes, and he had seen his grandmother do this before. Grandma said you never know when a baby will all-of-a-sudden learn to roll over and fall on the floor. Amelia was squirming and thrashing about, though Raymond was relieved that she had stopped crying. Before he ventured down the stairs to get supplies for Amelia's care, he wiped her right hand clean with a little of his own saliva and pushed her thumb into her mouth to keep her quiet until he could get back upstairs.

He had no choice but to walk by the stove and the old rocking chair to get to his parents' room. He could smell the blood before he saw it. It smelled like copper tasted when he sneaked a lick of cocoa off the kettle before he washed it...sharp and tangy. He doubted he would ever lick a copper kettle again, no matter how much chocolate might be stuck to the side. When he saw the blood, Ray had to steady himself against the table. Without warning, he felt his knees buckle and his vision go black. He remembered this happening to him once before, when he'd been tasked with holding a chicken's neck between two nails in a stump while his father lopped off its head. He'd been fine until Brownie, the fox terrier with one brown patch on his back, came along and scooped up the detached noggin into his mouth and crunched so hard that Raymond could feel it in his bones. His father had told him then to put his head between his knees, so that's what he did now. In a few minutes, his vision had cleared and he worked up the courage to approach the bedroom door. He could hear muffled voices in the room so he knocked softly. He didn't want to make anyone jumpier than they already were.

"Pa," Ray whispered to the closed door. He followed that up with a soft rap of his knuckles. He got no response so he knocked a little louder, and this time he called for them both.

"Pa. Grandma." Ray said. "I need to ask you about Amelia." The door cracked open, and Lillian poked her nose through. Ray caught a glimpse of his mother lying motionless on the bed. Her arms from the elbows down were wrapped in bloodied cloths, some of which appeared to be Amelia's diapers. His father sat beside his mother with his head in his hands.

"I thought we told you to mind the baby. Where is she, boy?"

Grandma looked about as worried as Raymond had ever seen her.

"She's fine," Ray told her. "I made her a pillow cage on my bed, like you showed me."

"Well, you need to get back up there, Raymond." Lillian pushed the door to close it, and Ray reached out to stop her.

"Grandma," Ray said. "I need some stuff to change Amelia and everything is in the drawer in Ma's dresser. And, what am I supposed to do about feeding her?" Ray asked.

"I'll be up in a minute. You take up some water from the pot on the stove but be sure to cool it a bit with water from the pump. Use some of it to wash the mud off you and save the rest for the baby. I'll help you get her situated as soon as I can." Ray was relieved to know his grandmother would help him. He was sure he could manage cleaning the baby on his own, but he had no idea how to feed her. He wasn't sure if cow's milk would sicken a baby but he thought probably not, since he and Leon drank it all the time. Babies are different, though, he reasoned, and he was glad that his grandmother was the one who would take on that risk.

It seemed to Raymond that his grandmother took an exceptional amount of time to get herself back upstairs to help him. Amelia May was sucking her fist with a passion; her little hand was red and wet over her knuckles where her gums were seeking comfort. Finally, he heard Lillian lumber up the stairs. She entered the room and placed a basket of soap, towels, diapers and a clean gown on the spindly chair under the window. She pulled out a soda bottle filled with milk and topped with a black rubber nipple, the kind they use to feed motherless goats or lambs.

"Will the cow milk hurt her, Grandma?" Ray wanted to be sure that Amelia May wasn't going to get the colic. When that happened, no one in the whole house got any peace.

"This is your ma's milk, boy. But cow's milk will likely be what we feed her from here on out," Grandma told him.

Both of these statements troubled Raymond. How did his grandmother get the milk from his mother and if she could do that, why would Amelia need the milk from the cows? Ray decided to ponder those questions privately. From the look on her face, Grandma seemed to have her own troubling thoughts to fret over. They worked together to clean up the child. When he finished wiping her little hands, the wet rags he used to clean the baby were pink from Leona's blood. He tried to be gentle, but the dried blood that was stuck in the crevices of her fat arms and around her nails took some extra scrubbing which Amelia May didn't enjoy. When at last the infant was clean and dry, Lillian plopped Ray down on the chair and put Amelia on his lap. She handed him the bottle of warm milk.

"Feed her the same way you'd give the bottle to a lamb. Then burp her when she's done. You've seen us do that often enough," Grandma instructed. She tossed a couple extra diapers at him.

"Use one of these if she spits up and save one for her bottom. I got to go see about your ma and pa."

Ray folded the baby into the crook of his elbow and stuck the nipple between the baby's lips. Exactly like an orphaned lamb, Amelia May latched onto the spigot and nursed with a vigor that surprised him. Amelia closed her eyes and grunted softly with each swallow. When the nipple collapsed from the powerful vacuum her sucking created, Amelia would whine and fuss to tell Ray that he needed to do something. He pulled the nipple out of her mouth and listened for the whooshing sound of air reinflating the rubber nipple. Once he was sure the nipple had regained its shape, he continued feeding the child. When she'd finished, Raymond pulled the bottle away from her lips and heard a wet pop as the suction was released. For some reason, he found the whole experience oddly satisfying. He wanted to tell Leon about it when he returned with the doctor, but he doubted that his brother would be interested in hearing about another of his domestic accomplishments. Like so many of the thoughts Raymond had that day, he kept it to himself.

The infant sated, little Raymond rearranged blankets and pillows on the bed to make a cozy nest for his baby sister. He laid her down in its center, then covered her with an old shirt of Leon's that had been hanging off the back of the chair. He pushed open the window as far as he could to try to let out some of the heat from the humid second-story bedroom. He'd sat back down to begin the vigil over his charge when he remembered he needed to burp her. Amelia made the process so much easier for him when she let out a hearty belch while he was lifting her to his shoulder. The warm air from the child's belly smelled sweet to Ray; it smelled like his mother's bosom when she pulled him close for a hug.

It was well after suppertime when Leon was finally able to drive Doctor Becker back to town. When he returned, Grandma was in the kitchen making eggs and bacon. That upside-down meal echoed the family's perception of what sort of day it had been; a day they all wished they could start over. If only having breakfast again could wipe away the anguish of the last several hours and alter the uncertain future the shattered family now faced.

"Boys," Everett began, "your ma is very sick. The doctor says she's going to have to go to the hospital to get better." Everett held Amelia on his lap; he was letting her lick egg yolk from his fingertip. The baby coiled her fist around the man's middle finger to pull his hand closer to her mouth. Ray never knew babies liked eggs. He wanted to stick his own finger in some yolk, too, to see if she would take it from him.

"What's wrong with her, Pa?" asked Leon in a low voice. The events of the day had knocked most of the bluster out of Leon.

"The doctor called it puerperal hysteria," his father told him. "He says it sometimes happens after a baby comes. Nobody knows why. It just comes on for no reason."

"Well, how long does it last? She's going to get better, isn't she?" Leon wanted some answers.

"Becker didn't know. I asked him that myself but he said we'll have to wait and see. He wants to get her to the hospital as soon as Grandma can get your ma's milk dried up."

Now Ray understood what Grandma was getting at when she told him that Amelia was going to be fed cow's milk from now on. His mother would be going away, leaving her family to figure things out all on its own.

"We'll be able to see her, won't we?" asked Ray.

"We're not sure what the rule about visiting is just yet," his grandmother told him.

"When Granddaddy Earl was sick, we got to visit him," Leon reminded her.

"That's true, son," Pa replied, "but your ma is going to the State Hospital and they do things different there."

The blood drained from Leon's head and he thought he might vomit what little he'd eaten for supper. He had heard plenty about the State Hospital from a fella whose father worked there. They had guards at that hospital. It was a place for idiots and the insane, and he knew his mother wasn't an idiot. Anger rose in the boy, and it pushed away all the sadness he had been feeling. He clambered up from his seat by the stove, toppling over the chair in his haste. It was the chair his mother was in when Grandma found her. He kicked the rocker against the wall and felt a fleeting satisfaction when he heard it crack. Leon looked down on his father; for the first time in his life, he understood how it felt to hate someone.

"You did this to her!" Leon accused Everett. "You couldn't stay away from her, could you?"

Everett looked at his older son with a misery that seeped up from his battered soul. He had lost so much this day, and now he was losing Leon along with his beloved wife.

"I told you having another baby was a bad idea," Leon continued to rant. "Now look what a mess we're all in because of you."

Pa sat there not saying a word. He acknowledged to himself that the boy was half-right. Amelia May's birth had sapped the life out of Leona and, as Leon implied, he had been a willing participant in her conception. What Everett couldn't tell the boy was that it was his mother who had longed so desperately for another child. She'd told him that she felt she would die if she couldn't hold a baby to her breast ever again, and now she might be dying because he'd given in to her pleas. Poor Everett had known another mouth to feed would stretch their meager resources, but he never imagined that they might lose everything that really mattered.

* * *

The Minnesota State Hospital in Hastings opened its doors to the unfortunate souls afflicted with mental derangements in 1900, the same year that Raymond Saxby came into the world. The state legislature had noted that the number of intellectually deficient individuals and the outright insane populations had overrun the three existing state institutions. In the late 1800s, funding was provided to expand the facilities in Minnesota. Around the same time, ideas about the care of mental patients were evolving away from the prevailing concepts of warehousing the populations in dank fortresses meant to protect the public from danger. New theories advocated providing a more engaging atmosphere in which the ill could participate in a safe, closed society that provided some social stimulation. These new institutions were still warehouses, albeit friendlier feeling ones, designed to isolate the patients from the wary communities they served. For those who arrived at the Hastings State Hospital in 1908 with visions of Bedlam in their minds, a very different reality greeted them. The hospital setting was serene and bucolic. Instead of a prison-like compound filled with dingy cells, Hastings featured cottages nestled under a canopy of trees. The first patients at the new facility were transferred to its pleasant buildings from the crowded institution in Rochester. Initially serving males, it opened to women for a brief time between 1905-1909. Leona Saxby was one of the women who entered the mental health system through its doors.

It took almost two weeks for Grandma Saxby to get Leona dried up and the baby weaned from her mother's milk. The nearly catatonic mother allowed the older woman to lactate her into a bowl twice a day. Lillian mixed the expressed fluid with the ever-increasing amount of cow's milk needed to feed the child. Every day, Leona's milk was less copious, and by the end of the second week, her dry, flattened breasts were secured in a padded binder, heralding the end of Leona's maternal duty and the beginning of her new identity as a member of the forlorn society of the insane. What remained of Leona's personality had drained out of her in the blood she'd spilt on the kitchen floor. She no longer fought her demons or gave them any consideration. She was as complacent as Lovely Lydia but without the purpose---Lydia was still providing for the family; Leona was nothing but a stone around their necks. To the extent that she could care about anything at all, she was relieved that the burden of failure she carried like an albatross could be set aside in a cottage filled with women like her.

With Leona gone, life in the Saxby household went on much as it had in the months after the baby arrived. For all practical purposes, she left them on the day Amelia was born, and each family member had established routine chores to pick up the slack that Leona's illness had created in the home. Grandma stayed with them a couple of nights each week to cook and do laundry. She and Amelia took over the marital bedroom on those occasions, while Everett slept on the outside porch until the weather changed and it became too cold. Then he made do with a pallet on the parlor floor. All conversation was distilled down to only what was essential to keep the household viable. "Do this. Do that. Yes, sir. No, sir," passed for communication among the family. Amelia May's gurgles and cries were the rare expressions of genuine emotions in those painful early weeks of Ma's absence. Ray found that it was in his moments of interaction with the baby that he felt most like himself. He was able to smile and laugh at her baby antics. Sometimes when she cried, Ray cried too--Amelia for her empty stomach, Ray for his empty heart.

Leon declared that he had no intention of returning to school, and his father gave him no guff about his decision. Everett knew that everyone in the area had heard about Leona's breakdown. He felt the stares and heard the whispers behind his back during his infrequent visits to town. Everett knew the pain Leon would suffer at school. If he could keep Raymond at home too, he would, but the child was still learning to read and write, so school was a priority for the boy. For his older son, however, Everett thought that hard work was the best medicine. He told the boy that he could quit his studies but that would mean that Leon must pull his weight at the farm. While Leon would have preferred to hop a train to just about anywhere else in the world, he had no money to finance his dreams. He also knew his father couldn't afford to hire help until his grandmother moved in and they could use the money from the rental of her cottage in town to pay for a hired hand. So, Leon agreed to his father's terms. He and his father worked side by side that fall to bring in the harvest in a practiced dance that required no words. Father and son were held together by a contract of need, not love. Everett recognized that one day soon, Leon would shed the need he had for his family and he, too, would leave them all behind.

"Raymond. Come on over here, son. We need to talk a few things over before you head back to school."

Lillian left her work at the stove and walked over to Raymond. She wiped her hands on her apron and reached over to take Amelia from him. He had been holding her in his outstretched arms and twirling her in the air. The baby's laughter had resulted in milky bubbles on her lips, and the spheres sparkled in the sunlight streaming in through the open door. Ray walked over to his father, who was standing on the outside stoop. Pa hooked his arm across Raymond's shoulders and guided him toward the barn.

"I thought you could help me fix the hinges on the gates. I picked up a couple new ones the other day when I was in town," Everett told the boy.

Raymond looked up into his father's haggard face. He would do whatever his father wanted. All Ray wished was for everyone to be happy again. "Sure, Pa. I can do that," replied the boy.

"Son," his father began, "when I was in town, folks were talking about what happened to your ma. When you go back to school next week, some of your friends might ask you about all that. That could be kinda hard on you, Raymond."

"I know, Pa. I don't care what they say," he lied, but it was one of those good lies that help people feel better so he thought God would forgive him. Raymond, who had been looking forward to school, now dreaded it. He had already thought about the questions he would be asked. He envied Leon for not having to deal with the morbid curiosity of his classmates anymore. Despite his misgivings, Raymond was aware that he needed to continue his own learning. He was just now getting so he could keep his letters facing the right direction to write a decent sentence, and he thought that arithmetic might have a purpose. His grandmother could help out with a lot of things, but expecting her to school him, with everything else she had to do, would be too much to hope for.

"Well, son, folks can be cruel and children can be the cruellest. If they start to get to you, remember that your ma is sick; that she didn't do anything wrong and there is no shame to what happened to her or where she's getting her care. Sick brains are no different from sick kidneys or livers; they're all part of our God-given bodies."

Raymond's mother had aged and shriveled since her illness, and he could see that his father was no longer the man he had been, either. His straight brown hair was wandering back from his brow; he was as thin and creased as his favorite work shirt, and his once ready smile only appeared in response to some silly antic of Amelia May's doing.

Ray thought over what his father said about sick brains and decided it rang true, but he still was stinging from his last year, when nothing more serious than mismatched shoes had made his school days miserable. He prepared himself to be treated like a biblical leper, as if his mother's condition could be spread like chicken pox or measles to anyone who came near him. More and more, he, like Leon, lived out an alternate life in his imagination.

The boy didn't want to talk about the subject of his mother's illness anymore. He wanted to get on with whatever came next. All he could think to say was, "Pa? Can I screw in the new hinges myself?"

"Sure, Ray," Everett agreed. "I'll just get them started for you." With that, the discussion was done and the work on the gate began. Ray only stripped one screw. When he finally swung the gate closed on its new hinges, he felt pretty good about the job he'd done.

The weekend before school started, Grandma Saxby came to stay at the farm full-time. She'd rented out her little single-story, brick cottage in town, near Estergreen and Sons Wagon Sellers, to a new dentist who had recently graduated from the University of Minnesota. Ray went with his grandmother one day to pick up the rent money, and he marveled at how the parlor had been transformed. Where the davenport once sat, a splendid chair-like contraption stood, surrounded by trays of shiny instruments. Doctor Quam let Ray climb up on the chair to try it out. Ray liked how the different parts of the chair could be raised and lowered with a foot pump. He thought the room smelled cleaner than anyplace he'd ever been. Dr. Quam smelled clean, too. His soft, pink hands didn't have a speck of dirt on them, not even under the nails. Ray noticed this as the doctor helped him get settled into the chair. He'd never seen a man with such clean hands. When the doctor smiled at Ray, his teeth sparkled in his mouth like an advertisement for his services.

"One of these days, you'll have to come in and let me do a check up on you, Raymond." Dr. Quam said this as he demonstrated to the boy how the chair functioned to position a patient for an examination. "You can't start good dental hygiene too early," he advised. "I tell all my patients, you have no idea how important it is to take care of your teeth."

"We'll do that, Doctor," replied Grandma. "Maybe when we come next month for the rent money."

The boy knew his grandmother wasn't worried about the condition of his mouth, but she did want to remind the young dentist that she would be back for the money that she was due. The extra income from the cottage was helping her family survive its new circumstances. Already, life around the house had improved with Grandma's presence, especially for Raymond. He still helped out in the kitchen and with Amelia May, but he no longer felt weighed down by adult responsibilities. He gladly hung the wash on the line, now that the dirty work of scraping diapers and wringing them by hand had been assumed by his grandmother. They were eating pie again, cookies, too. And they had fresh jam for breakfast, smeared on hot, fluffy pancakes. It was almost better than when his mother ruled the kitchen, except for the love. Lillian was full of cooking expertise, but it couldn't make up for the hugs that used to come as a side with his mother's meals.

* * *

Life for Leona took on its own routine. Her days at the asylum started with breakfast in the cottage dining hall. Rows of women with lank hair, wearing muslin shifts, sat on benches lined up along rectangular tables where they were served oatmeal and a boiled egg. Leona's tablemates seldom bothered with conversation. Many, like Leona, had nothing to say. Others simply screamed or babbled or cried until they were led away, only to return at the next meal to repeat the same incoherent mutterings. Breakfast was followed by alternating hot or cold baths that were thought to both calm and stimulate the patient's nervous system to produce therapeutic relief of their psychotic symptoms.

Each morning, Leona was led to a room laid out like a dormitory, where tubs lined the walls in place of cots. She was stripped down naked and placed in a deep tub filled with ice cold water. Over the tub, a canvas cover was stretched and lashed down to discourage any thoughts of escape. Only Leona's head emerged above the tub through a hole in the canvas. Her dark hair was wrapped in a turban to keep it dry. A wet head was thought to be an invitation to all manner of physical ailments that might complicate the patient's well-being. Leona would be left in the tub for hours on end. It was not uncommon for an attendant to hand feed her during the long hours of hypothermic treatment. When she was finally released from the tub, her teeth would be chipped from chattering, her skin blue and wrinkled from submersion in the cold water for so long. She would be returned to her bed where she would sleep under heavy blankets for the rest of the day, rising only for supper as prescribed by the attendants. The next day would bring the same routine. The only difference was the temperature of the water they put her in and the color of the turban they wrapped on her head.

Social interaction and meaningful work were hallmarks of the therapeutic process at the Hastings Hospital. After a month of enforced baths and isolation from toxic stimuli, Leona was assigned an occupation. The Hastings facility operated as its own self-contained town. There was a farm and a dairy to produce food for the residents, a laundry to process clothing and linens, and a kitchen to prepare their meals. Every patient who was able was assigned an occupation within the system. It was thought that work routines instilled a sense of purpose into the lives of the residents. Leona became a baker. Her specialty was bread, for she had made it so often in her life that it required no thought on her part. The physical acts of kneading the dough, punching it down, and kneading it again before shoving it into a hot oven were rote for Leona. She didn't want to think...about bread or anything else. The days became weeks, the weeks became months, but Leona's mood never changed. No amount of frigid baths or hot loaves of bread could fill the vacuum Leona had experienced since the birth of her baby girl.

Leon and Ray were standing by the sink, sticking their dirty hands under the water pump to wash for supper, when their father came in dressed in his Sunday clothes. It was a Thursday; the boys were certain they knew where their father had been in his fine coat and hat. Thursday was his day to visit Ma at the hospital. Sometimes, on a Sunday after church, when the family looked its most presentable, Everett would take them all out to see Leona. Ray liked the outside of the place where his mother was being treated; it was pretty, with large rolling lawns and big shade trees where they could bring her out with them for a picnic on the grass. Little Amelia would sit propped up by a blanket on the cool lawn under the autumn trees and squeal with delight when a golden leaf fell within her reach. She loved to pick them up and crumple them in her hands to hear the crackling sounds they made. Ray had to constantly watch that the baby didn't stick the dried leaves in her mouth. Still, the beauty of the grounds could never make up for the sad lives that existed inside its walls. Raymond wondered what they would do during visits in the winter. He didn't much like going inside that place or seeing the broken people who lived side by side with his mother.

Everett tossed his hat onto the kitchen table then pointed to the chairs, indicating that the boys should sit down.

"Boys," Everett said. "Have a seat. We need to talk." Raymond knew that whatever came after this sentence was rarely good. The last time they needed to talk, it heralded the beginning of their current disaster. Leon refused to sit. He leaned against the new Hoosier cabinet Everett had bought for his mother days before Amelia was born, acting disinterested in what their father had to say. Leon pulled a smoke from his pocket and lit it with a match he struck against the side of the stove. He closed his eyes as he inhaled and shut out all but the relief the nicotine gave his ragged nerves.

"Leon, please," implored Everett, "sit down with me and your brother. This will only take a couple of minutes but I want you boys to know what's going to happen in a few months. It's about your ma."

Leon reluctantly tossed his half-smoked cigarette into the fireplace and joined his father and brother at the table. He leaned back in his chair, balancing it on its two rear legs. If his mother were there, she would have his hide. She had always been very careful about maintaining the furniture and had told the boys many times not to sit in the chairs this way, that it would weaken them. Leon thought that the furniture was no longer his mother's concern, so why should he care if it broke. She ate off benches now, surrounded by lunatics and morons. He knew. He had seen them himself when his father insisted that he walk his mother back to her room after one of the family's visits.

Little Raymond allowed himself to think that something happening with his mother meant that she would be coming home soon. When he had seen her on the last visit, she had told him that she was baking bread every day. In the boy's mind, that showed that she was improving. The last couple of months that she had been home, she could hardly eat bread, let alone bake it.

Everett began to explain. "I talked with the administrator today. There's going to be some changes at the hospital. All the women are going to be transferred sometime in the next year or so to the hospital in Anoka."

"Anoka? Where's Anoka?" asked Raymond.

"It's far enough away that we won't get out to see her much anymore. Not until she comes home," Everett told him.

Leon looked up at the ceiling and rolled his eyes in contempt for the naivety of his father's statement. "She's not coming home ever and you know it." Leon snarled the words at his father. He was tired of false hope. Why couldn't they all just face the facts. Leona was lost to them, and in her place was a baby that needed constant attention. If only his parents had been smart enough to see this coming when they decided to have another child. He couldn't believe how short-sighted they had been. He thought that adults should know better. He decided then and there that he was never going to have kids. Not a one.

Raymond, who normally tried to keep his mouth shut when Leon said hurtful things, became angry at his brother for giving up on Ma. "You're not a doctor! You don't know anything, Leon!" Tears clouded the child's eyes. More than anything, he wanted to smack his brother in the nose and watch the blood dribble down his chin. More than that, he wanted his mother home. Most of all, he feared that Leon was right, that he'd been right from the start and so why should he be wrong now? The realization crushed the young boy.

Everett struggled to stay calm. Leon was hurting and had no way to harness the pain, other than lashing out. He didn't blame the kid. He felt that way himself, but he had to believe that Leona would rally and return to them one day.

"Well, I wanted you boys to know the situation. There's nothing I can do to change it. We can't bring her home. She's not ready. I'll check out the best way to get to Anoka so we can see her now and then." Pa turned to address Leon directly. "You remember, Leon. No matter where she is, she's your mother and you are to think about her and talk about her with respect. You hear me, boy?"

Leon nodded his head and grabbed his coat. He pulled his tobacco out of the inside pocket and headed for the barn. "I got chores to do," he called back to them. Everett and Raymond watched him go. Everett motioned for Grandma to hand him the baby. He needed her sweetness the way Leon needed his cigarettes. Ray was left without anything to comfort him.

* * *

It was not unusual for Leon Saxby to hike into Hastings proper to explore the displays in the shop windows or to meet up with friends at the old Ramsey Mill ruins above the Vermillion River. There were rumors that the ruins were haunted, and nothing could be more enticing to children than the chance to happen upon a ghost. It became an informal meeting place for the town's youngsters to get together to swap cigarettes, gossip about one another or simply escape the mundane routines of daily life. Leon had been going up the hill to meet his friends for several years. Now that his mother wasn't around to tell him "no," Raymond begged his brother to take him along.

It was a late fall day in 1909. The sky was crystalline blue. Not a wisp of a cloud was anywhere in sight. All the leaves from the dogwood trees had been driven to the ground by the winds and rains that pounded the area the week before. On this day, a persistent breeze scattered the leaves in every direction and whipped them through the old stone structure. The ruins were once a gristmill that had been erected in 1856-1857 by Alexander Ramsey, the first governor of Minnesota, at a time when he had pivoted from his political pursuits, such as persecuting Indians. At its peak in 1894, it produced 125 barrels of grain each day. Part of the operation included a copper shop and a storage facility, all of which burned to the ground on December 22, 1894. It was rumored among the children of the area that the fellow who set the fire had been consumed by flames of his own making when the stored grain exploded from the heat. They said his fire-blackened ghost still ran up and down its four floors, trying to escape. When the wind came through the cracks just right, it sounded like a moan, which added considerably to the staying power of the story. Raymond's mother hadn't approved of Leon going there, but he had gotten too old for her to control his ramblings. While she couldn't curtail Leon, she had strictly forbidden her younger son from playing in such a dangerous place. She worried that the charred beams could fall from what was left of the open roof or that the stone walls would crumble to the ground and either trap her boy or outright kill him. Leona had come to Minnesota from southern Illinois with her mother two decades earlier, after her father had been killed in a fire at a sawmill. Any building that had been touched by fire brought back those memories for Leona. She didn't want her boys anywhere near those ruins. But their mother was no longer around to object, and Leon didn't see what it could hurt to bring Raymond with him. Maybe the kid could make a friend there. He knew that his brother was shunned at school. He also thought that a couple hours away from his grumbling grandmother and demanding baby sister might do them both good.

Most appealing among the old stone buildings was the area that had housed the copper shop. The town boys would rake through the debris to find pieces of the melted metal, which they used as a form of currency among themselves. Years of this activity had mostly depleted the ruins of the precious globs, but now and then a victorious cry would echo through the walls, announcing a find as exciting as a hunk of gold. Leon had fashioned a ring he wore on his right middle finger from a nearly intact piece of copper tubing he'd found a couple of years back. Raymond always coveted that ring. He wanted to find a treasure for himself.

"Do you think we'll find copper?" Ray anxiously asked his brother. "You'll help me find some. You will, won't you Leon?" Leon was already thinking that bringing Raymond had been a bad idea. He'd hoped that his brother would be satisfied to simply come with him. If the kid was going to badger him the whole time they were there, he should have left him behind.

"Listen, runt," Leon told him, "almost no one finds copper anymore. What you need to find here is a friend or something. Besides, the idea of coming here is to get away from people whining at us. If you plan to whine at me, you can go home now." Raymond was stung by Leon's admonishment. He vowed he wouldn't say another word about finding copper because if he didn't find a piece this time, he wanted Leon to bring him back for another try. He decided he would quietly dig around on his own.

When they arrived at the ruins, the boys split up. Leon pointed out to his little brother where to dig for the best chance to find the copper globs, while Leon wandered into the carcass of the old mill building. Inside, a ring of fellows about his age were squatted down on the dirt floor, throwing dice against a fire blackened wall. They looked up when Leon entered.

"Got any smokes, Saxby?" inquired Carl Carlson. Carlson was the one who owned the dice. No one trusted Carl because he won a little more often than it seemed like he should, but since he had the only dice in the group, the other boys had no choice but to tolerate him. Leon pulled a few hand-rolled cigarettes from the breast pocket of Granddaddy Earl's jacket. The old flannel-lined topper had become his favorite. He liked that he could still catch a whiff of his grandfather's pipe smoke in the worn plaid creases. He had admired Granddaddy Earl. He'd been an ornery son of a bitch who didn't take shit off of anyone.

"Got these here ones," Leon replied to Carl. Leon laid the cigarettes on a piece of stone so they wouldn't get filched or stomped on.

"OK, then," Carl told him. "You want to make a wager?"

"What do you got to bet, Carl?" Leon asked the other boy.

"I have actual money," Carl told Leon. "Let's see. A pack costs five cents so how about four smokes against a penny?"

"If you got money, why don't you buy your own, Carl?" Herbert Delois asked him. Herbert was a red-haired, pasty-faced fellow Leon had known from his schooldays. His old man was the attendant at the hospital. It had been Herb who told Leon all about the state hospital and the patients it served. Leon felt that Herbert probably looked down on his family since his mother ended up in that place where Herb's father worked.

"Why don't you stay out of it, Herb." Carl told him. "I don't see you putting anything into the pot." That put Herb in his place. Herb didn't have tobacco or money. His parents made him save whatever change he came to have in a can under his bed. If they heard the can jingle without permission, the boy was required to pay them a penny of his own money as a fine. Herbert crossed his arms over his chest and looked over at Carl.

"I'm not stupid enough to waste my money playing with loaded dice." He smirked when he said it and tried to look tough. He didn't want the other fellows to figure out that he was so controlled by his parents.

"If you're stupid enough to say crap like that, Herb, you'll be lisping it without any teeth from now on," Carl shot back.

Leon came to get away from bickering, not to listen to these two go at each other. "Shake that elbow, Carlson," Leon said to get the game started.

The other boys crowded close to watch the action. First Leon was up a penny, then down eight cigarettes. When the match was called, Carl and Leon were even. It had been a pleasant waste of time with no penalty for either boy to pay. The boys stood to go when Leon remembered that his brother was still over in the copper shop. He hadn't given him a thought until now and wondered if he'd found anything. Probably not, thought Leon, or runt would have been racing over here to tell him.

"I got to go find my brother," Leon told the boys. "He's hunting for copper."

"Hey, Saxby," Herbert called as Leon started for the outside of the building, "you know they're transferring your ma out of here in a few months? My father told me the women are all going to Anoka."

"Yeah. I heard," Leon called back.

"You know why?" Herb asked him.

"No idea, Herb. Makes no difference." Leon hated Herb for bringing up the subject within earshot of the others.

"My old man told me the reason," Herb taunted Leon. "You know how they separate the men and women by that wire fence?" He laughed and glared into Leon's face. "Well guess what? The women were letting themselves get fucked through the holes in the chain link. He said it was the damnedest thing he ever saw. They were squealing like pigs, my pa said." Herb laughed again and looked over at the gang of boys for approval. They covered their shocked smiles with their hands and cast their eyes away from Leon.

Leon stopped in his tracks. The anger and humiliation boiled up inside his body until it popped out on his forehead in beads of sweat.

With a slow, deliberate march, he returned to stand face-to-face with Herbert.

"You're about to get fucked yourself." Before Herb could register the threat, Leon hauled off and blasted the other boy in the mouth. He heard a crunch; he didn't know if it was Herb's teeth or his own bones and he didn't care. Before Herb could hit the ground, Leon was all over him. He grabbed the boy's ginger hair and used it as a handle to raise his head above the ground before he yanked it back down, slamming it into the packed dirt floor. Herbert was screaming, his bloody spittle sprayed Leon in the face. The other boys gathered in a circle around the fighters, yelling encouragement to Leon. Carl was trying to pull Leon off Herbert, but he didn't work at it too hard. Herbert had it coming, in Carl's view, and judging by the shouts of the observers, so did everyone else there.

From fifty yards away, Raymond heard the commotion and went running to see what was going on, hoping that someone had found a significant treasure. It would be exciting to be part of such a find on his first trip to the ruins. As he got closer to the noise, he was able to discern that these shouts were angry. He heard his own brother's name being yelled over and over again. The small boy butted into the agitated scrum. Flailing around in the dirt was his brother, covered in blood and on the verge of homicide. Ray didn't mind if Leon killed Herbert...no one liked Herbert, but he didn't want his brother to go to prison for murder. Ray screamed at the top of his lungs. "LEON! STOP IT!" The sound of Raymond's voice brought Leon to his senses. He pulled back from Herbert, who lay whimpering and limp on the ground.

"Don't you ever talk about that place to me again," he said to Herbert. "If you bring it up again, I'm going to finish what I started." Herbert looked up through his swollen eyes and nodded that he understood. Everyone there, and especially Herbert, knew that Leon meant business.

Leon turned to his shaken little brother. With a smile he asked him, "Did you find anything good, runt?"

Ray shook his head. No. He hadn't found anything good this time, but at least he'd found his brother before he killed that other kid. He reached into his pocket to retrieve a worn handkerchief. He handed it to Leon. "You better get that blood off your face before we get home," he advised his brother.

Leon took the cloth and winked at his younger brother. "This is our secret, right?" he asked. Raymond gave Leon a little salute and tucked the secret into that place in his mind where all the other unspoken deeds were stored.

3

St. Paul, Minnesota 1994

Dwight's family considered church to be somewhere to kill time while Christmas or Easter dinner roasted in the oven. Nominally Methodists, they chose to have Dolores' funeral at the Fairmount Avenue Methodist Church in St. Paul, where she and Raymond had married back in the thirties. The old brick building had lovely stained-glass windows; the center panel depicted Jesus giving comfort to one of his flock. It was flanked on either side by somewhat incongruous scenes of farmers at work. Ray had been thankful for those windows on the rare occasions when he visited the church. They gave him something he could examine if the sermon lacked interest or went on for too long. He would sit there wondering why the farmers had been chosen when there were plenty of prophets and angels that could have taken their spots. He always tried to sit far in the back, where his wandering eyes wouldn't be too obvious to his pew mates. In various iterations, the church had served the city's non-Lutheran and non-Catholic populations for about a hundred years. By 1994, its congregation had dwindled to a few dozen white-haired believers who came as much for the Wednesday card games and coffee as they did for spiritual sustenance. Most had heard all the preaching they would need to secure a berth in heaven. For them, the church was more of a waiting room for what would come next. Like most folks, Raymond disliked funerals. He would have preferred to opt out of attendance at such functions. Unfortunately, the older he got, the more funerals came to be as inescapable as death and taxes; in fact, he noted that the three things always went hand-in-hand. Well into his nineties, he had been to more than his share, and he felt that after he buried Dolores, he shouldn't have to attend another funeral until they dragged him back here in his own casket for a final good-bye.

At the time his mother died in 1994, Raymond's son, Dwight, and I had been keeping each other company for several years. Our circumstances were such that we seldom spent more than a few hours together at any one time. He lived as his father's caretaker in their bungalow near Como Park, and I lived with my two sons in a little house in White Bear Lake. He was quick to point out that my house was conveniently located a short stumbling distance from the White Bear Bar, a rowdy place I had never been to and had no intention of ever going. I would laugh along with him when he joked about how smart I had been to choose such a responsible location, saving me from the possibility of a DUI. I later moved to a lovely, old, stucco foursquare not far from the Payne Reliever, a notorious strip joint in east St. Paul. This gave him an even more salacious reason to rib me. "Location, location, location," he would say with a devilish grin. The reality was that I ended up in those neighborhoods because they were the areas that I could afford on my nursing salary.

Dwight would occasionally drive out to visit me in White Bear Lake when my teenage sons were out at a time that coincided with his father's bingo night at the home. After a teasing suggestion that we walk the two blocks to the bar, Dwight would turn on the television and plop down on the couch. We would spend an hour or so watching a Twins or Vikings game while we consumed Cheez-Its and Coca Cola, a culinary passion that we both happened to share. Often, after he left, I would spend the rest of the evening brushing cracker crumbs from my bed, where we usually ended up if I was confident that the boys had plans that would keep them away until Raymond's bingo game ended at nine o'clock. When Dolores died, I was anxious to support Dwight in his grief and planned to be at his side when they lowered his mother into her grave. Dwight squirmed when I asked him about the service.

"You know, Fiona, Dad wants to keep it very small and quiet," he told me. "Just family. I wish I could invite you but I don't want to do anything to upset him...He's so frail...I just want to get him through this."

Dwight had a tiny tear streaking down his cheek, and I watched it as it disappeared into his moustache. At forty-seven, he was a fine-looking man. His full head of reddish-gold hair was repeated in a curly version on his broad chest, and I loved running my fingers through it, searching for the scar he wore like a medal from his time in Vietnam.

Of course, I understood. Whatever his father needed was fine with me. When I asked him what I could do to help his family, he told me that his father thought I made the best meatloaf he had ever eaten.

"Maybe you could drop off a meatloaf," he told me.

Raymond liked that mine were soft and easy to chew. He also loved the sweet tanginess of the slightly burnt catsup I smeared across the top. So that's what I did. I dropped off one of my Betty Crocker specialties, along with a sympathy card, and waited to see if the changes in their lives might mean that Dwight would have more time to pursue our awkward relationship.

Hastings, Minnesota 1910

It had been eighty-four years since Ray had lost the other important woman in his life. As the latter months of 1909 waned, the family visits to the Hastings Hospital became fewer and brief. Leona was becoming a stranger to Raymond. He would hug her goodbye before she was led back from the cottage dayroom to her dormitory, hoping to feel her love for him in the desperate embrace he offered. More and more, her limp body gave him nothing back. She was still beautiful to him, but it was a strange, haunting beauty. Her skin was pale from the time she spent inside the cottage, and that paleness caused her dark eyes to stare out from her expressionless face like coffee stains on a white linen tablecloth. Her deep auburn locks were no longer piled on top of her head the way she had worn them at home. Now they hung down her back in a single braid that bounced in rhythm with her gait. But that was the only bounce left in Leona, and even that was less pronounced as the months wore on. Her hair became stringy and dull, her skin ashen. When the date for the transfer to Anoka was, at last, imminent, the woman Raymond remembered as his mother had disappeared into a spectral shell.

Leona's transfer away from them was scheduled for sometime in June 1910. Amelia May had just turned two. To Everett's great delight, she was a tiny replica of her mother. Her sparse baby hair had been replaced with soft, dark waves, shot through with sparks of fire where the sun shone the brightest on her head. She was a gregarious little child who never had an inkling that her birth had changed the substance of her family. For Amelia was like any two-year-old; the world and all those in it existed only for her pleasure. Everett rarely told the child "no," despite his mother's concern that too much indulgence might cause the child to turn out exactly like Leona. Lillian thought that Leona had long lacked self-control, and she had never forgotten how the girl had trapped Everett into marriage all those years ago. She secretly harbored the opinion that Leona had ended up right where she should be. Raymond was ten that summer, strong enough to be a substantial help on the farm and old enough to recognize a certain anticipation of relief in himself and the rest of the family that accompanied the upcoming transfer of his mother. And Leon was still with them. Almost sixteen, he had the same swagger that Everett displayed as a younger man, though he lacked Everett's agreeable nature. His desire to get out from under his father's roof only got him as far as the barn, where he knocked together a room for himself out of one of the vacant sheep pens. He fought off the cold of the frigid winter by packing straw between the studs of his makeshift walls and re-purposed a fifty-gallon drum into a primitive wood stove with a flue he made from cast off tin roofing pounded into a cylindrical shape. A floor of uneven barn planks and a simple pallet for a bed finished off his abode. The arrangement worked for Leon, and for about an hour, Ray thought that Leon's departure for the barn would mean that he would get the bedroom all to himself. The very same day that Leon hauled his meager belongings out to his new room, Everett moved himself off the davenport in the parlor and up to the depression in the bed that had been vacated by Leon. His brother had been a fitful sleeper, but Pa slept like a dead man so, all in all, it was an improvement in Ray's circum-stances.

It was well before sunrise when the household was awakened in the early morning hours of June 25, 1910. Everett had left word with the hospital to let him know when Leona was leaving for the train station. When he heard Brownie barking, he pulled back the muslin curtain in the room he now shared with his younger son and peered out the window. The full moon cast the yard in long shadows. He could barely make out the fox terrier running back and forth across the path that led from the road to their place. Beyond the darting dog, he saw the outline of a wagon coming toward their house. The sound of wheels hitting ruts and the jangle of horse tack jarred him fully awake. Beside him, Raymond stirred from a deep sleep.

"What's going on, Pa?" Raymond asked. "Why's Brownie barking?"

Everett was puzzled himself. He reached his hand over and tousled the boy's already disheveled hair. "Not sure, Ray." his father told him. "You go back to sleep, now."

It seemed an ungodly hour to move the patients from the hospital, but Everett silently acknowledged that he had never truly understood the way the hospital operated. Perhaps they had arranged an early train just for the patients so that they would have the station all to them-selves. That made a lot of sense, when he thought about it. He pulled on his britches and an old work shirt that was hanging from a nail in the wall beside the bed. He could hear whoever was down in the yard doing his best to quiet the dog. Everett descended the stairs and was met at the bottom by Lillian. She had a cap over her hair that made Everett think of paintings he had seen of Betsy Ross. He could picture his mother sitting in the rocker, sewing a flag. He was startled from that fleeting vision by a sharp knock at the door. He opened it to see a middle-aged man doing a little dance on the porch to discourage Brownie from nipping at his heels. Everett stepped out to the porch and closed the door behind him, leaving his mother with no option but to plaster her ear against it so she could hear what was being said.

"Go on, dog!" Everett growled to Brownie.

The dog backed off, looking injured at being reprimanded for simply doing his job. Leon, too, was awakened by the commotion. He stood outside the door of the barn, situated about one hundred feet away from the house, and the little dog ran over to take shelter behind Leon's legs. The boy shooed Brownie into the barn, then shut the bottom half of the Dutch door to contain the whining terrier. He walked across the yard to the front porch to find out what had brought such an early visitor. His white union suit glowed like a lantern in the moonlight, giving him a ghostly presence as he approached the men.

"Mr. Saxby?" the man inquired. Everett nodded his affirmation.

"I'm Everett Saxby. What can I do for you?" Everett felt his mouth go dry. He looked over at Leon, who he could tell was concerned. In a nervous gesture he couldn't control, the boy kept trying to jam his hands into non-existent pockets on his long johns.

"I'm from the hospital, sir. I'm afraid I have some disturbing news for you, Mr. Saxby," the man explained.

Everett motioned for the man to sit down on the porch swing. He settled himself onto an old stump they kept by the swing as a table for tea or beer. Everett tried to get Leon to go back to the barn, but he wouldn't budge.

"I can hear whatever he has to say," Leon informed his father. Everett sighed his consent. The boy leaned against the porch railing. Whatever came next, Leon would hear it standing up.

The man took off his hat and stared at his feet.

"As you no doubt are aware, sir, your wife has never responded well to treatment. We were hopeful that a change in her care situation, specifically the upcoming move to Anoka, would have a positive effect on her recovery but she had been steadily slipping into a deeper melancholia over the last several months. Mrs. Saxby was terrified of leaving the area and all that she knew. Nothing we said to her seemed to help alleviate her terror. Even a regimen of laudanum was ineffective. In fact, she was unable to tolerate the drug after the first few doses. Mr. Saxby, I'm sorry to inform you that we found your wife just after midnight. She had made a noose from her sanitary rags and hanged herself from a hinge on the door. I'm so very sorry, Mr. Saxby."

The man fidgeted with the hat in his hands, sliding the brim in a circle through his fingers as he talked. When he finished his report, he stood up, placed the hat back on his head and offered his hand to Everett. Everett stared at him in disbelief. She couldn't be gone. Not his Leona. After taking several moments to compose himself, Everett stood and shook the man's outstretched hand.

"Thank you for coming out this early to let me know," Everett told him. "When can we bring her home?" he asked. Before the man could reply to Everett's question, Leon pushed away from the railing he had been leaning against for support. He turned on his father.

"Why are you thanking him?" he cried. "Why? Their job was to take care of her. All they did was make her sicker and now she's dead." The boy was shaking from shock and fury.

"Isn't that why they call those places asylums? Because they save people from themselves?" The words came out with such force that spittle flew from Leon's mouth. He wiped his chin with the back of his hand, then rubbed it dry against his leg. Everett attempted to reach out for Leon, but he shrugged off his father's touch and turned for the barn. When he had traveled about twenty feet, he stopped and called back to his father.

"Soon as we bury her, I'm leaving. You hear me? You better find someone to take over my work here."

Everett hung his head and mumbled his apology to the messenger. "You must forgive the boy. This is a shock for him...for all of us."

The man put his hand on Everett's shoulder in a gesture of condolence. "You have my sympathies, sir. I'll have someone contact you later today so that you can make arrangements to retrieve your wife's body."

The man boarded his wagon and turned it toward town. When he heard the sound of the wagon and horses moving along, Leon opened the barn door to let out the dog, who barked and antagonized the horses all the way to the road.

"Retrieve your wife's body." Those were words Everett never thought he would hear. In his mind, Leona was always going to return to them, alive and whole. He couldn't imagine what their lives would be like without her. He never once stopped to consider that they had been without Leona for nearly two years or, worse, that Leona had been without herself for even longer. Everett went back into the house where a stoic Lillian held out her arms to her son.

"I heard," she told him. He laid his weary head against his mother's bosom and cried as he hadn't done since he was a young child seeking comfort in her lap.

* * *

In 1867, a group of nine forward-thinking women from the Hastings Methodist Church formed an organization to establish a cemetery close to the river. They called the thirteen-acre plot Lakeside Cemetery, and it was here that Leona was buried on June 27, 1910. Everett and her sons brought her body from the hospital to the farm in the wagon they used for all their transportation chores. They moved the big table from the kitchen into the parlor and laid her on it in her closed pine casket for the day and a half until the burial. All around Leona's body, life went on. Pa and the boys worked the farm; late June was not a time when they could let things go. There were cows to milk and eggs to collect. Stock still had to be fed and weeds needed to be pulled from the furrows in the corn field. The men in the household were grateful for the distraction. Not a word was mentioned among them about how Leona had died. It was silently agreed that any discussion of the subject would only make the reality worse.

Little Amelia May had no idea what was in the big box that stood so prominently in the parlor, though she did register a pervasive sadness in the family. To compensate, she performed various acts of silliness in an attempt to coax smiles from her father and brothers. She tried standing on her head and dressed up the dog in some of her discarded baby clothes, but nothing she did seemed to lighten the mood in the household. Only Grandma Saxby was capable of smiling; Grandma went about her tasks just as she had on any other day---cooking meals, beating the carpets, churning butter. Her biggest complaint was that commandeering the dining table for Leona's bier had made doing her work in the kitchen damned inconvenient, especially when she had so much cooking to do for the funeral. She voiced her displeasure only to Amelia, who was equally disturbed by the table's presence in the parlor. Grandma assured Amelia that by the next afternoon, things would be back to normal. In the meantime, Amelia made a little fort under the table that held her mother's remains and watched the household activities from there.

Grandma Saxby was wrong. Things did not get back to how they had been in the past. The day after Leona's burial, Leon did his morning chores and then spent the rest of the day readying himself for his long-anticipated escape. He made a backpack of sorts from a burlap gunny sack and some rope. What he couldn't pack, he passed on to Ray. To his disappointment, Leon was taking everything he'd hoped to acquire. The only thing of value that he was going to inherit from his brother's departure was the room in the barn. He would finally have his very own space, at least for the summer. Pa said that he was too young to tend a fire in the colder months, that he would need to bunk in the house for the winter. To Raymond, on this late June afternoon, winter was a lifetime away.

Ray watched as Leon struggled to stuff his favorite old jacket of Granddaddy Earl's into the pack. Raymond pointed out that the sleeves extended beyond the hole in the top, but Leon told him it didn't matter. He had to put a piece of canvas over the pack anyway, in case of rain. For some reason, Raymond was much more affected by the idea of losing his brother than he was by his mother's death. He and his brother were bound together by secrets and deeds they had vowed never to share with their parents. The boy couldn't conceive of telling his secrets to Amelia. He wished he could go with his brother, that he could be small enough to crawl into the pack and burrow down beneath the clothes, like a leprechaun he'd seen in a storybook.

"Where are you going?" Ray asked. "You'll write me, won't you Leon?"

"I don't know yet. But I think I'll get to St. Paul and figure it out from there," Leon told him. "And sure, runt. I'll write you soon as I know where I'm going to end up."

This made Ray feel better. He was glad he no longer wrote his own words backwards because now he would be able to send a letter back to Leon; he could still have his brother in his life, if only from a distance. That evening, Leon went up to the house for his final meal before leaving at dawn the next morning. He, his brother and father ate their fried chicken on the front porch, Everett on the swing and his two boys sitting on the steps. The table was now back in the kitchen where it belonged, but they couldn't rid their minds of its most recent function in the household. Amelia and Lillian suffered no such compunction. The sound of high-pitched laughter and clinking cutlery floated from the kitchen table out to the porch where the male contingent sat.

"You got everything together you think you'll need, boy?" Everett asked his older son.

Leon nodded. "I think so, Pa."

Everett looked at his son in a way that he hadn't since Leon was the tiny child he'd carried around on his back when he went out to inspect the farm. His son was a strapping lad, almost six feet tall; his face had taken on the angular contours of a man's, with the hint of a dark beard shadowing his cheeks. Everett was disappointed in himself that all this had occurred without him noticing. So much had happened in the last few years that he had left Leon to grow up on his own. He remembered when Leona had just given birth to their first child. They had anticipated nothing but happiness for their boy. When he was born, the baby looked so much like his mother that he was named for her, and as he approached adulthood, that resemblance had returned. The pale hair of his childhood had changed overnight to his mother's dark auburn hue, but the boy had Granddaddy Earl's whiskey eyes and Everett could see just a trace of mist clouding them now. He knew Leon was hurting. Leaving the farm would only distract the boy from the pain, but maybe that's all he would need to get past his sorrow.

Everett stood and handed his plate of chicken bones to Raymond to hold. He reached into his trouser pocket and pulled out a small leather sack he normally used to hold ammunition for his 30-30 rifle. He handed it to Leon.

"Here you go, boy. I figure you're going to need a little something to get you by until you find work."

Leon pulled apart the rawhide strings that held the pouch tight and peeked inside. There were crumpled paper bills and a couple silver dollars tucked in the bag. Leon shook his head and handed it back to his father.

"I can't take this," he said. "You need this to pay for help around here."

Everett refused to take it back. "You'll do me a favor by keeping it, son. I won't be able to sleep a wink, worrying about you out there on your own. At least with this, you can get some food and maybe a ticket to wherever you think you're going."

The young man nodded to his father and extended his right hand to thank him. Everett grabbed the boy's hand and pulled him into a long, overdue embrace.

"We love you, Leon. We all do. Your ma, too. Maybe her most of all. Be careful, son. You can always come back and we'll be glad to have you."

Everett went directly from Leon's arms into the house, leaving Raymond holding the plate of stripped bones. He sat the plate up on the flat porch rail to keep the dog from grabbing it and looked over at his brother.

"Hey, Leon," he said. "Can you teach me to smoke before you go?"

Leon cracked a one-sided smile at his little brother. "Sure, runt. Let's go out to the barn."

Well before the first traces of sunlight licked the morning horizon, Ray was up to see Leon off. He walked with his brother to the dirt road that bordered their property. They strode ahead at a leisurely pace; there was no hurry. The rest of their lives would start as soon as they parted at the road. Both brothers lingered in their last few moments together, sharing a smoke under the waning stars. When they came to the fork where Leon would go forward and Raymond would go back, they stopped and looked each other in the eye.

"I'm going to miss you," Raymond told his brother. "I'm going to miss having you to talk to. It won't be the same."

"I know, runt." Leon clapped his little brother on the back. "I never thought I'd say it, but I'll probably miss you, too." He laughed and gave Raymond a gentle punch into his shoulder. "Here," he told Raymond. Leon drew the copper ring from the ruins off of his little finger where he had been wearing it since his other fingers had grown too thick. "You always wanted this and now it's yours," he told Ray. "It's a magic ring. Talk to it when you need to tell me something and it will keep your secret until I see you again." He handed Raymond the piece of copper tubing that was shiny and smooth from years on Leon's hand. The younger boy slipped it onto his middle finger.

"Thanks, Leon. I promise not to lose it." Ray's voice caught in his throat as he fought back his emotions.

"Yeah, you better not lose it, runt." He smiled and looked out at the road ahead. "Okay, I got to get now," Leon told him. He picked up his pack and tied it to his back, then started down the road to town. Raymond watched him go until he rounded the curve and disappeared into the glare of the rising sun.

No one heard from Leon for several months until two letters arrived postmarked from Duluth. In the letter he had written to his father, he explained that he was sharing a room in a boarding house in Duluth that had inside bathrooms down the hall and actual hot water running through its taps. He had kicked around at a couple of different jobs: a ditch digger for water lines in the streets of St. Paul, then a coal tender in a hotel boiler room in Duluth. He finally found a promising position at a brewery overlooking the Duluth Harbor and its new aerial transfer bridge. He told his father that he never thought he would get sick of smelling beer, but that was before he worked around the aroma ten hours a day. He reassured Everett that he did much more smelling than he did drinking so he shouldn't worry that his morals were slipping.

In his letter to Raymond, Leon told of the journey itself, some of it by rail and some by foot, until he reached the shores of Lake Superior. He described a lake that went on for as far as you could see, a lake so big that it made Duluth a major shipping port for the upper Midwest. Tucked into the letter to his brother were two crisp, new, beer bottle labels from the Geiger's Brewery. In the middle of a red star on the label was a representation of the building where Leon worked. Raymond carefully positioned the labels between pages of his mother's old bible to keep the new from wearing off of them. It gave him a certain contentment to be able to open his mother's bible to see the very place where he could imagine his brother working. It felt to him that Ma had wrapped her paper arms, full of heavenly grace, around Leon and she would keep him safe until Raymond could go to find him.

4

———

"There's a war coming in Europe, Mama. I heard the fellas at the bank talking about the Germans and the English getting at each other." Everett informed his mother of the news he'd heard in town. Four years to the day after Leon left the farm, an Archduke of Austria and Hungary was assassinated in Sarajevo. For reasons Everett didn't understand, that event had caused such disruption in Europe that major alliances had banded together to fight against each other in what would come to be called The War to End All Wars. In Hastings, Minnesota, in the fall of 1914, those events were so remote that they served merely as topics of conversation when too much good weather gave the locals little to talk about.

"Well, they can just keep all that silliness over there, where it belongs," Lillian replied.

Everett was helping his mother string a temporary line for hanging the laundry. The poles for the old system had rotted away where they contacted the soil and Everett had set new ones in cement to keep them solidly in the ground. At six, Amelia May was learning to write, and she was delighted when Everett let her scratch out her name in the wet cement at the base of the poles.

"There you go, darling girl," he told her. "Now your name will mark this spot forever." Amelia hugged her father around his knees, then squatted down to poke a stick in the gray slurry to check if it had dried.

"Now, now, Amelia. You can't play with that anymore today," Everett said. "You don't want to mess up your name, do you?" Everett pulled the girl up and tossed her stick to the ground.

"How about you, Mama? You want to immortalize yourself, too?" Everett asked his mother.

Lillian was pleased that Everett and the children had finally shaken off the malaise brought about by Leona's death. It had taken four years for Everett to start teasing her again, an encouraging sign that meant Everett was getting back to his old self.

"No thanks, son," she teased him back. "The only time I want my name etched somewhere permanent is when I join your father in the cemetery."

Another encouraging sign was that Everett was showing some interest in a youngish widow to whom Lillian had introduced him at church. The woman was thirty-five to Everett's forty years of age and while she was likely past her prime childbearing years, she came with three robust teenage sons and a four hundred acre farm a bit farther from town than the Saxby place. Raymond knew the boys from school. He neither liked them nor disliked them. Mostly, he had never paid them any attention at all. He was annoyed when his grandmother asked him about those boys and what they were like. Grandma seldom asked him about specific individuals unless she had some ulterior reason to seek out the information, and he was pretty sure this situation would be no different. Whenever she was able to corral him alone in the kitchen, she pumped him for details on the widow's sons.

"You know the Blume boys, don't you Raymond?" asked his grandmother.

He nodded to her. "Sure. I know them. You know I do, Grandma," Ray reminded her.

Grandma gave him an encouraging smile to try to elicit information from the reluctant boy. Ray had turned fourteen a few months earlier. He wished he could show his brother that he was no longer the worthless runt Leon knew before he left. Raymond had shot up in the last few months. His wrists and ankles protruded beyond the hems of his clothes, and Pa had promised that before school started, he would have Grandma sew him some new shirts and a couple pair of trousers to accommodate his elongated body. He hadn't measured himself, but he was sure he was over six feet tall now, a good three inches taller than his father. His voice was getting deeper each time he opened his mouth and, like his brother before him, he had lost the baby fat in his face. He had soft blond whiskers sprouting from his cheeks and over the top of his lip, along with a few pustular eruptions of adolescence scattered across his forehead. Where Leon's coloring had darkened as he approached adulthood, Ray stayed fair; his hair was as straight and pale as corn silk. The blue of a crisp Minnesota sky in January was captured in the color of the boy's bright eyes, perched above an aquiline nose. He flashed those eyes now at his grandmother.

"What do you want to know about them for?" he asked her.

Raymond knew perfectly well why his grandmother was interested in the widow's sons. She was hoping they'd be Pa's sons in the near future. He calculated that if his father married the widow Blume, he would acquire one hundred acres for each of his new family members, along with a big brick house and all the help the new sons could provide.

"They're fair enough fellows," Ray told his grandmother. "I've never had any problem with them. The middle one is a different sort, though. He seems quiet; not all there, if you know what I mean."

Lillian thought about this appraisal. "Tell me again, how old is this young man?" she asked her grandson.

"I don't know, Grandma. Maybe thirteen, but a backward thirteen, if you get what I'm trying to say."

He explained as best he could without outright insulting the younger boy for his strange, immature ways. Ray had been on the receiving end of scorn from his classmates for most of his childhood and, for that reason, he was inclined to give the boy some latitude in his assessment.

"Well, look at you!" Grandma exclaimed. "You were a quiet little mite yourself just a few years ago, weren't you, Raymond?"

Ray knew that his grandmother had convinced herself already that nothing would do but for Everett to hijack Mrs. Blume into matrimony before someone else beat him to the punch. As he wondered what Leon would think about such an arrangement, he twisted the copper ring around his finger to secretly telegraph his concerns to his brother at the beer factory a million miles away.

When Everett first encountered Arabella Blume chatting with his mother at a church picnic several months earlier, he'd thought she was a comely woman, if a bit well-padded for his taste. Mrs. Blume had borne five sons over a span of six years, three of which had survived past infancy, and the corset around her waist failed to disguise the toll those pregnancies had taken on her body. He couldn't help but notice that she was holding a plate of chocolate cake, layered with thick fudge frosting. He surmised that such indulgences probably added to her zaftig figure. Lillian had taken a keen interest in the widow and had called him over to meet her and her boys. He pulled Amelia May away from a gaggle of little girls in Sunday dresses to make the woman's acquaintance.

"Mrs. Blume," Lillian said with a sugary smile on her lips, "I want you to meet my son, Everett, and this is his youngest, Amelia."

Everett tipped his hat to the woman and was rewarded with a bright smile that redirected his gaze away from her proportions and onto her lovely face. She had smooth, olive skin and bright green eyes that twinkled when they met his.

"Very nice to meet you, Ma'am." Everett offered a shy smile of his own.

"Oh, please," said Mrs. Blume, "do call me Arabella and I must call you Everett. Your mother speaks of you so often, I feel I have known you for years."

"And you could have, Arabella," Lillian told her through her upturned lips, "if only he would come to church more than once or twice a year."

Lillian was sure she was handling this encounter just right. Everett cocked his head at his mother then turned to face the woman.

"Yes, indeed. Arabella, then, it shall be," Everett replied.

Lillian was so pleased that she could hardly interrupt her grin to introduce the widow's sons. "And these are her boys, Frank, James and Walter," his mother said as she pointed out each one as his name was recited.

Everett offered his hand to each boy in turn. He thought the middle son, James, seemed a little off in some way. He was a good-looking youngster, maybe a bit younger than Raymond, but he appeared disengaged from his surroundings and wouldn't reach out to shake hands with Everett. He only cast his eyes downward and grunted a soft greeting. Feeling ignored, a rare situation for Everett's daughter, Amelia made her presence known.

"I'm Amelia May," the Saxby girl informed her new friends. "I'm six!"

The adults chuckled at the child's greeting, and Everett lightly tugged the girl's braid to remind her to keep her peace until spoken to.

"Well, I am six!" Amelia retorted to the gentle reprimand.

She was delighted when this statement elicited a laugh from all but James, who only gave her a vacant stare.

A couple of summers had passed since Everett first heard the story of Albert Blume's demise. One of the more prosperous farmers in the area, he had been pulling a new, state-of-the-art disc behind his team of horses when his wife became aware that the sky was darkening in the distance. The faint scent of ozone was freshening the air. She knew rain was on the way. When she went outside to round up her boys, she heard the rumble of thunder and saw thunderbolts light up clouds that were so low they hovered flat against the far-off horizon. Once the boys were safely inside, Arabella ran out to the field where Albert was cutting under last year's weeds and spent barley with the still-shiny disc.

"Come on in before you get wet," Arabella called to him.

Albert looked at the clouds and figured they wouldn't be over them for a bit. "No," he told her, "I can make one more go-round. I hate to go in when it's still dry. I'll be in shortly. You go on back."

He smacked the horses with the reins and continued with the next patch of stubble. He had plowed under a couple more rows when the first drops of rain fell on his dusty back.

"Alright then," he said to himself. "Time to get ourselves to the barn." He unhitched the horses and watched as they made their way to shelter. As he was removing the harness from the metal disc, a bolt of lightning speared itself into the piece of steel he was touching, shooting Albert through with enough electricity to light up every house in Hastings. He was instantly killed. When Arabella and Frank slogged through the rain to see what was keeping him, they found him splayed out next to his newest farm implement, smoke still wafting from the burnt soles of his muddy boots.

In response to his mother's prodding, Everett began to attend church more regularly. He had dropped away from his long-held belief in a benevolent God after he'd lost his wife in such a traumatic way; he had no use for a vengeful God or any church that told him he must accept "God's willy-nilly will," as he called it to Raymond. He didn't think much of some of God's decisions, but he was willing to reconsider church now that attendance might offer him more than just an hour of wasted time on a Sunday morning. He and Amelia began to sit in the pew behind the Blumes on their weekly visits. Raymond had long since come to regard his brother's outlook on matters of religion as his own. He preferred to stay home to hunt rabbits on the sabbath. Everett and his daughter eventually moved up to sit beside Arabella and her boys after a couple months of polite nods and gestures of interest between Everett and Mrs. Blume. Lillian Saxby watched the fledgling relationship from her customary perch in the choir loft. She enjoyed the elevated view of the church proceedings and, especially, she enjoyed being witness to the next chapter in Everett's life.

Courtship under the watchful stares of ninety or so church members became so awkward that Everett decided he either had to go back to skipping church or he had to ask Arabella Blume to be his wife. His mother reminded him daily of what a lovely person Mrs. Blume was and wasn't it a shame she had to raise those boys on her own? She pointed out what a choice piece of land Mrs. Blume had for her farm and wouldn't Everett love to have such a place himself one day? Her relentless encouragement made Everett feel like a doomed steer, cornered in the slaughtering pen. He knew in his heart that he had no love for the Blume woman; his capacity for that kind of love had faded along with his memory of Leona's face. Still, Arabella was easy enough on the eyes, and he could imagine lying on her generous body for carnal comfort at the end of the day.

In an embarrassing nod to romance, Everett Saxby and Arabella Blume married on Valentine's Day, 1915. Hours before the ceremony took place, Everett rode into town to lay sprigs of holly on Leona's grave. It was the only decent looking foliage he could find in the deep winter month of February, but he knew Leona would appreciate the effort. He told her that she would always be his one love but that he had to take comfort where he could find it so that he could go on for Raymond and little Amelia. For the first time since Leona's death, Everett felt released from his bond to his late wife. That sense of freedom lasted about fourteen hours, until Arabella led him to her room in the big brick house.

All the heady anticipation of marital bliss was obliterated when Arabella instructed Everett on how to undress, where and how to hang his clothes, what places on his body to wash, and with which soap, and how to enter her from behind so that she wouldn't have to witness any part of what he was doing. He had seen more tenderness between mating hogs. He realized as he rolled to one side of the bed after the consummation of his marriage that he had made a mistake that day that would last the rest of his natural life. Before he could surrender to sleep and end his waking nightmare, Arabella demanded that he go wash himself again so that he wouldn't stain her expensive linens.

Combining the Saxby and Blume homesteads was both an emotional and physically arduous task. Everett's family had been ensconced on the farm for three generations, since Lillian's family had emigrated from Sweden decades ago, long before she and Earl inherited it from her father shortly after their marriage. While their personal belongings inside the house were limited, over fifty years of discarded agricultural refuse littered the old barn and outbuildings. It had been decided by Arabella that the Saxby farm would be turned over to tenant farmers, despite Everett's wish to ask Leon if he would like to come back to take over its operations. Arabella insisted that the income from proven farm tenants would be much more valuable to them than anything Leon could produce. She further mollified him by pointing out that the farm would still be in the family and if he wanted to repossess it someday, he could.

Everett found it less aggravating to go along with Arabella's wishes. She was a woman of very definite ideas, and she could make a man's life miserable if he objected to her plans. After six months of marriage, Everett was convinced that Albert Blume had run headlong into a lightning bolt just to get away from the constant nagging. Everett silently acknowledged that he had made his bed and now he would have to lie in it. The fact that it was a rather luxurious bed helped Everett to accept the consequences of his new marriage. The big house had electricity, something he could never have afforded to install at his farm. Arabella was placing an indoor commode on the second floor of the house and was talking about the possibility of an indoor bathtub as well. She hadn't mentioned it to him before they married, but Arabella Blume Saxby was a wealthy woman, at least by Hastings standards. Albert Blume hadn't been a particularly successful farmer. It had been his wife's money all along that made him appear so to the rest of the town. She was the only surviving daughter of the owner of several small spur railroad lines throughout the Midwest. When her father died a widower several years before, Arabella became one of the few well-off women in the Hastings area who didn't have her family name painted on the side of a building, like the Smeads or the Pringles. For the first time in his life, Everett didn't have to constantly worry about how he was going to feed his family...the problem had become how to keep his family from running away from Arabella's iron fist.

Despite her wealth, Arabella was not one to hire help when newfound familial resources could augment the labor that was needed to manage her farm. She was eager to welcome the Saxby family into her home, but she made it clear that there was a hierarchy that must be respected and expectations that must be fulfilled. Lillian, who had been such an advocate for the marriage, was the first casualty of Arabella's demands. In place of a fine room in the new house, Lillian was relegated to a service room off the kitchen. The room had not been wired for electrical service like the rest of the house, and it had a draughty window and a narrow mattress for her to share with Amelia. When Everett proposed bringing in the beds from his place to make the room more comfortable for his mother and daughter, Arabella would have none of it. Anything that couldn't be washed in a tub or dried on a line was considered by the new Mrs. Saxby to be contaminated and forbidden entry into her home. Everett was able to bring some of his own livestock and tools to his new abode, but the rest was to be sold or left behind for the tenants. Arabella subscribed to the idea that fine people required fine things in their lives and the sooner Everett shed the detritus of his old life, the sooner he would meet her image of a suitable husband.

"I'm staying behind. I'll work with the tenants," Raymond told his father as he helped him transfer some equipment into Arabella's large stone barn. Most of the moving would have to wait for spring, but the livestock couldn't be left behind. Already, Raymond could see that there would be problems with the horses. King and Queenie had never known any other home than the Saxby place and after the work day, the horses automatically headed for their stalls in the old barn, two miles away.

Everett had made this devil's bargain for the betterment of his family, and he had no intention of allowing Raymond to throw away the opportunities this new life could provide. "Ray. Listen to me, son," his father implored the boy. "It's always hard to make changes but I need you to trust me. This is going to be a better life for all of us. It's going to take some getting used to, is all."

Ray could tell his father was trying to talk himself into it. He knew that his grandmother was disappointed at her station in Arabella's home. If she had anticipated a life of leisure as she entered her sixties, she was forced to deal with another reality. She went from caring for four at the old farm to having to prepare the food and do the wash for eight. Lillian was loath to admit that she had miscalculated in her assessment of Mrs. Blume. She vowed to endure the situation for Everett's sake. As long as she arrived at church every Sunday in full view of the other congregants in a new Chalmers Model 24 horseless carriage, she could put aside her own aspirations of comfort for the good of her family.

* * *

Raymond, too, had some adjustments to make when he moved into the big house.

"That's my drawer," Frank informed Raymond. "Get your stuff out of there."

Ray had put his few items of clothing in an empty drawer in the room he shared with Frank on the second story of the big house. "Where am I supposed to put my clothes, Frank?"

Frank looked around the room and kicked an empty apple crate over to Raymond's feet. "Use that," he told him.

Ray did as he was told. He could understand how Frank might feel. He didn't like sharing a room with a stranger, either. Ray was determined that if he had to be in this situation, he would do his best to make it work. Both his father and his grandmother had lectured him on the importance of compromise as the two families learned to adapt to one another's ways. Though to Ray, it was pretty clear which family would do the compromising.

When his mother married Everett Saxby, Frank was sixteen. Arabella intended that her oldest son should continue his schooling so that he could someday attend the University of Minnesota. Raymond, she told Everett, was not a boy who would profit from advancing his education, and she proposed that since he was fifteen, Ray should become a regular hand on her farm. With Arabella, it was always her farm, not their farm. When Everett protested that it should be up to Ray to decide, Arabella suggested that the boy's future could be determined by a coin toss. Because Ray didn't actually care one way or the other, he consented to her idea and, of course, he lost the throw. His time as a student came to an end in Jun, 1915. He would toil alongside his father and the seasonal help needed to work a four-hundred-acre operation. Walter, Arabella's youngest, was only ten so he would return to school for at least four more years, and that left only James' future to decide. Everett let it be known that there would be no discussion about his Amelia May. She would complete at least eight grades before he would reconsider the subject of her education. On this point, Arabella relented.

Ray and Everett were working together in the milking barn when the subject of Pa's new sons entered their conversation. "How are you getting on with the other boys, Ray?" his father asked him.

"Well," Raymond offered, "Frank pays me very little mind as long as I keep my belongings under the bed where he doesn't have to look at them. He reminds me a lot of Mama` (Arabella insisted the Saxby children call her by a maternal moniker with an accent on the second syllable). He wants everything perfect looking at all times...I don't hate him...I guess we tolerate each other the best we can."

Everett nodded his understanding of Ray's situation rooming with the older boy. "And James?" Pa asked.

Raymond thought a moment before he responded. "I don't quite know what to make of that fella. Do you know what he does, Pa? He sits under the stairs reciting multiplication tables for hours. Then, he goes to the bookshelves and takes out each book, opens the front cover, sniffs it, closes it back up, then puts it back on the shelf. It's the damnedest thing I ever saw. When I asked him why he does that, he just gave me that dead-eyed stare and grabbed the next book."

Everett shook his head. "I know, son. He is a strange little fellow but he seems harmless enough."

Raymond agreed, but the behavior bothered him. "I guess so, Pa, but he seems like he might end up living in a cottage at Ma's old hospital, if you ask me."

Everett didn't respond to that remark, but he had to agree that it was a distinct possibility. Then Ray offered his opinion on the youngest, Walter.

"Walter's just plain worthless as tits on a boar. No wonder Mrs. Blume wanted you to marry her. Not a one of her boys will do a lick of work." Everett silently agreed with Ray's assessment of his marriage.

The brightest development in Ray's new living arrangement was the 1914 Chalmers automobile that Arabella had purchased months before the marriage. She had no interest in driving it. She considered driving an automobile unseemly for a woman, but she enjoyed the stares and waves she got as Everett drove them into town for the weekly shopping trip. Everett tried to teach Frank how to operate the car, but the young man had no patience for anything he couldn't master in under an hour. Getting the feel of the clutch, throttling the engine, using the brakes, all rattled the boy. He hated the way Raymond and Walter laughed when he caused the car to lurch and die after traveling less than twenty feet.

James was interested in the car but not as a mode of transportation. If he wasn't watched, the boy would have the hood rolled back and engine parts positioned in a perfectly straight line along the floor of the barn. Everett became so frustrated with James' mechanical aspirations that he had Arabella build a garage to the side of the house, one of the first garages on a farm in the area. He put a lock on the swing door and kept the car safely stowed away from the boy's destructive hobby. When he did allow James near the car, he watched as the youngster disassembled the engine; then Everett supervised him to be sure he put it back together. It was the one activity Everett did with the strange child where they were able to relate. James had no use for words, but he was a natural with his hands. Everett thought the boy might have potential after all.

Unlike his step-brothers, Raymond took to driving as if he'd been born for the activity. Everett took him along on his trips to town and taught him how to operate the vehicle. On these excursions, Everett would venture to some side road and let Ray practice his skills. Since his wife objected to Raymond learning to drive, the activity became a covert bonding time for father and son. Other times, Everett would bring James along with them to give the quiet lad some time away from his strange, solitary activities. On one such occasion, the Chalmers rattled and clanged to a stop on a forlorn dirt road, miles from town or the farm. Everett was positive the gas tank was properly filled, but the engine seemed starved for fuel. Without prompting, James opened the hood and began to remove and inspect the parts. He crawled under the car and examined hoses and wires. Within twenty minutes, the boy had the car purring again and they were on their way. Ray and his father both gave James a clap on the back, a gesture he didn't really appreciate as touch was bothersome to the boy, but he recognized in his bizarre way that he was being rewarded for a job well-done. It was the first time Ray and Everett had seen the boy smile.

* * *

Despite Arabella's decree that James would continue school, when the end of the 1916 school year approached, the school voiced a different opinion on the subject. They told her that, while James appeared bright enough, his antisocial tendencies and unsettling habits were becoming too disruptive for the other students. The principal told her that he would line up the chalk in its tray so that it sat perfectly straight and in order, from large pieces to small. If the teacher or another student used a stick and didn't return it to its proper place, he would become upset, storm up to the board and wipe all the chalk onto the floor. He refused to read any word that started with the letter "q." This was a minor inconvenience since so few words started with this letter, but it was another sign of his idiosyncrasies. He also had a peculiar affinity for arithmetic. As soon as the teacher wrote a problem on the board, James would shout out the answer before she had a chance to explain the concept. Other than required reading, these outbursts were among the few verbal expressions James made in the classroom. He was usually mute. School officials told Arabella that James was worthy of an education, just not in the Hastings schools.

"I am so insulted I could spit nails!" Arabella complained to her husband when she returned from the school conference. "How dare they tell me James cannot return to that school full of rural riff-raff."

Everett tried to look sympathetic. In reality, he'd wondered why

James had been allowed to attend classes as long as he had. Arabella continued her rant.

"He's a special child! They have no understanding of his genius," she complained to him.

Everett didn't entirely disagree with her. He thought the boy had talents, just different ones from those that his mother valued. Her tirade gave him a chance to bring up an idea that had been formulating in his mind.

"You're right, dear," he began. "James has a very specific aptitude. He's a genius for mechanical puzzles. Now that automobiles are more and more plentiful around here, maybe the best thing to do is let him develop his skills for repairing engines."

"That sounds so low-class to me," Arabella replied. "I had planned for him to follow Frank to the university."

Everett had long since learned not to argue with his wife. He simply put his arm around her shoulder and told her, "Let me work with him a bit. If my ideas for James don't lead to something he can hang his future on, we can talk about getting the boy a special tutor."

Arabella was relieved that Everett would take over her concerns about her troubling middle son. "Now then," she said, "we should have a glass of sherry to relax before Lillian and Amelia serve supper."

Supper wasn't served that night by either Lillian or Amelia. When Arabella and Everett went downstairs to pour themselves an aperitif, they heard Amelia screaming in the kitchen. They went to investigate and found the girl crouched over her grandmother. Lillian lay sprawled out on the kitchen floor, a well-done rump roast spilled from its pan beside her. Horrified, Everett tried to rouse his mother but her eyes were rolled back in her head, and he knew she was gone. His indomitable mother, the one person he had always thought invincible, went to her maker with yellow potholders on her hands. For the first time, Everett noticed Lillian's legs. Under her skirt, which had hiked up over her knees in the fall, her calves were swollen and discolored; just above the tops of her boots, shallow ulcers pocked her ankles. Her high-topped shoes were left unbuttoned to accommodate her edema-tous feet.

Everett was sickened by the sight of his mother's hidden physical condition, and Amelia was beside herself with shock. When the adults asked her what had happened, the eight-year-old told them that Grandma had asked her to go out to the porch to get a couple of onions and when she came back in, she saw her grandmother wobble with the roast in her hands, then collapse to the floor.

"I thought she slipped," Amelia said through sobs. "I tried to help her up but she wouldn't even try! Is she dead, Papa? Is Grandma dead?" the distraught child asked her father.

Everett folded the child into his arms. "You were a good girl, trying to help your grandma," her father told her. "You know, sweet girl, Grandma loved having you in the kitchen, learning by her side. You can always be proud that you were the one who was with her when God called her to heaven."

The child dissolved into tears and fell against Everett's chest. Behind him, Arabella pulled the potholders from Lillian's limp hands and picked up the steaming roast. She threw it into the sink. As she surveyed the scene of the dead woman on the linoleum floor, slippery with splattered grease, she shook her head in annoyance.

"Christ...what a mess," was all she had to say about the passing of Lillian Saxby.

With both his mother and his maternal grandfather struck dead while going about their everyday business, Everett began to wonder if the same fate awaited him; if his time would be suddenly cut short. It made him think about what mattered in this life. He was only a few years younger than Grandfather Anderson had been when he suffered a heart attack and died on Easter so many years ago, and while Dr. Becker couldn't say for sure without cutting into Lillian's chest to examine her heart, the doctor told Everett that very few other causes of death will hit so quickly and completely as a heart stoppage. He explained to Everett that the condition of her legs further indicated a problem with her circulation. The only other possibility Becker offered was a cerebral hemorrhage.

Everett could imagine his mother having a defect in her occasionally cold heart but never in her brain. She had always had a steel trap mind. He blamed himself for putting her in a position where she was working overtime at an age when she should have been content to sit on the porch and crochet doilies. He blamed himself and he blamed Arabella, who had treated Lillian like a servant or, at best, a poor relation. Everett had been increasingly unhappy with the bargain he'd made for a brick house and four hundred acres. Now he was miserable from loss and guilt, much as he had been after Leona's death.

"I'm going to insulate that service room for Amelia and pull the electric lines over there so she can have comfort at night like the rest of us," Everett told Arabella one morning at breakfast a few months after Lillian died. "Either that, or I'm going to sleep in that room and Amelia can make a pallet up in your room. I'm not about to let you continue to treat my daughter with the same indifference that you treated my poor mother."

Arabella stopped chewing the chunk of toast and pumpkin butter she had in her mouth. She looked at her husband with disbelief. "What did you just say to me, Everett?" She nearly choked on indignation. "Let me remind you that this is my house and I make the rules about what goes on in it. You stick to the barn, Everett, and leave the household arrangements to me."

Arabella rose from the table, stuffing the last of the toast into her mouth. Everett wondered how she could get the food past her pursed lips. The thought brought a hint of a smile to his face. She slammed the plate on the counter and whirled to face him. Her anger exploded when she noticed his sly smile.

"Why are you smirking at me?" she screamed at him. "Do you know how lucky you are to have all this?" She waved her arms at the well-appointed room around them; the electric lights were giving her raging green eyes a demonic glow. "You impoverished, miserable old Job's turkey!" she wailed at her husband.

With that ridiculous insult ringing in his ears, Everett couldn't help himself. He burst out laughing and told her through his sniggering, "You, woman, have taught me more about the true value of principles and compassion than all the bible stories put together. There's not a scrap of furniture, an electric fixture or water closet in the world worth the price of being dominated by the likes of you. You can take your brick house, your four hundred acres and your pompous, gentrified ways and stuff it all up your generous backside...the only generous thing about you, I might add," Everett informed the irate woman. "The children and I will be out of here as soon as I can make arrangements."

Everett stood to grab his hat. Any worry he felt about displacement was pushed aside by the feeling of release his declaration had stirred in him. "About goddamn time I stood up for my family," Everett told himself.

Arabella couldn't believe what was happening. Her money and position had always shielded her from the repercussions of her controlling ways. "What will people say?" she screamed at him.

Everett thought for a moment before he told her. "They'll say 'What took Saxby so long to come to his senses?' I should never have let visions of feather beds and indoor commodes trap me in this pretty prison. I'm done, Arabella. There's no more to be said about it."

That afternoon, when Amelia came home from school, Everett shooed her and Ray into the little service room off the kitchen that held the remnants of his mother's existence. Her bible lay on the dresser, held open to the last passage she'd read by the weight of her tortoise-shell hair brush. Silver and gold hairs sprung from the brush and caught the afternoon light that filtered in through the draughty old window. Her Sunday shawl was draped over the bedpost, just as she had left it, and her calfskin gloves hung from the back of the single ladderback chair that she and Amelia had alternately shared. Everett sat down with Amelia on the broken-down bed, covered by Lillian's faded marriage quilt, and indicated to Ray that he should sit in the chair.

"Mind your grandmother's gloves, there Ray," he told his son. Raymond slipped the gloves from the wooden rail and handed them to Amelia, who sat stroking the soft, black leather with her small hands.

"Children," he began, "I am like any other man. I am loath to admit that I have been wrong. But, by God, I couldn't have been more wrong than to marry Mrs. Blume. We're just too damned different, her and me. I intend to end this marriage and get us back to a life that means something to our family. We are, all of us, done kowtowing to the likes of the Blumes."

Ray and Amelia sat quietly, waiting for an explanation about what this new, meaningful life would look like for them, but Everett offered no more details. Finally, to break the silence if nothing else, Ray spoke.

"Pa, what are we supposed to do in the meantime?"

Everett hadn't thought this part through. He lowered his head and held his chin in his hand, considering the best way to handle the period of discomfort that was on the horizon. "I suspect the next few weeks will be damned difficult for you two. Best you stay as polite as you can and only complain to me if any of the Blume bunch gives you grief. I have some ideas for our future that will take a bit of time to work out." Everett rose from the bed and pulled both children into an embrace. Even Ray, at sixteen, welcomed the physical demonstration of his father's commitment to his children and surrendered to the man's fierce hug.

PART II

THE BIG LAKE

5

Dr. Quam was gradually outgrowing Lillian Saxby's modest cottage in Hastings. In the years since he had entered into his arrangement with Lillian, the young dentist had married and produced four children with his wife Mary, a local girl who knew everyone in Hastings. Her connections help convince wary townspeople that a yearly trip to the dentist, even if no problem was evident, was a valuable expenditure. At a time when removal of natural teeth was considered the best way to protect one's health from disease and infection, Dr. Quam was an advocate for preserving a God-given smile. Anyone who entered his practice for a dental concern left with a small container of Johnson and Johnson dental floss and instructions to use it daily. While most patients had no intention of running string between their teeth, they valued the sturdy waxed string for its ability to stick to itself and form tight knots. Some used it as thread to mend heavy materials such as leather or tarps. Dr. Quam did his best to convince folks to use the floss as it was intended, but he also recognized that if they didn't, it meant that they would be back for a toothache or an abscess that would fatten his wallet. When Everett came to speak to him about the rent shortly after Lillian's death, Dr. Quam informed Everett that he was looking for larger quarters for his expanding practice and growing family. Soon after his declaration to Arabella that he and his children would be leaving her farm as soon as arrangements could be made, Everett went to Dr. Quam to speed the doctor's departure from the cottage. It was time to inform the children that they would be moving to the town, a departure from the rural life they had always known.

Everett had retained unlimited use of the Chalmers as neither Frank nor Arabella could drive it and she refused to sit in it alongside him for any reason that could be avoided. If the price of removing Everett and his common offspring from her sight was acquiescing on the use of the car, Arabella thought it a bargain. This meant that Everett was no longer expected to attend church, and Sunday mornings once again became a time of quiet reflection for him. While the Blumes sat on a hard pew, Everett roamed the countryside in the Chalmers. He used the car as a means of escape from Arabella as often as he could. One weekend afternoon, Everett piled his children into the car for a brief trip into town for a phosphate at the ice cream parlor. As the Saxby children settled themselves onto the seats, James stood watching them from the front steps, a worried look on his freckled face.

"James," Everett called to the boy, "want to come along? We're going to the ice cream parlor." The boy simply nodded his head and made himself comfortable in the back of the automobile, next to Amelia.

The automobile not only afforded the family ready transportation, it became the perfect venue for planning the "next adventure," Everett's term for his upcoming separation from Arabella. "I've spoken with Dr. Quam," he told them as he drove into town. "He is going to vacate the cottage by the first of the month and we will be moving in shortly after that."

Raymond was surprised. He had expected that they would be going back to the old farm. "What about the livestock and King and Queenie?" he asked his father.

Everett could tell by the boy's voice that he was concerned about these animals he had known all his life. "Well, they will be going back to our farm. The only difference is that the tenants will be caring for them instead of us. This will be best for them and the income from the tenants will help us get ourselves established in town," he told his children. "I have given this next phase of our lives considerable thought. Actually, it was James who helped me come up with this idea."

Upon hearing his name, James turned his head away from the passing scenery to listen to what Everett was saying.

"What with all the automobiles around now and how often they break down, we're going to start a filling station and automobile repair shop at the cottage. We can put the gas pump out front by the street and convert the carriage house into a garage for the repair shop. I just need to put in a little stove for warmth in the winter and we'll be good to get started." Raymond looked over his shoulder to see Amelia's reaction. The girl shrugged in a noncommittal way, but young James had a rarely seen smile on his face. Everett continued. "I've spoken with James' mother and she has consented to have him live with us. He will be our main mechanic and I've ordered a manual on repair work so we can both figure things out as we go."

In fact, Arabella had made taking James one of her conditions for Everett to retain the automobile. Everett could keep the car as long as he took the embarrassing boy with him. After the humiliating episode with the school principal, Arabella considered her middle son a social liability. She offered to help Everett with the startup costs of his new business in return for James's room and board and vocational training. It turned out to be an arrangement that suited all concerned, except perhaps Raymond.

Raymond thought this all sounded promising, but it also seemed like he was being displaced by his younger step-brother. "What about me, Pa? What am I supposed to do?" Raymond asked.

"Don't worry, son. We're going to need someone to man the pump out by the street and wait on folks while James and I work on the cars. You'll be the face of our new business, Ray."

This sounded like a do-nothing proposition to Ray...the kind of position offered to the weak link. Raymond decided in that moment that the time had come to seek his fortune elsewhere. He would write to Leon for advice. The thought of his brother made him aware of the now-too-small copper ring his brother had given him years before. He cupped it in his hand where it rested against his chest on its rawhide cord. It felt warm in his fingers from the heat of the skin that lay between the ring and his heart. Leon would tell him what to do.

* * *

"You'll give your brother our love, won't you, boy?" Everett asked Raymond. Father and son walked to the car parked in the carriage house, each carrying a piece of luggage ready for Ray's departure on the train for Duluth. Ray stopped to watch James, who was painting over the side of the carriage house that had served as an advertisement for Dr. Quam's dental practice. Broad strokes of deep green paint were covering the yellow boards where Dr. Quam's somber face advised the townsfolk to "Take care of your teeth."

"Hey there, James," Raymond called to the younger boy. "What are you going to put on there once you get it painted?"

When James turned to engage Ray directly, Raymond was amused to see the flecks of green paint sharing space on the boy's face with his multitude of freckles. James's red hair was shaggy on his neck, where it poked out from the old newsboy cap he was wearing to protect himself from the sun. The boy's upturned button nose gave his countenance a playful demeanor, but James was all business when he informed Ray of the new signage. "Saxby and Son Automobile and Engine Repair," James proclaimed in his monotone style of speech. That simple statement told Raymond that he was making the right decision to leave. He was not the son who had the knack for auto repair.

"Sounds good, James. You guys take care," was all Ray said to the boy as a final farewell.

Once at the station, Everett bought Ray's ticket for the first leg of his journey and handed him his suitcase and duffle. "You write as soon as you get settled in, boy," Everett told him. "Let me know if you and your brother need anything." Ray nodded to assure his father he would be in touch. "I'm going to miss you, son," Everett admitted to his sixteen-year-old child. The last thing Raymond wanted was for either one of them to surrender to emotion and make a scene. To move things along,

Ray gave his father's shoulder a brief squeeze of affection before he stepped up onto the train.

Raymond gestured farewell to his father from the entrance to the economy coach, then slipped inside to find his seat. He tossed his bags into the overhead luggage compartment and sat looking out the window as the train slowly pulled away from the only life he had ever known. The excitement of the uncertain circumstances that lay ahead of him caused Ray to lose his appetite for the light meal Amelia had packed in his duffle. His stomach was churning with the anticipation of leaving home for the first time in his life. The only thing he chewed that day was the skin around his nails, an old habit he'd developed during his mother's illness that comforted him in times of stress. Long before Raymond reached the depot in Hinckley, Minnesota, his nails were gnawed to the quick; the skin was chewed away from his bloodied cuticles on both hands and the trip was only half over. He bought Black Jack gum from the depot store to distract his worried mouth and arrived at the Duluth train station just as the streetlights were going on in the Zenith City. From the smeared window above his seat, Raymond saw the much-changed figure of his big brother doff his bowler hat and wave it frantically at him from the side of the platform. Leon was fully a man now, thought Raymond. It had been six years since he had seen his brother. The man he saw on the platform was a bit shorter than himself, with a fine dark handlebar moustache, a broad chest and winning smile, dressed in a black three-piece suit. Leon had changed in many ways, but his rich amber eyes shot out sparks of greeting to his brother. Raymond would know those eyes anywhere.

"I hardly recognize you with those fancy duds on," Ray told Leon when they embraced on the platform. "You still have Granddaddy's jacket?" Ray asked his brother.

"Well, hell yeah! I wear that thing now and then, but to meet my baby brother after all this time calls for looking sharp." Leon held out his arms and turned in a slow circle to show off his rakish form. Ray laughed and let out a soft whistle.

"They wouldn't know you in Hastings, Leon."

Leon looked Raymond over and arrived at his own conclusion. "I probably would have walked right by you if I'd seen you there myself. You're no runt anymore, Ray. You're taller than me and still growing, I bet," Leon told him. "How's Pa and Amelia?" he asked. Before Raymond could answer, Leon grabbed one of his bags and tossed Raymond the other. "Come on, runt. Let's get you settled in, then go get a drink or something."

Leaving the grand French Norman style depot, Raymond swiveled his head from side to side to take in the unfamiliar sights of Duluth. He had never expected it to be so impressive. Growing up, he'd always thought of Duluth as a place situated at the ass-end of the earth. He'd been surprised when he received the letters his brother sent from this strange, faraway city at the edge of nowhere. He'd wondered why Leon had decided to stake his claim in this place. From the looks of things around him, Raymond had seriously underestimated Duluth.

"Can we walk over and look at the lake?" Ray asked his brother.

"Right now?" Leon asked, puzzled that Ray should want to do this, rather than hurry for a drink.

"After all you told me about it in your letters, I can't wait," Raymond told him.

"Listen," Leon explained, "let's come back tomorrow when it's lighter out. Then you can see as far as the horizon. Now, being after ten o'clock, you won't see much more than the lights. You can see those from the Incline on the way to the boarding house. Trust me, little brother."

The young men made their way to Superior Street, where Leon guided his brother into a base station for the Duluth Incline Railway, a streetcar-type service that provided passage up the steep slope of Seventh Avenue West. On the six-minute journey from the station, the car traveled 509 feet of elevation in just a half a mile. Raymond had never imagined that such a short trip could be so wondrous. He could see the lights of downtown Duluth and the ships in the harbor below. Even in the dark, the Aerial Transfer Bridge stood tall in the distance.

"How's that bridge work, Leon?" asked Ray.

"I'll show you tomorrow but it's really special. Hardly any of these bridges in the whole, wide world," Leon bragged. "People, autos, wagons...they go into a cart that's carried over the harbor, then deposits them on the other side. Kind of like a gondola across the water."

Tired as Ray was after the trip from Hastings, he could hardly wait for the night to be over so he could explore this amazing new environment. And, to have Leon by his side made the adventure all the sweeter for the boy.

* * *

When Ray arrived in Duluth shortly after the Fourth of July festivities of 1916 were celebrated throughout Minnesota with a new fervor of patriotism brought on by concerns over the escalating war in Europe, he came upon a city in the throes of industrial expansion. In the recent past, Duluth had become the busiest port in the United States, surpassing even New York for the tonnage that passed through its harbor. Iron ore and steel from the mines and mills across the Mesabi and Vermillion Ranges were loaded at the Duluth docks onto freighters that transported the raw materials to factories far and wide. At those destinations, the ore was turned into instruments of war for the allies of Britain. That ore also became the ships used to carry the goods across the Atlantic to fight the Germans, and domestically the steel made from the ore helped build the cars, trucks and tractors now in high demand in the United States. The need for consumer goods such as refrigerators, new stoves and iron beds also contributed to the continued lust for ore that could be transformed into these objects. Skyscraper buildings, held together by rebar and steel beams, were changing cities throughout the country from horizontal expansions into vertical wonderlands where one could view the world from unimaginable heights. In 1915, U.S. Steel put its Duluth plant into operation and developed Morgan Park, on the city's outskirts, as a company town for its workers. Newspapers were touting Duluth as one of the fastest growing cities in the country, thanks to its proximity to iron reserves and its big, accessible harbor that made it possible to get the ore almost anywhere it was needed. Not even the slag generated by the steel mills went to waste. Under construction in 1916, as Ray was settling into his new life in Duluth, the Universal Atlas Cement Company was soon utilizing the ore slag from the steel plants to manufacture its in-demand product for the myriad of new concrete roads, dams and buildings springing up in every corner of the United States. This was the Duluth that Leon sacrificed a half day of work for so that he could acquaint his younger brother with the town he had come to love.

The next morning, Raymond carried his shaving kit and hairbrush down the hall from the room he shared with Leon on his first night in Duluth to the communal bathroom used by all the tenants on his floor. Leon's experience with electric lighting, indoor plumbing and water closets originated in a similar boarding house, but Raymond needed no such introduction after his eighteen months of living in Arabella's modern farmhouse. He knew which faucet was hot and which was cold. He knew how to pull the chain from the elevated tank to wash away bodily wastes in a cleansing whirlpool of water. He thought of all the buildings he had seen on his ride up the Incline; literally thousands of houses, large and small, were crammed, side by side, on the slopes above the city. Below, in the downtown district, handsome brick and sandstone buildings marched right up to the vast lakeshore and along the edge of the harbor. It boggled his mind to think that waste from all these places was washed away in a flush. "Where did it all go?" Ray wondered. Until he found out, Raymond decided that he would avoid swimming in the big lake as a precaution should the watery refuse end up in its depths. He later learned that he needn't have worried. The lake was so damn cold that even at the height of August, almost no one dipped so much as a toe in the frigid waters of Lake Superior.

A line of five men stood waiting for the bathroom when Ray arrived at its location down the hall. With the exception of one very short, middle-aged fellow with a swarthy complexion, the other men were young, about Leon's age. Ray was anxious to make the acquaintance of these fellow boarders but found, when he tried to speak to them, only one seemed to understand his greeting, and this blond-haired raga-muffin replied to Ray's morning salutation with a heavily accented "Ya. Gut morgen." Or at least that's how it sounded to Raymond. The blond fellow said something in a guttural language to the man in front of him, and they both turned to Ray and gave him a suspicious smile. Unsure of the communication protocol of foreigners waiting to use the water closet, Ray just nodded, then turned his eyes downward to examine the stains on the well-trod carpet runner.

"Jesus, Leon. Does anyone in this building speak English?"

Back in the room, Raymond described his encounter with the other men, waiting in the hallway line. Leon laughed before telling his brother, "Yeah. Sorry, Ray. I should have warned you. This entire town is filled with filthy immigrants from all over the goddamn world. It's all the mines and mills that brings them in. Better get used to it."

Apparently, from his tone, Leon disapproved of foreigners invading his turf, but to Ray, the mix of people only added to the allure of this surprisingly exotic town. Riding the incline car back down to Superior Street later that same morning, Raymond listened to the voices around him converse in strange tongues. Hastings had a few immigrants among its population, but they mostly kept to themselves on their farms and in their churches. Here in Duluth, Raymond had the giddy feeling of being on a trip through Europe while still being able to read the road signs and the morning paper in his native language.

"So," Raymond began as he and Leon walked over to the docks to view the lake and the aerial bridge as promised. "What group is the biggest? Foreigners, I mean?"

Leon had only been with his brother for less than a day, most of it spent sleeping, and already the boy was displaying the same bone-headed enthusiasm for meaningless information that had made him annoying back on the farm.

"What's it matter? All I know is that when you add all the Finns, Danes, Poles, Swedes, Krauts, Croats, Wops, and all the other riff-raff, you got yourself a whole lot of troublemakers, itching to take the food right out of our mouths."

Leon's attitude was likely shared by most of the native white population living and working in Duluth. For decades before the industrial boom hit this part of Minnesota, ethnic scorn had been reserved for the Indians from the surrounding tribes, mostly Ojibwe and Chippewa, with some leftover for the descendants of the French fur traders with their fancy names that somehow never came out of a person's mouth in one piece. Now the townsfolk had to spread that scorn thinly over so many newcomers. It was easier to simplify the process by hating all foreigners. Period. Although, as talk of war became more urgent in the bars and workplaces, a special suspicion was focused on the Germans who were especially prominent where Leon worked, the Geiger's Brewery. Leon didn't like the way they spoke to each other in the language of the enemy. Who knew what they could be planning? Maybe they would do-in innocent drinkers by poisoning the brew. Leon was no fool. He would keep his eyes peeled for sabotage along the production line. Meanwhile, his idiot little brother was prattling on about how fun it was to try to guess where these strangers came from.

"Is there someplace I can buy a world map, cheap?" Raymond asked.

The boys were heading back to town after Leon took his brother on the short trip across the shipping way via the transfer bridge. Raymond had been a little disappointed that the ride in the suspended cart was not very far from the water. By the looks of the bridge, he'd thought he would be high over the lake during the ride. Leon explained that the height of the bridge was not for the actual transfer of people and their needs, it was to allow the huge ships to pass under it without incident. Leon was annoyed that Ray asked so many questions, and now, he was asking about a map.

"What do you need a map for?" Leon wanted to know. "You planning a trip someplace?"

Ray took no offense to Leon's sarcasm. He rather enjoyed hearing it after so many years apart. It made being with Leon feel like old times.

"No. I'm about as far from home as I plan to get for a while," Raymond responded. "I just want to keep track of all the different people and where they come from. For instance...do you know where Croatia is? I never even heard of it before!" Raymond exclaimed.

Leon shook his head at his brother. "Don't know and don't care," Leon told him. "But I do like Wop food. Let's go get some spaghetti at this little place I know."

Raymond had no idea what spaghetti was, but he would try to like it for Leon's sake. "Okay," he said. "But I still want a map." Raymond ended his first day in Duluth sucking slippery noodles from his fork and splattering red sauce on the brand new shirt that Pa had bought him just for the trip.

* * *

Everett had given Raymond a modest amount of money before he left Hastings, much as he had for Leon when he struck out on his own. The boy figured that he would offer Leon half of it for putting him up and use the rest to hold him over until he found a suitable job. Leon was pleased to get the cash. He had been living shoulder to shoulder with undesirables so that he could save money for an automobile. Ray's money and his knowledge of driving would help Leon attain this goal of personal mobility. Ray felt it was only fair to share his money with Leon. He was helping him get settled, and Ray was confident that he would be self-supporting soon enough. Duluth seemed to have plenty of jobs to go around. He was more concerned with finding a job that he would enjoy going to day after day. It appeared that a smart fellow, who could speak English and work hard, pretty much had his pick of occupations. Raymond wanted to ask some of the fellows at the boarding house about their experiences at various workplaces, but Leon would allow no fraternization with the foreign element and Raymond couldn't understand their broken English anyway. He would take a few days to wander around town, learning the layout and asking the locals about job prospects.

The boy explored the streets of Duluth from the harbor to the outlying neighborhoods. On one of his longer streetcar adventures, he ventured over to Morgan Park where he discovered a marvelous building that had all the accoutrements of a modern town under one roof.

The recently completed Lake View Store was built of concrete blocks manufactured by the cement company owned by US Steel. It had celebrated its grand opening on July 20, 1916, just the week before Raymond arrived in Duluth, and housed everything a person could ever need. There was a butcher shop, grocery, a hat store, and a general store for odds and ends. Raymond stepped into the hat shop and perused the isles, looking for the hat he would buy when he had the means. He fancied a stylish gray Homburg with a black grosgrain band. When he tried it on, he looked at himself with satisfaction in the mirror. That satisfaction only increased when the sales clerk approached Ray from behind and tipped the hat to a jaunty angle over his left eye.

"Would you like to wear it out or should I box it for you, sir?" the clerk asked.

The embarrassed boy handed back the hat and informed the man, "Just looking today." The clerk smiled and told Ray that it would be waiting for him when he returned.

One could browse furniture or hardware and pick up hygiene supplies from a pharmacy. Every kind of clothing was available for both men and women. On the upper level, a billiard room, dentist office, barber shop, bank and auditorium were some of the offerings. Even the basement had a shoe store and ice-making plant to conveniently supply the residents of Morgan Park with a way to keep their ice boxes cold. Raymond had never even conceived that such a place was possible. The huge space enabled Ray to lose himself in dreams of consumer delight. He thought about all the things he would purchase from this very building once his wages started rolling in. Maybe he should try to find work at the steel plant that built this company town, with its shopping extravaganzas and broad boulevards lined with modest, but handsome, homes.

On the streetcar back to the boarding house, he asked everyone who made eye contact with him if they could give him advice about getting hired in Morgan Park. Sometimes, they answered him with a polite recommendation, but mostly they acted as if they had no under-standing of what he was saying, which was probably true.

When Raymond walked in the door of Leon's room, he was anxious to tell him of his discoveries in Morgan Park, but Leon had an announcement of his own.

"Where you been, runt?" Leon asked his brother. Raymond was

excited to tell him just that, but Leon had other plans. "Come on," he told his brother. "There's been an accident on the transfer bridge. Let's go see what happened."

Nothing ever brought the light to Leon's eyes like someone else's tragedy.

"How do you know?" Ray questioned his brother. "We can't see that far from here, at least to tell what happened."

There he goes again, Leon thought, full of useless questions. "I passed a fellow coming in just now who told me about it. The streetcar operator told him," Leon explained. "Grab your hat...I want to see what's going on."

From the top of the incline railroad, it was possible to make out a huddle of cars, people and horses mingling near the harbor below. Clearly, something interesting had occurred, and Raymond was now as determined as Leon to get down the hill to be part of the action. The boys waited impatiently for the carriage car to make it to the top of the hill where Leon's boarding house was located. There were numerous people, mostly men who lived in the rundown rooms available in this area, waiting to join them for the descent.

"Don't be shy about muscling your way in, Ray. Just follow me so we get a spot on this car," Leon advised.

Turns out, Leon had been wise to warn his brother. When the car opened to admit passengers, a crush of malodorous bodies nearly pushed Ray aside, but he held his ground, and just as the doors started to close, he was pulled into the carriage by the strength of Leon's left arm. Ray could tell by the excitement on the faces of his fellow passengers that Leon wasn't the only one who enjoyed an unfortunate event now and then. The packed rail car groaned under the weight of its load, but it arrived safely at the bottom of the hill in just a few short minutes. The car dislodged its travelers, and they moved almost as a single organism to the site of the bridge landing or at least as close as they could, given the crowd that was already milling around the loading area for the ferry car.

"What's going on?" Leon asked the first familiar face he saw in the crowd.

A rough-looking fellow in a stained denim jacket and a battered wool cap smiled at Leon, exposing the holes in his mouth where he should have had teeth. Raymond had a fleeting image of Dr. Quam advising folks about oral hygiene from the side of the carriage house back in Hastings. "Seems a car got out of control and ran through the barrier and launched itself, right along with the horse and wagon in front of the car, into the lake," the man gleefully reported.

"Anybody hurt?" asked Leon.

The grizzled man grinned again. "Oh, the fellow driving the car got pulled out of the lake and the wagon driver was standing aside so he's fine but that damn horse wasn't so lucky. Hard for it to pull itself out of the deep when it's got a wagon full of creamery barrels anchoring it to the bottom."

Leon and Ray lingered for a time with the other onlookers, but most of the real spectacle had finished by the time they'd arrived at the accident site. Ray could read on his brother's face that he was disappointed to have missed the daring rescue in which the Duluth Boat Club's rowing coach dove into the canal and pulled the car's driver from what would have been a watery grave.

"Let's go, runt. We missed all the fun," Leon told him. "I need a drink before we head back. You okay with that?"

Raymond had no interest in drinking, but he wanted for Leon to feel that the trip down the hill hadn't been in vain so he tipped his hat to his brother and told him, "sure."

Before Raymond arrived in Duluth, he had never been inside a saloon in his life. His Methodist mother had been staunchly opposed to the use of alcohol, though Grandma Saxby had been known to tipple when the spirit was weak or a special joy needed celebrating. Pa had kept a bottle of low-grade whiskey hidden under a pile of hay in the barn for those moments that required fortification. He never realized that both his sons knew where he kept it and had sipped from its dusty neck just to try out the taste. Raymond concluded that the taste was vile, but Leon could overlook that for the effect of warm determination a stiff drink could instill in a man. After his six years of working in a brewery, Leon had developed a genuine thirst for beer, but he also enjoyed an upgraded version of Everett's whiskey when he was in the mood for serious drinking. One of the establishments that Leon preferred was the Pickworth, a pub next to the brewery where he often ate after his shift on the bottling line.

Leon led his brother into the pub and settled the boy at a table in front of the long, wooden bar. Raymond was taken with the magnificence of the room; a huge fireplace sat silent and dark against one wall and the ceiling was a grid of recessed rectangles, bordered by handsome wood frames. It was opulent and down-to-earth all at once. Ray could see why it appealed to the working public who might live in near squalor but could feel a part of the economic boom in their public spaces. He was mesmerized by the light reflecting off the endless bottles behind the bar. That kaleidoscope image of sparkling glassware would stay with Ray whenever he thought about this day of mishaps in Duluth. Complementing the visual splendor, the place had a smell all its own: a hoppy, malty musk that permeated the woodwork and the floor, where enough brew had been spilled since the last mopping to stick to the bottoms of their shoes, making a suction noise with every step.

"You want a beer, Ray?" Leon asked.

Raymond shook his head. "No thanks. I think I just want a ginger ale or something like that," Ray told his brother.

Leon gave the boy a quizzical look and replied, "Suit yourself."

Leon placed his order at the bar and stood waiting for service with his sight set on the front door. It seemed every fellow who entered knew Leon. He was glad-handing and back-slapping with five other young men who toasted Leon with their drinks. Leon motioned with his head toward Ray, sitting alone at the table a short distance away. The men swiveled their heads to view Leon's companion and then in unison, raised their glasses to Ray and saluted him with "Brother!" When Leon's order arrived on the counter, a short, balding fellow in a checkered waistcoat helped Leon carry the drinks and a couple of generous slabs of ham on rye bread to the table.

"This here is my baby brother, Raymond," Leon told the fellow.

The man nodded and smiled at Ray, then extended his hand to the boy. "I'm Henry. Good to meet you, Raymond." Henry sat a sandwich and a glass of pale amber fluid on the table. "Ginger ale must be for the baby brother," Henry said as he slid the glass close to Raymond. "When you get all grown up, come on back for a real drink," Henry advised the boy.

Pleased with himself, Henry gave Leon a wink, and Leon laughed at Ray's expense. "By the time he's that grown up, won't none of us be able to get a drink in this town," Leon remarked.

The sad fact was that the city of Duluth had fallen prey to the fanaticism of the Temperance Movement. It was widely expected that in less than a year's time, the city would be dry like its neighbor, Superior, on the Wisconsin side of the shipping channel. The Minnesota legislature had passed a law that enabled local ordinances to govern the distribution and use of alcohol, and Duluth's freewheeling ways were soon coming to an end.

"All the more reason to drink up now!" advised Henry. And that's what Leon did for the rest of the evening. He guzzled six beers to Raymond's two ginger ales and smoked a cigarette for every beer.

When it was time to head up the hill, Leon staggered his way to the door, trying to pull another smoke from his pocket as he went. The pack dropped in a puddle of slopped beer on the dirty floor and Leon raged at his brother to pick it up. Ray wondered if Leon was going to go through another phase of blaming him when things went wrong, but he let the thought slip away and retrieved the soggy cigarettes and handed them to his brother.

"Son of a bitch," was Leon's response when he fingered the damp pack. He tossed the cigarettes into a spittoon and pulled Raymond outside. "Let's go. I need to get me some more smokes."

The boys started to cross the street to get Leon's tobacco at a nearby store when, from out of nowhere, an auto with no lights on to spot them, came racing up behind the young men. Hearing the engine noise, Ray pushed his brother out of the way of the car. In doing so, he managed to step into a deep rut that wedged his shoe like a vice. When Raymond fell, he heard a snap and felt a piercing pain shoot through the bottom half of his right leg. He'd never broken a bone in his life, but he was sure this misstep had changed that one bit of luck he had enjoyed.

* * *

Leon was mostly sober by the time that Raymond was ensconced in the orthopedic ward at the Duluth Hospital. He watched over Raymond, who drifted along in a painless sleep induced by a dose of morphine. When he woke hours later, his right leg was sealed in an elevated plaster cast that reached above his knee. A blurry-eyed Leon was slumped in a chair beside his bed.

"You're still the luckless runt you always were," Leon told the injured boy. Raymond had to agree.

"How are we going to pay for this?" was what Raymond wanted to know. Ray was fairly positive that the money he had left from Pa wasn't enough to cover a hospital stay.

" We'll worry about that when they come after us," Leon told him. "In the meantime, I'll write Pa to see if he can send us some money to help out."

Ray looked at his brother through the watery tears in his eyes. He wouldn't outright cry---that would only add to his misery--but he was horribly dejected that his new life had been derailed so soon after it had started.

Leon got to his feet and ruffled his brother's hair. "I got to go, runt. On account of you, I never did get my smokes."

Raymond gave his brother a weak smile before he closed his eyes and drifted back into the arms of Morpheus.

The week spent bedridden in the Duluth Hospital was one of the longest in Ray's young life. In one sense, it was interesting to watch the hustle and bustle of the doctors and nurses flitting in and out of rooms to administer treatments and medications. In other ways, it was terrifying to hear the screams of agonizing pain emanate from the rooms near to his or to watch the bandages be changed on the burns suffered by his roommate on the left. Most terrifying of all was the dreaded bed bath. Each morning a young woman would cart in her basin, towel and flannel to clean Raymond of nonexistent dirt. This, after handing him a bedpan he attempted to use with discretion under the bed linens. As if this humiliation weren't enough, whenever this lovely vision in an apron and starched cap ran a warm cloth up his thigh, Raymond's body reacted with manly vigor. Raymond would turn beet red from shame, but the girl simply continued as if nothing was amiss.

"I'm so sorry," Raymond told her.

The young nurse smiled at the boy and arranged the covers neatly over him. "It happens to most every man who isn't on the brink of death," she told him. "It's natural. It means you will be out of here soon."

Raymond was glad to hear his health was intact and that he would soon be released back into the world, but he would also miss this daily touch in the most intimate places on his body. The bed bath experience was one of alternating angst and pleasant anticipation for the boy, and it was his first experience with how a woman's soft hand could arouse his base desires.

A few days before Raymond was to be released from the hospital, a severe-looking woman with a matronly air visited him at his bedside. A pair of wire-rimmed glasses sat above her pinched nose, and she took in Ray's situation with beady, mud-brown eyes that hinted at disdain for her wards. The tightly wound coils of salt and pepper hair covering each ear only added to her harsh demeanor.

"Raymond Saxby?" she asked him. Ray tipped his head in a gesture of affirmation. "Mr. Saxby, I am the hospital social worker. I've been asked to help you arrange for care at your home." She paused a moment. "You have a home, do you not?"

Ray only nodded again. This woman was so intimidating that he had trouble getting the words to form in his mouth.

"Tell me, where do you live and with whom, if anyone?"

Ray explained that he lived with his older brother on an upper floor in a boarding house at the top of the hill. He watched as her frown deepened with every word he said.

"I see," she said. "That is an unfortunate situation for one recovering from a leg fracture. Do you have any means of support?"

Ray wasn't sure how to answer this question. Obviously, he wouldn't have any money until he recovered and got a job. "I can't work until I get this thing off my leg," he said motioning to the cast.

"Of course. I'm not stupid, Mr. Saxby," the woman huffed. "What I meant was, do you have anyone, such as a parent, to help pay for your care?"

Ray tried to explain his circumstances. "My brother wrote my Pa to ask for help. We haven't heard back yet but I think he can spare something."

He wasn't sure of anything where money was concerned, but he wanted to please this harridan and get her out of his room as soon as possible. The woman busily jotted down notes on her well-used clipboard as Raymond talked. When she had finished her scribbling, she looked down at him as she handed him a piece of paper.

"The hospital will help you arrange transportation up to your residence. It would be unwise to use the incline in your condition. We will also contact someone to serve as a caregiver for when your brother is away at work during the day. You will need help with meals and ambulation until you learn to maneuver on your own. You and your family will be expected to reimburse any and all expenses for the services provided but we can work out an installment plan if needed. Do you have any questions?"

Ray was working to process all that she had said. He did have questions, about almost all of it, but when he opened his mouth to speak, the only thing he said was, "What's ambulation?"

The dour woman finally softened her lips. "Walking, Mr. Saxby. Ambulation means walking."

The paper she had given him had a date written at its top. He would be released from the hospital in two days' time, the time it would take to make arrangements with his unknown future caregiver.

Her name was Inka Siskanen, a Finnish, socialist, Unitarian beauty of nineteen who agreed to offset some of the wages owed to her for English lessons from the bedridden boy. She planned to attend nursing school as soon as her reading of English became more proficient. Providing cut-rate care for Raymond could help further both of these goals. The moment she walked into the room at the boarding house, Leon was aggrieved that it was his brother who would be ministered to by this fetching girl. He could imagine relaxing his rigid attitude about immigrants for this blond beauty with skin so fair that she seemed to be transparent against the sun streaming in through the dirty window. Her hair was like fine, white silk that framed a face blessed with wide-set pale blue eyes and rose-colored lips, puffed out from her mouth in a natural pout. That pout was quickly replaced by the most disarming smile Leon had ever seen. He was disappointed to see that it was Raymond the girl was smiling at. For his part, in the very back of his mind where only his most private thoughts resided, Raymond was thinking about a warm flannel inching up the thigh of his injured leg. He smiled back at this lovely woman who would have him ambulating in no time.

Leon rushed over to the young woman to introduce himself. "Hello. Welcome, Miss Siskanen," Leon said. "I'm Leon, the brother of the sad little fellow over there, and he's Ray."

Leon was doing his best to point out how juvenile his brother was, not that Ray could possibly be competition where women were concerned. Inka Siskanen looked past Leon to consider her patient, lying in the Murphy bed that took up much of the space in the room. She gave Raymond a once over with those pale blue eyes, noting that he looked perfectly capable of caring for himself in all ways but walking and she had plans to remedy that problem in a few days' time.

"Ya, Mr. Saxby. Tank you." She offered her small soft hand to Leon, who held it in his own a moment too long. "I am happily to be hilp, ya?"

Leon suddenly found that the sound of her broken English was like delicate music floating through his head. Her voice was a high, clear pitch, like a songbird announcing a spring morning. The girl lifted the basket she had at her side, which Leon hurried to take from her hand.

"Please," he said, "allow me to help you with that." Leon placed the reed basket on the top of the crowded dresser, where his bowler, Ray's newsboy cap, and penknives, coins and cigarettes cluttered the surface. "You must have enough stuff in here to last a week," Leon joked in an attempt to elicit one of those heavenly smiles. He was rewarded when Inka laughed.

"Oh, ya!" The girl exclaimed.

From the basket, Inka pulled out a small parcel. Wrapped in flour sacks over newspaper, it contained a strange sort of pie that Inka called Karelian. Inka put the disk of baked dough onto Raymond's lap, using the newspaper as a serving tray. Raymond noticed that the paper was filled with strange words that stretched impossibly long and were filled with bizarre dots and symbols over the letters. The indecipherable words reminded him of how English looked in his early school days. Must be Finnish, he thought.

"You vill like, ya?" she told him.

"I'm sure I will but what's in it?" Raymond asked. Inka smiled at Raymond as if at a child balking at his supper.

"Is Finniss foot for mornink," she told him. "Rye flour vit podado inside."

The next package she removed from the basket was a small jar filled with a yellow mixture. She produced a spoon from the pocket of her apron and smeared the mixture over the top of the pie on Raymond's lap.

"Now, what's that?" he asked.

"Gootest part. Budder vit egg," she told him.

Raymond smiled, then lifted the treat to his mouth. He rolled the bite of dough and topping over his tongue, exploring the taste. "First rate," he exclaimed. "Leon, you need to try this."

Leon reached down and pulled the savory pie to his lips. The rich, still warm combination of potato, butter and egg on the crusty rye was an explosion of familiar flavors put together in a surprising new form.

"Did you cook this?" Leon asked the girl.

"Oh, ya," she told him. "I cook tis foot."

Leon laughed. "You mean food," he corrected her.

"Ya," the girl demurred, "I neet many hilps vit Engliss!"

Leon decided that he would pay her extra to bring him one of these delicacies each morning, along with the provisions she brought to Ray to sustain him through the day.

"Listen, Miss Siskanen. Ray's right. These are first rate. Bring me one each morning and I'll pay you extra for your efforts. Can you do that?" Leon asked the smiling beauty.

"Oh, ya," she agreed. "I brink more in morninks."

As Inka and Leon negotiated the breakfast arrangement, Raymond devoured the pie and its buttery topping. He was anxious to get Inka all to himself. "You better get going, Leon. You're going to be late," Raymond reminded his brother, not really caring if he showed up tardy for his shift.

"Yes. Right." Leon looked Inka Siskanen in her lovely eyes and tipped his bowler hat to her. "Thank you for your help, Miss. When you return tomorrow, I will have your pay for the week and the extra for the pies. Good day," he told her. He turned and exited the third floor room, passing immigrant strangers in the hall who now seemed a little less suspicious after his encounter with Inka Siskanen.

Raymond looked at the other two parcels that sat on top of the dresser. "What else have you brought me?" he asked.

Inka pointed to the other packages covered with newsprint. "Tat von is bread for noon," she told him, "and tat's von for now."

She unwrapped the flat item and pulled out a book. To Raymond's delight, it was *Tom Swift and His Airship*. The young woman ran her hand over the cover of the book, brushing imaginary dust from its surface.

"Vee vill read, ya? You hilp me vit Engliss vords."

Inka handed the book to Raymond. He turned it over in his hands, losing himself in the cover art displaying the fantastic airship. When he opened the cover, the mystery of where she had obtained the book was solved when he noted the paper pocket for the checkout slip from the Duluth Public Library.

Raymond and Inka spent the morning reading aloud to each other. When it was Inka's turn to announce the passages in her clean, clear voice, Raymond would stop her to explain the differences between English consonants and her Finnish take on them. "Watch my lips, Miss Siskanen," Raymond advised. He showed her how a word such as *with* differed from how she said it. He had her purse her lips to make the sounds for "w" as opposed to placing her teeth against her lips for "v." It slowed the pace of the adventure Tom Swift was enjoying to correct the lovely Inka, but Tom Swift was merely a vehicle for his interaction with the girl. Ray was almost disappointed to see how quickly she was able to change her diction. He wanted the lessons to go on forever. He was also dismayed to think about how he would miss her when his leg healed and he no longer needed her help. The only negative part of the day was when he was required to ask her for the old milk can he was using for a urinal. Though she turned her back on him while he used it, the sound of his urine stream hitting the tin bottom made him feel like an infant in her care, and he burned with humiliation for them both. Inka was not so delicate. She simply took the can from him, popped the top back on and gave him a look of compassion.

"Bedder now?" she asked him.

Because Ray had been holding his water for so long as a way to avoid her help, he had to agree. "Yes. I do feel better but I'm sorry you have to do that," he told her.

"I am nurse, ya? This is vat I do."

Raymond was pleased to hear that Inka had learned the "th" sound. He guessed the other sounds would come to her eventually. He was definitely in no hurry for her to acquire perfect English. He loved the way she focused all of her attention on his face when he endeavored to show her how to shape her words. He could look into those eyes forever.

The last chore for Inka before she left that first afternoon was to measure Raymond for a set of crutches her father had offered to make for the boy. She carefully laid a piece of string from his armpit to the sole of his foot and marked the length with a knot. She had him make a fist and noted where it fell on the string, marking where to place the handle on the crutches.

"Vee vill have for you in some days," she told him. She then packed up her basket and bid her patient farewell. "Vee vill read more soon, ya?" she said as she packed the book to take with her. "I try alone now at my house to read."

Ray held his hand up to acknowledge her parting wave. Who would have thought that breaking his leg could be such an enjoyable experience?

By the end of the first week under the care of Inka Siskanen, Raymond was ambulating, as the social worker had promised, around the small room at the boarding house. He was able to propel himself down the hall to the bathroom on the sturdy birch crutches Inka's father had fashioned for him. Each morning, the Murphy bed folded away, both Leon and Raymond awaited the soft knock at the door and vied to be the one to greet her. Owing to Ray's infirmary, it was usually Leon who admitted Inka and took her basket from her arms. It might have been his fevered imagination, but it appeared to Ray that Leon and Inka shared an intimate look of pleasure in each other's company. This made Raymond feel broken in places other than his leg, and he envied his brother's age and charm. He supposed Leon's mustache, muscles and chiseled jawline didn't favor his own cause when she compared the two brothers side-by-side. Being six years older, Leon certainly must look like the better prospect. He also had a real job and money, augmented by the funds Pa had sent to the boys from the auction of the horses and livestock back in Hastings. When Leon handed Inka her wages at the beginning of the next week, their hands touched in a way that promised more than a week's pay. The implications of that touch broke poor Raymond's heart.

As Raymond's condition improved, so did Inka's English, and soon Tom Swift had completed his adventure, leaving his mother's old bible as the only book left for Raymond to use for her instruction.

"I vill go to library soon for new book," she told Raymond.

He didn't think she would ever sort out "w" and "v" but otherwise, her use of proper English consonants was coming along.

"You vill not need me much but I can still bring book from library, ya?"

That remark was a double-edged sword to the boy; her nursing of him would soon end due to his improved ability to care for himself, but at least he might see her once or twice a week to exchange the books she promised to obtain for him.

" I really appreciate everything you've done, Miss Siskanen. I was wondering if you would like us to read from the bible today? It's all I've got here right now."

Inka placed a hand on Ray's shoulder. She told him, "I only read bible for the vords. I do not believe in God."

Ray was shocked. How could someone who looked like an angel not believe in God? He certainly had his own misgivings about religion, but he wasn't sure he could just out-and-out reject the idea of a supreme being.

"You don't believe in God?" he asked the girl with a shock in his voice that made her laugh.

She shook her lovely head and said, "Ya, no God for me."

Ray was confused. He knew she went to church regularly. That was the reason she left early on Wednesdays...to get to her church meeting.

"But you go to church!" he blurted out.

"Ya. I believe in church but not God," she told him.

This was one of the most contradictory statements Raymond had ever heard. What the hell was the point of a religion without a God? He didn't want to attack Inka's values, but he had to have an explanation.

"Why on earth would you go to church if you aren't worried about getting into heaven?" he asked her.

"Oh, Raymond," she began. "I am Unitarian. Vee meet for community. Vee vorship goodness in man. Same as you vorship goodness of God," she told him.

That statement did little to further Ray's understanding. "So you think man and God are the same?" he asked.

Inka smiled at the boy. "I tink dere is no God, only man who can be good, like idea of God. Vee do not need God to tell us to be kind and fair to von and otter. At my church, vee believe in hilping each otter to live in kindness and respect for all peoples."

Ray considered her words. "Okay. So that's what a Unitarian is? I never heard of Unitarians," Ray told her. "Are all your people like this?"

Inka shook her head. "No. Most Finn are Lutteran. Ya? You know tis church?" she asked the boy.

Ray nodded. "Yeah. My Grandma was Lutheran," he told her. "Her family was from Sweden."

Inka was visibly delighted.

"Ya! Sveden! Wery close to Finland! But my people come here to be free from old vays. At Wirginia, in da nort of here,"(Ray could hear her diction slip the more worked up she got) "we yoin vit Reverends Risto and Milma Lappala to be Unitarian and practice social yustice."

Her eyes were gleaming as she went on to tell Raymond of her family's beliefs.

* * *

The Siskanen family came to Northern Minnesota when Inka was ten years old. Her parents emigrated from a village where it was not unusual for America to be the aspirational destination for young Finns looking for work opportunities and freedom from Russian influence, specifically, conscription into the Russian Army. As Inka explained to Ray, Finns generally advocate for social justice and socialist ideals. Her family was active in labor politics in the home country, and when they settled in Virginia, Minnesota, in 1907, to take advantage of the plentiful mining jobs available on the Mesabi Range, they continued to pursue their values of equality and justice for the miners who made up their new community. Originally Lutheran, her parents' progressive ideals eventually alienated them from the conservative values of their church. They gravitated toward the new Unitarian Church started in Virginia by Finnish-American, Risto Lappala, a one-time minister for a Congregational Church who had been excommunicated for heresy. The exiled minister found a spiritual home in the Unitarian Society, where Christian values were tied to conscience, not doctrine. The Reverend Lappala and his wife, Reverend Milma Lappala, were commissioned by the Unitarians to begin a mission to the Finnish people of Northern Minnesota. Due to its Nordic population, the values of social justice and humanism were already in place, making it a good fit for the teachings of the society. This was the church that Inka's family joined in early 1912. And this is where Inka Siskanen found that doing what was right for her fellow man was its own reward. She no longer felt that an angry God was necessary to guide her through life. The fear of God's wrath for making a mistake was replaced by the joy of choosing a path of goodness born from her own sense of fairness and integrity. Inka liked everything about the Unitarian Church except its insistence on changing the words of traditional hymns to suit its own purposes. She felt that it was a form of cheating to steal the songs of others when they could just as well make up their own hymns. Then again, maybe it was good socialist practice to share the musical wealth. At any rate, it was a minor point that Inka could overlook for the greater good of her Unitarian community. And it was certainly offset by the acceptance of women in leadership roles among the Unitarian brethren.

Raymond was fascinated by what Inka had told him. He remembered how Leon had rejected religion back when he was so young. The difference between Leon and Inka was that she had found a way to reconcile the need for spiritual companionship with the rejection of the vengeful God. It sounded like a good trade-off to Ray. He had taken the opposite path; he had rejected religion but maintained his belief in God on the off-chance that if there was a heaven, he might have a shot at getting in. If he lived as Inka proposed, doing what's right for the sake of his conscience, he should get into heaven on those merits alone. Should it turn out that there was a God, surely He would value good deeds over good faith.

"Do you still have things like Christmas?" he asked her. Ray couldn't imagine a life without holidays.

Inka smiled indulgently.

"Ya. Vee have holiday vit tree and presents. Only, is Vinter Solstice celebration. Christmas is vat church makeup to use old Nordic holiday in new vay. Vee have Christmas since before there is Christ."

Ray nodded as if he understood.

"And vee have spring celebration. Is for new life, like Easter, ya?" Inka told him.

"With eggs and treats?" Ray asked. Inka laughed.

"Ya, Raymond! Many eggs and treats for spring happiness!"

Ray liked the concept of all the good parts of religion without the hateful negativity he remembered from sitting in the pew behind the Blumes back in Hastings. Arabella had fancied herself a pillar of her congregation, but Ray had to admit he'd never known a more Godless human being in his whole life.

"Maybe you could bring me some stuff to read about your church," Ray ventured. "But it has to be in English!" he advised her.

"Of course, Raymond. And vee can read together, ya?"

Ray smiled and nodded, "Ya. I'd like that."

6

St. Paul, Minnesota 1995

When Dolores died, Raymond found that she had taken the
rhythm of his days with her. For the last several years,
he'd scheduled his activities around his daily visits to the
nursing home. He would be up by five-thirty for a breakfast of coffee
and instant oatmeal, which he enjoyed over the Pioneer Press on the
sun porch in the warm months or at the kitchen table next to a space
heater when a chill crept into the air. With his magnifying glass in
hand, he would spend hours reading about the interesting and
mundane activities of the world at large and the city of St. Paul in
particular. Just as he had been captivated by immigrants in Duluth all
those years ago, Raymond was intrigued by the changing names in the
local section of the paper. Where earlier editions were crowded with
names sounding Irish, Scandinavian or German, the current pages
were overwhelmed with Nguyens, Vangs or Trans. On his weekly
pilgrimage to the local market with Dwight, he came to notice that the
majority of his neighborhood had been depleted of Andersons and

Dooleys, and the sidewalks were increasingly home to small, dark-haired children with almond eyes and soft brown skin. At the market, he often had to reach over these children's ancient grandmothers, dressed in mismatched florals and plaids from Savers or Goodwill, to get a box of Minute Rice from the shelf above the bulk grains, stacked in ten pound bags like cord wood. He wondered how many people must be in a family to use up a ten-pound bag of rice. He was confident he hadn't used ten pounds of rice in all his years of life. His neighbor's daughter was a real estate agent over on the east side, near Lake Phalen. She had told her father that it was not unusual for several of the Laotian immigrant families to live in a single, two bedroom house. She had one listing where the entire basement had been converted into a tiny farm; chickens, a small pig and raised beds of dirt, growing greens and herbs, thrived under lights strung across the underside of the main floor of the house. His neighbor told Raymond that his daughter had no idea how to describe this unlikely bonus feature in the multiple listing service information sheet. To her surprise, the property sold quickly when the Pham family fell in love with the chicken coop and onion patch hidden next to the ancient furnace under the house.

Raymond found these new immigrants to be as resourceful as the European versions he had encountered back in Duluth. He also found that his admiration for immigrant determination was not always shared by his long-time friends or family. Dwight had spent a couple of years in the military at the height of the Vietnam War, and he had an entire vocabulary of unsavory terms for the Asians who cluttered the aisles at the grocery store.

"We need to move you out of this area, Dad," Dwight told his father for the hundredth time. "With all these gooks, I get flashbacks just buying milk," he complained.

Raymond patiently ignored Dwight's animosity towards the newcomers. He'd seen it all before. In a few years, there would be some new tribe to bitch about, and from what the Pioneer Press indicated, the next group in line for derision would be folks from Somalia, elegant black strangers with names straight out of the *Arabian Nights*. When Dolores had been at home still, they would play a game of counting people who seemed to be from some exotic location as she drove the old Buick along Front Street, guessing where their home countries might be. As the years progressed, it became easier to count the dwindling white folks and attempt to guess when they might leave the neighborhood. He missed Dolores and all the silly games they played to amuse one another through the years.

With Dolores gone, Raymond lost his internal clock. He slept late and napped at the strangest times. He found himself slumped over cold coffee and yesterday's paper, wondering why the Twins had lost again on exactly the same plays as the previous day. He gave up matching his socks and turned his undershirts inside out to hide the stains and postpone the laundry. He missed going to the nursing home. He hadn't been aware while it was happening, but the daily visits had given him a reason to shave and put on clean clothes. He'd looked forward to the dessert he ate with Dolores in her room each evening before Dwight arrived to take him home. A frozen dinner at the kitchen table with his taciturn son did little to cheer Raymond in the months that followed Dolores's funeral. He was losing weight and purpose with each passing day.

"Listen, Dad. I'm having Fiona come over after work. She said she'd bring you a home cooked meal but then I want you to make yourself scarce. OK?"

Raymond nodded. He would retreat to the bedroom upstairs and fiddle with the rabbit ears to get a channel on the old black and white TV next to his bed. WCCO always came in pretty good or maybe KSTP would have a strong signal. He'd make do.

"She's a nice girl," Ray told his son.

"Yeah. She's OK," Dwight replied.

Ray wondered why the woman bothered with Dwight. He didn't think she would if she made the effort to take Dwight's full measure. He was glad for her short-sightedness, though. It meant an occasional dinner of fresh food and cake from scratch, simple joys that gave a man hope.

"Mr. Saxby!" I called through the glass window in the door that evening. "It's me. Fiona. I've got your dinner here."

I watched as the old fellow rose slowly from the threadbare recliner and made his way to the door where I stood with the foil-wrapped casserole in my hands. I raised it to the window so he could see it. Instantly, his watery blue eyes lit up like a dimmer switch had been turned up behind them. An equally bright smile erased years from his face. He shuffled hastily to admit me. I watched him trip over the throw rug he used to wipe the snow from his shoes, and I was relieved to see him catch himself and regain his balance. For an instant, with his thin frame and long face, he reminded me of Fred Astaire, executing a dance step to entertain me.

"Well, well, well! Dwight said you were coming," he told me. "And look what you brought!"

It was a little routine we went through whenever I provided his dinner. He acted like it was a complete surprise, even though I knew Dwight always told him I was coming with food in hand. He pulled me into the house and shut the door on the cold outside. The room was stifling hot. I shed my coat and my cardigan sweater before a hot flash could drop me in my tracks. I had recently entered the magic years of hormonal mayhem. I carried the hotdish into the kitchen and sat it down. Just seeing how nicely he had laid out the settings on the kitchen table choked me up. Tears and sweat were constant threats in those days, but one of the nicer points of my acquaintance with Raymond was that he never commented on my fickle moods or perspiration.

"Dwight called a bit ago," Raymond reported. "He says he's finishing up a late run and will be here as soon as he can."

I smiled at Mr. Saxby and asked him if he would mind if I put the food in the oven to keep it warm. He seemed more than pleased to add extra heat to the house. I turned the oven on low and stuck the chicken and noodle goulash inside. I reached over the sink to crack the window.

"Do you mind?" I asked him before I raised the window an inch.

"No. Go right ahead," he said. "I'm feeling warm just having you here." Mr. Saxby could be a charming flirt when food was the passion he anticipated enjoying.

"Did Dwight say what kind of call he was on?" I asked him.

"No. Just that he'd be a little late," Raymond replied.

"Well, if it gets too late, we'll just go ahead, the two of us," I assured him. Raymond looked relieved. Dwight was known to be very late on occasion.

* * *

I'd met Dwight Saxby years before. I had recently relocated from a clinic in White Bear Lake to become the nurse-manager at an office in the same consortium in St. Paul, over on the east side, where I would eventually move after my boys graduated from White Bear Lake High School. I would no longer need to be in an excellent school district or close to their friends, and because my old car often broke down, I planned to buy a house within walking distance to the new clinic. It was at this new clinical assignment that I met Dwight Saxby, when a medical emergency at my facility brought his paramedic unit to my door. The patient was determined to be having nothing more serious than a panic attack, but the patient's evaluation allowed enough inter-action in that twenty-minute call to feel the sparks pass between us. Later that week, as I vacuumed the floors and hauled out trash after hours to augment my income, I heard a knock at the locked doors. When I went to investigate, there was Dwight Saxby in his uniform, looking through the glass with concern on his face. I opened the doors, and he smiled at me. Another spark hit me right between the eyes.

"I was driving by and saw the lights on," he told me as an explana-tion. "I was worried maybe there was a problem."

I smiled back, delighted, and in spite of my better judgement, I asked him if he would like to come in.

"Sure. Just for a minute," he said.

We spent the next two hours sitting in the conference room eating a pizza from the place two doors down in the strip mall where my clinic was located. We washed it down with Cokes from the liquor store next door. Under the harsh fluorescent lights flickering overhead, I fell in love with Dwight Saxby. We laughed about the antics of patients and bonded over the adrenalin rush of handling emergencies. I was touched to hear him tell of his devotion to his parents and how he helped them with the chores of daily life now that they were both elderly or infirm. It helped immensely that he was so handsome in his uniform. I wanted to reach out to feel the golden ringlets that peeked out from the vee of his shirt. My opportunity for touch came when he rose to leave. A tiny speck of pizza sauce sat like a beauty mark on his chin.

"Oh, oh," I said. "You need a little clean up here."

I reached up with a napkin in my hand and touched it to his face. He responded by taking my hand in his and pulling me closer. It was the first time that a first kiss had been what I'd always hoped it could be. That night started a relationship that I was never able to define. Sometimes you don't really understand what's in a medicine...you just know that you need it to feel right. At that time in my life, Dwight Saxby was my medicine.

About an hour after I arrived with Raymond's dinner, Dwight called to say he wouldn't make it. It seemed that a Snowy Owl had been injured out at the airport, and Dwight, in his capacity as a volunteer for the Raptor Center, had been called out to rescue the bird and deliver it to the sanctuary. When Mr. Saxby told me of this development, I shrugged my shoulders and told him, "Let's eat!" Over Tastee white bread and chicken casserole, I made polite conversation with my unlikely date.

"This chicken is pretty good," he told me. "We used to raise chickens at the farm in Hastings."

I'd known he started life in that river town, but I hadn't heard that his family had farmed.

"Oh yeah?" I remarked.

He spooned another mouthful of savory noodles into his mouth. When he finished his lengthy bout of chewing, he cleared his throat to speak.

"Oh sure," he told me." We had chickens, cows, horses, sheep. All kinds of animals. We ate everything except the horses and the dog."

He chuckled when he looked at me to see if I was shocked. I wasn't. I had a rural background myself. I winked at him and replied tit for tat.

"Some of your new neighbors apparently like to eat dogs best of all."

He smiled before he spoke. "You mean those Orientals we got so many of now?"

Feeling sheepish for the mild ethnic slur I had just lobbed his way, I hurried to claw it back.

"Well, I was just joking. I shouldn't have said that about your neighbors."

He laughed then. "I heard about one of those families that has a whole farm in the basement, with chickens and a pig. Gotta hand it to folks trying to make a new life in a strange place," he told me.

Then he regaled me with tales of his early adulthood in Duluth. Over weak coffee and dried out store-bought cookies that made for perfect dunking, Raymond Saxby drifted back to an America on the brink of World War I.

Duluth, Minnesota 1916

Raymond found after a couple of weeks of confinement in the upper level of the boarding house that he could make his way down the stairs with the use of his crutches and the handrail. He perfected a hopping technique that got him up and down efficiently. He became so adept at conquering the steep steps that he could take them almost as fast as when unimpaired by his broken limb. Soon, he was back to exploring his limited neighborhood when Leon was at work. Miss Siskanen no longer came by each day to care for him, but on the days when she was expected, Raymond would meet her at the door with a look of pain and loneliness on his face. Inka Siskanen could tell by the grit and mud on the bottom of the boy's cast that he wasn't sitting idly in the room, waiting patiently for her to bring him her latest find from the library.

"Hello, Miss Siskanen. Please come in. I've been waiting for you all morning," Ray told the young woman.

Inka came through the door, but she left it open behind her. The

more recovered Raymond became, the more Inka treated him as a business obligation. It was already quite inappropriate for a single young
woman of moral standing to visit a man unaccompanied in his rooms.
Injury or infirmity of either party acted like a chaperone, but Ray was
now past the point of incapacitation. For Inka to maintain respectabil-
ity, boundaries had to be enforced.

"Ya. Hello Raymond. I can only stay for few minute," she told him.

From the pocket of her coat, she produced another library book for
him. "You have been farmer, ya? You vill like dis book." She handed the
boy a worn copy of Willa Cather's *O Pioneers!*. "I have read. Is goot
book," she offered.

Raymond took the book from her hands. He wanted so much more
from her than this damn book. He wanted to touch her face and wrap
his fingers in the spun silk of her hair. He wanted to taste her breakfast
on a kiss. He wanted to take her hand and walk along the shore of Lake
Superior in the moonlight, until the lights in the city went out when the
sun broke the horizon. He wanted to tell her how much he loved her.
All he said was:

"Thank you. I'm sure I'll enjoy it."

She nodded her agreement.

"I get my cast off next week," he said to her, thinking this announcement might make him more appealing in her eyes. Inka smiled to hear
of this development.

"Is goot, Raymond! You vill be vorking soon, ya?"

Ray knew he should be happy, but all he could think was that he
might never see her again. "Yeah. I'll give myself a few days to get the
strength back in my leg and then start looking for a job. I was thinking
about some of the things we talked about. Maybe I could go to your
church some day..."

The bright notes of her laughter surprised Ray. Why would she be
amused at the suggestion of attending her church?

"Oh, Raymond," she explained. "All our sermon is Finniss. You
vould understand notting. I tell you otter Unitarian Church for Engliss,
here in Dulut."

Inka had missed his point entirely. He wasn't that interested in hearing what the Unitarians had to say; he only wanted a way to keep Inka in his sights, and he thought the church might be a perfect excuse to see her in her own environment. She had cut him off at the pass. Dejected, he thanked her again for the book and watched from the doorway as she walked away from him and down the stairs. When he heard the front door to the lobby close behind her, he felt that his only hope for happiness had left as well.

Inka's last visit to Ray at the boarding house came just a day after his cast had been removed. She had come by to see him the day after the procedure and had found him doubled over with cramps in his withered limb. After hobbling to the door to admit her, he collapsed on the floor and writhed in pain, clutching his atrophied calf muscles as they raged against the weeks of disuse.

"Sorry," he murmured through his moans. "This damn leg has been in a Charlie horse since I stood up this morning."

Inka helped him back to the bed, but it seemed there was no position that relieved the intense spasm that pulled his muscles so tight that his toes splayed out from his foot like the prongs on a worn- out garden rake. Inka raised his pant leg and began to massage the contracted flesh. Her practiced hands coaxed the muscles to relax a bit; Raymond fell back onto the pillow and sighed.

"That helps some. Thank you, Miss Siskanen."

As soon as Inka took a break to allow her hands to rest, Raymond was doubled over once again. "What am I going to do?" he asked the girl.

"No vorry. I vill bring someting to hilp." Inka stood to go. "I be back soon," she told him.

She couldn't get back soon enough for Raymond. The pain in his leg was so intense that he completely forgot about the pain in his heart.

A basket full of heavy, hot stones was what she brought back with her. It must have been a chore for the girl to carry this heavy load up the stairs, and Raymond had no idea how they were supposed to help him. He thought some morphine would have been a simpler solution.

"What are those for?" he asked her when he stopped groaning long enough to speak.

"You vill see," she said.

Each stone was wrapped in flannel cloths and then again in newspaper to preserve the heat. Inka had Ray lie on his stomach with his pant leg raised as high as it could be pushed. She again massaged the muscles up and down his limb until it relaxed enough that he could keep it stretched out straight. Then, she applied the hot stones all along the back of his leg, from the thigh to his ankle. Instantly, Ray felt immense relief. The heat thawed the rigid cramps and soothed the pain. He could wiggle his toes and flex his ankle again. This girl is a wonder, he thought. How did she know this would help?

"Where'd you learn to do this?" Ray wanted to know.

Inka explained that Finns in the old country had what she called "saunas," and they had brought the practice of using hot rocks and steam to relax muscles and increase blood flow with them to Minnesota. She described the little sheds made of wood and the fire that heated the stones that would hiss and steam when a bucket of water was thrown on them. She laughed about it getting so hot in the room that it brought people to the brink of heat exhaustion before sending them running naked into the ice cold water of whatever stream or lake was closest. She lifted a rock from Ray's leg to show him how smooth and flat it was.

"From sauna, ya," she advised him.

Ray was impressed. He thought that maybe people should be more open to the gifts immigrants brought with them to America.

* * *

Within weeks of having his cast removed, Raymond was recruited through Leon to become a driver for Geiger's. With the anticipation of Duluth becoming dry, the company wanted to expand to as many other locals as possible. Ray loved driving; it couldn't have been a more perfect job for him, and it put minimal stress on his still weak leg. He was assigned to a Model T panel truck and given a hand dolly to help move the heavy barrels in and out of the saloons in his territory across the Iron Range. For the first few weeks of his route, he was supervised by Arvid Sivertsen, a first generation Iron Ranger of Norwegian descent. Having grown up in the Minnesota Arrowhead, Arvid had extensive knowledge of every dirt road and short-cut in the area, and he used the time he saved in travel to drink away the hours in the establishments he supplied. So inebriated did Arvid become by the end of the route that Ray wondered how the fellow ever made it back to Duluth in one piece.

"Watch out for this stretch in the rain, Ray. Gets downright swampy. Cut through on Bearskin if it looks like rain."

Arvid was an atlas of backroad detours. By the end of the two weeks spent riding with Sivertsen, Ray was confident he could manage on his own. Arvid showed him where he was likely to encounter impassable snow in the winter and where the ice could make a jaunt up a small hill almost impossible. He pointed out areas where trees were likely to fall and cut off the road and instructed him on how he could use the chain he kept in the truck to drag most of the timber he encountered off to the side, clearing the path for the vehicle. He told him of all the places he could get fuel for the truck, an important detail in a place where towns were sometimes miles apart or closed up tight before the sun went down. And Arvid introduced Ray to all the saloonkeeps and bar owners from Biwabik to Hibbing. Ray wasn't one to drink, but he'd never felt so welcome in his life as he did when he arrived at the door of some rundown slosh house with his full barrel on the hand truck, ready to swap it out for the empty cask. Nothing brought a smile to the faces of weary miners like beer. Even the long ride back to Duluth, through the desolate forests and along the lakes and streams that interrupted the landscape, was a special joy for Ray. He used those hours enjoying the scenery and daydreaming about the life he wanted with Inka Siskanen. He was nearly sorry each time he saw the aerial bridge come into view, knowing he would have to confront the reality that Inka was probably rubbing some other man's broken limbs and feeding him Finnish pies with egg on top.

In the year that followed Ray's injury, subtle changes began to appear in the relationship of the two brothers. Leon had become a supervisor at Geiger's. He thought it bad form to fraternize with the staff; that included his own brother. More and more, Leon left Ray on his own when he returned from his delivery routes. Some days Ray would find a note telling him that his brother was managing a late shift. Sometimes he would share the room with Leon for a few minutes in the evening, watching Leon clean up and change from his work clothes into his dapper "going out" costume. Leon never told Ray where he was going...just out. All he knew was that his brother no longer invited him along. Ray, of course, developed friendships of his own and occasionally had simple outings with the friends he had made at the brewery and in the pool hall, where he became a proficient player who frequently walked home with a few extra coins in his pocket. It was on one of these evenings, roaming about with a trio of German boys Ray had met on the loading docks at Geiger's, that Raymond discovered one of Leon's covert activities.

"You're buying, Saxby," Ernst advised him after Ray had collected his earnings from the poker game the four regularly played on Tuesday evenings in the boarding house parlor.

The three Germans had immigrated as little children with their parents. Though they each spoke German at home and amongst themselves, they were proficient in English. The poker game had rules they had all agreed to: no bets higher than a nickel, no chewing tobacco (the parlor lacked a spittoon) and no conversation in German. If Ray couldn't understand what they were saying to each other, there might be the temptation to assume the Germans were setting him up. This rule was insisted upon by the German boys. The sentiment surrounding their country of birth had turned toxic in the recent months, and German immigrants were eyed suspiciously everywhere in Minnesota. Duluth was no exception. The Minnesota legislature created the Commission of Public Safety in response to the Zimmerman Telegram, a secret message from Germany to Mexico, seeking an alliance against the United States. Outraged Minnesotans did their best to restrict the activities of anyone who even hinted at Germanic affiliation. They would have censored Mexicans too, but none could be found in this northern land so close to Canada. The Commission banned books, prohibited labor rallies, forbad speaking out against the war and outlawed gun ownership for aliens. South Dakota, a neighboring state to the west, made it illegal for the German language to be spoken within the state, even among families in their own homes. If Kurt, Stefan and Ernst were perceived to be conspiring against their good American friend, even in a matter as frivolous as a penny-ante poker game, it was a short leap to thinking that they could betray his country as well. The German boys kept their language to themselves and opted for Anglicized versions of their names. There wasn't much they could do with Kurt, but Stefan became Steve and Ernst adopted Ernie as his nickname. They stopped eating at places that served German food and went so far as to shun the very beer they made at the brewery. If they drank at all, Kentucky bourbon was their order of choice. Can't get more American than that, they reasoned.

"Alright, gentlemen," Ray said as he dropped the coins he'd won into his pants pocket, "where should we go?"

The other boys lapsed into German for this discussion of food. Some things, like food and sex, required speaking from the heart, and their hearts only knew their native tongue. It appeared to Ray that they had reached a consensus.

"Let's try that dinky Italian place just down the hill," Steve suggested.

"Is it cheap?" Ray wanted to know.

"Should be," said Kurt. "They only got noodles and bread."

Ray calculated that he could cover that. He had extra change from the pool hall in his pocket that he'd won the night before. Kurt gathered the cards into a neat deck and placed them back on the bookshelf, which was cluttered with some of the many newspapers read by the citizens of Duluth. Conspicuously absent were the papers in foreign languages, so prominent in the town just a short time ago. In their place were flyers urging residents to buy Liberty Bonds to help defeat the enemies across the sea. It was implied that some of those enemies could be much closer to home---maybe in the house across the street or even the room across the hall. Kurt, Steve and Ernie could feel suspicious eyes boring into the backs of their blond heads wherever they went, but the wop diner promised to be a safe place to grab a meal. The

Italians aroused suspicion too, so who were they to complain about the clientele?

On the short walk to the diner from the Incline Station, the four boys ribbed one another and laughed as each one out did the next at hurling insults. It was cold and blustery on that evening in October 1917. The boys had bundled up to brave a wind off the lake that carried the promise of snow by the end of the night. Raymond had his new, plaid wool jacket buttoned to the neck, the lapels flipped up against the wind. The big, stiff collar had the effect of blinkers, obscuring all but his vision for what lay directly ahead of his path. He hadn't noticed them as he walked past the window. If he had, he would have never gone in.

On the way to a table along the back wall of the restaurant, Ray pulled up when Steve asked him, "Hey. Isn't that your brother?"

Raymond cast his eyes over to the table where Steve was looking. There, in his best suit and his face glowing from the light of a candle that sat between them, was Leon. Across from him was Inka Siskanen. Her hand rested on Leon's wrist. His other hand covered hers. Raymond felt every drop of joy he had dreamed for himself and his future with Inka Siskanen drain away, leaving only his curdled blood to sustain him. He thought his heart might stop then and there.

"Are you alright?" Ernie wanted to know when he saw Raymond's face turn white before his eyes.

"No." Ray told him. "I feel sick all of a sudden. I'm going back."

Ray dug into his pocket and handed his companions back the money he'd just won from them. And the pool hall money as well. "Keep the change," he told them.

"You sure?" a skeptical Kurt asked.

"Yeah. I'm sure," Ray told him.

He turned around and started for the railcar to take back up the hill. It was then that he realized he had no money left for the fare. Rather than return to the diner to grab some change, Ray hiked up the steep slope. It took him forty minutes to get to the top of the bluff, his weak leg aching with pain. He used the darkness and the privacy of the lonely path to cry the entire way.

* * *

"Inka. It isn't safe anymore for you to be a socialist." Leon was trying to talk some sense into the stubborn girl between bites of lasagna. "And you absolutely have to stop all that anti-war talk or there's going to be trouble for you. Your family, too."

He tried to convince her to be reasonable. She had heard the rumors, more than rumors, about secret organizations that were documenting every statement made by every person against the war. Statements coming from the ranks of immigrants and socialist were likely recorded in red ink. The girl's face took on an expression of firm resolve.

"Vee come to America to be free. Now you say vee must send our men to fight. Vee must not say vat is in our minds? No, Leon. I vill not be silent about vat I belief is true."

Leon couldn't understand why she wouldn't put her safety first or show any concern about how his association with her might damage his own reputation. If she would just marry him and give up her propensity for sedition, he was positive they could have a bright future together.

Leon was aware that her beauty blinded him to reason, just as her convictions blinded her to reality. It had been a mistake to fall for an immigrant. He'd known that all along, but when she first came to the room that morning to care for Ray, all he could see was a loveliness that eclipsed his distaste for her origins. When he'd finally saved enough money to buy an old car, it enabled him to take Inka for rides in the country where they could be alone, just the two of them. It was in that car, on a summer evening, high above Lake Superior on a secluded lane, that Inka Siskanen removed her shirt dress and allowed Leon to loosen the laces on her corset. When she slipped the clothing away from her slender body, Leon was paralyzed by his own desires. She was truly the most beautiful woman he had ever seen. Her skin was as pale as milk; her soft breasts were punctuated with rosebud nipples, and her slender hips flared away from an elegant waist. She would not allow him to touch her, though to see her this way was enough for Leon to regard the act as a promise of what might come. They had agreed that it would be a mistake to tell Ray about their relationship. They both knew that the boy harbored his own desires for Inka, and she worried that the situation would hurt or confuse her former patient. She had a true affection for the kind boy who met her once a month at the library to pick out the book they would share over coffee at the Unitarian Church. Inka wanted to wait to see if she and Leon could work out their differences before doing anything that might damage the relationship between the brothers. The young woman had been exposed to closed minds and discrimination before, and it was no secret that Leon shared some of those inclinations. It was important to her that Leon love her for the person she was and for what she valued, not in spite of it.

Leon could see that he and Inka were at an impasse. What started as a pleasant meal at the Italian diner had deteriorated into another philosophical stand-off. He loved and hated her fierceness all at the same time. He called for the check. He knew that no amount of warmth from the candle between them could thaw the ice that hardened her blue eyes. She was a confounding woman with a type of Nordic hard-headedness he had glimpsed before in Grandma Saxby. Leon helped Inka into her coat.

"Let me take you home," he implored. "It's too cold for you to take the streetcar when I can drive you there."

Inka shook her head.

"Well, then. I'll walk you to the pick-up spot."

He was determined to smooth things over before she left his sight. On this point, Inka relented. As they walked past other diners to the exit for the street, they passed a table with three young men Leon vaguely recognized from work. He thought they were friends of Raymond's so he tried to duck an encounter, concerned that they might tell Ray who they had seen him with. The short one rose from the table and stuck out his hand.

"You're Ray's brother, right?" the fellow asked.

Leon nodded that he was.

"Glad to meet you. I'm Steve. Say, your brother was with us earlier but you might want to check on him. He took real sick just after we came in. Said he was going home. Tell him we said thanks for the supper."

Again, Leon just nodded. He placed his hand on the small of Inka's back and guided her to the streetcar stop. They waited silently together in the cold. Finally, Leon spoke.

"I think Ray knows."

Inka dropped her eyes to the sidewalk at her feet. "I am sorry. He vill be sad. I am sorry I am von to make him sad. He is sveet boy."

There was nothing for Leon to say. He helped her up into the trolley, then returned to the old Ford parked in the street. He had to use the hill to roll the recalcitrant car down the grade before popping the clutch and starting the worn-out engine. He would need to remember to park it facing down a slope with winter coming, the only way to ensure a dependable start. The car appeared to hate the cold as much as he did. For now, even with the damp wind whipping through the weathered canvas top, Leon drove aimlessly around the city. He was in no hurry to get home to his brother to explain his love for Inka Siskanen--a love that would never have happened if Ray hadn't been such a luckless runt and broken his leg.

"You should have told me, Leon."

Ray was sitting on his side of the Murphy bed when Leon came in that night. He was fully dressed and at his feet were his two bags, packed with all he owned. Leon was pained by the sight of his forlorn younger brother. He hadn't wanted to hurt the kid, but that was just the point. Raymond was still a kid. Leon was twenty-three, and Inka was now twenty. How the stupid seventeen-year-old runt could imagine for one minute that she would be interested in him was beyond Leon's comprehension.

"She wouldn't let me, Ray. She didn't want to hurt you. We didn't plan for it to happen. It just did."

Raymond scowled at his brother. "Yeah. But if you had told me, I wouldn't have had to find out this way--with my friends standing right there with me."

Ray was mad. He wanted to knock Leon on his ass and he was big enough to do it, but he knew that wouldn't change Inka's choice. Leon cracked a condescending smile before he spoke.

"If you think I care what those lousy Krauts think you're a bigger idiot than I thought. You shouldn't be carousing with that traitor scum anyway."

Raymond pulled himself up off the bed and shouldered his duffle. In his left fist was his battered suitcase; in his right fist was all of his pent-up anger. He hauled off and punched Leon with such force that he was laid out on the rag rug before he knew what hit him.

"I'm going to go stay with Kurt. His folks said I could drop by anytime and now's the time. If you need me, you and your APL friends will know where to find me."

Ray left the room before Leon had a chance to pick himself up off the floor. At the top of the hill, waiting for the railcar to take him down to Superior Street, Ray pulled the copper ring hanging by the rawhide string from his neck. The force of the yank cut into the tender skin above the back of his collar, and Raymond felt it burn when the cold wind touched the wound. He sat the suitcase down and freed the ring from its broken string. He reared back his arm and flung the ring as far as he could off the hill. A distant ding of copper meeting granite stung his ears. And then, there was no sound but the whoosh of wind through the trees around him. He vowed he would never again tell Leon his most private thoughts. That he'd shared his feelings for Inka with his brother had been a mistake. All these months, Leon must have been laughing at him behind his back. He only hoped that Inka hadn't laughed, too.

* * *

Summer and fall of 1917 were months of divisiveness in Duluth and the surrounding mill and mining towns that made up the Range. Anti-war and isolationist sentiments were melting away in favor of pro-war involvement and xenophobia. In particular, the socialist-leaning Industrial Workers of the World became a target for the Duluth battalions of the Home Guards and the American Protective League, quasi-military organizations of civilian patriots working to stamp out sedition in the area. Leon was a member of the Home Guard and hoped that the availability of his automobile would make him eligible for the elite APL Motor Corps, a group of citizens tasked with rooting out pro-German and anti-government activities in areas as far as the Canadian border. His affiliation with these organizations contributed to his estrangement from both his own brother and his socialist, pro-labor lover, Inka Siskanen. Inka's family were either members or supporters of the IWW. They were proud to be called Wobblies, the derisive term for participants in the labor organization. Inka's brother, Arto, had been at the IWW headquarters on August 18, 1917, when a mob led by the Minnesota National Guard destroyed the office, breaking the windows with bricks, splintering furniture and burning books and literature intended to educate workers about their rights. Three Wobblies were beaten and killed. Arto escaped with black eyes, bruised ribs and a new understanding about freedom in the land of the free. Despite the protests to the authorities that their constitutional rights had been flagrantly violated by the mob as uniformed police stood by, the Duluth authorities refused to indict anyone for the crimes. Public sentiment was on the side of the mob. When Inka told Leon about Arto's experience at the hands of the National Guardsmen, Leon was not surprised. He urged her to disavow her involvement with the labor movement. He told her he was afraid for her, and he was. But he was also afraid for himself and his status in the Home Guard if his relationship with Inka became known to his compatriots.

It angered Leon that the two people he cared about most were the first two he had to consider putting on his list of violators of the war laws. He was enraged at them for placing him in this situation, making him choose between his personal relationships and the needs of his country. Raymond, he knew, had no real opinions about the war one way or the other, but he did have a genuine soft spot for the underdog and most of those were the immigrants he had befriended, like Kurt or Stefan, who couldn't wash the German off just by sanitizing his name to Steve. Leon thought he would need to have a real heart-to-heart with his brother to impress upon him just how serious the political implications of ill-advised friendships could be in the pro-war climate. He had no idea how to handle Inka.

Two days after he saw her board the streetcar following their disagreement over candlelight at the Italian diner, Leon waited for Inka on the steps of her school, The Finnish Work Peoples' College. He pulled his hat low over his face and ducked his head down between his lapels. The school was on the list of places to surveil by the APL, and he would do what he could to avoid being seen in enemy territory. When Inka advised him that she had given up her desire to go into nursing in favor of studying Marxist theory in English and Finnish, Leon considered it treason--if not to America, at least to him. He was sorry he had ever made Ray help her improve her English skills. She was using those very skills to undermine the country that had given her a home. He would offer her one final opportunity to make a choice that could save both of them from trouble and humiliation.

"Why are you here?"

Inka was not pleased to see Leon loitering on the steps of the school's three-story brick building, doing his best to hide his face. She recognized him in an instant. She was sure whoever he was hiding from would, too, if they saw him pacing back and forth in front of the radical institution's entry. He had an unmistakable strut that marked him like a tattoo.

"Please, Inka. Can we talk?"

He looked from side to side, scanning the area for anyone who might report him for being there. The sound of her voice, angry though it was, stirred his emotions. He had seen the naked breast that gave air to that voice, and the memory grabbed his heart like a vice. Why did she have to be an immigrant agitator, and why did there have to be a war that made her opinions a threat? In normal times, who would even consider a woman's views on such matters as anything other than nonsense? Why couldn't they just love each other and get on with things?

"Oh, Leon. I am tired. Vee vill not vork. Too different, you and me," she told him.

She was tired. The last few months had been a series of painful events for Inka's community. Since May, the IWW had been under constant harassment or outright attack. Their leaders had been arrested, Finns had been charged with draft evasion, and new ordinances allowed IWW members to be arrested as vagrants. Frank Little, one of the organization's national leaders, had been tortured and killed in Montana. He was left hanging from a railway trestle with a note pinned to his long johns warning others of what could happen to war resisters and agitators. Arto had been beaten and the IWW headquarters in Duluth destroyed. And this very day, Leo Laukki, the publisher of the paper Inka read every afternoon and the administrator of the very school where Leon had come to confront her, was indicted for conspiracy. Inka was weary of being berated for her beliefs, and she was tired of Leon leading the charge to change those beliefs. Couldn't he comprehend that beliefs, by their very nature, were not meant to be fickle? Why couldn't he understand that she and her family had come to America to escape just this type of suppression?

"Go avay, Leon. Before your friends see you," she advised him. "I vill say notting to you."

Inka picked up her satchel of books and moved away from the building with obvious determination to avoid any further contact with Leon. Heartsick and frustrated, he ran after the retreating girl but she would not turn back, no matter how earnestly he implored her.

Raymond found that he enjoyed life in the Hofmann household. Kurt had seven younger brothers and sisters, all American citizens, born on American soil. They loved to tease their older brother by pointing out that he was an alien and that when the round-up came to purge the area of undesirables, they would bake him brotchen and mohnkuchen with saws and files folded into the dough to make his escape from prison. They started to call him "Dough Boy," not for the reference to the army recruits streaming off to training centers to learn the occupations of war, but because dough would be the instrument of his salvation. If he couldn't escape with the tools hidden within the pastries, at least he wouldn't starve.

Raymond did what he could to help out around the house. He washed dishes and helped Mrs. Hofmann hang the laundry, jobs that were familiar to him from the days of his mother's illness. Handling the sheets and shirts, overalls and underclothes, all brought back the feelings he'd experienced as a young boy trying to cope with a wrenching loss. This time, the loss was Leon, the person he had always felt closest to. For reasons he couldn't explain, the chewed cuticles that had been his constant companion for many of the last months with his brother were healing and his nails were no longer bitten to the quick. Raymond came to realize that much of what had passed for love between the brothers was actually anxiety. Without Leon in his daily life, his nervous tics melted away. He didn't miss Leon. It was Inka he longed for. He worried from a distance on her behalf. He read in the paper each day about anti-immigrant sentiment. The conversations around the supper table in the Hofmann home reinforced how frightening it must be for immigrants who were perceived as hostile to America. Mr. and Mrs. Hofmann struggled with English, but they steadfastly insisted that the children speak only English, even at home. The parents worried that slipping into German speech at the wrong time or the wrong place could bring scorn to their children or bring the APL to their door. They were aware of other German families who had been visited by authorities who confiscated books written in German and insisted a family show its loyalty by purchasing Liberty Bonds. It only made matters worse for the law-abiding citizens of German ancestry when an actual spy or conspirator working on behalf of Germany was rooted out in the raids. Everyone became guilty by association, even if there was absolutely no association. The very fears so many immigrants had come to the United States to avoid were now an everyday fact of life in their American homes.

"I'm enlisting," Kurt told Raymond over the clothesline in his mother's backyard.

It was one of those balmy early November days that are as precious as gold to Minnesotans, a last reprieve from the harsh cold to come. Raymond wasn't sure he'd heard right. Kurt had a mouth full of wooden clothespins jumbling his words.

"What's that?" Raymond asked.

He reached over to pick a clothespin from Kurt's lips. He used it to secure a pair of Mr. Hofmann's tattered dungarees to the line. Kurt pulled the pins from his mouth to speak unencumbered.

"I said, I'm enlisting. Next month. 'Least that's the plan. Me and Ernie are going in together."

Ray sat the wet laundry in his hands back down in the wicker basket at his feet. "Why are you doing that? Why not just wait for them to call you up?"

On June 5, 1917, every man between the ages of twenty-one and thirty had been required to register for the draft. On August 24, 1917, every man who had reached twenty-one years of age after June fifth was also required to make himself known to the draft board. Raymond knew that Leon had registered, along with all the other young men he knew within that age range. Kurt, Ernie and Steve were no exceptions. They would get called up eventually, so why rush the inevitable?

Kurt shook his head at Raymond's naivety. He told him, "It's the only way to prove that I support America. If I go voluntarily, maybe it will keep the Home Guard and all the others away from my family. Ernie thinks that, too. All our folks are scared. We gotta go sometime anyway, so maybe this will help."

What could Raymond say? Maybe it would make things better for Kurt's family if he signed up now.

"Do you think I should go, too?" Ray asked Kurt.

Kurt wagged his head from side to side, his shaggy blond hair falling over his eyes. "No, Ray. You sit tight. You won't even be eighteen for several months. Give your leg more time to get strong. Besides, my ma kind of likes having you here to reach things on the top shelves."

Raymond laughed. It was true. He had grown taller with each passing month. At six feet, two inches, Raymond Saxby towered over the tiny Mrs. Hofmann. The next tallest person in the household was Mr. Hofmann, and Ray had a good three inches on the railroad man. He also supposed that with Kurt gone, the family would appreciate the modest amount he paid for room and board. He decided that he would increase the money he paid them as soon as Kurt left.

"Do you think you can do it, Kurt? Kill a fellow German, I mean?" Ray asked his friend.

"I don't even remember Germany, Ray. I'm as American as you are. I just have to work harder to prove it."

* * *

More and more, Leon spent his nights roving through the outskirts of town with other members of the Home Guard. One evening in late November, his friend Henry invited him to ride along with the elite Motor Corps, a group of agents that had been given the authority to arrest slackers, spies and agitators. It was rumored that actual Pinkerton detectives made the directives for this law-enforcement organization. The rural areas north and west of Duluth were filled with trapper shacks and obsolete logging camps where draft dodgers and other undesirables could hide out with little fear of detection. It was thought that from these safe houses, German sympathizers and spies were using a communication network to work on behalf of Germany against the interests of the United States. Going after this scum seemed like a pretty good time to Leon. After his breakup with Inka, he needed a way to vent his rage. By busting the immigrant trash from their hideouts, he could unleash his anger while he helped his country.

"We're going to break up into teams," Henry told him, "four men to a car. Keep your eyes peeled for any lights you see coming from behind the trees. We'll check out anything we see. If you find something that needs dealing with, fire a shot into the air to alert the rest of the team."

Henry had a look of glee emanating from him at the prospect of a night on the prowl with a gun jammed into his waistband. He had been rejected by the draft board as unfit for service due to loss of hearing in one ear, the result of purulent infections of his eardrum as a child. He wouldn't even turn his head if someone approached him from the right, so profound was the loss of hearing on that side. The fellows at the brewery teased Henry about his handicap. They told him he could only listen to discourse from the left which, of course, meant he was a commie sympathizer. Henry chuckled along with his buddies, but he also felt shame at being physically inadequate to fight for his country. At least he could serve the cause by bashing insurgents hiding in the woods and be back to his own bed in time to roll onto his wife before falling into a post-coital slumber.

For Leon, the night rounds brought back memories of coon hunting with his father and Granddaddy Earl, back when he was just a boy. The dark around him, the sharp smell of pine sap and the sounds of owls hooting from a distant tree aroused the same sense of anticipation he'd relished on those long-ago nighttime outings near Hastings. Warren Padgett would set his Redbone hounds loose, and their howls would send wildlife scurrying for cover. The sight of a fat coon, perched in a tree with the crazed dogs scratching at the trunk below it, had always given Leon an almost sexual thrill for the kill to come. He felt that thrill now, even as the cold November night froze the mucus running from his nose; his blood was hot and that's all that mattered. The men drove through the bleak night on backroads and logging trails that coursed through the piney forests. Two hours had passed, and not a lick of rabble had been found. They treated their disappointment with sips of whiskey from a flask Billy Wright had strapped to his lower leg. The longer the night wore on, the lighter Billy's step became. He had just screwed the top back on after a piss stop and a round of Old Grand-Dad when Leon tapped him on the shoulder.

"Hey Billy. There's a light off in the distance." Leon pointed to the west, through a copse of trees.

Henry, Billy and Charlie peered through the dark in the direction where Leon looked to make out the faint glimmer of a lantern moving away from them.

"Ok. Quiet all of you. We don't want them to know we spotted them."

The autumn wind was rustling the boughs of the tall pines and scattering leaves that the aspen and birch trees had dropped a month earlier. The natural sound was the perfect cover for the noise of the automobile. With the lights off and the car slowly advancing toward their prey, the men pulled their guns and readied themselves for the encounter to come. More than likely, it was just some trapper checking his lines, but the anticipation of the possible arrest of a slacker mixed with the alcohol in their blood to heighten all their senses. Leon could see the shape of every tree. He could smell the sweat pouring off Charlie, and he could hear each breath Henry took through his pursed lips. He could feel his own heart hammering in his chest. He felt alive in a way he hadn't experienced for weeks, not since he'd lost Inka.

The distant light began to flicker erratically. It moved quickly and disappeared over a ridge. Knowing they had been spotted, Henry threw on the headlights and pushed up the speed of the pursuit. They were in unknown territory, and the dirt road would not lead them to whoever was trying to escape.

"Hang on, men!" Billy shouted.

He veered off into the woods, the car jumping like a rabbit over the rocks and branches that littered the forest floor. At the top of the ridge, they could discern a group of men racing for the face of a cliff.

"Why the hell are they boxing themselves in against the cliff?" Leon wanted to know.

The closer they came to the hillside, the more detail they could see through the darkness. A small shack huddled under the rocks that jutted out from the rugged slope. A couple old cars were parked under the trees, one so rusted it was frozen in time, the rubber tires disintegrated into the dirt under it. Neither the light nor the men were seen. Billy pulled his gun and fired into the air. If any other teams were around they would be here shortly. In the meantime, he hoped the gunshot would flush out whoever had run for cover. It was quiet except for the sounds of the night in the woods, small animals running through fallen branches and trees struggling against the wind.

"OK. We're going to split up. Two of us will go through the shack and the other two need to look around outside. Keep your guns ready at all times."

Henry gave the orders, and the others nodded in grim understanding of their roles.

"Saxby. You come with me. Since you don't got a gun on you, you can hold the light while I keep us covered."

Leon saluted Henry. He hoisted the kerosene lantern from the back of the auto and lit the wick. Heavy, black, acrid smoke filled the air. Leon carefully dialed back the wick until the smoke cleared and a steady light illuminated the grounds around them. The door of the shack was ajar. Leaves were swirling their way into the small building. Billy walked over to feel the hood of the old car that sat next to the rusted heap.

"It's still warm," he told them.

"OK. They got to be around here," Henry told them. "They can't get back to town anytime soon without that car."

Henry and Leon carefully approached the ramshackle cabin. Inside, the light brightened the room, and Leon could see a small table littered with pamphlets and books. A small device that looked like some sort of hand-cranked printing machine sat beside the table. The language on the papers was foreign, but it looked an awful lot like the writing he remembered from the newspapers Inka had wrapped around her stuffed breakfast pies. The same funny dots hovered over letters in ridiculously long words. Then again, maybe all foreign languages looked equally complex, thought Leon. Tin plates sat discarded on the floor. The only food left on them was a dried out crust of dark bread. A pot-bellied stove sat in a corner. When Henry opened it, a few coals still glowed red in the graying ash.

"Yeah. They been here recently. Must be camping out here doing whatever they're up to," Henry remarked.

Leon pointed to the literature on the table. "My guess is they're making propaganda. Look at that crap on the table."

Henry shuffled through the papers. Unsure of what he was looking at, he used his arm to brush the papers onto the wood planks below him. He picked up the press and crashed it against the floor. Pieces of metal and springs shot off in all directions.

"Hey, Leon. I got a better idea. Pick up that paper crap and shove it in the stove."

Leon smiled his approval. "Good thinking," Leon said.

When he fed the stove the sheets of incoherent writings, the coals caught the paper and they flared into flame. With the door of the stove open, the room was lit from corner to corner. They searched under the beds, but no other hiding places were apparent. The only other furniture in the room was an old highboy dresser, crammed against the back wall. The drawers contained blankets and some well-worn sweaters but little else. They pulled most of the contents to the floor, searching for anything that might be hidden on the undersides of the drawers but found nothing suspicious.

"Where the hell did those guys go?" Henry was puzzled. No sooner had the words cleared Henry's lips than they heard the shouts outside. "You stay here and finish burning those pamphlets. I'm going to see what's going on," Henry ordered Leon.

Leon was fine with missing the excitement happening near the car. He was finally warm after hours in the cold. He held his hands palms out to the warmth from the fire, and he could feel his whole body relax. His face burned from the thaw, and the frozen snot liquified and dripped down into his mustache. He reflexively mopped it with his sleeve. He was about to shut the door of the stove when he heard Billy call him.

"Hey Saxby. Come on out and join the fun."

He heard laughter and groans from the men outside. He slammed the grate closed on the pot-bellied heater. A rasping noise accompanied the rusty hinges on the stove door. Then another sound was faintly heard. It wasn't the stove. Leon was sure of that. It seemed to be coming from the old dresser. "Rats, probably," Leon thought. "Strange, though. We just went through the whole thing," he told himself. He went over to the furniture to investigate, hoping a rat didn't run out and crawl up his pant leg and send him screaming like a schoolgirl out of the room. At first he heard nothing and then a muffled noise that sounded like a suppressed cough caught his attention. Leon couldn't imagine what he could be hearing. The shouts from outside were growing and in the distance, he could hear the roar of another engine coming their way.

"I'll be right out," Leon shouted through the open door of the shack. "Just need to check something."

Leon went to the dresser and pulled out each drawer again. Nothing capable of making a sound was in them. Next, he scooted the dresser from the wall a couple of inches. He felt a rush of cold air brush his face. Surprised, Leon pulled the dresser farther away from the timber siding.

"I'll be goddamned," he gasped.

A hole about two feet square connected the cabin wall with the side of the cliff it had been built up against. When he stooped to explore what he had found, he saw it--an entrance to a cave. Before he could back his head out of the dark opening to shout to the others, a hand clamped over his mouth and dragged him into the dank hole. In an instant, he was looking into a face that he knew.

"Leon. It's me. Arto." Behind Arto squatted Naldo. Both of Inka's brothers looked at him with pleading eyes. "No say anyting, Leon. Vee don't vant to hurt you," Arto told him.

"If you hurt me or you don't hurt me, you're still caught so you might as well let me go," Leon advised.

Inka's brothers knew that what Leon said was true. They would be hauled from their hiding place and sent to prison.

"Please Leon. For sake of our sister, let us crawl back in hole. Vee vill tell her how you safe us, ya?"

Leon was torn. He wanted to drag the brothers out to prove what a valuable addition he would make to the Motor Corps, but he also liked to think that someday, when all of this war business was over, he and Inka could resume their romance. "What difference would a couple loose Finns make one way or another?" Leon asked himself. Leon shooed them back into the dark hole and carefully dragged the dresser back into its place against the wall. He hastily gathered the remaining blankets from the dresser, then carted them with him outside. Leaning against the automobile were two ragtag men with their hands tied behind their backs. One had been hiding under gunny sacks in the rusted car, and the other had jumped into a shallow hole and covered himself with dried brush. He was found when Charlie stumbled into the hole and fell right on top of the prostrate fellow. The men from Leon's unit were lounging against the auto that had come in response to the gunshot. They, too, had a ration of whiskey that was being passed around.

"Get your ass over here for your share, Saxby," Henry yelled to him.

Leon carried the blankets over to where the men stood.

"Took your time in there, Leon," Billy commented.

"Hey. I'm not stupid. It got warm in there once we burned them commie papers. I brought these out to keep the next set of foreign trash from using them."

Leon threw the blankets on the ground and opened his fly. He urinated a steady stream onto the moth-eaten wool. His companions laughed, and a couple joined him in defiling the blankets.

"Let's get these bastards back to town," Billy said. "We got some serious drinking to do."

Leon argued with himself all the way back to Duluth. He knew he had helped the enemy, but he also knew Arto and Naldo. They weren't spies. They were just a couple of ignorant Finns who probably were pushed to do whatever they were doing by the damn IWW. Maybe he would go by the office of those worthless agitators and launch a rock through their new window. Maybe that would make up for the harm he did to his country tonight. He would have to think on it over a drink. If he didn't get too drunk, he might do some more thinking over the belly of a fair maiden at one of the female boarding houses in the Tenderloin. That should clear his head.

7

Raymond stood on the station platform with Kurt's family to wave him off to his training as a United States Army recruit. Kurt would be traveling on his own. Ernie had decided to wait until his number was called up. He had read too much about mounting casualties in the trenches to justify going in before his time. The frigid December morning reddened the noses of Kurt's younger siblings, noses already inflamed from constant wiping on woolen cuffs to remove the liquid effluent of sadness and fear they felt for their beloved brother. This very depot had greeted Raymond when he arrived in Duluth eighteen months earlier. What had seemed a wondrous portal to a new adventure on that July night in 1916 now stood as a foreboding abyss that was devouring young men and spitting them into harm's way. If Kurt sensed this foreboding, he didn't show it. His shaggy blond hair had been sheared tightly against his scalp, and the pale bristles sticking out from his head glistened like tiny icicles in the winter sun. He was jovial and excited to be leaving the Duluth area for this first time in almost twenty years. He and his parents had journeyed by train from New York to Duluth on the final leg of their travels from a remote German village that had been their ancestral home. Once settled, the Hofmanns found no reason to venture beyond the nearby town of Cloquet to visit distant relatives who had followed them from the old country.

Mr. Hofmann patted his eldest son on the back and ran his rough, cracked hand against the stubble on the boy's head.

"Knock it off, Pa," Kurt told his father with affection. "You're gonna rub off what hair I got left."

The older man smiled, kissed his own fingers and placed the kiss on the boy's cracked lips. Kurt's mother refused to spend her last few moments with her son on wasted emotion. Renate Hofmann busied herself packing the remaining space in his bag with pastries, dried fruits, sausages and cheeses, wrapped securely in waxed paper and flour sacks. From her apron pocket, Renate pulled out a bright red cap she had knitted from the remnants of an old sweater of her own and pulled it over her son's tender scalp.

"This was to be for Christmas. You need it now," she told him. The woman looked relieved to offer these tangible gestures of maternal devotion to her departing child.

"Thanks, Ma. It's exactly the color I wanted. I won't wear it in the trenches, though," he told her with a wink. "It would turn my head into a bullseye."

A look of horror filled Renate's face. How could she have been so stupid as to not think of that? She reached up to snatch the cap from Kurt's head, but he grabbed her by the wrist to stop her.

"Ma! I was only kidding," he said. "I love it and I'll think of you every time I put it on." Kurt grabbed the sides of the cap and tugged it down tightly over his bare ears. "Ahh. Better already," he told her. He kissed the tiny woman on the top of her headscarf, and she caressed his ruddy cheek with her hand. "Love you, Mama," he said.

It was only then that a tear leaked from Renate's eye. The young man couldn't understand what everyone was getting so worked up about. He was only going to Iowa, at least for now. Kurt left the tight circle of family gathered around him and approached Ray, who stood apart to give the family the space it needed to say goodbye.

"You'll watch out for them, won't you, Ray?" Kurt questioned.

Raymond nodded. "Sure thing," he replied.

Kurt's smile dissolved into a serious expression. "I'm gonna write to them in English, to be safe, you know? The kids can all read it but if they have any trouble with words, you'll explain, right?" Kurt asked his friend.

Raymond smiled and looked a little puzzled. "I don't speak German. You know that," Ray replied.

Kurt laughed. "No. I meant that if the kids have trouble with an English word, you can explain to them and they can tell Ma and Pa in German. Golly, Ray. I don't expect you to become a translator all of a sudden."

Kurt lifted his eyes to look over Raymond's shoulder just as Ray felt a hand grasp the back of his plaid coat. From behind him a voice he recognized cried out, "Thought I seen that ugly jacket before!"

Ray turned to look into the face of his brother. Leon dropped the bag he was carrying to the cement platform and held his gloved hand out to his younger sibling in a formal greeting. "How you been, Raymond?"

Ray was torn between throwing his long arms around Leon and knocking him on his ass. "What are you doing here, Leon? I thought you were only interested in German spies, not families sending their sons off to fight for America."

Ray's words and tone telegraphed that he was in no mood for the possibility that his brother might belittle his German friend and the family that had taken him in. Leon smirked at his brother.

"Always asking questions, aren't you, Ray? I'm getting on that train for the same reason as your friend. I'm off to Camp Dodge. I enlisted a couple of weeks ago."

Raymond felt his knees go weak; for a moment he processed what this might mean. Leon could die in a faraway place, among nameless men and muddy trenches. His anger at his brother over Inka Siskanen was nudged aside by the possibility of losing Leon yet again.

Leon pushed past Raymond and offered the same hand his brother had rejected out to Kurt. "Leon Saxby," he told the blond man in the bright red cap. "I guess we're headed to Camp Dodge together."

Kurt had heard some unflattering stories from Raymond about his brother, but the man standing in front of him, offering him cama-raderie in their shared adventure, seemed a beacon of goodwill. Leon's smile dazzled in the morning glare; Kurt's younger sisters whispered behind their hands to one another. From their adoring eyes, Raymond could tell that Leon's charm and good looks were stealing their affec-tion with a minimum of effort on his part.

"When did you decide to sign up?" Ray asked. "I thought you were going to wait until they called you."

Leon focused his smile on Ray.

"Here's the thing, little brother," Leon began. "It might be all over by the time they get to me. I want to do my part, you know? Only cowards are fixing to wait until they don't got a choice. Ain't that right, Kurt?"

Leon threw his arm over Kurt's shoulder and pulled him away from Ray, over to where the German family was observing the encounter. The Hofmann girls tittered to have Leon so close to them. They thought he looked like a picture of Francis X. Bushman they had seen on a poster outside the Strand movie theater on Superior Street. Leon introduced himself to Kurt's family. In a brief explanation to his parents in their native language, Kurt told them that he would be accompanied to Iowa by Raymond's brother. The look of relief that erupted on the faces of Kurt's mother and father broke through any barrier erected by the obvious cultural differences displayed by the Germans.

"Ya! Ya! Ist gut!" Kurt's father exclaimed, all the while pounding Leon on his back in appreciation. Kurt's mother rambled on in words that were lost on Leon and Ray, but the gist was unmistakable--they were happy that their boy would not have to march alone into the jaws of war.

When the train pulled away at last, headed south to St. Paul before making the ultimate journey down to Des Moines, Raymond's feelings of envy and bewilderment jangled his nerves. Leon's surprise presence at the depot had changed Ray's role of supportive friend, who would watch out for Kurt's family in his absence, into that of a child with nothing to offer but a wan wave goodbye. Needing to redeem himself in his own mind, Raymond squared his shoulders and approached Mr. and Mrs. Hofmann.

"Leon will take good care of Kurt," he told them, "and I'm going to take good care of you. Starting right this minute...let's all go for a nice breakfast...on me."

Raymond knew he could ill-afford to buy a round of restaurant food for ten people, but the investment in his self-esteem and the looks of appreciation from the Hofmann girls were worth the cost. In the excited scurry to the diner, Raymond regained his status as the family saviour and Leon was reduced to being a fellow passenger on the train to Des Moines.

* * *

Leon settled into his seat by the window and watched the frozen landscape pass by. After transfering to a different train in St. Paul, the real journey began. Leon's thoughts mimicked those of the trip. A series of stops and starts and round-about detours took Leon through the events that had led up to his enlistment. When it was discovered by a different squad of Motor Corps volunteers that the shack Leon had searched concealed the entrance to a hidden warren of caves used by dissidents, Leon's actions that December night were questioned by his compatriots. His explanation, that he had no reason to suspect anything troubling lay behind the old dresser in the shack, was accepted by the crew he accompanied on the raid. But privately, Leon acknowledged that he had betrayed his country when he let Arto and Naldo slink back into the moldy dark behind the dresser. It ate at him like a cancer. He was unable to forgive himself for putting his desire for a woman, who was herself a traitor, above his sworn duty to the security of the United States. He would never admit what he had done to anyone. If Arto or Naldo spilled the beans, he would deny their claims and denounce them for the dirty anarchists that they were. He would have to think about how he would handle the incident if Inka re-entered his life. For now, he struggled to rectify his actions that night with his principles. It had been this sense of inadequacy that propelled Leon into the enlistment office two weeks after he let Arto and Naldo go. He would make up for his error in judgement by entering the war on his own terms.

That he was on his way to serve his country sitting next to someone whose cousins he would likely, and willingly, slaughter in a few weeks made Leon shake his head in brooding agitation. He'd much rather have a real American, someone he could count on, sitting at his side.

"Christ! What's that smell?" Leon asked Kurt, who sat with a greasy parcel, pulled from his overstuffed duffle, carefully balanced on his lap..

"Blutwurst." Kurt said. He lifted the paper and offered a chunk of reddish meat to Leon. "Want some?" Kurt asked.

"It stinks. What's it made of?" Leon didn't think it looked or smelled appetizing at all. He marveled at some of the crap foreigners tried to pass off as food.

"Meat and blood, mixed with oats," Kurt explained. "We eat it all the time."

Leon wrinkled up his nose in disgust.

"Who the hell eats blood? Sounds like that vampire book someone wrote a while back," Leon told Kurt. "What kind of meat? Beef? Pork?" Leon didn't think it smelled like either.

"Horse, I think," Kurt replied. "It's really cheap and okay if you spice it right. My ma makes good blutwurst," Kurt assured Leon.

He again proffered the meat to Leon who shook his head vigorously in a declining gesture. Kurt raised and lowered his shoulders in response to Leon's dismissal and took a hefty chunk of sausage into his mouth. He chewed with contentment.

"Christ! I can't believe you can stomach that stuff."

Leon thought about the prospect of eating King, the old plow horse back on the farm in Hastings. He had recently received a letter from Amelia, stained with tears, telling him that King had died. Pa and Amelia had heard that Brewster Smith, the tenant who bought the plow team from Everett, planned to sell King's carcass to the rendering plant. This bit of news plunged poor Amelia into fits of despair, and she begged her father to do what he could to provide a proper burial for their old equine friend. Feeling silly for the sentiment he had to display, Everett went over to the farm to pay the tenants to bury the old horse in a giant hole behind the barn. She wrote to him about how Pa had laughed when he told her the story of Mr. Smith digging the hole and hollering for help when he discovered that he had dug so deep that he couldn't climb out. It wasn't until the next day, when Everett returned to help slide the horse into the hole, that Smith had been found. Pa always said that Ol' Brewster needed to think ahead a little more and wasn't this a perfect example of what he meant?

Leon had laughed to himself when he'd read Amelia's letter, picturing the distraught Smith clawing his way up the side of the horse's grave. But watching Kurt, chewing away on horse meat that could have been King's distant relative, made Leon feel like he was observing a savage or a cannibal. Germans must be a different type of human, thought Leon. And that should make killing them a whole lot easier.

Kurt was oblivious to Leon's discomfort. When his mouth was finally clear for talking, Kurt went on to describe all the many forms that blutwurst could take: different meats and blood, different grains in the mix, even a version where it was mixed with liverwurst and potato called "Tote Oma."

"Tote Oma? What's that mean?" Leon wanted to know. Might as well learn some German words. They might come in handy down the line, he reasoned.

"Dead Grandma," Kurt replied.

Leon didn't want to hear any more of Kurt's family recipes. Thinking about King was bad enough. The last thing he wanted to consider eating was a dead grandma.

* * *

Minutes after twelve AM on April 13, 1918, Raymond was rousted out of a sound sleep by the voices of children singing "Wie schoen dass du geboren bist," a birthday tradition in the Hofmann household. In the bed Ray shared with Kurt's two younger brothers, a small body on either side of him threw back the blankets and pushed him to his feet.

"What's going on?" Raymond asked in mock puzzlement.

Mr. and Mrs. Hofmann and their five daughters laughed and pounded on the door to the boys' attic room at the top of the stairs.

"Come out, geburtstagkind!"they shouted in unison.

Having lived with a family of ten for the last several months, Raymond was familiar with the traditions associated with a German birthday celebration, as he had already witnessed four such events in the household. What he didn't anticipate was what came next. When he opened the door to accept his birthday salutations, fifteen-year-old Mathilda cracked an egg over his sleep-mussed head.

"Hey! What's that for?" he cried, this time in genuine surprise.

Mathilda handed Ray a towel to soak up the sopping mess running into his ears. "Honestly, Raymond, I don't know!" The girl laughed. "It's just what we do for eighteenth birthdays," she told him.

Mrs. Hofmann interpreted the baffled look on Raymond's face and offered her own explanation. "To make babies come," she informed Ray.

Ray feigned shock. "Then I better get every bit of this mess off me!" he cried to the delight of the family gathered around him.

After accepting well-wishes from his foster family, Raymond was released back to his place in the crowded bed and listened to the complaints of his young companions who told him he smelled like undercooked breakfast. Raymond drifted back to sleep thinking the exact same thought.

Turning eighteen meant that Raymond was required to register for the draft, which he dutifully did later that week. Despite appraising himself as a rather passive person, Ray harbored thoughts of patriotic glory at the prospect of joining all the other young men who had gone to war. In letters received from both Leon and Kurt from the training center in Camp Dodge, Iowa, Raymond and the Hofmann family learned what life was like for a military recruit. Ray had to admit that it sounded like a fairly good time. His brother and Kurt wrote about enjoying the routines of sports and drills that took up many of their hours. They were both playing baseball, and it turned out that Kurt was a fine catcher with an arm that could whip the ball to second base with precision and speed. No one dared an attempt to steal second when

Kurt was behind the plate. Leon, for his part, had a knack for laying down awkward bunts that confounded the efforts of opposing teams to anticipate where he would place the ball. His skittering bunts often advanced baserunners into scoring position. To their teammates, Kurt and Leon were as revered as professionals Bill Carrigan and Ray Chapman for their baseball abilities. Their natural athleticism made them both standouts in bayonet drills, and they wrote of how they would plug their ears with wads of cotton to muffle the roars of the big guns they were learning to operate.

Leon told of the large contingent of Negroes that had arrived on base; he had never realized that there were enough Negroes in America to bother drafting them, but recruits from more southern states, such as Illinois or Missouri, educated Leon on this matter. Apparently, Duluth wasn't a place Negroes had come to in substantial numbers, despite an active campaign by U.S. Steel to bring them up from the South to work in the mills for substandard wages. He calculated that there were more Negroes in the camp, training as soldiers, than he had seen altogether in all his years in Duluth. The white recruits only interacted with the Negroes on limited occasions, which Leon thought was still too much contact for his comfort. Leon stayed away from trainees he didn't trust or understand, but Kurt was the exception. He couldn't shake the Kraut kid who stuck to him like a pale shadow. The one good thing about Kurt's devotion was that he readily helped Leon with odious tasks. Kurt stuffed scratchy straw into Leon's mattress and threw Leon's uniforms into the water with his own, saving Leon the need to struggle with his laundry. If Kurt was shining his boots, he pulled Leon's off his feet and gave them a polish while he was at it. When Leon was quickly singled out for his sharpshooting skills and the managerial acumen he had acquired at the brewery, Kurt beamed with pride at his friend's accomplishment. And, when the orders for deployment arrived after three months of basic training, Kurt was overjoyed to find that he would be fighting in Europe side by side with Private Saxby.

The physician doing the fitness exam for the military draft board took Raymond's leg in his hands and turned it back and forth at the knee. Raymond winced with pain everytime the rotation pulled the tendons tight in his calf.

"Does that hurt?" the doctor wanted to know.

"No. Not really."

Raymond hesitated a second too long before he uttered the lie. The doctor looked at Ray in an attempt to gauge his veracity.

"Close your eyes, Saxby," the doctor instructed. Raymond complied.

The medical man then manipulated Ray's leg again. At first, he gently put the leg through a series of range-of-motion maneuvers meant to ascertain Ray's flexibility, and then, in an abrupt move that caught Ray off guard, the doctor gave the withered leg a mighty twist at the knee while holding his foot in place.

"Christ almighty!" Ray cried out, despite his vow to remain stoic throughout the examination.

"That's what I suspected," the physician told Raymond. "This leg would never hold up to the rigors of combat. Good news for you, son. You're unfit for service."

The doctor dropped Ray's leg onto the table where he sat in his underwear and threw his clothes back at him. He handed Raymond a slip of paper.

"Give that to the man at the desk in the room down the hall," he told the boy. "Next!" the doctor called to the line of young men waiting outside the infirmary door.

This was not good news to Raymond. His daydreams of heroics in the service of his country limped out of the office with him. The leg that had served him well enough in the last few months now ached with every step from the manhandling he'd suffered at the hands of the doctor. When a cramp hobbled him on his way back to work, he thought of Inka Siskanen and her wonderful warm stones. Walking half a block released the cramp, but the ache remained. He was happy that at least his clutch leg was in perfectly fine shape, and he fired up the delivery truck to finish his route, knowing that his contribution to the war effort would be limited to supplying beer and soft drinks to thirsty miners across the Iron Range.

Within an hour of leaving the examination room, Raymond had

come to terms with his rejection from military service. Once he cleared his head of visions of glorious warfare, he had to admit that he couldn't imagine shooting at people who reminded him of the benevolent Hofmann family. The Hofmann daughters had baked him the tastiest cake he had ever eaten as a treat for his birthday. Sitting around their kitchen table, eating sausages and potatoes seasoned with good humor and just the right amount of dill, Raymond felt almost German himself.

It was three months after Kurt and Leon left Camp Dodge before they were heard from again. The first letter arrived at the Hofmann home in a battered airmail envelope with exotic stamps decorating the upper right corner, and it contained two sheets of onion skin thin paper, one from each of the boys. Leon's letter to Ray told him of the long, boring oceanic crossing to France and of how he became an expert poker player on the voyage, arriving on French soil with enough money in his pockets to buy a woman for himself and Kurt, too, as a special reimbursement for all the boot licking his sidekick had provided over their months together. When Kurt declined, Leon wrote to Ray that he was left with the enviable decision of how to spend his windfall--whether to buy liquor or twin girls, assuming such a human commodity existed in the coastal city where they had landed. It turned out that liquor was the better purchase because once he had drunk enough of that, one woman had been plenty. Leon proudly related that he had been promoted to corporal and that he was on track to make sergeant by the time they completed training for the trenches. Raymond was amused that he could see through the paper the letter was written on just as well as he could see through Leon's words. The only part he believed was that Leon had likely been promoted because of his age and experience. At twenty-four, Leon was practically a senior soldier.

In his missive to his family, Kurt inquired as to the health of his parents and siblings. He told them that he was well and that the voyage across the Atlantic had brought back memories for him of the long ago trip from Germany. He specifically remembered that the rough waters of the earlier crossing had made him green with nausea from the rolling motions of the sea. He told them he had forgotten all about this peculiar illness until he threw up chipped beef on the mess hall floor on the first night out from the New York Harbor. Ray's brother had laughed at him, he wrote, but then, like the true friend he was, Leon brought him a mop to clean the revolting slop from the floor. He closed his letter by sending them all his love and added a P.S. telling them that Leon was a star. He would soon be supervising their unit. Kurt wrote that he was so honored to be Leon's friend and that he would be proud to serve under such a man as the soon-to-be Sergeant Saxby.

Late July 1918 in the Cote d'Or region of France was a time of relative calm for the American troops training under the watchful command of the French Army. The skies were blue, and the breezes indolent with the fragrance of wildflowers and meadow grasses. It was not so different from the environment at Camp Dodge, but the days were infinitely warmer than they had been in the Iowa winter and, unlike a midwestern summer, the threat of mosquitos was minimal even in the long nights of July. Rows of soiled white tents, laid out in symmetrical order along paths lined with hardy flowers the color of butter and lip rouge, gave the encampment the almost languid feel of a holiday escape. Even so, beyond the tents and flowers, men learned to string barbed wire and dig trenches. They learned to lob hand grenades and feed ammunition into the Chauchat machine guns, unreliable weapons, but light and easy to carry into battles on the backs of infantrymen. On August 2, 1918, Leon Saxby realized his ambition to become a sergeant in charge of a platoon made up of four squadrons. He named Private First Class Hofmann as his unofficial aide, and Kurt did all he could to support Sergeant Saxby in his leadership role. Kurt made sure that Leon looked the part. He shined his boots, cleaned his gun and washed his mess kit with a fervent determination to demonstrate his loyalty to Leon. Leon appreciated that he was finally being treated in a manner that his abilities demanded. For his efforts, Kurt was elevated to the rank of corporal by the powers that be. When he finished sewing the new set of stripes on Leon's sleeve, he proudly added a stripe to his own.

"You'll be helping with grenade training for the new boys today," Leon advised Kurt.

They had assembled the new men in rank and file formation under the watchful glare of a couple of French and American officers who were directing the training of newly arrived troops from Camp Dodge. Kurt had shown that he was the most efficient man in the camp when it came to the distance and accuracy of grenade deployment. His catcher's arm had caught the eye of a young lieutenant who still had to shave around his boyish blemishes. The young officer immediately nabbed Kurt and placed him in this role, to be overseen by Sgt. Saxby. Two squadrons, made up of ten men, were cut out from the larger group standing in formation. They followed Kurt and Leon to a distant meadow where training trenches and make-shift bunkers had been erected. The first order of business was for Cpl. Hofmann and Sgt. Saxby to familiarize the troops with the mechanical operations of grenades.

"Back home, you may or may not have been introduced to grenade warfare," Leon told his charges. "Grenades haven't been used much by American forces until we joined the British and French during this engagement. Grenades have been shown to be extremely effective weapons for the style of trench fighting that you men will experience out in the field."

Leon held up a long, pipe-like object to show his charges. "These here are stick grenades. The French love these babies and they are pretty useful for close-in deployment." He turned to his corporal. "Cpl. Hofmann, show the men the proper technique for throwing the sticks."

Kurt grabbed the weapon by its lower shaft, and all watched as the object flew end over end into the distant ditch. There was no accompanying explosion as all the training devices were dummies, meant for instruction only.

"We don't see many of these stick grenades now," Leon went on. "Mostly, our army uses the Mk 1, or the Mk 2, if we can get our hands on them. They are called fragmentation grenades." Leon held the pear-sized object up for his men to observe. "See the sections carved into the body?" he asked them.

The transfixed soldiers nodded in unison.

"The weapon is designed to have a fuse that is lit by manipulation of the lever and cap. This action ignites the charge inside the casing, giving you enough time to throw it at the enemy before it explodes. The striations in the steel body come apart during the explosion and send the shards in all directions. Very damaging to anyone or anything near it."

Kurt had the soldiers assembled in a loose circle. He ducked into the center of the observing men and held out the dummy grenade for them to see.

"Watch Cpl. Hofmann. He's going to show you how to activate the device," Leon told the soldiers.

Kurt slowly went through the operation of the hand grenade. He showed the men how to pull the pin out by the ring, slipped over the middle finger of the left hand, being sure to hold the lever tightly against the casing until the grenade was released in an arc towards the enemy.

"Be careful to keep the lever depressed. Releasing that is what ignites the fuse," Kurt told the men.

He demonstrated the throwing stance, both from a standing and from a kneeling position. "Always follow through," he told them. "Then immediately take a cover position. If you're throwing a grenade, the odds are good that someone is shooting back at you."

Sgt. Saxby offered another bit of advice. "Remember, men. These are fragmentation grenades and they blow apart and send the metal missiles in all directions. If you're close at all, you could get shrapnel in you. Another good reason to duck and cover when using these things."

Kurt nodded vigorously. "That's right," he said. "One more thing. We got any lefties in this group?"

One young man raised his hand.

"Okay. We got a special technique for you fellows."

Kurt demonstrated how the grenade is inverted and the pin disengaged by the right middle finger for the left-handed soldier.

"Alright now, troops. We're going to spend the time before the mess call to do some practice with these things. Corporal, divide the men into two groups. I'll take one outfit over there," Leon indicated a distant field with a cock of his head. "And you stay here with the others," Leon ordered.

The next couple of hours were spent learning the components of the grenades in detail. That instruction was followed by practice with pipes and rocks before actual dummy grenades were placed into the grips of the soldiers.

"Jesus! You got an arm on you!" one admiring fellow told Kurt. "You play ball much?" the kid asked.

"Catcher," Kurt replied.

"I wouldn't try to steal on you, Corporal," the rookie remarked.

"Well," Kurt told him, "this isn't a game. One of these bastards can blow your ass to kingdom come."

It was early September when Leon learned that he and his platoon of nearly fifty men were to be transferred to the 90th Division, known by the moniker "Tough 'Ombres" for the "TO" patch worn on their shoulders. Originally a group of soldiers from Texas and Oklahoma, the Tough 'Ombres were a fierce unit that had sustained major casualties on the Western Front and needed replacements from newly arrived troops to replenish their ranks. The cushy training assignment at Cote d'Or had indeed seemed a vacation in the sun for Leon and Kurt when they contemplated the chaos ahead. The 90th was in place to engage German forces in what was to become the only offensive of the war launched by American troops. They were led by Gen. John J. Pershing. Leon and Kurt arrived at the troop staging area on September 10, 1918. In two days time, the Battle of Saint-Mihiel would begin.

* * *

Raymond's routine during September 1918 went on much as it had in the months since he had been denied entry into the military by the draft board. He picked up occasional night shifts on the production line at Geiger's to help make up for all the men lost to training camps and deployment to the European theater. Ray mused about the terminology of war. He had no understanding of the word "theater" as a description for such a colossal scene of suffering and death. The battle pictures printed in the daily papers detailed the destruction of men and property on a massive scale. To call the devastated landscape a "theater" seemed absurd to Ray. Theater was supposed to be make-believe. When people died in the theater, they reappeared at the curtain call, good as new. War was real, and the dead of war were dead forever. Ray hoped with all his might that his brother and Kurt would be around to take a bow when this fight was over.

The more men Duluth sent away to fight, the more the men who remained were branded as slackers. So few of Raymond's friends were still in town that he gave up seeking fellowship among those his own age and increasingly depended on the Hofmann family for company. This affiliation brought its own problems for Ray. Being of enlistment age, without a hope of service and living with a family of Germans, Raymond became a frequent target for scorn.

"Why the hell are you still here, Saxby? You a draft dodger or maybe you like Germans more than Americans?"

He was confronted more and more about his situation as he went about his daily business. It didn't matter to those who monitored these things that the Hofmann family members still at home, with the exception of Mr. and Mrs. Hofmann, were citizens of the United States. It didn't matter that Ray walked with a limp that resulted from the stunted growth in his injured leg. It only mattered that he was a young man not bound for war who had chosen to live in the bosom of "the other side." In this hostile milieu, fear and watchfulness became as ubiquitous for the Hofmann family as bread and water.

"Are you working nights again this week?" Mathilda wanted to know.

Ray first met Kurt's younger sister when she had been a chubby cheeked girl with perennially chapped lips and stringy, dishwater blond hair, corralled in braids that fell half-way down her back. She now wore those braids coiled over her head, like a milkmaid advertisement he had seen on a dairy window. Her face had slimmed and her body had transferred some of the extra flesh of her child's frame onto the curves of her figure, signalling her emergence into womanhood. Ray wouldn't have given her a second look only a year ago, but he now found himself watching her from the corner of his eye whenever he had the chance.

"Yeah. I think I'll pick up a few shifts this week, if I can. It works okay for me if I can do them on the nights when I have shorter routes the next day. We can use the money," he told her.

Mathilda was aware that she felt more than a brotherly attachment for Ray. She had admitted as much to Lena, her next younger sister, when the girl had caught her darning Ray's only sweater.

"It's strange that you do darning for Ray but you don't want to do a thing for the rest of us," Lena chided her sister.

Mathilda barely looked up from her yarn before answering Lena. "Raymond always says 'thank you'," Mathilda replied to the snide remark. "You should try it sometime."

Lena was unmoved by the argument that Ray had better manners. "You're sweet on him, aren't you?" Lena came right out and asked.

"Maybe a little," Mathilda admitted. "I wish he was here more," she said to the self-satisfied Lena.

Mathilda much preferred Ray's presence at the house in the evenings to anything his money could buy. Lena considered Mathilda's situation.

"Well, Raymond is about the only boy left around here who isn't totally crippled or feeble-minded. I suppose you don't have much choice."

Mathilda shook her head at her sister's remark. "I think maybe I would be taken with Raymond even if I had all the choices in the world. But don't you dare tell him I said so!"

Lena saw this admission as something worthy of exploitation. She went to their shared room and pulled a pair of ragged stockings from her drawer. She returned to the parlor and flung them at Mathilda.

"Patch these up for me and I promise not to say a thing," she told her sister.

Mathilda picked up the stockings from the arm of the davenport where they had landed and placed them on the top of her pile of items to mend.

In the month of September 1918, every adult citizen in Minnesota was required to purchase a specific quota of Liberty Bonds to help finance the war effort, a hardship for most of the population living the hardscrabble existence of just getting by. An ad hoc organization calling themselves the Knights of Liberty joined already existing groups such as the American Protective League and the Motor Corps to ensure that the residents of Duluth did their share. Young men like Raymond, of age and uninvolved in pro-war activities, were confronted almost daily. If the young man was an immigrant and actively resisting conscription, the consequences could be dangerous. As if this environment didn't make life hard enough for those who disagreed with the zeal for combat, the United States Immigration Act of 1918 broadened the definition of anarchists to include just about everything Raymond supposed that Inka Siskanen believed in. Raymond knew that Inka had no romantic interest in him, and he had accepted this reality. The ready encouragement he received from the blossoming Mathilda Hofmann stirred his ardor in a way that he was sure was reciprocated. Mathilda was a simple girl who could comfort him, though she would never challenge him the way Inka had. This realization was both reassuring and disappointing for Raymond. Around Mathilda, his body felt alive, but with Inka, he had experienced an arousal of both his body and an intellectual curiosity that he never realized he had. She had frustrated him on dual fronts, and he had found that frustration exhilarating. Raymond had dismissed Inka to the back of his mind, to the place he'd set aside as a child long ago for unfulfilled dreams and unsaid words, until one September evening, when an event reported on the front page of the paper startled him with concerns for her well-being.

Olli Kinkkonen was neither a young man nor was he old. He was a Finnish immigrant of thirty-six years of age who assumed he had escaped the horrors of enforced military service when he left his village in Finland for a settlement of like-minded countrymen on the outskirts of Duluth. He worked for a time as a logger in the rich forests blanketing the rolling hills that stood watch over the great lake. Eventually, he came to work on the docks that serviced the giant ships laid up against the shores of Lake Superior on the Minnesota side of the shipping canal. Like many of his Finnish brethren, Olli was an avowed socialist who saw acts of war as imperialistic grabs for power and money. He was also a naturalized American who proudly displayed his citizenship certificate on the wall of his dilapidated boarding house, right above his headboard. Next to it, he had pinned a faded photograph of his mother holding him on her lap as a little child in his christening dress. He sat on his bed to relace his boots, glancing up at the certificate he'd studied so hard to get years before. Soon he would have to take it down. He had resisted the constant pressure to answer the call for enlistment, but now he was required by law to register for the draft. Olli had no intention of doing the very thing he had come to America to avoid. He saw wars as staged conflicts that enriched the few while the many suffered or died thankless deaths. He wanted no part of it. He wasn't alone. Many young men of Finnish extraction held the same views. Olli decided he must act on his principles, and he did the nearly unthinkable--he renounced his United States citizenship, refused to register for conscription and planned for his return to Finland. Five other like-minded Finns of Duluth had recently done the same.

When word reached the Knights of Liberty that such a blatantly disrespectful act was being committed by the ungrateful Finns, a vigilante group went out looking for the foreign trash to educate them on the errors of their thinking. Of the six men the Knights searched for that day, only Olli Kinkkonen was found. He was sitting on his bed, preparing for his departure. The quiet man was dragged from his boarding house and thrown into a car that transported him and his abductors out to Congdon Park. There, Olli was stripped of his shirt and surrounded by hostile men crying for his humiliation. Others heated a slurry of viscous, black tar over a fire made with fallen branches, dried out from the unusually parched months of the fading summer. Another couple of enterprising fellows were plucking the feathers from ducks they had rounded up from nearby Tischer Creek.

"We get duck for supper on top of a bit of fun this afternoon," one excited fellow pointed out.

"We should of run these fuckin' Finns out of here years ago," another remarked. "Nothing but a bunch of slackers. The whole lot of them."

Everyone there, with the exception of Olli Kinkkonen, nodded in agreement. Blistering tar was sloshed on to Olli's bare torso, and he was rolled on the bed of feathers laid out on the ground beside the dead ducks. He cried out in pain from the searing of his flesh. His moans were interrupted only by his plaintive pleading in a language the tormentors could not understand. If they had, it would not have mattered to them. There was nothing Kinkkonen could say that would have convinced them that he was worthy of mercy. He was draft-dodging filth in their eyes. Worse, he was someone who was denying any loyalty to America by renouncing his citizenship. If these men ever stopped to consider that they themselves were armed with tar and hate in the place of a military occupation, no mention was made of this irony. Their indignation was righteous and Olli's degradation, complete. Later that day, someone from the group telephoned a local paper to claim credit for tar and feathering Kinkkonen. The paper later received a letter to back up its claim, just in case the phone call was dismissed as a prank. Olli Kinkkonen then disappeared for two weeks.

His body was found a fortnight later, hanging by the neck from a tree near the serene landscape of Lester Park. Hidden in his shoes, authorities found four hundred and ten dollars. This was the money he planned to use for his fare to Finland and to start his new life in his old homeland. His death was ruled a suicide, but almost everyone knew the truth. No one hangs himself with money in his shoes. The money didn't change his ultimate fate. He was buried in a pauper's grave in Park Hill Cemetery. The cash disappeared into thin air.

Inka Siskanen was one of the mourners who came to watch poor Olli be lowered into the soil. She made up her mind, standing there, by his grave, that she would leave Duluth to fight on a different front. She would go to New York City where she would follow in the footsteps of her outspoken socialist heroines, Mary Jones and Emma Goldman. If the anti-sedition laws caught up with her there, she was more than willing to be deported from America, the price demanded to stand up for her people, people who longed for nothing more complicated than fair wages and a life of peace. This is what she told Raymond when he went to see her shortly after he'd heard about the death of her countryman.

"Will you write to me, Inka? So I know that you're okay," Ray asked the resolute young woman who told him of her plans while they sat on her porch, drinking scalded coffee that had been sitting for hours on the stove in Inka's kitchen.

Inka shook her head. "No Ray. Not because I don't vant to. It is to be safe for you and Hofmanns, ya? You understand, Ray?"

Reluctantly, Ray told her that he did. "You'll be careful, won't you?" Ray implored the girl, whose blue eyes and soft features had taken on a hardened resolve.

"No, Raymond. I vill not be careful. I can do notting important if I am careful."

Inka took Ray's coffee cup from his hand and leaned over to kiss the dear boy on his still soft cheek. His downey whiskers tickled her lips, and she smiled at his sad face.

"You be safe, Raymond. I am glad vee do not fix your leg too good. I am glad you vill stay here and be avay from var."

* * *

The 90th Division entered the Battle of Saint-Mihiel on September 12, 1918, as part of the I Corps, in an offensive assault from the right side of the battle arena. These troops stretched from Pont-a'-Mousson west towards Limey. They were supported by tanks, aircraft and artillery that added to the hellacious fury unleashed that day. The 90th Division was led into the chaos of brutal battle under Major General Henry Tureman Allen, a seasoned leader who had served the United States in military endeavors from the Mexican border to the Philippines. His experience contributed to the gains his troops made when the day came to a close. In a sagging tent the night before the engagement was to begin, Leon and Kurt did what they could to ready themselves for their first real taste of warfare.

"I think the men are ready," Kurt proclaimed to his friend and superior in rank.

Leon didn't look up from his focus on his rifle and ammunition. He was careful to check and recheck every bit of his equipment. The activity took his mind off his fear. He had spent what he could of the day in a state of quiet meditation in the fleeting moments between encouraging his men for combat and squatting over a hole dug into the dirt to relieve his anxious intestines. The more Leon wanted to run, the more his bowels did what he couldn't do. He was unable to eat, and what liquid he could stomach poured through him in a watery slurry of undigested muck. Only his focus on the small details that he could control--his gun, his bayonet, his ammunition and his uniform--allowed Leon to function at all that day. He was beginning to understand the mindset of the slackers who had argued that war was barbaric and an affront to civilized society. He had seen shattered men brought out of battle on stretchers and in pieces on wagons. Though it was a thought he would never reveal, he had a new respect for those reviled men who refused to play the military game. Being scorned for a time seemed a reasonable trade-off for being alive and in one piece.

"I'm not sure anyone is ever ready for the possibility of death but we'll know by this time tomorrow," Leon replied to his corporal. "How about you? You ready?" Leon asked.

It boggled his mind how Kurt went about his business as if he were just going for a pleasant hike the next day. He wasn't sure if the younger man was fearless or stupid. He suspected Kurt was a little of both.

" I'm ready," Kurt replied. "I know we got good officers, good equipment. And I got my good friend--you, Leon. We'll look out for each other."

Leon kept on polishing the bluing on his rifle. " Yeah. Let's hope you're right," Leon answered in an absent-minded reply.

He suddenly doubled over at the waist and grimaced.

"Shit!" he said. "I can't believe I got anything left in me to crap!"

Leon laid his gun down on his pack and scurried out of the tent, unbuckling his britches as he ran for the latrine. When he left, Kurt went over to examine Leon's rifle. He picked up the old rag Leon had been using and ran it along the barrel in a gentle caress. The barrel felt smooth and cool under his hand where the sergeant had rubbed it to a spotless shine. He laid his cheek along the stock and smelled the oil that had been massaged into the wood. It smelled like Leon.

On the night of September 12th, it started to rain. As Leon assembled his men at dusk for the march to the St. Mihiel Front, the drizzle that had softened the soil under foot for most of the afternoon became more and more insistent. Mud on the soles of the men's boots crept up to their ankles as the downpour increased. Through the dark, wet night, the men found their way forward by holding onto the pack of the man directly ahead. Like ants, they marched single-file in a quiet, determined advance, each man lost in his own thoughts and fears. With no light to illuminate their path, the men stumbled through the scrub brush and sole-sucking mud until they reached a crest that overlooked the front below. A sea of fire and flash was evident as far as the eye could see. The constant barrage of artillery blasts shook the ground beneath their feet, and many had to cover their ears with their hands to insulate tender eardrums from the overwhelming concussive forces that could shred the thin tympanic membranes in a soldier's head. Kurt made plugs of mud and horse manure that he stuffed into his own ears. He couldn't hear Leon's orders, but the cacophony around him rendered verbal communication useless. In any case, he didn't need to hear. He had spent so much time with Leon that he could read his lips and body gestures with ease. Sergeant Saxby was making it known that his men were to advance to the trenches vacated by the retreating Germans. From there, they would support the troops to the rear as they marched forward to join the assembled ranks before pushing into the territory held by the German forces.

The weather was as much of an enemy as the German opponents. Trenches dug six feet wide and equally deep now presented obstacles reaching eight feet down into the mud and as much as fifteen feet across. The French Renaults used to transport men and supplies disappeared into the earthen channels where they remained hopelessly mired in the sludge. Horses carrying artillery supplies on caissons slid down into the ruts in the slippery soil. The exhausted animals fell silent, and the trenches eventually became their graves. The sight of a frantic horse struggling in a muddy pit eight feet below brought to

Leon's mind Amelia's letter about the burial of poor old King. Seeing the crazed animals flail in the mud distressed Leon in a way he hadn't anticipated. He could explain the horror of what they would encounter to his troops, but the ignorant horses must have been filled with unexpected terror.

He pushed his troops forward through the devastated landscape. When mired in a rut that reached over their heads, Leon and Kurt showed their soldiers how to climb out of the ditch by using their own bodies as ladders. With Leon standing on Kurt's shoulders, he reached down to hoist man after man up to solid ground, just to repeat the procedure at the next set of trenches, some so filled with rain run-off that the men stood up to their armpits in fetid, brown water. In the worst cases, the water swirled with blood and shredded entrails from men and horses. Nothing had prepared any of the men for the mind-altering cataclysm they encountered with each yard that they advanced. When the next night descended onto the scarred earth, the relative quiet brought with it a different doom. Now, the cries and moans of the wounded could be heard, and their pleas came from every direction. Some cried for rescue; others begged for a well-placed bullet to end their agony.

When Leon finally lifted the last man from the last trench he would confront at the end of the long day, he slid down off of Kurt's shoulders and fell against the side of the sodden bank that would be their refuge for the night. Kurt crumpled down next to Leon. They were both so encrusted with mud that they could have been anyone, but each knew the other by voice and gesture. Lying side by side on the wet ground, they felt like twins fighting for survival in their mother's womb.

"That was a hell of a day," Kurt mused under his breath.

"Yeah," Leon replied. "Good thing I was empty or I would have had the shit scared out of me."

He laughed then just for the fact that he was still alive, and Kurt laughed, too. The cold night and the drenched clothes that stuck to every inch of their bodies shook them with chills. They scooted closer to one another to conserve what little warm remained beneath their uniforms. In a place where sleep should have been impossible, they fell into the grace of unconsciousness. When Leon awoke later, he had no idea where he was or what time it might be. For an instant, he thought he was back in his room in the barn at the Hastings farm. The familiar smells of earth and horseflesh were comforting until the acrid scents of gunpowder and decay assailed his senses. He opened his eyes to a waning blackness that enveloped him. Beside him, Kurt moved, and Leon remembered all at once where he was. He shifted his weight to take the pressure off of his aching hip. In doing so, he dislodged Kurt from the side of his body that Kurt had been propped against. Kurt stirred awake and waited for his eyes to adjust to the dark of the trench.

"What's wrong?" Kurt asked. "Are you okay, Leon?"

Kurt pushed himself to a sitting position against a sandbag he had been using as a pillow. In the soft light of the approaching dawn, Kurt could make out Leon struggling to remove his boot.

"Here," he told his friend. "I can help you."

Leon extended his leg towards Kurt. "Thanks," he said.

The energy Leon expended wrestling with the boot had tired him, and he allowed his torso to rest against the dirt wall behind him.

"Why are you taking this off? Are you hurt?" Kurt questioned Leon.

Leon shook his head. "It's nothing. Just a blister, I think. From all that marching with holes in my sock."

Kurt smiled. "Could have been a lot worse after what we seen yesterday. Let me have a look."

Kurt carefully pulled the sodden leather boot from Leon's foot. There was just enough morning light peeking into the trench for Kurt to see an area of pinkish stain covering the heel of Leon's ragged sock. The blister had broken, and it seeped, raw and wounded, from the white flesh visible through the hole in the wool. Kurt carefully rolled the old stocking away from the lesion and off of Leon's toes. His pale foot stood out against the dark mud that surrounded them.

"The blister on your heel has popped but there's a big one on the ball of your foot. Just here."

Kurt used his finger to prod the bulging pocket of fluid under Leon's big toe.

"Christ! That hurts like a mother!" Leon cried.

"Shush." Kurt told him. "Try to keep your voice down. No telling who's out there."

Kurt found his canteen strapped to his side and poured a small amount of clean water over the oozing skin on Leon's heel. Leon recoiled from the sting but kept his cries safely clamped behind clenched teeth. From a small tin kit stowed in his knapsack, Kurt pulled out a tiny container of Vaseline and a roll of gauze wrapped in crinkly blue paper. Kurt wiped his dirty hands as clean as he could on the inside of his jacket under his armpits, the only place on him not covered with mud. He tore open the blue paper with his teeth after he smeared a goop of petroleum jelly over the blister. Carefully, he rolled the bandage over the sore and around Leon's ankle, just like his mother had done for him as an injured child. He ripped the gauze, again using his teeth, and secured it with a tidy knot tucked below the hollow of Leon's ankle bone.

"Thanks, Kurt," Leon said with a sigh. "That feels a lot better."

Kurt just smiled and nodded to his friend. "We need to do something about this one, too," Kurt said, referring to the nasty bulge on the ball of Leon's foot. "I should open for you. Take the pressure off."

Kurt did the only thing he could think to do. He bent his head to Leon's foot and sucked the soft flesh between his incisors and bit a tiny hole in the blister. The salty ooze flowed against Kurt's lips and he found himself resting his cheek on the instep of Leon's arch. When Leon closed his eyes and sighed, Kurt hesitated for only a moment. Before he could think about what he was about to do, he did what had been in his heart for months. He lowered his mouth to kiss the soft flesh of Leon's delicate arch and then each of his toes. Leon's shock was immediate, but he was helpless to pull away. A soft groan escaped his lips. He felt himself harden behind the buttons of his fly, and his shame was eclipsed only by the stunning realization that no one had ever touched him with such gentleness or devotion in his entire life.

He sat bolt upright and pulled his foot away from Kurt's grasp.

"What the fuck was that about?" Leon cried.

Kurt was unfazed. In a soft voice he said, "You know what that was about. Don't tell me that you don't."

Leon scrambled to find his dirty sock and yanked it back onto his foot. In his haste, he dragged it over his bandaged heel and the friction made him scream in pain.

"Son of a bitch!" he yelled.

Kurt struggled to slap his hand over Leon's mouth to quiet his outburst, but Leon knocked him away.

"Get the fuck away from me, you fucking queer!"

Leon's face reacted with terror as Kurt approached him, holding Leon's boot in his hand.

"Here. You're going to need this," Kurt said, as if nothing unusual had happened.

In the time it took for Kurt to draw his next breath, Leon had sprung to his feet and was charging towards him. He had grabbed his gun by the barrel and was swinging it in an arc as if he intended to crash the rifle butt onto Kurt's head.

"Look out!" Leon screamed.

Kurt pivoted his body to the side, and he caught a glimpse of a figure, with a bayonet fixed to the end of a German carbine, leaping into the trench behind him. The German slammed Kurt to the mud with the momentum of his jump from the ground above. He kicked the corporal squarely in the temple with his right boot as he advanced on Leon with the bayonet raised above his head, ready to drive the blade into Leon's torso. Leon fell to the side to avoid the weapon, but the German soldier reacted with the fluid moves of a dancer anticipating his partner's next step. Backed against the dirt wall behind him, Leon had no room to swing his own weapon in defense. He tried to fire the rifle from his hip, but he fumbled the bolt. Leon swiveled the gun to a horizontal position in front of him, holding it across his body like a staff, in an attempt to ward off the imminent attack.

"Leon!" He heard his name screamed from what seemed like a mile away.

Leon never took his eyes off of his attacker. When the German reared his arms back to drive the bayonet home, a blur of brown flew up between Leon and the German. Kurt hurled himself at the charging Hun, taking the large knife into his own body just below his left nipple.

In the moment it took the German to pull the blade from Kurt's chest, Leon had righted the bolt on his rifle. He pulled the trigger and heard the explosion. The German was blown back with such force that he ricocheted off the side of the trench. The blast went right through the man's body and put a crater into the earthen wall behind him. He dropped his gun and crumpled onto Kurt's bleeding chest.

The entire episode had taken seconds from start to finish, but for Leon, time had slowed to a crawl. It seemed a lifetime ago when he had noticed the shadowy figure approaching the trench. The adrenaline coursing through his system was urging his heart to pump blood to his brain with such force that he thought that his eyes might be blown out of his head by the pressure. He watched in awe as the muddy footprints around the German filled with seeping blood. It wasn't until he heard a soft gurgle that he thought of Kurt.

Leon dragged the dead man off of his fallen comrade. With each contraction of the boy's heart, a new wave of blood bubbled up from the wound. Kurt's eyes were closed, but they fluttered open when Leon pushed his arm under Kurt's head to raise it off the cold ground. Leon clamped his other hand over the chest wound in an attempt to stem the bleeding, but he knew it was futile. The lad's face was chalk white and serene. In his repose, the corporal looked like the nineteen-year-old innocent that he was.

"Kurt," Leon softly whispered the boy's name. "We'll get help. You'll be okay. I promise." Leon told the boy the lie as he cradled his head in his arms.

Kurt Hofmann took another ragged breath. He used it to whisper, "Leon. My Leon."

The boy's body went limp, and the weight of his head rolled it to the side. It was hours later when two of Leon's men found him still rocking Kurt's body in his arms. Leon's tears had rinsed some of the mud from the dead boy's face.

8

St. Paul, Minnesota 1995

"We're out of cookies," I told Mr. Saxby. "Guess that means it's time for me to clean things up in here."

Dried-out noodles and wilted salad sat in their serving bowls on the beige Formica counter, patiently waiting to be dumped into the garbage can hidden under the sink. Beneath the bowls, years-old stains and circular scars from Dolores' wayward Virginia Slims pocked the already worn surface. In places, the veneer had begun to wear off completely. The exposed gray layer, peeking through from the friction of a million wipes of the washcloth, looked like dark circles under weary eyes. I wondered if Mr. Saxby or Dwight even noticed. I suspected that houses aged around their inhabitants in the same way that people do, a wrinkle at a time, not readily perceived by those who love them.

"Do you want to save this little bit of hotdish?" I asked him. "You could maybe mix it in with a can of chicken noodle soup."

I raised the bowl and tipped it to his eye level to show him the meager cupful remaining in the dish. Mr. Saxby smiled and gave me a thumbs up. He rose from his chair and straightened the vinyl tablecloth with his bony fingers. The brown spots on the back of his hands made me think of the dot-to-dot books I had loved as a child. I mentally connected the spots on his left hand and was delighted to find that they could be made to resemble the Big Dipper. I watched him amble over to a cabinet above the stove where a jumble of old plastic butter containers was stored.

"Good thing you're so tall," I said. "I would have needed a step stool to get those."

Raymond carefully extracted a bowl from its nest and then rummaged around until he found a top that would fit. It didn't match the bowl, but it would work. Very little in the old kitchen matched; pots without lids were covered by tin pie pans, and glasses came from jelly jars or McDonalds' giveaways. Mr. Saxby had taken his milk with dinner in a glass featuring the Hamburglar making off with a Big Mac. The coffee mug he'd used for dunking his cookies had been a promotional item from a gas station on Snelling, a remnant of a time when gas stations gave out dishware and green stamps. A man in a uniform would check your oil, pump your gas and wash your windshield, then hand you a gift when you drove away. Raymond hadn't driven since his cataract surgery had gone wrong in 1979, but he still had the avocado green mug he'd scored on his last visit to the station.

"Save the salad, too," he told me, but I had to shake my head at that request.

"Oh, I don't think that would be any good by tomorrow. It's got dressing on it and that turns it into mush."

He laughed and scratched his head. It, too, was covered with sun spots, but I couldn't connect those dots because his height prevented me from playing my game.

He smiled when he told me, "Dolores always saved it and, you're right, it was mush the next day. She told me it was good for me anyway and I should just go ahead and eat it. I never did know that it was the dressing that caused it to get all floppy. See, even an old dog can still learn a thing or two."

I ran hot water into the sink basin and swished my hands through the water to get the suds whipped up into a nice froth. An old plastic wash tub on the counter would have to serve as a rinse container. No double sink in this old house. The sink stopper was nowhere to be found, but Raymond showed me what to do. He jammed another used butter cup into the drain hole.

"This works," he said. And sure enough, it did.

"I've got it from here, Mr. Saxby." I gave him a smile and tried to shoo him to his easy chair, but he was having none of it.

"Now, now. After all the work you did bringing me dinner and listening to me drone on about the old days, you earned some help with cleaning up."

He grabbed a tired towel from its home on the stove handle, then waited patiently for me to produce the first clean dish for him to dry. I supposed he'd done this task many times with Dolores. He was slow and deliberate so I paced my dishwashing production to match his drying speed.

"Dwight missed a fine meal. I hope that damn owl appreciates what he sacrificed to save it." He winked at me as if putting a period at the end of his sentence, then picked up the rinsed mug with his towel.

"It seems like Dwight is always running off to save something," I replied, a bit miffed that his son still hadn't appeared at the door.

"Dwight's got too many fires going. One of these days, he's going to get burned," Raymond muttered under his breath. I wasn't sure what to make of that comment, but if Raymond was anything like me, he didn't get to see as much of Dwight as he wanted.

I suspected Mr. Saxby was standing by my side, helping with the dishes, just to have someone to be with and something to do.

"You're off work tomorrow, aren't you?" he asked me.

I normally had a three-day weekend, having decided that Fridays would be my gift to myself. Where I worked, everyone worked a thirty-two hour week; being the manager, I was able to get Friday as my day without pay. What I lost in wages, I made up for with the sheer luxury of being able to go to the bank when the lines were short or to the supermarket when everyone else was at work. On a rare occasion, I could take my boys camping with the extra day off at the end of the week.

"I'm usually off on Fridays but tomorrow I have to go in. We've got lots of staff out with the flu. The vaccine didn't work all that well this year," I explained.

He dropped his head to examine the water in the rinse tub before he declared, "I get that shot every year. You young people have no idea how bad the flu can be," he said. "Ever hear of the Spanish Flu?" he asked me.

"Of course," I replied. "Let's hope nothing like that happens again."

Raymond nodded in agreement. He leaned against the counter and got a faraway look in his rheumy eyes.

"Yeah. That was a really bad time. Most of 1918 was bad," he mused. Then, he told me just how bad it had been.

Duluth, September 1918

It felt to Raymond that he had spent a good part of 1918 standing at the railway station, waving goodbye to the people who meant the most to him: first, Leon and Kurt, then Ernie and Steve, and now Inka. He helped her step up onto the steps of the train car and handed her her bag. Behind him, Arto and Naldo stood jabbering to each other in Finnish as Inka's parents dabbed at their eyes with the backs of their hands. Disapproving glances from passersby, and an occasional hard stare, alerted the brothers of the need to converse in English. The fate of Olli Kinkkonen was still fresh in the minds of the immigrant population, and most did what they could to deflect notice from those who might do them harm. The Siskenens were not easily intimidated, but even they had tried to keep a low profile since the recent lynching incident. Raymond hoped he wouldn't soon be reading Inka's name in the paper, identifying her as an agitator of national importance. The women she idolized had nefarious reputations in the eyes of the public and, even worse, the United States government. The activities of old

Mary Jones and Emma Goldman showed up often enough in the news rags that Raymond's concerns for Inka were justified.

"You really want to do this?" Ray asked Inka on the drive to the station.

When Leon deployed, he'd left his car in Ray's possession and told him that he could outright have it if he didn't make it back from Europe. After all of the Siskanen family had piled into the car that morning to see Inka off, Ray had found the old car difficult to start but Inka knew just what it needed to turn over the engine.

"Let it roll down da hill and pop clutch!" she advised him.

It was a not-so-subtle reminder to him that Inka had been driven about in this car many times with Leon. He tried not to think about where they had gone or what they had done on those excursions.

"Vee hafe talk about this, ya?" she responded to Raymond's question about leaving. "I must go. Here, I can do nothing. New York is destiny for me," she resolutely told him.

Ray had absolutely no idea what his destiny was supposed to be, and he was pretty sure that Inka didn't either. At one time, he'd been sure that his destiny was to marry Inka and become a Unitarian, and look how that turned out. Regardless, he knew she would do what she thought was right, and who could complain about that course of action? Now, realizing that he might never see her again, he marveled at her fearlessness. From what he'd read, New York seemed a chaotic place full of danger and the unknown. It wasn't a place he would ever choose to go.

"You're a brave woman. Just don't be too brave for your own good," he said, more to himself than to her.

Inka kissed him on his forehead, then turned to her family standing below, waiting to watch her depart.

"Hyvasti!" she cried and, in unison, the Siskanens sang it back to her.

With the farewell still on their lips, Inka turned and disappeared into the coach. That was the image that Raymond carried with him when he thought of her--a strong, defiant beauty who was always a bit too brave for her own good.

With so many men gone, Raymond could have worked double shifts everyday, and he often did. He had little else to do or anyone left to do things with. When he wasn't making far-flung deliveries or filling in on the production line at the brewery, he spent his time hunched over the kitchen table at the Hofmann home, eating a quick meal or playing cards with the family. More and more, as the other family members drifted away after meals to other pursuits, Raymond stayed at his place, Mathilda across from him with the card deck in her hands.

"Let's play five hundred but maybe only go to two-fifty," Mathilda suggested.

The Hofmanns loved this version of rummy, but it could take forever to play a complete game. It was getting late, and Ray knew he had to get up extra early the next day for a delivery somewhere way-the-hell-and-gone.

"You do the adding," he told the girl. "You need the practice with your arithmetic," he teased.

In reality, Mathilda could add long columns of complex sums in her head but everyone made her write the scores down, so they could be content that she hadn't shaded the results in her favor. The Hofmann children were loving but not always trusting of one another. Mathilda laughed at his remark and reached across the table to pat him on his hand. He playfully grabbed her by the wrist and held it tight. With his thumb, Ray stroked the soft skin on the underside of her arm and felt her steady pulse tap beneath his fingers. Its beats were like Morse code, sending him a message he couldn't quite decipher. He released his grip and motioned for her to hand him the deck.

"I'll shuffle. You can do the adding up of all the points but I better shuffle. I've seen how slippery you can be."

With their eyes locked over the scarred table, Mathilda slowly slid the cards over to Raymond. When her fingers touched his, he could have sworn he felt a shock shoot through his body. If her fingers could make his body feel that way, no telling what the rest of her might do to him.

As Ray doled out the cards, Mathilda asked him, "Do you want to make it interesting? Play for pennies?"

Raymond shook his head. "Money won't make it interesting," he advised the girl. "I think if I win, I want a kiss."

Mathilda looked up from the cards she had been arranging in front of her. A half-smile formed seductively on her mouth.

" Well then, I hope I lose," she declared.

Raymond set the cards down on the table. He rose and offered his hand to the girl.

"Let's go outside and see if there are any Northern Lights."

Mathilda grabbed her shawl and willingly accompanied Raymond into the cool autumn evening. They didn't mind that there was no show in the sky that night. They had other joys to behold.

* * *

The golden leaves of October usually exhibited their beauty against the crisp blue skies of fall; like an arboreal Narcissus, boughs laden with color dipped towards brilliant reflections of themselves in the lakes and rivers of the northland. This spectacle foretold of the hardship of a winter to come, but it softened the brutal promise by imbuing the landscape with a glorious reminder of the summer sun, captured in the amber foliage on the trees. Over the weeks, the leaves would drop, along with the temperatures, and the long nights of winter would capture more and more hours of the day. But 1918 was not a usual year; the summer had been a season of continuous heat that had scorched the grasses and withered the crops. For a second year running, rain visited the region as if it had somewhere better to go and that's what it did. The clouds blew by without shedding a tear for the farmers below and instead dropped their sustaining moisture on other fields and other forests. The northern reaches of Minnesota were bone-dry as October came; brush crackled underfoot and the leaves gave up their homes in the trees long before the dog days of August had spread green algae blooms across the tepid waters of the area's lakes. Raymond carried large jugs of water with him every time he went out on a delivery; a backfire, or even a flint thrown from a tire, could spark a blaze in the dry grasses that lined the roadways. In an area that depended on the railroads for so much of its transportation of people and goods, cautious railmen saw to it that trains were followed by cars loaded with water to douse the frequent fires that caught the vegetation alongside the tracks. October 1918 was the driest anyone could remember in this place where too much water was the usual incitement for anxiety.

"Hey there, Raymond."

Dewey always greeted Ray with the same words whenever he appeared at the door of the Northeast Hotel in the lumber town of Cloquet. For the last few months, he had added the tagline of "Hot enough for you?" to his usual greeting.

"How's it going, Dewey?" Ray pushed the door to the hotel open with his foot and wedged his shoulder through the slice of air separating him from the boardwalk outside. Much like the ambiance of the Pickworth in Duluth, the Northeast had a saloon on the ground floor with a polished, dark wood bar stretching along the far wall and intricate tin ceiling panels separating the drinking establishment from the hotel rooms above. Ray had started out early for Cloquet on the morning of October 11, 1918, hoping to get most of his route done before the heat of afternoon combined with that of the truck's engine to make driving especially miserable. He hated the way his clothes would stick to his body like a soggy second skin, particularly where the sweat accumulated behind his back and under his thighs. Sometimes, the seat of his britches was so wet that he tried to keep his back to the wall, lest someone think he'd had an embarrassing accident with his bladder. On this day, the heat and humidity were so intense for this time of year that Raymond gave up any pretense of propriety and embraced the sad state of his appearance.

"Before you say a word, Dewey, I didn't piss myself. I'm too dried out to make a mess this big," Ray told the grinning saloonkeeper.

"Ain't that the truth, boy!" the big man bellowed. "Come on, boy. Let's get that keg hooked up."

Dewey swung open the drop-down section of the bar counter and came over to hold the door open wide enough for Ray to enter with his hand truck. The thick brick walls of the building offered a semi-cool refuge to its patrons, and ceiling fans pushed the air around the room enough to suck away their sweat but not the odors that came with it. The musk of beer and bodies assailed Ray's senses, but he couldn't complain. From the rings of soaked cotton under his armpits, he was sure he smelled worse than most. Dewey tossed the boy a white towel he had been using to dry beer glasses before he carefully stacked them on a shelf behind the bar.

"Thanks, Dewey," Ray said when he caught the towel with his free hand.

He mopped his brow and dragged the cloth behind his neck. When he looked at the towel, it was brown with the mud that had formed above his collar. "Shit," Ray mumbled. "Sorry, Dewey. I got your towel all messed up."

Dewey wasn't fazed. He took the towel from the youngster and flung it behind the counter.

"Plenty more where that come from," he said. "Let's get this put away and then what do you say I pull you a nice cold root beer?"

Ray ran his fingers through his hair where it had fallen limply into his eyes. He raked it back off his forehead with his shirtsleeve, rearranging his hair and sopping up the moisture on his skin with a single gesture.

"That sounds like the best offer I've had all day," Ray replied. "Thanks, Dewey. You make the drive out here almost worthwhile," Ray joked to the genial bartender.

"Hey, Dew. Better keep some buckets handy. I hear one of them Great Northern locomotives started a fire out by milepost 62. They got it out but another train will be by and who knows what that will do." This piece of news was delivered by a grizzled old man with hands so bent by arthritis that he could barely clutch his beer mug. Already drunk before noon, the man stayed on his barstool only by wrapping his ankles around two of the three wooden legs below him.

"You mark my words," the drunk said to no one in particular, "gonna be a helluva inferno one of these days. So damn dry, I ain't seen nothin' like it."

Before he could offer any more ominous predictions, his dirty head fell forward onto the bar rail, knocking his hat to the ground.

"Shitfire," he declared, a gnarly grin splitting his face. "See, even the shit's on fire!" he laughed at his own pun, then promptly crashed to the floor as he reached to retrieve his hat. He was asleep before anyone thought to help him up.

Dewey shook his head. "See what I got to put up with?" he asked Ray.

"Yeah. He's kind of a calamity, isn't he? Want me to drag him out of the way?" the boy asked the barkeeper.

"Nah. Just leave him there. He'll come to in a bit and then he'll be screaming to finish his beer," Dewey told Raymond. "He's a pain in the ass but he's right about one thing--conditions are ripe for a nasty fire. They been putting out small ones right and left all month. Just a matter of time before one gets out of hand," Dewey reported.

"You be careful driving back, son," the bartender advised. "Now, let's get you that root beer."

The rich foam tickled Ray's lips, and the sweet drink only made him thirstier than he'd been when he walked in the door. He wiped the foam off his mouth with his well-worn cuff.

"I gotta get going, Dewey. Miles to go, as they say. Thanks for the drink but do you mind if I grab some more water before I head out?"

Dewey nodded his consent. "Take all you need, kid. See ya next week."

Ray guzzled down two full glasses of room temperature water before he left to continue his route. Iver, at his next stop, acted as if a man asking for a glass of water was a significant cause of the ongoing drought. Ray had no intention of giving the dour Swede any reason to blame him for the sorry state of the world. Raymond stowed the hand truck in the back of the vehicle and lashed it down to keep it in place next to the kegs. He started the truck, put it in gear and headed southwest in the direction of Moose Lake, twenty-six miles away. He had several stops to make, everyone always needed more beer, and he planned to spend the night near one of the towns at the end of his route. With the full kegs out of the way, he could stack the empties and make room for a pallet on the floor of the truck to serve as his bed. It wasn't his favorite solution, but it beat driving back to Duluth on the dark gravel roads where a flat tire could turn into a major event. It also meant that he could find a nice, out-of-the-way spot near a river or lake and spend the evening fishing. He always lugged a frypan with him for just these sorts of occasions. Raymond had little time for recreation, and he grabbed it when he could.

Nightfall found Ray camped out on a shady patch next to the Willow River. After the long day of wrestling beer kegs and glad-handing with his customers, Ray was more than ready to peel off his sweat-soaked shirt and dip his body in the cool water flowing by his campsite. He had gone well-beyond Moose Lake, all the way out to Askov, and had made it back to the outskirts of the town with a couple of hours of fishing time to spare before dark overtook the sky. Tomorrow morning, he would start out early for the return trip, stopping in Barnum to pick up a fellow he'd met earlier in the day who needed a ride to the Duluth harbor. Ray was always willing to extend a ride to someone who could keep him company, especially on the trip back to town. As payment for the ride, this fellow had offered him a homemade stick lure he'd whittled expressly for snagging muskies. Raymond didn't care about payment, but he did care about catching a muskie. So far, none of the big fish had been interested in anything Ray had tossed their way. He told the Hofmanns that if he ever got one of those giants he would stuff it and hang it on their wall, but Renate Hofmann had other ideas. She told him that stuffing it would be a fine idea, though with bread crumbs, vegetables and pork belly before she baked it in the oven. The two had agreed to disagree.

The morning of Saturday, October 12, 1918, started out muggy and warm, but Raymond felt an ache in his right leg that acted like a barometer when a change in the weather was coming. He didn't consider his injured leg to have many good qualities, but it was handy to have some advance warning about the weather. Many times his knee predicted rain well ahead of the presence of clouds, and he was able to grab his oilskin slicker before he left on his route. The Hofmann children had laughed when they'd observed him preparing for rain on a sunny morning, but so adept was Ray's leg at announcing an upcoming storm that, before long, the kids would consult Ray before planning their day.

"What's your leg say, Ray?" the kids would ask.

If they were around now, Ray would have to tell them that something was about to change. The ache in his leg wasn't the only sign that got his attention that morning. The smell of smoke permeated the air. For weeks, fires had been smoldering in the bogs around the area of Moose Lake, giving the air the smell of Scotch whiskey when heated up to make a hot toddy. A peaty, thick odor of simmering swamp had competed with the smoke from dozens of little grass fires to pollute his lungs all yesterday. Ray hoped that his leg was telling him that a good rain would come their way to subdue the volatile conditions.

The morning played out at a leisurely pace. He had no more deliveries to make once he made it back to Duluth later in the day, and he sincerely hoped that he would be able to take Mathilda to a movie in the evening. He was sure she would want to see some silly romance when he was more interested in watching cowboys shoot each other and fall down dead in the dust from the tops of stagecoaches. He would see a romance, though, as long as it enticed Mathilda to hold his hand in the dark. Ray had the truck loaded and ready to depart his lakeside retreat when he decided to try a little more fishing from a fast-moving stretch of water he had noticed the day before. He grabbed his pole and hiked about a half mile back down river to a spot where rocks and boulders created little eddies in the river. He was out of bait, but that didn't matter. All he had to do was flip over some rocks on the bank to find a worm or two.

Two hours of killing time on the banks of the Willow River produced nothing more than a sunburn and blisters on his hand from where he'd brushed against stinging nettles. He rubbed mud on his hand to quell the itch. He smiled in remembrance of his Grandma Saxby when he smeared the muck across the back of his hand; she'd prescribed mud for just about every skin condition he could think of. By noon, Ray had picked up his passenger in Barnum and was coming close to Cloquet when the two men felt their stomachs complain from lack of food. Ray had planned on a breakfast of fish but had ended up stewing the very nettles he'd sworn at hours earlier for assaulting his hand. They proved to be as disagreeable to eat as they were to harvest, and he was more than willing to take a break for a quick meal of something actually edible. Milo Sobieski, his companion for the day, knew of a place that sold pasties.

"What the hell is a pasty?" Ray wanted to know.

"Oh. You never had one? It's like a pie you can hold in your hand. The ones I like are filled with beef and potatoes. They're pretty tasty, Ray. I think you'll like it," Milo told him.

Ray was sure he'd never had a pasty before, but from the way Milo described it, it sounded a lot like one of Inka's breakfast pies. He was game to try it. It had to be better than nettles.

Milo and Raymond sat on a patch of dried grass under a scruffy tree with enough leaves left on its branches to offer a bit of shade. Ray stretched out his cantankerous knee and rubbed it through the denim of his dungarees.

"You got a bum leg? That why you limp a little?" Milo asked.

Ray nodded. "Yeah. Broke it a year ago and it still hurts me some. I did a lot of growing when it was broke and now it's a little shorter than the other one. It hurts today because the weather's fixing to change. At least, I think so."

Milo cocked his head. "I heard about that. Mostly from old folks. `Oh, my lumbago's acting up. Gonna rain,' my grandpa says sometimes. But you know, it does feel cooler now than yesterday. At least, not near as humid."

Milo stuffed the rest of his pasty into his mouth. When he finished chewing, he licked his fingers clean before taking a swig of water from one of the jugs Raymond kept in the truck. By early afternoon, Ray had the truck just outside of Cloquet when he noticed that a strong wind was rocking the vehicle from side to side. What had started as a warm fall day was now turning blustery; a dry wind whipped the air around them. Leaves skittered across the road and branches swayed overhead.

"Look out," Milo advised. "I think I see a limb down just beyond the curve."

Ray hadn't noticed it. He'd been watching what was left of the leaves on the trees get blown into the sky. What caught his attention was a plume of gray smoke in the distance. He turned his head to tell Milo of the distant fire when he spotted more smoke over Milo's shoulder. Raymond pulled the truck over by a berm running alongside a field of potatoes and climbed on top of the truck's cab. He was alarmed to see signs of fire in three directions--more alarmed when he thought he could see the orange of flames flaring beyond Cloquet.

"I think we got a problem out where we're planning to drive," he said to Milo. "Climb up here and have a look for yourself."

Ray extended his hand to Milo to help him boost himself up to where he could see in all directions. Milo took in the smoky vista but displayed no concern.

"Oh hell, Ray. It's been like this for the last two months. Fire everywhere. We'll be fine. It's just another day in paradise," he said. "Come on. Let's get going. This is nothing worth worrying about."

Milo hopped off the truck. The dust flew up from the plowed berm where he landed beside the field. Ray helped himself down with care. He couldn't afford to give his knee any more grief.

By the time they reached Cloquet, even Milo had to admit that the sky looked ominous, particularly northwest of the town. Huge, black clouds of ashy smoke obliterated the western sky, and the residents of the town stood open-mouthed in the streets, watching the spectacle of destruction inch closer to them with each minute that passed. Factory whistles blew warnings, and runners from the fire department ran up and down the streets, pounding on doors and sounding the alarm that folks better get busy evacuating the coming inferno.

"Jesus Christ!" Milo cried. "We better get out of here!" he screamed at Raymond.

Ray agreed, but the question was where to go. The streets were jammed with horses, automobiles, and folks carrying children on their hips. Wind blew sawdust and ash from burning lumber, piled near the mills, through the air and into the stunned eyes of the panicked citizens. Ray watched in terror as a woman carrying a small child screamed and dropped her baby to the ground. When she turned, he could see that embers had caught the hem of her dress and flames raced up the back of her skirt. She fell to the ground, rolling over and over in the dirt while her child wailed near her. When she finally lay still on her back, the baby crawled over and patted his mother's face. She rose from the waist and embraced the little one with her dirty arms. Her personal fire was out, but in the few seconds she'd spent batting out the flames on her dress, the approaching fire had gained purchase in the lumbermill two blocks away. Huge orange spikes leapt into the sky; embers from the burning lumber danced dangerously above wooden buildings and piles of logging refuse. Raymond no longer believed in hell, but he thought if it existed, it couldn't be any more frightening than the scene that unfolded before him.

Gusts of fierce wind buffeted the truck, and Ray and Milo had to huddle against the windward side of the cab to keep the vehicle upright.

"What do you think we should do?" Ray asked his companion.

A panicked Milo was wide-eyed with fright. He reached over and grabbed poor Raymond by shirt. "You gotta save us!" he cried with such ferocity that spittle flew onto Ray's face. "You got to get us out of here!"

Raymond saw some sort of official walking through the street, approaching each stalled car. The man waved his arms and mimed his instructions with his hands. In some cases the noise was so loud from the cacophony of whistles, snorting horses and automobile engines that verbal communication was nearly impossible. In other cases, gestures were all the officer could offer to recent immigrants who wouldn't understand what he was saying even if they could hear his advice.

"Hang on, Milo. Let's find out what they're telling folks to do," Ray said in the calmest voice he could muster.

When the officer climbed onto the running board next to Raymond's window, he could see that the fellow was just a boy. His face was dirty; faint tear tracks ran down his cheeks, betraying his brave demeanor, but the boy was all business and professional in his tasks.

"Where you headed, sir?" the boy asked him.

"We're on our way back to Duluth," Ray said.

The stony faced youngster shook his head. "Don't think that's gonna work for you today, sir. The winds are merging several fires between here and Duluth. The only good way out is by train or maybe the river but even that is unlikely. They're pushing lumber into the St. Louis River to try to get some of the fuel away from the town," the officer reported.

That this youngster, maybe not even his own age, could be so composed in the face of literal disaster amazed Raymond.

"So what do you suggest I do, Officer?" Raymond asked him.

"Well, if you got enough gasoline in this thing, maybe you could help round up folks and bring them to the train station."

Ray only hesitated for a moment. "Sure. We can do that but I got to get the empty kegs out of the back," Ray told the kid.

"Right. Pull over there and I'll get someone to help you."

The boy pointed to a patch of bald dirt next to a rundown building that advertised rooms by the week. Raymond nodded and started the truck. As soon as he came to a stop where the officer had indicated, he jumped down from the cab.

"Come on, Milo. Help me with these things."

Milo followed Raymond to the back of the truck. Ray turned his back to Milo to unlatch the doors to the storage area where the kegs and hand truck were stored.

"Grab this cask," Ray ordered, but no one answered or approached him to take the load from his arms. When Ray turned to look for Milo, he spotted him running like a scalded cat towards the train station. "Yellow bastard," Ray mumbled, almost wishing he could find the good sense to be a coward, too, and save his own hide.

The intensity of heat and fear ramped up all afternoon. Word was that as many as fifty fires had been pushed together by hurricane force winds into an unholy blaze of destruction that was spreading over the northland. Raymond had agreed to use his truck, and the large cargo space it provided, to bring people to the depot from the more isolated areas outside of town. Trains that had been on the tracks when the inferno began were held in Cloquet by the station master. As soon as one was filled with women and children, it was released to travel out of the danger zone--a rapidly expanding spread of raging flames fed by the detritus of the logging operations and sawmills that proliferated in the towns and villages this side of Duluth. Ray was happy to hear that they were using a "women and children first" system. At least that Milo bastard would have to wait his turn.

On his way out of town for the third time of the afternoon, Ray could barely see the road in front of him. The searing heat made his eyeballs feel like they would sizzle in his head if he didn't continuously splash water in his face. His lungs struggled to suck in the rancid air; it smelled of brimstone and roasted meat. Driving by a small dairy, he saw the bodies of cows smoldering in the black dirt as the hay in their barn caught fire and turned the wood-plank structure into a torch that shot huge flames through the billowing clouds of smoke. The officer who had commandeered his truck assigned a fellow to ride along with Raymond to help direct him to the homesteads on the outskirts of Cloquet. If a road didn't lead to a bar or saloon, Raymond was as lost as a blind man. The only roads he knew were those of his beer route. His helper was having almost as much trouble finding his way as Raymond. The day had turned as dark as India ink from the smoke that covered everything like a heavy, black blanket. It was impossible to gauge the time of day. Any direction he looked, it could have been midnight, though his stomach told him it was closer to supper time.

The truck unexpectedly bumped and slid to the side of the road where it teetered at the edge of a deep irrigation ditch.

"Son of a bitch!" Ray yelled. "Didn't you see that?" he asked his hapless guide.

When he climbed down to inspect his truck, Ray could see through the haze that the body of a mangled sheep lay just behind his rear wheels. That explained the bump.

"We're okay," Ray told his helper, "but you have to keep a better eye on what we're driving into. Can't even help ourselves if we're stuck in a ditch."

Edgar, his assigned companion, wiped the soot off of his face with the tail of his grubby shirt. "Ya. I know," he said, half-mad at himself and half-mad at Raymond for calling him out. "I do better."

Edgar searched the side of the road for a long branch, eventually finding one about eight feet long on a fallen tree. He used his foot as leverage to crack the branch off from the charred limb, then he clambered up on the hood of the truck. He laid out flat on his stomach along the length of the hood.

"Okay," he yelled to Ray. "You can go now."

Raymond inched the truck back onto the road. In front of him, Edgar swept the path ahead with his stick, swinging it side to side, searching for obstacles or even ruts in the road that could impede their progress. Raymond considered that his blind man metaphor was apt; they were feeling their way along with the help of a makeshift cane.

"Edgar? Is it much farther?" Raymond wanted to know.

They had driven so far into the disaster zone that fire had erupted in the dry fields on either side of the gravel road they traveled. Ray figured this would be the last rescue run he could make before he ran too low on gas to consider carrying on with his efforts to bring homesteaders to safety at the Cloquet train station. He wasn't even sure that the depot was safe. For all he knew, Cloquet itself would be burned to the ground by the time he was able to return to its streets.

"Not sure, but it's maybe half mile to turn-off to Brozovic place. Hard to see landmarks in this damn smoke."

Both Edgar and Ray had covered their mouths and noses with some old rags they found behind the seat of the truck. The filthy rags had mopped up spilled beer and engine oil, but they were better than breathing in the fumes of smoke and gray ash that made the air around them thick enough to chew. On the last run into town, the same boy who had asked Raymond for his help ran up to him as he waited for the refugees to exit his truck. The town was in a state of pandemonium. It had been bad when he'd first arrived hours earlier, but now it had definitely descended into a deeper level of hell. Buildings burned randomly, as if caught aflame by burning arrows sent down from above by blindfolded angels seeking vengeance on Sodom and Gomorrah. In an ironic twist, a Catholic church raged with fire while a whore house a block over sat safe and sound.

"Say, sir!" the boy shouted to Raymond. "Can you do another run? How's your fuel holding out?" the boy asked.

Ray hopped down out of the truck, and Edgar scrambled off the hood and over to the side of a smoldering building, where he peed what little fluid his dehydrated body had processed onto the side of the charred wall.

"Let me check," Ray said to the official. He pulled a yard-long piece of wooden dowling that he used to prop open the hood from the floor of the cab, wiped it clean with his hand and jammed it down into the gas tank. His gauge stopped working miles ago, after they hit the sheep on the road. Ray guessed that the wires had rattled loose. He looked at the faint line on the rod and could see that he had a few gallons left. How long it would last depended on where they planned to send him and whether or not he got stranded in a line of slow moving traffic. He'd hope for the best.

"Yeah. I still got some fuel," Ray informed the kid. "Where you want me to go?"

"You know these Brozovic folks? They're Polish, too, right?" Ray asked Edgar.

It seemed likely that all these Poles might be related or something. The thought made him wonder about Kurt's relatives. He remembered them talking about distant family living in the Cloquet area. He hoped they'd gotten out of this mess in one piece. He hated to think of Mathilda being sad or Renate crying over relatives she loved but clearly couldn't tolerate to visit very often. The relatives put a bit too much faith in the church and pressed Renate join them in their devotion. Renate respected their religious convictions, but she had other things to devote herself to--things like trying to keep enough food in the house to feed eight growing children. She did thank God for Raymond, though. He gladly pitched in to help keep the household running and handed over more than a fair share of his paycheck every week. He also distracted her from the hole in her heart where she buried her anxiety over the fate of her oldest child. It had been weeks since there had been any word from Kurt or Leon. Ray was anxious about them, too. As long as no telegram arrived, he could at least imagine that they were still alive someplace where there was no post office box in which to drop their letters home. That's what he hoped, and then he put it out of his mind. He couldn't help them with his thoughts, but he could try to help out where he was. And today, that was in the middle of a battle as big as anything happening in the fields of France.

"Ya. I know 'em," Edgar replied. "They only been here couple years. Nice family. Lots of kids. Slavs, not Poles, ya?"

They eased their way forward. In places they could see as far ahead as a couple hundred feet, and in others, they struggled to see past their noses.

"Okay. Turn is just ahead," Edgar hollered.

'Right or left, for Christ's sake?" Raymond yelled back.

"Right. Right here!"

The delivery truck swung right and followed a faint track toward a small cabin that sat in cultivated fields on three sides and backed up to a tall stand of pines and denuded aspens that were engulfed in flames. Raymond sounded his horn, hoping it would lure the occupants out of the house and into his truck before all hell broke loose. He calculated that it would be only minutes before the cabin caught or the embers from the trees would set the dried corn stalks in the field ablaze. If that happened, the family would be lost, along with him and Edgar.

"Where the hell are they?" Ray asked

"Don't know. Maybe gone already," Edgar told him.

Raymond was tempted to turn the truck around and get his ass out of there before another minute passed. He wanted to, but he didn't.

"We better take a quick look," he said to his companion.

"Okay. But it better be quick," Edgar shot back. Ray could only nod his assurance that it would be quick. He wanted a chance to survive as much as the next fellow.

The men took the rags from their faces and soaked them with water from the jugs in the truck. Raymond thanked God that he had made a habit of carrying water with him. They retied the wet rags to cover their airways, but they had to squint hard to keep their eyes from involuntarily shutting out the irritating smoke.

"You try the root cellar and I'll check the cabin," Ray commanded.

"Ya," Edgar said, and he scurried off to search underground for the family. He knew this might be a place folks would think was safe, but he'd heard men in town talking about people being found roasted like pigs in a pit where they had taken refuge in cellars.

"Tomasz! Magda!" he screamed down into the hole. But no answer came. He ventured into the earthen vault and kicked around in the dark. No one was sheltering in the root cellar at the Brozovic place.

Raymond fared no better in his search of the cabin. It was small and tidy and empty of humans, though a fat yellow cat sat licking its paws on one of the beds in the loft. When Raymond tried to coax it to him, it squealed and slashed his hand with its claws.

"You had your chance," Ray told the surly animal.

The men emerged from their searches in time to see a flaming branch fall onto the roof of the cabin. Here and there, stands of dried corn were catching fire around them. A sudden burst of updraft sucked the air from the ground where they stood and pulled the fire closer to them from all directions.

"We need to go now!" Raymond told Edgar, and Edgar gave him no argument.

They turned to run for the truck, but to their horror, the truck had erupted in flames and in the seconds it took for them to appraise their situation, what was left of their gas exploded. Ray's delivery truck disintegrated into fiery missiles that shot out everywhere.

"Run!" Edgar screamed.

Ray looked around him, trying to keep his panic in check. His throat was so dry he choked on his own tongue when he tried to swallow. The fire was all around them. Then he spotted it. About fifty feet away, half-hidden by a stone shed, was what had to be a well.

"Over there!" Ray yelled, pointing as he did to the well by the shed.

Edgar raised his eyes to see where Ray pointed.

"We'll cook in the shed," Edgar said.

"No. Not the shed. The well. We can try in there."

Edgar saw no other option. He took off running for the well, Raymond right on his heels.

When they got over to the well, they could see that it was a circular structure made of rock. It rose about four feet off the ground and was maybe five feet in diameter. Over the top was a large sheet of canvas that was damp in spite of the searing heat. Ray pulled back a corner of the wet cloth and was shocked to see the upturned faces of the Brozovic family staring back at him. Two adults and four children stood in the shallow well water. The adults were in up to their thighs, and the kids had water reaching to their chests or necks, depending on their ages. Both adults had a baby in their arms: twin girls who looked exactly the same, down to the black smudges on their tiny faces. In his free hand, the father had the well bucket. He had been tossing water up onto the canvas to keep it wet in the hopes that it would not catch fire. So far, it had worked. Raymond could see burn marks on the top of the cloth, but they hadn't scorched through.

"You vill save us?" the mother asked.

"No." Raymond told her. "Looks like you're going to save us."

When the parents looked up through their makeshift canvas fire blanket, they could see the inferno raging right up to the backs of the men above.

"Ya! Come! Come," Mr. Brozovic motioned them down into the well.

The men dropped into the dank shelter and breathed a sigh of relief. They might all perish in the end, but at least they had a chance. Raymond pulled the canvas cloth back over the hole and took the bucket from the father.

"Here. I'll do that," Ray told him.

He spent what seemed like a lifetime tossing water up to wet the cloth covering their refuge. Water splashed back down on everyone, keeping them cooled as the world above them sizzled and baked in the intense heat. No one spoke. Only the babies were unfazed. They clapped their little hands and squealed with delight when the water rained down on their baby heads. After what must have been at least three hours, the adults agreed that it should be safe to poke a head through to check their surroundings. Edgar clambered up onto Raymond's shoulders and tried to see in the waning light. It appeared that the only things left alive, fauna and flora alike, were the nine other humans with him, standing in the well.

The early morning light of Sunday, October 13, 1918, revealed just how fortunate the family in the well had been. The stand of woods behind the cabin was reduced to blackened rubble that steamed and smoldered under still gray skies. Any sign of the cabin itself had been completely obliterated. Where the barn had been, half burned carcasses of Holstein cows were found within the stone footprint of the structure. About forty yards from the barn lay the bloated form of a plow horse. It was impossible to tell what color the horse had been in life. Every inch of the body was covered in crusty soot. When Raymond reached his hand over to touch the horse's flank, the creature's entire corpse collapsed into itself; the dessicated flesh dissolved into ash, and a rush of foul gases escaped into the air. Raymond recoiled in horror. He never imagined that the benign poke of his index finger could produce such utter destruction. Where a body the size of a truck had been just seconds before, a small pile of ash now covered the ground. The only things left among the ashes to remind him of the horse were the odds and ends of metal rings and buckles from the horse's harness. Ray picked up a still warm tack ring and slipped it into his pocket. From now on, this would be his good luck ring. For the rest of his life, Raymond carried the piece of brass with him, mixed in with his quarters and nickels. Whenever he felt like things were getting upside down in his life, he would jangle the metal ring against his pocket change and be reminded that he was a survivor. Ray had to jangle that ring far too many times in the final months of 1918.

Hiking into town from the Brozovic farm, Raymond and his bedraggled companions were able to see the scope of destruction the fire had wrought on the countryside. None of the farm buildings that had dotted the fields remained. Remnants of charred stone footings were all that were left where the homes of the family's neighbors had existed less than twenty-four hours before. Oddly, where structures as large as homes were reduced to rubble, a pair of pristine long johns, hanging from a line, waved in the breeze like a flag of surrender.

"I wonder if their owner made it out," Ray mused to Edgar.

"At least we did," Edgar told him.

The family trudged behind Raymond and Edgar in stunned silence. There were no birds in the trees that morning. There were no trees left where a bird could perch. There were no sounds of crickets or frogs; no cows bellowed to be milked. No horses whinnied; no sheep bleated. The only sounds to be heard were the crunch of their footsteps and the whines of the children asking for food, and even those cries were subdued by shock and fatigue. They were nearly to Cloquet when they heard a car approaching from the direction of the town. As it came closer, Raymond could see a sign in the window designating it as part of the Motor Corps. The auto stopped a few feet from Raymond. In the car were two men. One offered a jug of water to the shabby group of survivors. When Edgar greedily grabbed for the jug and swung it to his mouth, Raymond tapped him on the shoulder.

"Hey. Let the kids go first."

Ray took the jug from Edgar's grasp and offered it to a girl about nine years old. She took two big gulps before she helped an even smaller child steady the heavy crockery to take a drink. There was enough water remaining after the family had each had their share to give a swig to Edgar and Ray. They'd had water from the well earlier, but it was tainted with mud and ash that made it taste like a wet version of the fire they had survived. The clean water felt like liquid life in Raymond's mouth. Instead of wiping the errant drops from his lips with his sleeve, Ray sucked them off with his tongue. He had a new appreciation for the most mundane of gifts: sunlight, fresh air, clean water and another day that he thought he might not see. He wondered if Leon felt this way after a battle. He wondered if Leon were still alive to feel anything at all.

"Get in," the driver of the car told the group. "We'll take you into Cloquet but I gotta tell you, ain't much left of the town. The Motor Corps is setting up tents and bringing in food. You folks will be ok there for a few days until we can get you to something more permanent," the driver reported.

The other official helped the family into the car. By piling children onto the laps of adults and babies on the laps of the children, all ten of the group found a place on the auto for the ride into Cloquet. Edgar, Mr. Brozovic and Raymond stood on the running boards and hung onto whatever they could for support. They bumped along until a massive expanse of charred ruins alerted them that they had reached Cloquet.

All along the railroad tracks that led into and out of town was a mile long line of burned out baby carriages, left behind by mothers who'd carted their children to the trains.

"How many made it out?" Ray asked the solemn driver.

"Over seven thousand. Far as we know, only five died here in Cloquet. I heard Moose Lake didn't do so well. They don't have a count for their folks but plenty died, a lot of them on the roads trying to get out."

Ray tried to imagine how it must be to lose so many people at once. Whole families were probably wiped out in minutes. He thought of the Hofmann family and was grateful they were out of harm's way, up in Duluth.

"Duluth is fine, though. Isn't it?" Raymond asked. "I doubt the fire would get all the way up there," he said to the officer.

"Well, son," the man said, "Duluth got pretty damned burned around the edges. Whole neighborhoods gone in places. You from there?" the man asked.

"Yeah," Ray said. "I sure am."

* * *

For the next five days, Raymond worked alongside other survivors to pitch the tents and haul the food and supplies needed to establish camps for those displaced by the fires. He had no way to get back to Duluth nor did he have any way to contact the Hofmann family to let them know that he was alive. He had no idea if they had been affected by the fires themselves, and he worried that might be the case. The Hofmanns lived on the west side of town in a dilapidated frame house with tar paper siding. It wouldn't take much to set it ablaze. Raymond's strategy for emotional survival was to hope for the best and then get on with whatever he had to do. For now, that meant driving tent stakes and settling distraught folks into makeshift abodes until better options were available. The fall season had been warm and dry, but winter would come in a few short weeks, bringing its own fierce hardships.

It was almost impossible to sleep in the overcrowded men's tent where Raymond bunked because incessant coughing rattled the men through the nights. Many had damaged lungs from the inhalation of smoke and ash, and their irritated membranes produced choking fluids in their airways. Phlegm spattered the dusty streets and filled the spittoons that sat at the entrance of the tents. Children went about wiping runny noses on tattered sleeves, and women discreetly spat into scraps of cloth. There were shortages of everything. Diapers, food, milk, blankets and clothes came in daily on trains from distant towns anxious to help the refugees, and as it became colder with each passing day, the need for these staples rose. Sanitation was minimal. Water for washing bodies was shared by family members and sometimes passed between families. Outhouses were overused and rank with the smells of human waste. The tent camps became breeding grounds for disease, where wounds became easily infected and a single case of food poisoning could spread unchecked and decimate dozens living in such close quarters.

"You don't look so good," Ray told Mr. Evers, the fellow charged with picking up trash that accumulated behind the men's tents.

"You don't look so good yourself, kid," the man replied. Raymond hadn't had access to a mirror since the morning he'd left Duluth, and he was sure Mr. Evers was telling him the truth about his appearance. Even so, Raymond wasn't coughing his lungs out or complaining about how bad his joints ached. He was tired; that went without saying, but he wasn't covered with beads of sweat and his bad leg was the only place his joints complained. Mr. Evers coughed and launched a wad of blood-tinged mucus into the trash heap piled in his wagon.

"Son of a bitch," the man said.

He pounded his chest with his fist until another hunk of phlegm was jarred loose. He spat that with precision right on top of the last expectoration. For a fellow no more than thirty-five, he seemed to Ray to be aging by the second.

"What are you doing right now?" Evers asked Ray.

Raymond thought it was pretty obvious that he was helping to load trash unto the wagon. "Just helping you, at the moment," he replied.

Evers coughed again. To Raymond, the man looked deathly pale and beet red all at the same time. His lips were as white as the under-belly of a dead fish, and his cheeks looked as if they had been scalded by an iron. Mr. Evers slipped down from the wagon seat and handed the reins to Raymond. The horse snorted and turned to look at his new master.

"I gotta go lie down a bit. My head is killing me," Evers told him. "I'm putting you in charge. You know where to take this stuff?" the man asked the youngster.

"Sure. I'll take care of it," Ray told him.

Four hours later, when Raymond went looking for Evers to ask him where he wanted Ray to stable the horse, he was told that the man was dead. He was the first camp victim of the Spanish Flu. By the next day, the sick were everywhere. People were shuffled out of their temporary lodging to make space for infirmories to isolate the ill, but the measure did little good in a situation where people lived cheek to jowl. The only thing the fires hadn't taken from the folks in the camp was their lives, and those were now being stalked by a greedy virus.

* * *

Mathilda had watched the sky blacken to the west and nonchalantly shrugged the potential danger off her young shoulders. Fires were part and parcel of the summer of 1918, but none had gotten out of hand. She sat on the sagging steps that led from the porch of the ramshackle house down to a scrubby yard enclosed in rusted chicken wire. A broken gate swung open on its hinges. Her chore that Saturday morning was to use whatever wool she could scavenge from outgrown sweaters to fashion winter socks for the family. As she sat and knitted, she acted as a referee for the younger children, who were using sticks to bat an old tin can back and forth in a game they invented as they went.

"Tell her that's not fair!" Franz cried to his older sister.

Apparently, Ina had used her foot to kick the can and, in doing so, violated a new rule that Franz made up as a consequence of her misdeed.

"You never said we couldn't kick it," Ina protested.

Mathilda hadn't been paying close attention to the game, but she was inclined to side with Ina. Franz was known to make a new rule whenever things went against him, no matter what game they were playing.

"She's right, Franz. You can't make a rule about something after the fact," his older sister told him. "Ina's score stands but from now on, no one can use a foot to kick the can. Only use the sticks. That's fair to both teams."

Ina's team cheered and stuck out their tongues at their opponents. Franz spit on the dusty ground, then pounded the spit into the dirt with his stick.

"You always side with the girls," Franz complained.

Mathilda shook her head at her little brother. "No Franz," she told him, "I always side with whomever is right."

A strong gust of wind scattered dust about the yard, and the children used their arms to shield their eyes. Mathilda's ball of salvaged yarn was caught in the wind and fell from her lap. It rolled down the steps and into the dirt.

"Damn!" she cried, scurrying off the steps to retrieve the wool before it could unroll any further.

She picked it up and plucked stickers and leaves from the woolly clump. Alice, only six, and still enthralled with swear words and the spectacle of parental punishment, ran up to her sister.

"You said a bad word. I'm gonna tell Mama," the child informed Mathilda.

Mathilda looked down on the smug youngster. "You do that and I'll make sure you get the socks with the stickers in them. Besides, Mama would have said the same thing. We've all heard her say that when she gets mad."

This seemed to put Alice in her place. The child whacked her stick against the bottom of her shoe and searched for a comeback. All she could come up with was a technicality.

"Mama says it in German so it's not the same."

Knowing she was defeated, Alice went back to the game, but the wind continued to gust and soon the children were all chasing the can as it rolled out through the gate and down the hill, propelled by a wind that was bringing cold air with it.

"You kids are done playing. It's too windy now. Put your stuff away and come on in the house," Mathilda told them.

She shivered when the cold air shot up her skirt. When she glanced to the west, she saw that the gray plume was being pushed their way and her nose stung from the sharp smell of smoke; her eyes itched, and she coughed from a dry irritation in her throat.

"Come on. Get out of this wind," she advised the children.

The children scuttled up the rickety steps running through the front door, the wind slamming it behind them. All but Franz. He stood on the porch with his hands on his hips and considered the darkening sky before informing his sister, "I bet you don't get to go to a movie tonight. I bet Ray gets his self killed in a fire."

Mathilda should have been shocked, but she wasn't. Franz was always proclaiming gloom and doom. Still, it did look as if this fire might be a threat. The wind was blowing harder every second, forcing dried weeds and household trash up against the side of the tar paper dwelling.

"Ray will be fine," she told the sullen boy, " but you're gonna get yourself killed by me if you keep talking that way."

Mathilda grabbed the boy by his arm, spun him around and used her foot to nudge his backside into the house. No sooner had they shut the door, than they were drawn back out to the porch by the sound of shrill whistles signaling a general warning to the residents. The whistles were followed by men in automobiles, going street to street, advising folks that a fire was out of control to the west of town and they all better be prepared to evacuate if the flames crept much closer.

By late afternoon, there was no doubt that the Hofmann neighborhood was in danger. Renate Hofmann wrung her hands and considered her options. If only her husband were home to help her manage their situation but, like most railroad men in this area of Minnesota, he had been advised that there would be no time off until the emergency was over. Mr. Hofmann worked incessantly, loading supplies into box cars for the relief efforts that would commence as soon as it was safe to travel to the burned communities. During his rare breaks, he helped refugees, smoke-stained and thunderstruck, disgorge themselves from overcrowded railcars. With nowhere to go, displaced families huddled against the sides of buildings and waited for whatever came next. That usually meant being directed to hospitals or public buildings, where they might be fed and comforted with temporary shelter among similarly stunned masses of fellow victims.

"Mathilda! Come child! We must go!" Renate told her daughter after Franz had told his mother that the men with the bullhorns were screaming for them to leave.

Mathilda ran to her mother, unsure of how they would manage their escape. What had been a dark tangle of roiling, gray plumes in the western sky was now a wall of black, being marched their way by fierce winds and angry, red tongues of flame that were blotting out the afternoon sun. The younger children cried in fear and, when told to gather their things, grew confused and petulant.

"Alice, no!" Mathilda told her sister. "We only have room for the things we need. Put the doll down and get your coat."

Alice wailed as Mathilda pulled the doll from the pillowcase the child was using as a satchel. "I don't want my coat!" the child screamed. "I want my Greta doll!"

Greta was nothing more than a stuffed sock with some yarn for hair and button eyes, but to Alice, she was the one friend she could rely on. Seeing the fear and sadness on Alice's little face, Mathilda relented.

"Ok. You can take Greta but you have to wear the coat, then. There's no more room to pack it."

A mollified Alice somberly agreed, sticking her little arms into the sleeves of a winter coat that had been handed down so often that it had been given a name. Mathilda buttoned Old Blue for the child before handing her the pillowcase, stuffed with the doll, a spare dress and underwear, before joining her mother in the kitchen.

"Mathilda. Can you rescue us with Raymond's auto?" Renate asked her daughter in a calm mixture of English and German dialect that Renate often used with her children.

"I know how to start it but I've never, ever, driven," Mathilda told her mother.

"If you can start, you can go," Renate told the girl.

"Okay," Mathilda replied, "but where are we going? Nowhere seems safe."

Renate looked over at Franz, who had spoken with the men sounding the alarm. Clearly relishing his role as man of the house, Franz hiked up his pants and looked his sister in the eye.

"They says we gotta go to the Amory," Franz declared. "And I know how to drive Ray's car. He showed me once," the boy boasted.

Mathilda believed Franz. Raymond was always eager to help the children learn new things but, at a time like this, the family's safety was more important than the ego of a puffed up ten year old.

"I'll drive," Mathilda told her mother. "If I fall down dead, then Franz can take over," she said, scowling at the disappointed boy.

"You could, you know. You could die," Franz told her. Mathilda didn't bother to engage in her brother's rhetoric.

"Get your things. All of you! Get your things. We are leaving in five minutes," Renate told them.

Eight, maybe nine, minutes later, Mathilda had the children push the car down a gentle slope until it rolled fast enough that she was able to start the engine. The gears grinded, and the car bucked and stalled several times on its short trip down to the corner where Mathilda tramped on the brakes to avoid a disoriented dog that had dashed into her path. Bodies and belongings flew forward against the windshield, but Mathilda managed to keep the engine running by working the clutch.

Once he had settled himself back on the seat next to his sister, Franz turned to the passengers in the back and declared with the seriousness of the confident man he saw himself to be. "Told you I shoulda been the driver."

On the streets closest to the Amory, automobiles were backed up for blocks and people on foot dodged between the lines of cars stopped on the roads. Refugees carried belongings in their hands and wrapped larger necessities in bedclothes, attached to stooped backs like military packs. Children ran after adults in hurried steps or were dragged along by outstretched little arms that struggled to maintain their grasp on a parent's skirt or coat. Tiny, flesh-colored trails streaked down the sooty faces of distraught infants and, sometimes, the mothers who carried them.

"I wonder if there will be any space left for the car by the time we get there," Lena said from the backseat of the old Ford.

"Maybe we should find a place to leave the car and walk the rest of the way," Mathilda replied to her sister.

Renate looked at the pandemonium around her. The automobile hadn't moved twenty feet in the last twenty minutes. Those on foot rushed by them; every one of them potentially taking a place in the Armory, leaving one less spot for a Hofmann.

"Mathilda is right. We are parking, ya?"

The children understood that their mother's question was really a statement. Mathilda began maneuvering the automobile out of its cramped position among the hundreds of others stopped on the road. It took her several attempts to find the gear for reverse, and when she finally had it engaged, she instinctively turned the wheel in the wrong direction to move the car out of traffic. The entire time that Mathilda worked to free the family from the congestion on the roads, Franz yelled out advice or criticism of her driving skills. It was all Mathilda could do not to stop the car in its tracks, haul the belligerent child out onto the street and smack him upside his empty head. Amid the cacophony of car horns and the shouting of her backseat drivers, Mathilda lurched away from the road, eventually pulling onto a patch of scrub beneath a leafless tree. She figured they would have to walk a bit more than a mile, but they could do that in half an hour. It could take four times that long to drive the distance, and even if they made it to the steps of the Armory, where would they park?

"Okay. This will have to do," Mathilda told her passengers, who piled out one by one, retrieving clothes and food from the floor below the backseat.

"It's stupid to leave the car under a tree," Franz told his sister. "It's going to get burned up."

Renate had come to the end of her rope with her son. She did what Mathilda had fantasized about doing for hours. She put down her armload of belongings and used the back of her hand to slap the child across the face.

"You will speak no more, Franz."

The boy started to open his mouth in protest, but Renate raised her arm to his face again and held her position until the boy came to realize that she was not bluffing. Franz hung his head and picked up his bundle. He obediently fell into line behind Lena as Mathilda led the family toward the Amory. Renate brought up the rear, herding little Alice along in front of her as she carried her youngest child on one hip and her carpet bag in her free hand.

The evacuated were huddled shoulder to shoulder in the largest room in the new Armory building, where their names were taken down for the records and space assigned to each family group. Most of those seeking shelter were women and children or grumbling elderly residents not too stubborn to leave their homes. With the military draft draining away the young and strong male population, the few capable men who remained in Duluth were sent to the lines to help fight the fast-moving conflagration that surrounded the city. Renate sighed in relief when her family at last was registered and directed to a small area in a corner of the brick building. She secured their space with a ring of blankets and clothes to serve as a boundary and realized that the family might need to sleep in shifts to be sure that they weren't robbed of what little they had managed to bring with them from home. She remembered the ocean voyage during her immigration from Germany. Those with nothing felt entitled to take what they needed from those who had anything at all. Renate was determined to keep her family and their belongings intact.

"Ugh. I can't breathe in here. It's so crowded there's no air left," Mathilda complained.

Her throat burned and her eyes watered from the stench of over-warm bodies and dirty diapers tossed into corners. Her head pounded from the stress of the day. Her knees and wrists ached from the exertion she'd expended wrangling the unwieldy old car. The girl slumped against the cool wall of their little corner and allowed her body to ease itself down to the floor. When she closed her eyes, they felt too big for their sockets and she could feel her pulse banging at them from the inside of her brain. Despite the heat of a thousand bodies around her, a chill contracted the skin over her shoulders and chest. She wrapped her arms tightly across her torso and shivered so hard that she could hear her teeth clack against each other in her mouth.

"Mathilda," her mother said. "Why do you rest? Here, mind Dieter for me."

Renate pushed the fair-haired tot over to her oldest daughter, who absently sat the young boy on her lap. She shivered again with such vigor that the child giggled. "Again!" cried Dieter to his sister. Instead of shaking the child with the involuntary spasm of a chill, Dieter was jarred on Mathilda's lap by a cough so violent that the distracted Renate snapped to attention. The woman snatched the boy off of the girl's legs and handed him off to Lena. With a mother's deft touch, Renate laid her cool palm on Mathilda's forehead. She felt her blood grow cold even as her palm burned from the fever of Mathilda's brow. Renate laid an old green and red patchwork quilt over her daughter, tucking it under her feet and tightly to her sides.

"You rest, ya?" Renate told the weary girl. "Children," she told the others, "your sister is not well. She is tired. Let her sleep."

Renate hoped that Mathilda would regain her health by morning, but long before morning came, Ina, too, was collapsed by her sister's prostrate form under one side of the quilt. A hallucinating Franz lay on Mathilda's other side. A large clearing of apprehension appeared around the Hofmann family, and a doctor was summoned. He had only to look into the blue-tinged faces of Renate's children to arrive at his diagnosis.

"They must all be moved to the isolation room," the doctor declared. "These children have the flu."

So began the longest day of Renate's life. She was forced to separate from her three ill children who were taken to a section of the Armory where they would be cared for with other victims of the Spanish Flu. For weeks prior to the fire, Duluth had been inundated with the deadly virus; movie theaters, schools, auditoriums, even funerals, had been closed in an attempt to lessen the population's exposure to the illness. These measures had been marginally successful until the fire forced the mingling of residents in close-quarter situations resulting in an upswing in cases of the deadly disease. In a cruel twist, this particular flu took as its victims the young and strong; hardy adults between the ages of twenty and forty were the most vulnerable, and death came swiftly to many of those afflicted. Renate had thought her children were safe. They were younger than the usual victims. She had worried more for herself and Friedrich, her husband, than she had for the youngsters. She fretted over what would happen to the family if she or Friedrich died and left them alone without the resources to survive. Now, she prayed that she could trade places with even one of those dear, sick children. As her son and daughters were carried away to the infirmary, she saw the fear in their watery blue eyes; their cracked lips uttered goodbyes on the faint whispers of ragged breaths. All that day, Renate and the remaining Hofmann youngsters sat quietly in their little circle of contamination, praying for the lives of Mathilda, Ina and Franz. They were shunned by those around them, but Renate didn't mind. She understood the fear and knew she would have the same reaction had her family not been the pariahs in the room.

Later that day, a cheer went through the crowded building when word spread that the winds had shifted and the ferocity of the fire was swiftly dying. Renate cheered with them. Perhaps God had listened to the impassioned pleas of the sad city's disenfranchised souls. For two more hours, Renate held on to that hope. Then, shortly before darkness fell on Sunday, October 13, a nurse came and stood just beyond touching distance to advise her that both Ina and Mathilda had died. Young Franz, whom the nurse described as a tough little fighter, appeared to have survived the disease. She was further informed that the bodies of her dear, darling daughters would be buried immediately in a mass grave, along with the many burn fatalities and flu victims claimed by that weekend of dual calamities.

Miraculously, none of the other Hofmanns became ill, and when they finally made it back to their dilapidated shanty, it too, had escaped destruction. A neighbor offered to drive the old Ford home for Renate, and a lethargic Franz made no protest that he should drive. The boy was weak from his illness and stunned by the loss around him. He was anguished by the words he had said to Mathilda, telling her that she could die. He couldn't take the hateful words back, and they would live on in his consciousness like a filthy stain he was never able to bleach away. The boy prayed for God and, mostly, Mathilda to look down and forgive him.

On the drive back to their neighborhood, they passed decimated blocks where fine homes had stood amid lush lawns and graceful trees. The fires had ignored the usual protections of social status and wealth. For a brief moment, some poor had been as fortunate as the rich. The losses from fire and disease had taken equally from both segments of society. For every mansion burned, a shabby home still stood. One such home was that of the Hofmann family. Renate did her best to be grateful for this blessing in a season of pain. Waiting on its steps, tired and disheveled, was her husband. He folded Renate into his arms, and they wept for their lost daughters. Two days later, they would learn that Kurt had died on the battlefield in France. A day after that, Raymond found his way to their door.

"They are all gone, Raymond. Mathilda, Ina and Kurt. All gone. My babies are all gone," Friedrich told him.

Raymond collapsed into tears, and a melancholy seized his soul--a melancholy that followed him like a homeless stray dog for years to come.

PART III

HIGHWAY 61

9

St. Paul, Minnesota 1995

I t was late when I finally left Mr. Saxby's house that winter night. I apologized for keeping him up so late, but he shook off my offering of regret with a chuckle.

"I haven't got that many nights left. Might as well use them up on a pretty girl," he said.

Now it was my turn to chuckle. "If you consider forty-five girlish, then you can count on me coming back for more compliments," I teased.

He just smiled and nodded his wizened head. "Bring meatloaf. With that burned ketchup on top," he suggested.

What could I say except "You got it, Mr. Saxby!"

He helped me with my coat, then handed me the scarf I used to keep the frigid air from seeping down my collar. When I opened the door, a blast of sleet stung my face.

"God. I hate February," I said, like a good Minnesotan.

He nodded again. "After almost eight years of February, you kind of get used to it," he replied.

It took me a moment to figure out the math. When I did, it depressed me even more to think that so much of one's life could be spent on the cusp of a spring that never seemed to appear on schedule. T. S. Eliot got it wrong. In Minnesota, February was the cruelest month, taunting with thaws that exposed the trash of Halloween and football season, along with deposits of dog waste in footpaths left by animals too timid to venture into the deep snow. The thaws never lasted. No sooner would the refuse be picked out of the slushy mud than a storm would come roaring in to slap the cautious sprouts of crocus flowers with a warning. Not yet. It's still February. Not yet.

"You drive careful, now. Watch the ice," he warned me.

"Don't worry. I'm getting good at this," I assured him.

After ten years in Minnesota, I had become adept at handling the adverse conditions of the winter roads, even in an old car with nearly bald tires. He smiled and blew me a little kiss off the tips of his yellowed nails.

"Sorry about Dwight," he called to me as I slid into the seat of my car. "That boy doesn't deserve you."

I waved and yelled over the roar of the cold engine, "You got that right!"

He laughed and closed the door, giving me a final wave before lowering tattered shades on the perennially dirty windows; the single-pane glass was opaque from years of grime. Like its owner, the old house had developed cataracts that put a film between it and the outside world. I had offered months before to give the windows a good wash.

"It will make it nice and bright in here," I told him, but he just brushed the suggestion away with the back of his hand.

"I don't notice them dirty and I won't notice if they're clean. No need to get worked up over something I never notice."

Mr. Saxby made this declaration with conviction. I had to admit, it was a pretty sound philosophy of life, and I tried to remember it every time I decided to iron only the parts of a blouse that would show under my sweaters.

The sleet turned into snow. It blanketed itself over a sheet of ice, making a simple walk to the mailbox a treacherous journey. I found myself lying akimbo more than once that winter, when snow covered patches of ice tricked me into a slippery ambush. Mostly, my dignity was bruised after one of these mishaps, but I found myself using an old ski pole to pick my way to the curb to grab junk mail that wasn't worth the risk imposed by the act of retrieving it. I thought of Mr. Saxby in those moments, glad that his mail was deposited through a slot in the front door of his old house. Broken pipes and broken hips were rampant in winter; plumbers and orthopedists made their livings on the ravages of the cold. So far, I had escaped both disasters, but I willingly put myself in peril when Dwight suggested we use one of my three-day weekends to do some skiing at a resort just outside of Duluth.

It was a bitterly cold morning when we started the trip up I-35 to Spirit Mountain. I had spent the previous week hounding the thrift stores in St. Paul, looking to find ski togs that I could pass off as gear I had owned for years. I found a pair of killer Spyder stretch pants and a nice purple Obermeyer jacket, still adorned with the lift tickets from resorts as far away as the Upper Peninsula of Michigan. Their slightly worn appearance and the bogus tags presented the illusion that I skied every now and then. In reality, I hadn't been on the slopes for a decade and I was apprehensive about my rusty skills. My previous skiing experience had been on Mammoth Mountain in California and, in the distant past, a place or two in Colorado.

As we made our way north, I anticipated a mountain range rising up to greet us. All I saw were relatively flat lands and stands of pines, planted in precise rows, that went on for miles.

"When will we see the mountains?" I asked Dwight. He kept his eyes on the road as he drove.

"What mountains?" he replied.

Now I was confused. Had I misunderstood the nature of our adventure? I didn't see Dwight as the Nordic cross-country type, and I knew I wasn't. I was in good enough shape to ride a lift up the mountain and allow gravity to pull me back down, but trudging across miles of terrain under my own power just wasn't what I'd had in mind.

"You said we're going to Spirit Mountain so I kind of assumed there would be mountains."

I tried to keep the sarcasm to a minimum. He reached over and patted me on the knee of my six- dollar pants and smiled at my remark.

"It's a Minnesota mountain. What it lacks in altitude, it makes up for with good snow. Think of it this way," he advised me, "it's such a short trip up and down that you can get in dozens of runs in one day."

While the actual skiing didn't sound that great, I was relieved to know that whatever skills I still had left would likely be adequate for Spirit Mountain. And I was getting to spend a long weekend with Dwight. That almost never happened. I intended to make the most of our time together in a cozy cabin, our stockinged feet warming by a fire and Irish creams in our hands.

I had moved to Minnesota from California years earlier, when an ill-advised marriage to a man twenty years my senior brought me to the St. Paul suburbs. When he retired from a California aerospace company at fifty-eight, he insisted that he needed to return to Minnesota to be near his elderly mother. I ended up hating him for his cruel ways, especially toward my beautiful boys, but I fell in love with my new state so I stayed on after our divorce. Besides, once I had moved away from California, I was financially unable to re-enter the brutal housing market in the Golden State; the amount of money it takes to buy property there is the real reason California is called "golden." So, as they say, I decided to "bloom where I was planted" and that was White Bear Lake.

On the morning we left the cities for Duluth, I was still coming to terms with the peculiarities of my adopted state, even after going on my second decade of residence.

"So, I was wondering," I started my question, "why does I-35 East go north and south?"

That made no sense to me. In California, if a road was designated as east, it went that way. Dwight glanced at me as if I wasn't just from another state but maybe a different universe.

"Because it's the version of the interstate that's on the east side of the cities. Thirty-five West is over in Minneapolis but they merge once you get up around Forest Lake and then it's just plain old I-35."

He drove for a few minutes before returning to the subject.

"Part of it is basically the same as the old Highway 61. You know, the whole Bob Dylan thing? He grew up in Hibbing," he said," up past Duluth."

I remembered the musical reference but never realized that Dylan was a Minnesotan. I'd thought that he was a hippie genius of indeterminate origins--someone who belonged to everyone.

"I didn't know that about Dylan," I told Dwight. "But your dad told me some interesting stories about traveling this area back in the day."

Now it was Dwight's turn to be puzzled. "He never said anything to me about hanging out up here. When was that?" he asked me.

I couldn't believe that I knew more about parts of his father's past than he did, but I was acquainted with many fathers and sons who rarely talked to one another, so maybe it wasn't unusual after all. Hoping I wasn't breaching a family confidence, I passed the time in the car by entertaining Dwight with his own family's stories.

Hastings, Minnesota 1919

Leon spent months laid up in a hospital in France. When the Armistice was declared on November 11, 1918, he was battling a case of gangrene that had moved from the bottom of his foot into his toes. For weeks, the doctors had tried to save his digits by debriding the festering flesh as it crept to the end of his foot, but the blackened skin resisted treatment and, in the end, Leon was forced to consent to a partial amputation.

"We've done all we can to save them, Sergeant."

Leon had argued mightily against surgery, but even he had to admit that losing a few toes would be worth the sacrifice if it put an end to his current misery.

"I understand," he told the young physician. "I'll still be able to walk, won't I?" Leon asked.

The doctor nodded. "Sure. Maybe with a limp but you'll be fine. Better off than most the men in here."

Leon looked around the ward. He acknowledged that he was lucky. The limbless, eyeless cripples he was housed with would have gladly changed places with Leon. What troubled him most was that his wound hadn't been the result of a combat injury. He would not be awarded a Purple Heart for an infected blister, brought on by miles of marching in wet boots and worn-out socks. His injury would get him only an honorable discharge and maybe a few free drinks back home but, at least, he would make it home. That was worth something. He looked down at the putrid stubs at the end of his foot. One of the last feelings he'd had in those toes was the touch of Kurt's warm lips. He shook off the memory of the contact, and his reaction to it, with a shudder.

Though the spoiled parts of his flesh could be cut away and incinerated along with the damaged limbs of his fellow patients, there was little that could be done for the rot in Leon's brain. He was awakened every night by either vivid nightmares that soaked him in sweat or by the anguished night terrors of his companions on the ward. In those moments of semi-wakefulness, the smell of his own rancid body parts transported him back to the battlefield; corpses in various stages of decomposition greeted him in his fevered dreams with rictus grins or fingerless waves hello. When daylight came to save him from his subconscious, the visions would recede, only to reappear at the sound of a dropped food tray or the backfire of an ambulance bringing more human wreckage to the overcrowded hospital. There was a term for it, the doctors explained to him. There was a term for the mental damage he had sustained. They told him he suffered from shellshock, a neurasthenia of war that imprisoned his mind in an endless loop of anxiety and fear. They explained that the imminent danger he anticipated at every turn was a falsehood manufactured by his overstimulated nervous system but that the fear he experienced was real.

"But how can I stop it?" Leon asked his physician. "How am I supposed to live like this?"

The well-meaning doctor patted him on the shoulder and advised quiet rest and long walks to clear his mind. When Leon pointed out that he was still learning to walk with half a foot and that long walks were not part of his current capabilities, the doctor just shrugged and encouraged him to read poetry to his sightless companions as a way to take his mind off of his own concerns. Leon considered poetry pointless at best and, in many cases, downright depressing. He decided to drink instead. Over the weeks of rehabilitation that followed, Leon learned to adjust his gait to accommodate his stump and he developed an appreciation for French wine, even the most mediocre of which could quell some of the torment of his anxious condition.

During the time Leon passed getting around on crutches and learning to walk again without the aid of the front portion of his left foot, he gained a grudging respect for his younger brother. Raymond had negotiated some of the same challenges that Leon now faced, but Ray had enjoyed advantages that Leon did not--the space in Raymond's shoe so long ago had been a temporary situation brought about by an oversized boot and, more recently, he'd had Inka Siskanen to nurse him through his time of immobility from his fractured leg. It caused Leon actual physical pangs of heartache when he thought of Inka; a tightness in his chest made it painful to draw a breath. He wondered if she would pity him for his disability or if it would stimulate a compassion in her soul that could lead to love; like Raymond, Inka was a sucker for an underdog. Leon was heartened to think that the corporal and mental vigor that he now lacked might be the key to Inka's affections. Maybe less could be more. That thought kept him going until he received a letter from Raymond telling him of Inka's relocation to New York and about the further losses in the Hofmann family from the Spanish Flu. Raymond wrote that Inka had effectively disappeared into the population of the great metropolis and refused to be found. This news made Leon angry with the girl all over again. In light of this development, being a cripple lost its only appeal for Leon and anger became the force that pushed him forward. He decided that he would not entertain feelings of sadness for his situation. Sadness was the poison that had killed his mother, and he had no intention of sipping from such a polluted cup of bitter brew.

Everett Saxby was gratified that Leon was coming home to them, if not completely in one piece. He had run into other boys who'd returned from service in Europe with injuries that far exceeded those Leon had suffered. Herbert Delois, Leon's one-time nemesis, stopped by the auto shop to have a tire repaired for his father. Everett knew the car, he had worked on it many times, but Herbert would have been rendered unrecognizable from his battle scars if not for the prosthetic that he wore. In place of half of his face sat a hand-painted copper mask that covered the horrendous cavity where his nose and eye had once been. Herbert had been peering over the top of a trench when shrapnel from a grenade caught him on the zygomatic arch and tore away the skin and muscle that comprised the right side of his face. The wound had become infected during his recovery in France, leaving physicians with no choice but to cut away the edges of the contaminated tissue, which included most of his nose and his right eye socket. His disfigurement had turned him into a monster to all but his closest friends and family; his young wife left him when she couldn't bear to have Herbert kiss her with lips that had been sewn back onto his mouth. Closing her eyes during the act of intimacy only flamed the horror of her imagination, stoked by the warm air that blew on her neck when Herbert huffed in passion through the crater where his nose should have been.

"I don't love you anymore, Herbert," his wife told him three months after he arrived home. "You're not the same man that I married. I can be your friend, but not your wife," she said to Herbert, as if this should be enough. It wasn't. He told her he didn't need such a friend. Still, Herbert was luckier than some. He had been fortunate to have a portrait mask made for him in Paris by an American woman named Anna Coleman Ladd, who dedicated her artistic talents to restoring the dignity of soldiers with severe disfigurements of the head and face. Herbert's mask, when he chose to wear it, bore a remarkable likeness to his former self. The thin, painted copper was molded to the contours of his bone structure and was held in place over his ears with glasses frames, incorporated into the mask. From a distance, Herbert appeared normal. Up close, the unblinking eye of paint and the rigid expression of the metal skin were unnerving to some who saw him; removing the device, however, could create even more discomfort in his viewers so, more often than not, Herbert strapped the artificial countenance onto his face when he chose to leave the solitude of his now-empty house.

"I hear Leon's coming back."

Herbert attempted to make awkward conversation as he waited for James to patch the tire on his father's car. James nodded and kept his focus on the task at hand. From his desk in the corner, Everett rose and walked over to Herbert. He extended his hand to the poor fellow.

"Good to see you, Herb. You doing okay?"

Herbert took the hand he was offered. Generally, people were hesitant to touch him, as if his condition were contagious, like the flu.

"I'm alright," Herbert said. "When's Leon getting to town?"

As usual, Leon hadn't been overly communicative with his father about his plans. Everett had learned from a brief telegram sent by Raymond that Leon would arrive in the Twin Cities sometime in early April. He had written that he would spend a day or two visiting with his father and sister, his first visit in almost nine years. Amelia only knew her brother from the pictures he sometimes sent from distant places, the most recent being a photograph taken shortly before he left Camp Dodge for Europe. She thought him handsome but aloof, his rifle slung over his shoulder and a cynical grin on his full lips.

"I guess he'll be here early next month but only for a couple of days or so. Then, he's headed back up to Duluth," Everett informed the man in the mask. "He lost part of his foot," Everett said.

Herbert smiled out of the part of his mouth that moved. "Lucky bastard. Wish that's all I lost."

James finished repairing the tire and placed it back on the wheel of Herbert's car. The boy found verbal communication an annoying distraction in most situations and especially when he was engaged in mechanical pursuits. He worked without uttering a word, only saying what needed to be said when his job was complete. He popped the assembled wheel and tire onto the axle and tightened the bolts with a few quick turns of the lug wrench. When all the lugs were in place, James cranked hard on the bolts until they were fully secure. He returned his tools to his worktable, where he meticulously hung up the instruments, from small to large, on a pegboard above the bench. Wiping his blackened palms on a rag he pulled from his back pocket, James finally called over to Herbert and his father.

"It's done," he said.

Herbert sauntered over to inspect the repair. "Looks good, Jimmy," Herbert told the younger man, who shook his head in correction.

"I'm not Jimmy. I'm just James," the boy informed his customer.

James looked at Herbert with intense interest. There was not a hint of disgust in the youngster's expression.

"Can I touch your steel face?" James asked.

Herbert smiled again. This time the smile was big enough to hike up the side of the mask.

"Sure, but it's copper," he said. "Do you want to hold it?" he asked the boy.

James silently assented by widening his eyes. He took the mask in his hands and turned it over to inspect the underside. He ran his fingers along the contour of the thin metal and examined the artistry of the paint. When he looked up at Herbert to hand him back his prosthetic, he grinned at the maimed man in one of his rare gestures of pleasure and offered a full sentence of approval.

"It's really nice work, Mr. Delois. It makes you look good."

Herbert refastened the device to his face and secured it behind his ears.

"Thanks, James. Glad you appreciate it." It was the first genuine acceptance Herbert had felt since he'd returned from the war in his altered state.

Much as he had on his journey over to Europe the prior year, Leon used the enforced captivity of the ocean crossing back to America to hone his poker and blackjack skills. He particularly enjoyed playing with men who had concussive injuries. These poor marks had at least some degree of diminished intellectual capacity from their brain injuries; many lacked concentration, others lacked the ability to use logical reasoning and some had trouble with memory, making it difficult to remember which cards had been played. Leon charmed these men into one-sided games that he invariably won if he were so inclined. He occasionally allowed himself to lose, not to enjoy the satisfied looks of victory on the faces of his incapacitated rivals, but so that he could count on them trying their luck against him the next day. Leon disembarked the troop ship in New York with a pocket full of small bills and heavy silver change that smacked him in the thigh every time he took a step with his awkward, half-footed stride.

At the Hastings Depot, Everett and Amelia waited for Leon's train to arrive on a damp morning in April 1919. He had wired his family from Chicago, telling them that he would be there in two days' time. He spent a night in the big city to see the sights and used some of his gambling winnings to buy himself a suit in the latest style for men of distinction. He had considered employing the services of a woman to comfort him but soon reasoned that spending his money on a good suit of clothes could lead to situations where payment for a woman's attention might not be needed. Despite his limp, Leon saw the man in the mirror for what he was--a handsome rake with a war injury resulting in minimal disability, a not-so-revolting handicap likely to bring him sympathy from the ladies.

Leon's war experiences had completely cured him of his infatuation with military life. Once he stuck his abbreviated foot down through the leg of the wool gabardine pants that came with his new suit, Leon felt physically renewed. He stripped off the rest of his uniform and wadded it into a bundle of fabric that he discarded down the trash chute in the hall outside his hotel room. The only things he valued were his stripes; he freed the chevrons from the uniform's sleeves with Grandaddy Earl's pocket knife. Those he saved, along with his marksmanship medal and a few battle ribbons he'd been awarded for participation in the French campaign. Leon was not a fan of participation awards. He would have preferred a recognition for heroism, but he saved his ribbons just the same. He knew they could earn him prestige with the uninformed souls back at home, where any medal carried by a returning soldier was accepted as a badge of honor.

From his view through the coach window, Leon scanned the Hastings platform for his family. His father would not have been recognizable to Leon if not for the hat that sat atop his head. It was the same hat Everett had worn since 1910, the one he used to wear when he went to visit with Leona at the State Hospital. Below the hat, a stooped Everett fondled a pipe in nervous hands, black grease embedded in every crack of their roughened skin. He was thin; his clothes hung on the forty-five year old man as if from a wire hanger. There was very little body mass to fill out the garments, and his face, while still rugged and appealing, had developed deep lines since Leon had last hugged him goodbye nearly a decade before. He was startled by the girl standing at his father's side. The little tot who had been baby Amelia May was now a comely girl who had grown to be her mother's child. She looked exactly like the studied portraits Leon had seen of his mother when she was only slightly older than Amelia. His sister had a mane of thick, chestnut-colored hair that hung down her back in braids. Her dark eyes radiated excitement and just a hint of the youthful rebellion he'd recognized in his own gaze as a child. She was the picture of Leona when Leona had still been herself. Amelia may have sucked the life out of her mother with her birth but at least that energy appeared to have survived in this vivacious girl, bouncing on the balls of her feet in her glee to become reacquainted with her brother.

"Is that him, Papa? Is that my brother?"

Amelia pointed at every uniformed man who emerged from the passenger train.

"No, child. I haven't spotted him yet," Everett told Amelia, and then, all at once, he saw his first born emerge from the steps of a rail coach two cars ahead of where they stood. Everett pointed to the well-dressed man walking in a manner that favored his left foot. His peculiar way of planting his heel on the ground and pushing off from the back of his shoe gave the handsome fellow a distinctive limp. But even with a limp, Leon still projected a swagger of confidence that Everett instinctively knew made the man his son.

"That's him!" Everett cried.

He grabbed Amelia by the hand and rushed to embrace his boy. Leon allowed himself to give his father a stiff hug. Everett enveloped Leon in his arms and kissed him on the cheek.

"Hello, Pa," Leon said. "Long time, no see."

Everett smiled and took the duffle bag from Leon, slinging it over his already stooped shoulders while still clutching Leon to his side.

"Too long, boy. Too long, indeed," Everett declared.

Leon then felt a tug on the tail of his new suit jacket. He unwrapped himself from his father's grasp and turned to see his baby sister grinning up into his face. Leon bent to examine the child who so resembled his mother. He stifled an unexpected urge to cry, so startling was the likeness.

"Hello, Amelia May. I'm your brother," he told her.

The girl beamed her affection to him in a look of adoration that lit up her face, just as Leona's had done in his memories of her from his long-ago childhood. Amelia put her arms around Leon's waist and rested her head against his vest. She hugged him tight for several moments before she pulled herself away and looked him up and down.

"Do the toes on your bad foot still hurt?" she asked him.

Leon gave the girl a pat on her silky head. "Of course not, Amelia. I don't have any toes on my bad foot."

Leon chuckled at her amazed expression and took her small hand in his.

"Come on," he said to her. "Show me everything there is to see."

Amelia and Leon walked ahead to the waiting Chalmers. Everett followed with Leon's bag, watching from behind as his daughter listened with rapt attention to the legendary brother she had long imagined meeting again. She hung on his every word, as if he were a god gracing her with a visit from the exalted realm of her dreams. His mother had loved him that way. She always called him her beautiful boy, her gift from the gods, and as a child, Leon had agreed with her. Everett wondered if experience had imbued Leon with humility, but before he could ponder his son's character any further, the train blasted the air with a shrill whistle to warn folks off the tracks. Leon crumpled into a protective crouch and clamped his hands over his ears. He sat there trembling until Everett knelt down next to him and put his hand on Leon's shoulder.

"It's okay, son. It's just the train."

Everett pulled Leon up and guided him to the car. Once seated in the automobile, Leon regained his composure.

"Loud noises bother me some...remind me of the battlefield. I'm okay now," Leon assured them.

He knew he needed to medicate his jagged nerves.

"You still keep a bottle of whiskey?" Leon asked his father.

Everett indicated that he did. "It's hard to get these days but it's a bit better than the stuff you used to sneak from the hay pile," Everett advised him.

Leon laughed then. "I didn't think you knew about that," he said.

Everett looked over at his son. "I know more than you think I do," he answered, before giving the young man a hearty slap on the back.

Leon was nearly reduced to tears for the second time in an hour when he walked into Grandma Saxby's old cottage. There, lying curled into a ball on a worn out blanket near the stove, was a faithful companion he'd never thought he would see again. Brownie raised his head and sniffed the air when Leon entered the kitchen. The old dog unwound himself from his sleeping position and stiffly hobbled over to Leon, his raggedy tail wagging with pleasure. When the dog finally reached Leon's outstretched hand, he licked his fingers and pushed his coarse-haired head against Leon's leg, telegraphing to him that he hadn't forgotten the friendship of their mutual youth.

"Look at you, Brownie. You remember me. I can't believe you're still with us." Leon scratched the head of the little fox terrier who pawed for more whenever Leon took a rest.

"He's mostly blind and deaf but still hungry all the time so he may have a ways to go," Everett told his son.

"Good old Brownie. Good old boy," Leon told the dog. He excused himself to use the bathroom, his head bent to hide the tears that had welled up in his eyes from engaging with this noble ghost from his distant boyhood.

At the end of the hall between the original bedrooms, an extension had been added to the cottage. On one side of the new addition was a bedroom for James and on the other, a bathroom with a flush-tank commode, a pedestal sink and a clawfoot tub, all decked out with shiny chrome fixtures and sitting on a floor of tiny hexagons of white tile. The walls were painted rose petal pink—obviously, Amelia had chosen the decor--and fragrant soaps scented the room with a whiff of lavender, another decidedly female preference. Just as Leon exited the bathroom, the door to the new bedroom opened and a lanky redhaired manchild stepped into the hall, bumping into Leon's shoulder. Leon wobbled on his unbalanced feet, before righting himself into a defensive posture.

"Hey! Watch yourself!" Leon hollered at the surprised boy.

James hung his head and dropped his limp arms to his sides.

"Sorry, sir," a chastised James told the stranger in his hallway.

Leon remembered suddenly that Everett's step-son lived with his father and his sister. This must be the lad, the quasi-family member whom Leon had never met.

"Are you James?" Leon asked the youngster.

The boy kept his eyes diverted from Leon's face and bobbed his head up and down.

"Sorry I snapped at you, James. You surprised me is all," Leon said to him.

Again, James nodded and stepped carefully around the newcomer, being sure not to touch the man as he worked his way to the kitchen. When she saw him, Amelia jumped up from where she was crouching down next to Brownie, feeding the old dog bits of scrambled egg. She ran over and gave James a hug. James applied a perfunctory pat to the girl's shoulder. He smiled down at the one person he could stand to touch.

"Did you meet my big brother?" Amelia asked the boy.

"Yes," he told her. James had no more to say about the visitor. " We should practice," he said to Amelia.

"Yes. You're right. Let's do it now before I have to start supper."

The girl picked up her arithmetic book from the kitchen table and handed it to James. He opened it to the page she had marked and sniffed the aroma of ink and pulp. It smelled to him like knowledge. Together, the pair worked for the next half an hour on long division. Amelia carefully used her pencil to show her work, as the teacher demanded, when she made the computations below the problem. James watched the girl struggle and corrected her as she went, carefully explaining her errors. He had made the calculation in his head as soon as he had seen figures on the page. It took all his control not to announce the answer to Amelia. He had learned that not everyone appreciated his easy way with numbers.

"Can you get me that drink now, Pa?" Leon asked his father.

Everett looked surprised by the request. "I didn't think you wanted it now," he said. "It's only eleven-thirty."

Everett opened one of the high cabinets over the counter and removed a slightly sampled bottle of Canadian whiskey.

"This okay?" he asked his son.

Leon took the bottle from his father, uncorked it and inhaled the biting aroma.

"This will do quite nicely," he replied.

He poured the water out of a glass that had been sitting on the counter and dried the rim against the leg of his woolen trousers. Leon hurriedly filled the glass with three fingers of the amber liquid.

"That's a stiff dose, son," Everett observed.

Leon sucked at least one of those finger-sized measures of whiskey into his mouth and swallowed it down. He could feel the pleasant burn of liquor accost the parasitic anxiety that bored into him like a tapeworm. He gulped down the rest and poured himself another, more modest, measure.

"It helps my nerves," Leon explained to his father. "Helps the pain, too."

Everett reached over to take the bottle back.

"That's enough for now," he said. "You better find another way to calm yourself down, son. You heard about the Eighteenth Amendment? You won't be able to buy any of your 'medicine' pretty soon."

Leon laughed at his father's naive acquiescence to the ridiculous law. He saw only potential in the situation.

"There's more than one way to skin a cat, Pa."

Leon looked around the kitchen and rubbed his stomach. "Who does the cooking around here? I'm starving."

James helped Amelia wash and dry the dishes after a supper of cold fried chicken, potato salad and peach pie, a meal the girl had been told had always been a favorite of Leon's. She had worked the entire day before, preparing all the foods she knew Leon liked.

"How'd you learn to cook like that?" Leon asked the girl as he sopped the last of the pie juice from his plate with a crust of homemade bread and a dab of butter.

"Did you like it?" she asked, clearly looking for a compliment for all her hard work.

"It was first rate, Sis. Just like I remember from the farm."

Leon gave his sister one of his disarming winks. Amelia blushed with pride. Everett handed his empty plate to Amelia to take to the kitchen.

"Thank you, darling girl. Your brother is right. That was a mighty tasty meal," he told her.

James followed her to the sink with Leon's flatware and his empty glass. Leon had been offered lemonade with the meal and nothing more.

"She learned from your grandmother. By the time that child was eight years old, she could handle darn near anything that needed doing in the kitchen," Everett bragged about the child's virtues after she disappeared from the dining room.

"How about the mute in there with her?" Leon cocked his head toward the kitchen. "He pulling his weight?"

There was something about James that Leon found unnerving. He couldn't figure out why such a strange bastard had been worth the trouble and money it took to build him a room. Why couldn't the kid just bunk in the garage, the way he used to in the old barn? Hell, there was even a real heater out there. That's more than Leon had back in the day.

Everett tamped the tobacco down in his pipe, handing the book of matches to Leon after he lit the bowl. Leon blew a stream of smoke across the table to the empty chair where James had silently eaten his supper.

"James is a little different, for sure," Everett tried to explain, "but you won't find a finer lad anywhere. And that boy not only pulls his weight, he does all the really heavy lifting around here. We wouldn't have what we do today if it wasn't for James. He's a mechanical genius. Never had a lesson. Just knows what to do," Everett told him.

Leon sat smirking as he watched the wisps of smoke from his cigarette drift up to the ceiling.

"I don't know, Pa. He looks like the type who'd take a mallet to your head when you're sound asleep. He gives me the willys."

Leon didn't like the fact that he would be sharing a room with the peculiar fellow during his stay with his father.

"Can't you move him to the garage while I'm here?" Leon asked.

Everett shook his head at Leon's request. "Tell you what, son. You can bunk on the davenport tonight but I have no intention of moving James out of his room. This is his home and he's welcomed you to share his space but no one's going to force you. You suit yourself on where you sleep but James is staying where he is."

Leon knew then that it would be a long night. His thoughts went to the whiskey bottle sitting in the kitchen cabinet, next to a jar of semi-solid bacon grease and a box of Arm and Hammer baking soda. At least he knew where he could find some relief.

When the Canadian whiskey ran out, so did Leon.

"I gotta get going, Pa. I need to see what the brewery plans to do about this prohibition situation. I was planning to get my old job back but now, I'm not so sure there will be any kind of job at all. Bet Ray is worried, too."

Leon used this as his excuse to escape the confines of Hastings and especially, his father's watchful eye on the liquor bottle. After the first night, Leon added a bit of water every time he helped himself to Everett's whiskey, and by the third night, its effect was so diluted that Leon awoke long before dawn to one of his fits of terror. Desperate, he rummaged through the quiet house until he came upon the only substitute he could find. In the petal pink bathroom he found Listerine, the elixir that Everett extolled as a sure-fire way to ward off the flu. The antiseptic compound offered more than fresh breath when guzzled for its high alcohol content. The fiery substance scorched his esophagus and smoldered in his empty stomach, but eventually the burning discomfort faded and a soft haze came over him, lulling him back to sleep. He slept late the next morning and was packed and ready to be taken to the train station by noon.

"Can't you stay another night?" Everett asked his son. "Your sister is going to hate it that she didn't get to say goodbye."

Amelia had left for school with her brother still snoring softly on the living room sofa. She left her father a note on the kitchen table saying simply, "We need more Listerine."

"Sorry, Pa. What with men returning now in droves, I've got to get back to Duluth and claim a job while I still can. You understand?"

Everett did understand and, secretly, he felt a certain relief to see Leon go. The boy had always been restless and contrary, and those traits made him disruptive in the household. Poor James had been retreating into his room as soon as he finished his work, taking cover like a turtle retreating into its shell. Leon slapped a walking liberty half dollar down on the table.

"Here. Give this to Amelia. Tell her I said to buy herself some nice ribbons or whatever it is girls that age want. Tell her it's for taking such good care of me while I was here."

Leon picked up his Army duffle and hefted it to his shoulder. "Let's go, Pa."

When Everett dropped Leon at the depot, he watched him until he disappeared through the doors, then sat in his automobile and waited until he saw the train pull away from town. He wondered if the retreating view of Leon's strong back and his herky-jerky gait would be the last memory he would have of his difficult son. He missed the little boy he used to carry on his back, a little boy who would clutch his sweaty hair like a bridle and cry, "Faster, Pa. Faster!"

10

She was an imperious beauty; lush, dark hair coiled into a thick bun sat low on her head, resting at the nape of her elegant neck. Leon's first glimpse of her was only from behind. She sat several rows ahead of him on the train bound for Duluth. He acknowledged that the woman could have the face of a horse, but he instinctively knew that her visage would be astounding in its loveliness. He could tell by the way she held herself--upright, proud and self-contained. Only beauty could imbue a woman traveling alone with the confident aura that she exuded. At least, that's how Leon imagined her circumstances. For an hour, Leon watched her from behind. He was fascinated by the way she brushed stray hairs back to the bun and wove them into the luxurious structure. Her hands were slender but strong; her nails, short and blunt at the ends of long, smooth fingers. Soft wisps of dark ringlets escaped the bun and teased him from her graceful neck. When he could no longer bear trying to imagine her face, he stood and moved forward into the smoking car ahead, just so that he could return down the aisle and catch her eye.

For a good ten minutes, Leon lingered on the platform outside the smoking car, observing the remnants of dirty snow as it melted away into the glistening mud beside the tracks. Here and there, spring flowers popped up in random areas free of shade and slush. Some were a brilliant yellow; some a faded violet color that made the yellow blooms near them all the more vibrant for the contrast. He thought about the woman on the train. Even from behind, she seemed to be a yellow bloom that stood out from the other lackluster souls on the train that day. He had to see her face to confirm his fantasy.

Leon tossed his cigarette butt over the rail and straightened his tie. He looked good. He was sure of that. With as much swashbuckle as he could muster, given the impediment of half a foot, Leon pushed open the door leading to his seat and ambled towards the woman. He cleared his throat and paused at the row of seats ahead of her. Her head stayed bent over the book she held in her lap, giving him only an abbreviated view of her face. Even so, Leon congratulated himself on his powers of intuition. She was stunning. Creamy, golden skin floated over the high cheekbones of her heart-shaped face. Sumptuous lashes, dark and feathery as if sketched around her eyes by an artist's delicate brush, fluttered on her cheeks as her eyes skimmed over the words on the pages. Leon cleared his throat again. He had to get a full view of this enticing creature. He hesitated in the aisle, willing her to respond to his insistent gaze. While he waited for her to raise her head, he allowed his eyes to linger on her body. Through the gape in her dark cape, she appeared robust in stature; taller and heavier than Inka but perfectly proportioned. Her full bosom tapered down to a tight waist, then her body gently widened again into hips that balanced her frame. From the hem of her white dress, small ankles, wrapped in thick stockings, rose up above her feet. She had kicked off her shoes in an unlikely gesture of abandon for a woman in public. Leon wondered if there was more abandon in her nature. He swore to himself he would find out.

The train swayed, and Leon felt himself falter. His hip slammed against the seat frame next to him, and he stumbled to his knees.

"Shit," he said loud enough to finally get the woman's attention.

She looked at him, down in the aisle on his new trousers, struggling to stand. Her eyes were the color of the chocolate frosting Grandma Saxby used to smear over pound cake. To Leon's utter humiliation, the woman sat her book aside and rose to approach him.

"You look as if you could use a bit of help," she said, smiling benignly over him in his position of submissive indignity.

Once she stood, he could see that she was dressed in a uniform. The dark blue cape he had seen over her shoulders was lined with red. A golden pin above her breast was engraved with the lamp of a Nightingale. She offered him her hand, and Leon took it. Better an awkward introduction than none at all, he thought. Once righted, Leon smiled back at her.

"Thank you for your help," he said to her.

"You're very welcome," she replied.

When she turned to retrieve her book, Leon became desperate to prolong the encounter.

"My name is Leon Saxby, by the way," he called to her. "And what might I call you... besides, Lovely?"

She looked at him with the tolerance of someone who had heard such lines before.

"You may call me Miss Pasquarelli," she replied. "Now, I really must return to my studies."

The woman settled herself back into her seat. When she picked up the book, Leon noted from its cover that it was a medical text about germ theory. This introduction was not going the way he had planned, but he would not throw in the towel just yet. He was consumed with attraction, even though her name had an off-putting immigrant connotation.

"I see you're a nurse. Did you serve in the war?" he asked her.

The woman exhaled a deep sigh from her slightly pursed lips. Clearly, she was annoyed by the persistence of his interruptions. She nodded without looking at him as she answered.

"Yes. I served in the Red Cross on a mercy ship. Now, if you'll excuse me..."

It was Leon's turn to be annoyed by her dismissive attitude.

"I was injured myself," he told her. "Lost part of a foot. That's why I fell just now. My balance isn't so good yet."

This declaration seemed to soften her attitude towards him. She raised her head to acknowledge his statement.

"Sorry to hear that, Mr. Saxby. Was it shrapnel?" she inquired.

Leon saw his chance. "No. It was an infection. From a blister, for God's sake. Looks like you're reading about the kind of germs that cost me my foot in that book you've got there."

He tipped his head toward the book on her lap. Miss Pasquarelli nodded an affirmation to his observation.

"Indeed. Infections complicated almost every injury I saw on the ship." She looked down to his feet, then smiled. "You are wearing shoes, Mr. Saxby. You must only have had a partial amputation."

Leon nodded to her. "That's right. Just about half. All my toes and the ball of my foot."

The woman returned her eyes to the pages of her book. "You were very fortunate," she told him. "Good day, sir," she said to indicate that her participation in the conversation had ended.

Feeling defeated, Leon started for his seat three rows behind hers when he stumbled again, this time catching himself before he fell. On the floor beneath him was one of her shoes, thrown into the aisle by the same jerky motion of the train that had caused his earlier mishap. He picked it up and tapped her on her shoulder from behind her back. She turned to see him offering her the errant footwear.

"Now that you've tripped me again, perhaps you'll allow me to offer you a cup of coffee in return for your shoe."

He flashed her one of his most disarming expressions as he handed her the black boot. Just as her fingers were about to grasp the laces, he snatched it back.

"I'm selling it to you too cheaply, miss" he said. "A coffee for the first fall and your Christian name for this one are the price of its return." He smiled so brightly that his eyes were closed in a handsome squint.

Her indulgence was wearing thin. "Mr. Saxby. I had nothing to do with your fall so I shall decline your offer of coffee but to thank you for retrieving my boot, I will introduce myself properly. My name is Rosella Pasquarelli and, as I indicated, I am indeed a 'Miss'. Thank you for your help."

Leon handed her the boot and again started for his seat. He stopped mid-stride and said to her, "But you did cause my fall, Rosella. I couldn't take my eyes off of you when I should have been watching where I was going. So, you see, it was your fault."

Leon said nothing more. For the rest of the trip, all the way to the depot in Duluth, Leon had to content himself with the daydream of removing the pins from that generous coil of raven hair at her neck and unraveling it down over her naked shoulders. In his mind's eye, he brushed the locks aside with his tongue to taste nipples as dark as her chocolate eyes.

* * *

Leon considered himself a forward-thinking fellow. The more he considered the changes that January 17, 1920, would bring to the brewery, the more he was glad that they had turned him down when he returned from Europe, expecting to resume work as a supervisor on the bottling lines.

"Sorry, Leon," Henry had told him over a filched beer, plucked off the line for having a crooked label.

Alcohol consumption was restricted in Duluth, had been for a while, but to Henry and Leon's mind, they were simply disposing of an imperfect product in a manner that minimized waste. To Leon's amazement, Henry had been elevated to the position of manager of personnel during the short time Leon had been serving in Europe. No one got a job, or kept it once it was secured, without Henry's approval. Now this old friend, who had been unfit to work as a soldier because of a scarred eardrum, was telling Leon that he was the one who was unfit to work in the brewery.

"I can't have you lurching around machinery when I got able-bodied men coming back by the dozens. Even those men will be let go soon enough. At least, most of them will be, when we switch over to strictly soft drink and candy production."

Henry sucked his bottle dry. He waved it at Leon. "Want another one?"

If he couldn't get his job back, Leon would take what he could get. "Sure," he told Henry.

Henry picked a warm brown bottle from the case of imperfect product and handed it to Leon. He pried the cap off with his belt buckle and took a gulp. The warm brew bubbled and foamed in his mouth and a small amount exited through his nose. Henry laughed at the sight.

" You look like a rabid dog," Henry joked to him.

"Yeah. Well, I kind of feel like one." Leon wiped his mouth and mopped the beer from the moustache he had been growing since his visit with his father and sister in Hastings. He was wearing this one like the English officers he had seen on the Front--a pencil thin line of hair that outlined his upper lip.

"You understand, don't you, Saxby? Things are going to get harder around here before they get better. I wish I could help you but it just ain't gonna work out right now."

Leon nodded.

"But it sure was good to see you. Take a couple beers with you when you go," Henry offered.

Leon grabbed four bottles and stuck them deep into his pockets. He rose to go, and Henry held out his hand to Leon as a gesture of finality. Leon shook it half-heartedly.

"What about Ray? You keeping him on?" Leon wondered.

Henry smiled then. "Oh yeah. He's already established good relations with the folks on his route and he's been pushing the soft drink market to the towns he serves. We'll keep him for now. We gotta see how this new business model goes. The near-beer and candy and all that."

Leon nodded again and left thinking that if he had shoved a toothpick in his ear back in 1917, he might be the one deciding who got work and who didn't.

It seemed that circumstances were forever forcing Raymond and Leon into a closeness that neither one enjoyed. Needing a place to stay when he returned, Leon shamed his younger brother into rooming with him once again.

"I'm your family. The Hofmanns are nice enough folks but I'm your brother and I need your help," Leon told the reluctant young man

when his money for rent ran out before he could find a suitable position. "I helped you. Put you up when you first got here. Remember?"
What could Raymond do but agree.

When Ray advised the Hofmann family that he was leaving their
home to live with his brother, Renate Hofmann cried as if she were
losing another child.

"Oh, no! You mustn't leave. He can live here, too," she said to
Raymond. "Your brother was such a good friend to Kurt. We would be
honored to have him stay with us."

When Ray told Leon of Renate's offer, he tossed his cigarette to the
ground and slowly lit another.

"Everytime I look at those people, I think of that hole in Kurt's
chest. And anyway, I can't stand being around a bunch of folks all at
once, especially when they speak to each other in German. Hell, if I
could get out of staying with you, I would. But, I need your help until I
get back on my feet--foot and a half."

Leon smirked at his little joke and saw the anguish on Raymond's
face. It made Raymond physically uncomfortable to see Leon's mangled
foot, and he surmised that he had no moral choice but to do as his
brother requested. Soon, the two brothers were back in a single bed in a
Duluth boarding house, waking up each morning mashed against each
other in the deep well at the center of the worn-out mattress.

* * *

The Emerald Caulk Horseshoe Company was founded in 1908 by a
Swedish immigrant with an idea that made city life for horses much
more comfortable. Lars Stenstrom lay awake in his blacksmith's hovel
each night listening to the clack of iron horseshoes assaulting the
cobblestone streets of his adopted city. The noise hurt his ears, and he
had to believe that the concussion was damaging to the horses' legs. He
wondered why someone hadn't come up with a product that could
muffle the incessant racket of steel slamming into rock whenever a
horse worked its way along the streets of Duluth. Once he decided that
this was a problem that he might be able to solve, Lars began experi-

menting with prototypes of cushioned horseshoes. He hollowed out the
street side of the shoes and used the space to try out a number of materials that could potentially soften the blow of impact. Like Goldilocks,
he found some materials too hard and some too soft. After months of
devoting his energies to the project, he finally arrived at a caulk that
seemed to offer the proper degree of support and cushion. His proto-
type horseshoes were quickly accepted by horsemen and civic leaders
alike, and the company he started with his one great idea took off.
Unfortunately, 1908 was also a year that saw an increase in the demand
for motorized transportation, and so Stenstrom's business was
becoming obsolete, even as it prospered. Quick-thinking Lars decided
that he would adjust to the times he saw ahead. By 1920, the Emerald
Caulk Horseshoe Company was using its forges to manufacture tools
for the very automobiles that were causing the horseshoe's decline.
During and after World War I, the business boomed. Emerald Caulk
Horseshoe Company hired Leon as a driver three weeks after good ol'
Henry turned him down at the brewery. To accommodate his handicap,
Leon strapped a block of wood to the clutch in the Emerald delivery
van and, with this alteration, he was able to shift effortlessly. It helped
that the van was a brand new Dodge--a state of the art vehicle that
started with a battery no matter what the temperature was, provided it
was pushing at least twenty degrees or the sun was shining down
directly on the hood to keep the engine warm as the temperatures crept
lower. No more hand cranks or coasting down a hill to turn over the
engine with this modern beauty.

"I want my car back," Leon told his brother as they lay in the dark at
the boarding house, trying to keep their bodies on their respective sides
of the bed. "I'm going to be needing it to get to work."

Leon gave his brother a jab to the ribs to send him back to his side
when Ray's body slumped towards his. Raymond was accustomed to
the feel of another human being tucked against him while he slept, but
Leon would awaken in a fright most nights when Raymond couldn't
avoid rolling over and coming into contact with his brother. Some
mornings, Raymond woke up to find Leon huddled into a ball on the
rag rug at the foot of the bed, his coat thrown over him for warmth.

"Okay. That old Ford needs a little work, though," Ray replied.

"Yeah? What kind of work?"

Leon had spent what money he had and was living on Raymond's paycheck until he got one himself. He would be unable to fix the car until the money rolled in.

"Tires need changing and there's a hole in the gas tank," Ray reported.

Leon took in this information and processed his options. "Well, Ray. That car had pretty decent tires on it when I left it with you. If you wore them out, you should be the one to get new ones. You do that, and I'll fix the hole in the tank."

Leon figured this arrangement was fair and would cost him nothing. He could have the hole welded in Emerald's workshop.

Duluth had been dry for over a year when Prohibition became a national phenomenon on January 17, 1920. On the evening before the amendment went into effect, one would never have known that alcohol was long prohibited in the Zenith City. Leon and Ray wandered the streets of town observing a spectacular bacchanalia, the likes of which they had never seen. More accurately, Raymond observed while Leon participated. For a dry city, there was an impressive array of spirits being passed around. Covert liquor merchants stayed open late to sell what stock remained, and folks drank with impunity. What they couldn't down, they squirreled away for the long, dry slog ahead. The lights were on in nearly every window they walked by, and inside tipsy revelers laughed and sang as if they were relishing their last night on earth. In the minds of many, it might as well have been. Prohibition officially began for the nation at midnight, but city authorities considered that to be only a suggestion. They, along with the rest of the population, were too busy drinking themselves into a stupor to enforce the new law. Tomorrow would come soon enough, they thought, and it did.

Friday, January 16, 1920, should have been one of the shortest days of the year in this far northern part of the United States but, on this occasion, it lasted until the sun came up the next morning. On the Saturday after, pharmacies did a brisk business selling aspirin and patented elixirs that could quell a headache by providing a little hair of the dog. Leon again resorted to Listerine, which Raymond found so disgusting that he offered his brother an idea.

"You should try mixing that with some of this."

Raymond pulled the top off of a bottle of a carbonated fruit concoction that the brewery was calling Spring Splash. The combination of scorching mouthwash and fruity fizz produced a still vile drink, but one that Leon could consume more readily than the Listerine alone. Leon could see the possibilities of Raymond's new product. He tucked his nascent idea for making bad alcohol better into his throbbing head.

By the time spring 1920 erupted through the winter snow, the brewery was sending Raymond up and down the corridor between Duluth and the Twin Cities with his supplies of soft drinks, candy and near-beer to stock the shelves of the saloons recently converted to soda parlors. He dropped Spring Splash, Lemon Lush, Ginger Jewel, Sassy Sarsaparilla, and Righteous Root Beer at establishments where such names would have been laughed off the premises just a few weeks earlier. He found that he was making more deliveries than ever and to destinations as far as the streets of Minneapolis and St. Paul. He not only transported his wares to the stockrooms of one-time taverns, he was adding grocery stores, pharmacies and diners to his route. Gas stations and general stores prominently displayed racks of candy nut bars, taffy treats and chewing gum produced at the former brewery. For Raymond, Prohibition was a boon that allowed him to expand both horizons and friendships through his far-flung delivery route. It even meant that he was able to visit with his father and sister in Hastings on his way back from Red Wing. He could overnight in his old bed at Grandma Saxby's cottage and reacquaint himself with the adolescent Amelia and quiet James, the backbone of the family's successful automotive repair business.

On one such trip south, engine trouble plagued Raymond's delivery van on every stop. The van would start in a cloud of black smoke, sputter along for a mile or two and roll to frequent stalls along the highway from Hinckley to White Bear Lake. It was noon when Raymond coasted off the spiral bridge and down onto the streets of Hastings. He had almost enough momentum to get him to the auto shop set up behind his father's house. A horse-drawn wagon threw Raymond a rope and pulled him the last one hundred yards to the garage with the Saxby and Son Automobile Repair sign painted on the streetside wall. His little sister screamed with delight when she saw who had been deposited in their yard by the milkman and his horse.

"Ray-Ray! You're here!" the girl cried as she ran to open the door of the delivery van.

Amelia wrenched open the driver's side door and pulled on Raymond's arm to extract him from the vehicle. He jammed his hand down into his pocket and flipped a coin to the wagon driver.

"Thanks, again," Ray told the young man in the white coveralls.

"My pleasure," the young man replied. "I had to bring out your three quarts, anyway." The milkman handed two bottles to Amelia, along with a warm smile and a playful wink. "For my best girl," he told her.

Amelia blushed just enough to signal to Raymond that his little sister was growing up. Ray grabbed the third bottle, and he and Amelia entered the cottage kitchen, where a large oak ice box stood waiting for the milk.

"I remember when I had to work hard to get three quarts of milk. Did you ever have to do the milking, Amelia?" Ray asked his sister.

She wrinkled her nose and shook her lush brown curls at her brother. "Of course not. That's why God invented boys!"

"What's wrong with the van?" Amelia asked as she prepared an egg sandwich for Raymond.

"You got ketchup?" he inquired. The girl opened a cabinet and extracted the bottle of red goop, handing it to her brother. "Thanks," he said. "As far as the van goes, which isn't very far right this minute," he joked, "I don't know what the problem is. I was hoping Pa and James could figure it out."

The girl bobbed her head up and down. "James can likely fix it. We haven't found anything yet that can stump him. Pa's not here, though. He's left for St. Paul, looking to buy some new tools for the shop," she told him.

Raymond considered this information. "You know, Leon's been

working for a tool company. He does deliveries down to the cities. I bet he can get Pa whatever he needs."

Amelia smiled. "I think Pa just needs to go to St. Paul now and then. Sometimes he brings home stuff in oil cans that isn't oil at all. He thinks I don't know but we figured it out when he yelled at James not to use the 'special cans of oil'."

Raymond and Amelia laughed. Even at just short of twelve years old, the girl knew what was what.

"Yeah. A lot of that kind of business going on these days," Ray conceded. "I think Leon can help with that, too. He's into 'special products' himself."

James ambled into the kitchen and pulled out a chair at the table.

"Raymond," he said to acknowledge his step-brother, a relationship once removed by the long-time separation of their parents.

"Good morning, James. I need your help, when you got a minute," he told him.

James poured a cup of coffee and added milk from one of the newly delivered bottles. He stirred in quiet contemplation, watching the coffee until every vestige of milk had been blended into the drink. Only then did he take a careful sip. "I saw you get pulled in," he replied. "I can look it over after I eat."

As expected, the delivery van was purring after about a half hour of tinkering.

"It's fixed," James told Ray.

Ray smiled. "You're a wonder, James. What was the problem?"

James wiped his smudged hands on a cloth he kept hanging from his back pocket. "Carburation," he replied. He offered no further information. The way James saw the world, "carburation" said it all.

"I wanted to see Pa but I can't wait around," Ray announced.

Amelia had hoped her brother would spend the night with the family. It was disappointing to hear him say he was leaving so soon. She was already planning a special meal in honor of her brother's visit, but she settled for packing him a supper to take on the road.

"Now that you got a telephone, you tell Pa I'll be in touch. Leon, too. Here. Write down your number."

Ray handed his sister a slip of paper with the telephone number for the brewery on the bottom. The top of the paper had an advertisement for Brewberry Buzz, one of the soft drinks Raymond distributed to his customers. Amelia tore off a corner of the paper and wrote down the number for the auto shop. She handed it to Ray, who slipped it into his shirt pocket. He patted his chest over the paper.

"Now I can get to you whenever I want," he told his sister, as he kissed her freckled cheek goodbye.

Raymond made it back to Duluth in fine time, stopping only briefly in Hinckley for gas. The delivery van ran as slick as a silk stocking all the way to Superior Street.

"Hey, runt. I'm home." Ray had been asleep for a couple of hours when Leon finally made his appearance at the boarding house. The younger man pulled the sheet back off his face and peered through sleep-crusted lids at his brother, standing at the foot of the bed huffing cigarette smoke into the stuffy room.

"Where ya been, Leon?" Raymond had the decency to ask the question even though he really didn't care to know the details of Leon's nocturnal activities.

"Get up and put some clothes on. I got something to show you," Leon ordered.

Despite the dark, Raymond could see the sparks flying from Leon's eyes. His brother spent more and more time roaming through the quiet dark of the city. Sleep brought Leon no solace, so rather than dreaming away the night in his bed or, worse, fighting demon nightmares, he used those hours to further his goals of financial independence. Leon reasoned that dreams were only as good as the actions they spurred. The less sleep he got, the more he smoked for the stimulant quality of the nicotine, which he inhaled the way a locomotive gobbled up coal.

Leon finished off two cigarettes in the time it took Raymond to dress.

"Come on. Hurry up, Ray!"

Raymond stumbled into his pants and slipped on his boots. When he bent to tie the laces, Leon erupted again.

"Oh, for Christ's sake, runt! Leave them be."

Raymond could tell by his voice that Leon wasn't mad, simply excited, and that wasn't always a good thing. Over their months apart, while Leon was serving in Europe, Raymond had grown into his own man. He hotly resented the way his older brother sought to dominate him the way he had as a child, and he specifically hated being called a runt by someone inches shorter than he was.

"You're the runt now, you know," Ray told his brother.

Leon snorted. "I'm not talking about your height, little brother. I'm talking about the fact that you're an intellectual pygmy. In that regard, you'll always be a runt." Leon laughed again, but to diffuse the sting of the insult, he threw his arm around Ray's shoulder and gave him a one-armed hug. "Hey. Come on, partner. I got something important to show you. We're gonna be rich, you and me."

Now, Raymond was mad and worried.

When they made it to the street, Leon tossed the keys to the old Ford to Raymond.

"I need you to follow me and bring me back here when we're done."

Parked behind the Ford was a large, boxy, black vehicle. From the design, Raymond instantly knew he was looking at a hearse. He wondered who'd died in their neighborhood until he watched Leon gingerly step up into the driver's seat of the death wagon.

"Jesus, Leon. What are you doing? Get out of there," Raymond said as quietly as he could.

He didn't want the lights to fly on in the surrounding apartments. He could see the article in the paper already, *MAN WITH LIMP STEALS HEARSE*. If they got caught stealing something, he hoped it would be bank money or jewels. He looked into the back of the vehicle and was shocked to see a pine box lying in the bed. He prayed that the coffin was empty.

"Settle down, Ray. I own this vehicle. Bought it this afternoon after I seen it sitting outside an undertaker's place that was going out of business. You believe that? An undertaker going out of business?"

Ray stood there, listening to his brother and shaking his head. He couldn't believe any of what was happening just now.

"So I stopped. I asked about it and they told me the undertaker died. You never think about what happens if the undertaker dies, do you?"

Again, Ray silently shook his head.

"For an extra few bucks, the old lady, his wife, I guess, threw in the box!" Leon said.

Finally, Ray found his voice and asked, "What are you going to do with it? Just so you know, I have no intention of going into the funeral business with you."

Leon laughed and started the vehicle. The older model Studebaker jumped to life with a roar. Over the noise, Leon called to Ray. "You'll see, runt. You'll see."

The streets were deserted and dark as Raymond followed Leon through the neighborhoods on steep back roads. When the houses ran out, Leon angled the hearse onto a gravel lane that wound through what was left of the forest on the west side of town. Here and there, burned out buildings stood silent vigils on charred lots, weeds erupting from the blackened earth. Soot-covered mailboxes at the sides of the roads acted as memorials to the families the fallen houses had once sheltered. Soon, even these remnants of civilization gave way to a section of forest that stood green and intact. Leon took a fork in a dirt path and led Raymond back into a sheltered clearing where a small shack sat up against the side of a cliff. Ray pulled up next to where Leon had halted the hearse. When Leon cut the engine, Ray knew they had arrived at their destination.

"What the hell are we doing out here?" Ray asked his brother, even though, on the drive out, Raymond had come up with a pretty good idea of why Leon needed such a vehicle.

Leon jumped down from the cab and wobbled on his abbreviated foot when it hit the ground.

"Come on, Ray. Let me show you around."

Leon produced a flashlight from his pocket and used it to light the path into the small cabin. Inside, Ray could see an old Franklin stove in a corner, opposite a wooden table with one leg broken off. The table was rammed against a wall to keep the corner from falling to the worn-out floor. A large, decrepit dresser, with a drawer hanging out in the middle of its chest, sat flush with the plank wall behind it. Leon approached the dresser and dragged it away from the wall. A hole, large enough for a man to easily pass through, was revealed. When Leon shined the light into the hole, Raymond could see a cave, and in the cave were barrels and jugs of what had to be illegal liquor or beer, lined up like soldiers at attention.

"What do you think, runt? It's something, ain't it?"

Raymond's suspicions were confirmed. Leon had joined the ranks of so many other citizens who thwarted the new amendment. He only wondered how his brother had accumulated so much product without anyone being the wiser.

"It's pretty impressive, alright," Raymond said. " Where'd you get this stuff? Or maybe, I should ask if this is your stuff?"

Leon laughed. "It is now!" he told Ray. "I stole it fair and square!"

For the next couple of hours, Raymond helped his brother drag branches and brush to hide the hearse in a shallow culvert behind a stand of pines about a hundred yards from the shack. Because of the darkness of the moonless night, it was impossible to know how well they had disguised the vehicle, but Leon told his brother that he wasn't too worried about its discovery. Since the end of the war, organizations like the Motor Corps had given up on patrolling these woods, looking for insurgent agitators.

"That's how I found this place," he told Raymond, "on a night raid with Henry and the boys, back in '17."

Raymond brushed the dirt and pine needles from his clothes. He was tired and wanted to get back to his bed. He had his own financial security to think about, and the next day promised to be a long one, with his route taking him over one hundred miles in all.

"So?" he asked. "Aren't you worried that the fellows who were with you that night will figure out that this is a good hiding place and want to use it the same way?"

Leon laughed. "Naw. I told them I went out driving around. Just checking things out, you know?" Leon pulled a stray leaf from the brim of his hat that had been batting against his ear and giving him an itch.

"I told them ain't nothing left out here, since the fire. They won't bother to look."

That answered one of Raymond's questions, but he had plenty more churning around in his brain.

"How'd you get all this stuff, Leon? Who'd you steal it from?"

Leon laughed again. When he finished his chuckle, a slow, sly grin hiked up one side of his mouth. "You heard of Robin Hood, right? Take from the rich...give to the poor? Well, I took from the slightly richer so I won't be quite so poor."

Ray could see that Leon was enjoying his scheme as he recounted the particulars to him.

According to Leon, he had been driving along a back road one day, taking his Emerald wares up to Hibbing to restock a hardware store, when he came across a couple of fellows hauling barrels in a wagon pulled by an old, swayback horse. When the men looked at Leon with wide eyes full of apprehension and guilt, Leon knew he had happened upon an opportunity.

"If you fellows want to get most them barrels where you're fixing to take them, you're gonna have to pay the toll. I'll take two of those and you can be on your way," he told them.

The looks of guilt were replaced on the men's faces by outrage.

"Yeah. How you gonna make that happen?" one of the men inquired of Leon.

Leon smirked and pulled a Colt M1911 from the seat beside him. It was his favorite souvenir from his time in the military. His most useful, too. Since the war, Leon felt naked without a weapon within easy reach. He gave the gun a little wiggle in front of the worried eyes of the boot-leggers.

"I can be pretty persuasive," he told them.

The men looked at each other and silently came to the conclusion that Leon was, indeed, pretty persuasive. They deposited two barrels of moonshine on the ground beside their wagon, then looked to Leon for direction.

"Thank you, gentlemen. It's been a pleasure doing business with you. Now scat!"

Leon fired a shot into the air just to let them know that he was locked and loaded. The old horse startled and took off in a gallop. Before it had gone seventy-five feet, the swayback nag tired and reverted to its lazy pace. By the time the wagon had retreated around the bend, Leon had the barrels loaded and concealed behind copper boilers he was bringing up to Hibbing--the very pieces of equipment folks needed to produce illicit drink.

One his way back to Duluth that day, Leon came up with his plan. He remembered the cave where Arto and Naldo had been hiding and reasoned that he could stash the liquor there, at least for the time being. The beauty of the situation was that no one he took from could report him to the authorities without incriminating themselves. Leon considered his reasonable seizure of a small amount of liquor to be nothing more than a business cost for his victims, like a highway tax for using the roads. He spent the next weeks of his deliveries looking for signs of bootleg traffic along his route and set out to use this knowledge for his own gain. Most of the liquor trafficking happened at night. Leon would determine a likely place for an ambush, hide his old Ford in the woods and wait for hours for someone to wander into his trap. Most nights were a bust, but often enough to make the effort worthwhile, he struck gold. He never took much, just a fraction of what was being smuggled, but like any good business, it was persistence that paid off. By the end of three months, Leon had a tidy stash of 'shine hidden in his cave.

Raymond listened to this story with a certain awe and respect for Leon's audacity. He had wondered where Leon had gone at night but had never suspected such an ambitious pursuit. He'd thought Leon was consorting with the ladies of the Tenderloin. Leon went on to explain his scheme for distributing his stash.

"I'm going to hide it in the coffin," he told Ray.

Ray shook his head. "Don't you think someone will want to check in there? Folks are hiding hooch everywhere and everything's getting checked," Ray reminded his brother.

"Oh. I thought of that, little brother. I'm gonna use rubber tubes to shape a container that will look like a body. Once I wrap it up in shrouds and throw in a dead squirrel under the thing, just the smell will convince anyone looking that they don't wanna rummage around any further."

Ray had to admit, it was an ingenious plan that had a chance of working. "So, what's my part in all of this?" Ray asked his entrepreneurial brother.

Leon clapped Ray on the back. "I can't steal and deliver at the same time, runt. You're gonna be the one making the deliveries with the hearse. No one will question such a sweet, baby-faced funeral assistant," Leon patted his brother on his soft cheek, " hauling around a dead body in such an odiferous state of decay."

As much as Raymond knew in his heart that he should run away from Leon's scheme just as fast as he could, there was something down-right exciting about the prospects of money and adventure that it offered.

"I'll think about it," Ray responded, his head nodding slightly as if tapped forward by his subconscious. "Let me think about it for a couple of days."

Leon smiled. He knew he had a partner in his new enterprise.

The original plan to fashion body-shaped containers from rubber tubes proved to be too difficult to accomplish. The rubber the brothers could readily procur, such as automobile inner tubes, was too unwieldy to manipulate into the arms and legs and torsos that Leon had envisioned. After brainstorming solutions over a bit of the very drink he hoped to peddle, Leon clapped his hands when Raymond offered a suggestion.

"Why don't we get Amelia to sew up some body shapes out of canvas. Then, we can stuff them full of bottles to fill them out and jam hay or sawdust around the bottles to smooth out the shapes and cushion the containers."

Leon hopped up and paced the room. From the far-off look in his eyes, Raymond could see the gears in his brother's head were spinning.

"Yeah. I like it. It gives us the ability to make bodies of different sizes and shapes. Just like the real thing. We can even throw some tits on now and then to change things up. Wrapped up in a sheet, no one's gonna be the wiser!" Leon was already counting on his success when he stopped to ask, "Do you think Amelia will do it? What if Pa finds out?"

Raymond had thought about his father as a complication but dismissed it as unlikely to derail the operation. From what Amelia had told him on his last visit, their father had no more reverence for the Eighteenth Amendment than any other red-blooded American. And, the spirit of capitalism had definitely seeped into his soul.

"For a cut of the action, I think Pa can be convinced to play along, maybe even more than that," Ray mused.

"Yeah. I'm pretty sure we can get the whole family working on this." Leon smiled. "What about that crazy bastard, James?" Leon wanted to know.

Now, Raymond smiled back. "James might turn out to be the most valuable asset of all."

Amelia May Saxby celebrated her twelfth birthday on May 1, 1920, by giving a gift to her brothers. Inside a cardboard box that had formerly been used as a shipping container for auto parts, she had carefully folded two canvas envelopes that would take on human form when filled out with moonshine. One shape was her idea of a "fat man" although, she pointed out, it could just as well be a fat lady when a couple of sandbags were stuck on to simulate a bosom. Leon made heads of paper mache, covered with hair scavenged from the brothers' trips to the barber shop.

"They look like creepy ghosts!" Amelia giggled to her brothers.

The hope was that these details would be unnecessary once the bodies were wrapped in shrouds. Even so, Amelia insisted on as much accuracy as possible, just in case an open seam in the shroud might reveal a place where hair should be. Both her brothers were impressed by the girl's larcenous spirit and enthusiasm for participation. For her birthday, the brothers gave her a pair of white mice.

"Now you're a farmer," they told her. "You're gonna raise the mice to give off the smells we need."

Raymond was concerned when he noticed his sister cooing to the rodents and sticking her finger into the cage to stroke their fur.

"Don't get attached, Amelia. This is business. No different than raising frying hens."

Amelia continued to rub her index finger against the side of one of the little white mice. "I know that, Ray," she said. "You'll give me a quarter for everyone of these animals that I provide."

Ray thought his little sister sounded more like she was forty than twelve, and that scared him just a touch. He hoped she didn't get a taste for a life of crime.

11

Duluth, Minnesota 1995

"There it is, over there."

Dwight cocked his head to the right side of I-35 to indicate the ski area. Through bare winter branches I could see mounds of raised earth strung together by a series of ski lifts. Dotted below the gentle runs were charming, octagon-shaped cabins sheltering under tall, old pines and leafless aspen trees.

"It's cute!" I exclaimed.

A feeling of relief flowed over me. Those piddly humps were going to be a piece of cake to ski. To my surprise, Dwight kept right on driving. When we reached the top of the grade, I saw the vast expanse of mostly frozen water that was Lake Superior. All these years in Minnesota and I had never seen the lake of Longfellow's legend. Huddled around its western shoreline was the city of Duluth. Tall smokestacks rose from the buildings and spewed great clouds of white steam into the frigid sky. The vapor appeared to freeze in the air and crack before my eyes. The shoreline was stacked with massive chunks of ice, pushed to the land by the winds that encouraged the waves to shatter the frozen surface into slabs, then pile them up like glittering Jenga blocks on the sand and rock perimeter. Between the jagged blocks of frozen liquid were graceful, curved heaps of ice, pearl-like and smooth, the result of solidified spray from the waves that licked the land's edge. There was a fierce beauty in the enormity of the lake and the white sculptures of frozen water that guarded its shores like sparkling towers of alabaster and diamonds. I was awed by the dazzling scene below me and also a bit confused.

"I thought you said we were going to Spirit Mountain. We passed it already," I advised Dwight.

He patted my knee again and told me, "Don't worry. It's still going to be there in the morning. I got a surprise planned for tonight."

I smiled at him and secured his hand to my knee. "Well, I love me a good surprise!" I chirped.

As we traveled down from the summit into Duluth, we passed under a huge chute that connected two sides of a factory. "What's that for?" I asked Dwight.

"They're for the taconite," he told me.

That only prompted me to ask another question. "What's taconite?" I had no idea what he was talking about.

Dwight thought for a moment before explaining what taconite was and why it was worth bothering with.

"You see," he said, "before World War II, this area produced some of the richest iron ore mines in the country. Hell, maybe even the whole world, for all I know. But, you know, all that ship and tank building for the war pretty much used up the readily available iron from these mines. To close down the mines would have ruined the city. Lives and businesses would have been destroyed, so the engineers came up with a way to get the iron extract out of the waste from the original mines. These plants crush up the waste to get out the residual iron and then shape it into pellets covered in clay. They bake the pellets into little marble things and ship it to steel mills all over the place. Then those guys melt the pellets into iron ore to make steel."

That was interesting, but making little pebbles of iron wrapped in clay seemed to be a lot of trouble to me, like an industrial version of appetizers or something equally tedious to produce.

"You know a lot about this," I told Dwight. "Where do they get all the clay?"

He laughed and squeezed my hand.

"Now you're just messin' with me," he said.

For the rest of the short drive down into Duluth, I studied the steep hills and marvelous lake in silence, happy for nothing more extraordinary than being someplace new and in that place with Dwight.

That night, we had dinner at the restaurant on the top floor of the Radisson Hotel. The view was spectacular in all directions because the Radisson had one of those trendy features that allowed the dining area to slowly rotate 360 degrees at the top of the building. After two drinks and the resulting need to visit the ladies' room, I found myself sorely disoriented when I tried to return to our table. Dwight was not where I had left him, at a prime location overlooking the Aerial Lift Bridge. I trotted around the dining room on the stationary track that bordered the moving section. When I finally spotted him, I was relieved until I set foot on the rotating floor and felt my unsteady inebriation ramp up to a new level. A spinning head, combined with a spinning floor, was not a good combination. I prayed I didn't fall down and make a scene. I wasn't sure how Dwight would handle a scene.

"I thought I lost you," he told me when I finally got to my chair. "Here. I ordered you another drink." He pushed the vodka tonic over to me and raised his newly filled CC-7 to give a little toast. "To fooling around," he said with a sly grin. "Get it...around?"

I wondered if he had worked on that line the entire time I had been trekking across the restaurant looking for him.

I raised my glass. "To fooling around," I echoed.

A huge slab of perfectly browned walleye appeared before me, and Dwight regaled me with stories of all the similar ones that had gotten away. I'm not sure how many times we made the rotation around the building that night, but every time I looked down at the city below, I tried to find one of the landmarks that I had learned of from Raymond

Saxby. I tried to imagine what life had been like up here before good car heaters and puffy down jackets. I tried to imagine primitive automobiles, moonshine and a world not yet familiar with plastic. Three vodka tonics helped quite a bit.

Duluth, Minnesota 1920

At the Saxby family Memorial Day celebration on May 30, 1920, the talk around the picnic table in Cascade Park was strictly business and good business, at that. In less than a month, Leon's fledgling criminal empire had successfully moved most of his liquor stash from the "Slackers' Cave" to grocery stores, private clubs, soda parlors, and thirsty individuals with ready cash. No one had stopped Raymond as he transported his sloshed ghosts to customers far and wide. He affectionately gave them that name because they literally sloshed when he drove around a corner. He laughed to himself that his ghosts had actual spirits inside them, making them more real than the real thing. His hearse seemed to attract no more attention than a stray dog would, making the rounds at night. Like a stray, people assumed that if they let it be, the hearse might wander in someone else's direction and threaten them instead. He began to think that he was tolerating the smell of a dead critter for no reason. One customer, a genuine undertaker who snickered out loud when he watched Raymond slide the lid off the casket, unravel the shroud and pull a canning jar of clear fluid from the leg of his canvas corpse, asked Raymond, "What're you gonna do if you get stopped and your friend there ain't got no body parts left?"

Raymond deftly shifted his bottles down the leg of the canvas form and rewrapped the shroud.

"Not sure, Mr. Biggerstaff. Maybe pass it off as what's left of a burn victim."

The man laughed again and unscrewed the top from his purchase. He offered the first swig to Raymond, but Ray had no interest. He had a lot of miles to cover through the rainy night, and he wanted to keep his wits about him.

"No thanks, sir. I have a lot of driving to do. Besides, the smell of that thing in the back makes me too sick to my stomach to consume anything. 'Specially that stuff."

Raymond gestured toward the jar the undertaker was lowering from his lips. The man nodded and handed Raymond the agreed upon amount of money for his purchase.

"I'd give you a tip, son, but you're already charging more than it's worth," the man stated. "But here's a bit of advice. Get yourself some Vicks Vaporub. Stick a glob up your nose and it will kill the smell. Makes all the difference. Believe you me!"

The man brightened when a thought surfaced through the dim light of the moonshine haze he had developed from his tippling. "Hang on, boy. I got some I can give you."

The undertaker skipped to the back door of the mortuary and let it slam behind him. When he emerged a few minutes later, he was holding a white cloth with a pile of viscous jelly sitting on it like a melted jewel. A potent menthol smell emanated from the glistening mound.

"Here. Stick it up your nose!"

The man scooped a glob onto his own finger and tried to apply it directly into Raymond's nostrils. Ray was surprised by the man's actions and pulled his head away from his reach.

"Whoa there, Mr. Biggerstaff. I can do it myself."

Raymond didn't want to be rude, but that man's hands had been stuck into who knows where on actual dead people. Mr. Biggerstaff passed Ray the handkerchief.

"Sorry, son. I'm so used to my customers not protesting anything I do that I just plain forget how to treat folks when they're still breathing."

When Raymond left the mortuary for his next stop, he did so with a good sized dollop of Vicks keeping the smell of a dead rodent at bay. Mr. Biggerstaff's tip proved to be a good one, and Leon liked the idea that it lent authenticity to the subterfuge of Raymond's disguise.

* * *

"Pa? Can I go explore the castle?" Amelia asked her father as the men discussed business that Memorial Day in the park.

Cascade Park, on the outer reaches of Duluth, was a pleasant piece of land that boasted a creek that ran through it and over a structure of rock, made to resemble a castle. The creek water poured out of the castle and cascaded down in a waterfall that changed velocity with the rains. On May 30, 1920, it was rushing from the structure and splashing loudly on the rocks below, propelled by recent showers and sparse remnants of still melting underground springs, clinging to shady crevices in the cliffs.

"Go ahead, darling. Just be careful."

Amelia whooped with joy to be on her own for a few minutes. This trip north was one she had anticipated for weeks and the first time in her memory that her surviving family members had all been together. Amelia recollected sitting under a table at her mother's funeral, but she had no memory of who was there that day. She had been told that the funeral had been the last day Leon had been with them. Not only was her family enjoying a reunion of sorts during this outing in Duluth, she was on her first trip of more than twenty miles from home. James, too, was able to make the journey. Leon consented to James attending when he was reminded that if there were car trouble on the way up, James would be the one who could get them out of that trouble.

Amelia carefully negotiated the slippery rocks leading up to the little castle so she could observe the water crash onto the ground below. She wished she could strip off every scrap of her clothing and let the water rush down over her loose hair and naked body. She settled for letting the cold water flow between her fingers. When she lifted her head to motion to her father that all was well, she could see that the men were engaged in a lively discussion. Her father and brothers made animated conversation, waving their arms, and James silently nodded along to whatever they were saying. That mute gesture of agreement was high praise, coming from James. She watched as James rose from the table and cleared a patch of leaves from the moist soil with the side of his shoe. He used a stick to make a diagram in the soft dirt. Too far away to see what James had drawn, she could only tell that her father and brothers were pleased. Leon, the one most reticent around James, slapped his former stepbrother on the back and grabbed his hand to give it a shake. Over the sound of the water splattering on the rocks below her, Amelia heard the group of men at the picnic table laugh. Even James was smiling.

Two weeks later, the Saxby family again gathered in force to discuss plans for its immediate future. Demand for their line of liquid product was far exceeding supply. Leon was down to his last few jugs, and he had called this meeting in Hastings to push ahead the building of the apparatus that James had sketched in the dirt at Cascade Park.

"I can't keep working twenty-four hours a day," Leon told his father and brothers over the kitchen table, all four men drinking strong coffee, courtesy of Amelia.

Leon felt an ache in his nonexistent toes and had added a generous slosh of moonshine to his cup. Irish-ish coffee, he called it.

"Besides, it's just a matter of time before I get caught by someone objecting to my road tax with an even bigger gun than I carry." His brothers and father nodded in synchronistic motion.

"Yeah. I been worried about just that thing," Everett replied. "We need to get started on the still but we need to go farther than that. We should use the farm. The tenants will work with us, I know. Crop prices are slumping more each day. They can help us and we can help them."

Everett had been thinking about the best ways to boost profits and hide their activities. For the first time, he consciously admitted that he and Leon had more than a little in common.

Both Leon and Raymond had lobbied their employers to allow them to extend their time in the Twin Cities area so that the family meeting could occur. "Our Pa is sick," was the excuse they used, and they knew if one employer checked with the other, they would get the same information on why the brothers had asked for a couple of overnight stays with their family in Hastings. Lying became an art form for those bent on circumventing the Eighteenth Amendment, and those who could do it with grace and panache were admired by their like-minded brethren. Leon was disappointed that he and Ray offered such a pedestrian tale, but Ray told him they should save their best lies for more threatening situations.

"The simpler the story, the easier to remember and keep straight. After all, Pa is in Hastings; we're having a family meeting. Only the sick part is a lie."

Leon could see the value of Ray's half-truth logic in this situation.

By the time his sons left the Hastings cottage on the morning of Monday, June 14th, to haul their legitimate wares to places like Stillwater, Red Wing and Wabasha, an ambitious plan for the family business was in place. James would build a still in the basement of the cottage, Amelia would bake bread and pies to mask the smell of cooking mash, and the tenants would hide the liquor under horse manure piles on the farm in the short term and grow the corn needed to produce the mash in the coming year. Leon told his father about a special strain of corn he had heard about when he'd been out in Stearns County. Minnesota 13, it was called, and it was rumored to produce a whiskey so smooth that it was actually better than some of the Canadian booze coming over the border.

"I know where I can get us a sack of seed," Leon advised his father. "It ain't cheap but I hear it's worth it."

It was agreed that the gas station would be the perfect cover operation to sell their product. They knew their customers well from all the years of servicing their cars. They knew who drank and who had a tendency to shoot their mouths off about every little thing. They knew who had the money to pay cash up front and who had wives sympathetic to the Temperance Union. They knew who to bribe to keep quiet and who to lie to. They knew Hastings from generations of interaction with its citizens. Knowledge could be a powerful protectant, Everett reasoned to his sons.

"What about the hearse? Do we even need it now?" Ray questioned.

In the short time they'd had it, Raymond had grown attached to the macabre vehicle. James, sitting quietly over his steaming cup and inspecting the grease under his fingernails, finally spoke up.

"We can convert it to a regular old van for hauling. We need something like that anyway," he said. "I just need to pull all that fancy wood stuff off of the sides."

The hearse was decorated with wooden wreaths affixed to the sides of the boxy backend.

"Then I'll paint it a nice color. Amelia can pick that."

Leon was pretty sure that this statement contained the most words he'd ever heard James say in one go.

When Amelia was advised that her canvas corpses were being retired so soon, she was disappointed. She liked that she had a role in the venture, and she'd been looking forward to raising the mice.

"That's not fair!" she whined. "I was supposed to get money for the mice!"

Her family watched her tear up, thinking she was being excluded from the fun.

"Relax, dear girl," her father said to console her. "You're going to have a crucial part in this operation."

He went on to tell her about her baking duties and, being just a pinch entrepreneurial herself, Amelia came up with the idea of selling what she baked at the gas station. It was agreed that she could keep whatever her baked goods brought in after the cost of supplies was taken out. That June morning, the entire family went on their way thinking about how their lives could be changed by the plan they'd hatched.

* * *

It was clear by the numbers of folks milling around in the streets that something was amiss when the brothers each arrived back in Duluth a little before noon on June 16, 1920. Clutches of raggedy men shouted at one another on street corners, and police strolled the walkways with batons in hand. "Settle down or break it up!" the policemen demanded of the groups of idle men engaged in boisterous conversation. Women, too, huddled their heads together to exchange frantic whispers.

"What's happening?" Ray asked Henry when he returned the empty van to pick up supplies for his local runs. "Folks are acting strange everywhere I look," Ray told his boss.

"You ain't heard, huh?" Henry declared this to Ray more than he asked. "Some niggers got lynched for rapin' a white girl."

Raymond felt the blood drain from his face. He remembered a picture that the paper had run a couple years back when the Finn was strung up in Lester Park. The slack body dangling below the cocked head and swollen face had never disappeared from his memory. A cold shudder involuntarily rolled his shoulders into a protective hunch.

It was Leon who knew the right people to ask to get the details of the incident.

"You know that circus you wanted to go to?" Leon reminded Raymond. "Those coloreds were working as roustabouts for that outfit. This white kid, Jimmie Sullivan, claimed he was robbed of twenty dollars at gunpoint by the coloreds and had to watch his girl get raped by a gang of them Negro fellows. Thing is, I know that Jim Sullivan from the docks. He's a gambler and the fellows I talked to said he didn't have a red cent on him to rob that night; he'd lost everything he had an hour earlier in a game of chuck-a-luck. He didn't have a decent roll all evening and he left the game mad. At least what they're saying. He and the girl approached the carnival men and tried to get something going with them but them black boys, they wanted no part of any trouble so Jimmie made some for them."

Leon shook his head as he related to Ray the story he had been told on the docks.

"What about the girl? Do you think the--you know--really happened?" Ray asked.

He felt he would dirty himself just by saying the word "rape" out loud. Leon shook his head again.

"I guess she got examined and there was no sign anything like that happened that night. She was known to be a loose sort, though. Just not that night."

"I heard it was a mob, mostly immigrants, thousands of them, who took those fellows from the jail," Leon continued. "Nobody tried to stop them. Cops just let them be to do what they wanted. The mob was screaming about the coloreds coming up here and taking jobs. Acting all uppity around town and looking at white women as if they had every right to. I'm glad we were down in Hastings when all this happened. It's a sorry situation."

The whole thing made Raymond feel sick to his stomach. The only saving grace was that Leon appeared to have grown out of his need to experience a vicarious thrill from the tragedy of others. He seemed genuinely aggrieved for the injustice suffered by the carnival men. Ray supposed the war had changed Leon's outlook on violence, if not on immigrants.

"I've never even said two words to a colored fellow," Ray told Leon. "Have you?"

"Not until Camp Dodge," Leon told his brother. "There was a slew of them fellows sent up from the south. They kept to themselves but were good soldiers, I can tell you that. I saw plenty of them at the Front, too. Fought as hard as anyone. Bled just as red as any white man and their innards was just as pink. I don't know why, but that surprised me."

Raymond processed this statement for a moment before declaring, "That makes sense, though, doesn't it? I mean an Angus and a Herford look the same on the inside. Just the hides are different."

Leon laughed. "Yeah. I guess bull is bull when you get right down to it. At least those colored fellows were real Americans, their families here centuries longer than most the Johnny-come-lately whites I fought with over there."

A pall of shame descended on Duluth after the horrendous circus incident. It was believed that a progressive city in the far northern regions of the United States would never stoop to such flagrant racial bigotry. The righteous veneer of racial harmony had been easy to maintain as long the coloreds stayed in the south. It was painless to be accepting of folks who lived hundreds of miles away but a different story when one of them was working a job right next to you, potentially robbing a friend or neighbor of gainful employment. The caucasian immigrants who made up so much of the workforce in Duluth during the early years of the twentieth century had weathered their own brutal battles of discrimination, and they felt they had earned their place in respectable, working class society. They had no intention of ceding their gains to dark-skinned, southern riff-raff, and it was awkwardly affirming for these marginalized, immigrant souls to finally have a group of people they could look down upon from their lowly perch.

Few known members of the Duluth lynch mob were ever held accountable for the crimes perpetrated on the Negroes that June night, and Duluth did what it could to erase the incident from its collective memory. The city would have been more successful in that endeavor had Raymond not encountered postcard scenes of the dead men, their half-naked bodies shown hanging from a street light and surrounded by smug rioters smiling up at the lifeless men as if admiring Christmas turkeys being displayed behind sanitized butcher's glass. These images appeared prominently propped up in the windows of storefronts for years after. It made the gentle crime of bootlegging seem almost quaint.

* * *

Not all of the 1920s roared. The early years of the decade saw depressed markets for agricultural goods and high unemployment, especially among returning veterans. After the demands of the war subsided, the farms many soldiers had left for their stints in Europe were barely able to sustain the families left behind. Military rejects with withered legs or busted eardrums had supported the war efforts in the domestic sectors, but without the demands for the equipment of battle, those jobs, too, had dwindled in a peacetime market. The Saxby family, long existing on the ragged hems of poverty, defied the trends. Their fortunes seemed to shine brighter with every passing day.

"I'm thinking of quitting at Emerald. I don't need that job anymore."

Leon was standing in the auto shop at his father's place, watching as James welded compartments for the concealment of liquor into the frame of Leon's new car. The Dodge, already fast and powerful, had been modified by James to give it more speed and torque than just about anything else on the road. Its drab exterior, solemn black and substantial, disguised its nimble ability to outrun competing moonshiners or the curiosity of law enforcement officers on the prowl for alcohol violations. Leon's favorite thing about the Dodge was that he knew its mettle. These were the cars that John J. Pershing trusted to pursue Pancho Villa through the rugged terrain on the Mexican border. So impressed was Pershing with the performance of the vehicle that he designated the Dodge as the official command car during the European campaign. Leon was conducting his own war of sorts, and he liked the solid feel of the deceptively staid automobile.

"Well, son," Everett began, "I never thought I would hear myself tell you to go ahead and quit but you're right. That job has served its purpose and now it's just holding you back."

Leon looked at his father with surprise. If his father had never thought he would encourage Leon to leave a perfectly good job, Leon had never thought he would hear him say something so uncharacteristic. But beyond the surprise of his father's words was the shock Leon registered when he looked into Everett's face. He was haggard and thin; wrinkles furrowed his skin, and his eyes had an eerie tint of yellow smeared across the whites. Everett was around fifty now, and it made sense that he should look a little worn.

Leon shook off his concern and replied, "I think you're right, Pa. I been thinking that, too. The holding me back part."

The job had served its purpose. Thanks to his tool delivery route, Leon had valuable contacts for liquor distribution all the way from the Canadian border to the corn stubble of Iowa. The big money, at least by the Saxby standards, was in moving their coveted product as quietly and efficiently as possible. With the help of the willing tenants at the old farm, the Saxbys had built a mini-empire that touched every part of liquor production: cooking, storage, distribution and sales. It was an open secret that their auto shop/gas station was the place to go for fresh-baked eclairs and three-level cakes filled with a jar of moonshine tucked into the hollowed-out centers of chocolate and spice. That had been Amelia's idea, and she was extremely proud of her inventive subterfuge. She called them "surprise cakes," but her customers called the confections "birthday miracles" that actually delivered on the wishes made on blown-out candles. Her baking business disguised the need to purchase large amounts of sugar for the fermentation process and covered the smell of yeast doing its work to convert sugar and grain into alcohol. Because of such ingenuity and determination to outwit the law, the Saxbys prospered in every facet of their illicit enterprise.

"I got to give Emerald notice. Two weeks is pretty standard, from what I hear," Leon went on. "I'll make a few final runs up in the Range before I call it quits. Maybe show a new fellow the ropes if they ask me."

Leon was grateful to Emerald for taking him on, disability and all, when so many other men had been lucky to pick up as much as a day job here and there. He had cultivated customers, for both bucksaws and booze, all over northern Minnesota. He welcomed a chance to let those customers know that, while he might be leaving the tool business, he could still be counted on to meet their needs for social refreshments.

The new man taking over Leon's route when he left Emerald was a swarthy fellow of about Leon's age of thirty years. He had the build of a boxer and a nose to match. His nostrils veered to the right, and he was constantly sniffling back the fluid that drained from his sinuses. Above full lips he had grown a coal black moustache as thick as Leon's was thin. Leon thought he looked like an organ grinder he had seen in Paris. Foreigner, he thought. But when the man spoke, he had no accent other than the one peculiar to Iron Rangers.

"Glad I could come with. Let me grab my hat just."

The slightly rearranged words of his sentences were verbal glitches Leon no longer considered strange. They were the way Rangers spoke...just.

"What's your name?" Leon inquired, more out of politeness than real interest.

"Joseph. Joseph Pasquarelli. You can call me Joe or, Joey, if we become friends"

The man grinned and stuck out his hand to grab Leon's in a firm shake.

"I know who you are. Everyone one knows about you," Joseph said.

Not sure what this fellow meant, Leon scratched his head and asked, "Why? Because of my goddam half a foot?"

Joe flashed a blindingly white smile.

"No. Not at all. You're known as the man who sells the lubricants for taking the squeak out of a nasty job."

Now Leon laughed. "So, everyone knows about my little side business, do they? I hope you don't get any ideas yourself."

Joseph shook his head.

"No competition from me. We're a wine family. We start on Saturday evening and keep going through communion and Sunday supper. Then we let it rest except for special circumstances, like the end of the workday."

Leon liked this fellow with his bushy upper lip and keen wit. There was something familiar about him, too--the unaccented English despite the foreign name, the dark hair and chocolate eyes.

"Tell me your last name again."

Some primal memory was knocking on the inside of Leon's skull. "Wake up. You know those eyes," his subconscious was telling him.

"Pasquarelli. It's Italian. My pa's Italian and my ma is Croat. I love pasta and potatoes equally. And wine." He gave Leon a good-natured smile.

Pasquarelli. It was all coming back to him. The exquisite creature on the train. Years ago now but still burned into his mind like the negative image that floods one's brain through closed eyes after peering into a bright light. Her radiance had seared a permanent scar on his memory. Her first name had never left him. Rosella. Rosella. Could such a woman be related to the organ grinder next to him?

"You gotta lot of family around? You know, drinking wine with you? Going to church?" Leon inquired. "A sister, maybe?"

A broad grin split Joseph's face, and he laughed again.

"Have I got sisters! Seven of them. And three brothers, too. I'm the oldest."

Leon thought of the dark ringlets flirting with him from the back of Rosella's neck. He thought of her slim ankles and stockinged feet.

"Seven!" he exclaimed. "I only got one, myself. Amelia May. Does one of your sisters go by Rosella, by any chance?" Leon asked this with caution, as if the question itself could cause the potential of her reappearance in his life to evaporate into the air between them. Why did hope seem to strangle possibility?

"Oh Christ! Don't tell me you know Rosella!" Joseph cried. "The only thing colder than a Minnesota winter is my beautiful sister," he said.

Leon cocked his head remembering the young woman, so self-possessed and composed.

"Well. I wouldn't say I know her. But I met a nurse on the train a few years back who went by that name."

"That's her. She works as a visiting nurse up in Hibbing and the surrounding area. That's where we're from. Hibbing. She can't tell our folks exactly what she does," Joe told Leon, "cause we're Catholic but I think it has something to do with helping folks to not have so many babies."

Leon didn't know what being Catholic had to do with having so many babies. It was his experience that most everyone of any religion had too many babies.

"She married? Your sister Rosella? She must be an old woman by now."

Leon tried to disguise his interest with a joke. Joe chuckled obligingly.

"She a ripe old twenty-four. In the work she does, all she ever talks to is women. No chance to meet decent men. My ma is scared to death the family beauty will die an old maid. She don't seem to mind, though. Rosella, I mean."

"I'm pretty decent. Maybe I could meet her again sometime," Leon ventured.

"I could likely arrange that but you better not say anything about your side business. There's so much in the papers about Italians killing folks over liquor that my Ma and Pa wouldn't be too happy to know that you're involved in any of that. Selling it, I mean. Not the killing part. Funny, though. They can bend the rules in a complete circle when it comes to wine!"

Joe smiled at Leon, and Leon felt like the luckiest man in the world.

* * *

Leon wet his fingertips and smoothed his officer's moustache down on his lip. He had trimmed it that morning, and little spikes of rebellious hairs poked out from his lip where he looked closely at it in the mirror. No amount of spit tamed the rebels so he resorted to plucking one particularly recalcitrant strand. The maneuver brought a tear to his eye. "Damn!" he said as quietly as he could from the washroom on the upper floor of the Pasquarelli home. He wanted to make a good impression with the family and most of all, Rosella. He figured that a dapper appearance might help sway Rosella in the direction of his charms, but swearing was sure to put off her devout parents. It had taken Leon over three hours to get to Hibbing from Duluth, and he fretted every moment of the drive that he would again face rejection from the lovely Rosella. He remembered the humiliation of falling at her feet, literally, on the train, and he could only hope that she had forgotten the particulars of how they had previously met.

A knock at the door of the bathroom startled Leon from his anxious reverie.

"Hey, mister! I need to pee!" came a young voice from the other side of the door. When he opened the door, two boys, about 10 and 12, rushed past him, the younger one jerking his pants down before Leon left the room. Sighs of relief from the bathroom followed Leon down the stairs.

"She's not here yet," Joe reported. "She was supposed to be here hours ago, for Mass, but she's still not here."

Leon nodded and sniffed the air. "Smells great," he told Joe. "At least it won't be a wasted trip if the food tastes as good as it smells."

Joe's mother had started cooking for this potential son-in-law three days earlier.

"She's made bakalar. It's one of my favorites but she didn't make it for me," Joe said. "She made it for you. Bakalar is a traditional Croatian dish made of salted cod and potatoes," Joe told Leon. "We usually have it on Christmas Eve or holidays but I guess Ma considers setting Rosella up with a man to be as good as any Saints' day!"

Joe chuckled, but all Leon could do was attempt to swallow his dry spit and he coughed when it didn't go down. Joe, mistaking the cough as distaste for his mother's recipe, sought to reassure Leon.

"Don't worry. You'll like it," Joe pronounced.

"I'm sure I will," Leon replied. "I just hope they all like me."

Well, maybe not all of them but at least Rosella, he thought.

"Oh, by the way. We don't got any cod so we use salted pike from Lake Vermilion. More bones but just as tasty."

Joe was anxious that his new friend feel comfortable, mostly because he didn't want to listen to his mother bawl him out if this encounter with Leon and Rosella didn't go well and he had contributed, in any way, to its failure.

As the meal wore on, Joe and his mother had plenty of reason to worry. The dinner, when Rosella finally showed up that Sunday afternoon, was fraught with tension. To the family's dismay, there seemed to be a subtle hostility between the two young people. Rosella, already on edge from her mother's admonitions for arriving late, seemed to take offense to every benign remark Leon made and his subjects for conversation were limited. Joe had warned him to say absolutely nothing about her job, lest her parents find out that she was working for the devil.

"Stay away from the war, too. It just makes her sad and maybe the whole subject of women voting. That will start my Pa off and that's never pretty. Pa and Rosella really go at each other on that issue."

That essentially left Leon with food and weather as the only safe topics of discussion that he could use to dazzle his prey. Because both the food and the weather were better than average, Leon found very little to say, and Rosella seemed as frustrated as he was with the entire situation.

* * *

Dragica and Geno Pasquarelli stood open mouthed over the telegram that she held in her shaking hands. With a whoop of delight, Dragica flung the piece of paper into the air above her shoulder and gave her husband a resounding kiss on the lips.

"She's married! Praise be to Jesus, Joseph and Mary!" she said, crossing herself with the incantation she had uttered.

Geno picked up the telegram and read it again--just to be sure. He gave his wife a happy wink.

"He's not Italian," Geno said without any real regret.

"Or Croatian," said Dragica, "but he's handsome, has a nice automobile and almost all his body parts!"

Dragica was mostly kidding. The foot bothered her in some way she couldn't explain but, since it didn't seem to bother her daughter or her new son-in-law, she let it go.

When he turned in his keys at the Emerald Caulk Horseshoe Company, Leon had done it early in the morning following his last day on the job. He wanted to be waiting for Joe when he came in for his first day on what had been Leon's route. He didn't think Joey, as his family and friends called him, would need words of encouragement on his new job but Leon did--need words of encouragement.

"You fill her up when she gets down around a quarter tank," Leon advised his successor. "If you have trouble starting it or it runs rough, jiggle the distributor cap. Sometimes it gets jarred loose."

Joey nodded. "Thanks for the heads up," he told Leon. "Well, I guess I better get going."

Joey started the Dodge van and smiled when it roared to life. "You take care, Leon!" he called over the noise of the engine.

Leon needed to remind himself why he had gotten up at five in the morning on his first day of freedom. "Rosella, you idiot. Rosella!" Before Joe Pasquarelli could put the van in reverse, Leon pounded his hand on the front fender. A startled Joe raised his head in alarm.

"What is it?" he asked. "Something wrong?"

Leon scrunched up his face so much that his nose was as twisted as Joey's. "Yeah," he said. "If I don't see that haughty sister of yours again, I think I'll die."

Joe Pasquarelli laughed. "You sure about that? She's a hard woman, my sister."

Leon had come to the realization that hard women were the only kind he liked for more than the hour it took to bed one.

"I'm sure," he replied.

Joe took a pencil from his breast pocket and tore a piece of paper from the upper corner of a map sitting on the horsehair seat beside him. He quickly scribbled an address.

"This is the address of the nursing agency where she works. Maybe she's there and maybe she ain't. She travels all over the place doing whatever it is she does."

Leon smiled in relief. "Thanks, Joe. I appreciate it."

Joe put the van in gear and slowly backed out of the garage. "Good luck, brother!" he yelled to Leon.

He was shaking his head the whole time he wished Leon luck. Leon wondered if Joe meant it when he called him brother, if he intuited more about Rosella's feelings for him than he did.

The frustration Leon and Rosella had endured during the bakalar supper started with the tiny fish bones that they had to delicately remove from their mouths and ended with a powerful sexual energy that had pushed them apart across the dining table. Like two strong magnets, the competing force of their desires proved to be mutually repellent--until it wasn't. When Rosella left her office that summer afternoon, blue cape slung over her shoulders despite the warmth of the humid day, she had been thinking of Leon. When he appeared before her, rising like a proverbial Phoenix from the concrete steps across the street from her office, she was sure she was hallucinating. She hadn't eaten since she'd had a bowl of runny oatmeal for breakfast hours earlier, and lack of nutrition and muggy heat sometimes made her vision hazy. But this was something different. There was no cloud or dizzying haze to obscure the acuity of what she saw. She was looking at what she had covertly longed for but never thought she could have.

She ran to him and he embraced her, kissing her on the lips in full view of whoever cared to see. The magnetic forces of attraction no longer repelled. They synergistically generated a heat that could only be quelled one way. The love-drunk couple went directly to the courthouse and sanctified their desire with a flourish of signatures on government documents.

Rosella was very late for work the next day, but all was forgiven when she showed her fellow nurses the ring she wore on her finger. Leon had guessed at her size and he was right. He knew he was right about Rosella in every way. When Leon came to her on their first night together, he saw that she had thrown every stitch of her clothing to the side of the bed with gleeful abandon, just as he imagined she would when he'd seen her stockinged feet on that train to Duluth a lifetime ago.

12

Midway through the decade, those operating cottage industry bootlegging enterprises were finding it increasingly difficult to compete with organized criminal syndicates that had overtaken the illicit liquor industry. Duluth and smaller shoreside towns on Lake Superior became ports of entry for highly prized liquor, smuggled in from Canada by large-scale traffickers. The little guy hoping to compete soon learned that being rich offered little benefit to a dead man. Hometown entrepreneurs eventually yielded their dreams of wealth to organized gangs with bigger guns and absolutely no compunction about using them on whoever stood in their way. With the trade to themselves, the warring syndicates stayed busy killing each other in order to secure more and more of the market for the illegal alcohol produced by their own stills or smuggled in from Canada by rumrunners. Small-time moonshine businesses, such as those operated by the Saxbys, came to be targeted by both law enforcement and organized crime. In the case of St. Paul, law enforcement and denizens of the underworld forged a gentleman's agreement that worked to their mutual advantage; as long as the violence was kept to a minimum, the syndicates could conduct their business in the city with impunity. In St. Paul, bribes were more efficient than bullets. The police force acted as a quasi chamber of commerce for high-level gangsters, greasing the skids for the use of syndicate products in most of the toney establishments in town and forcing the small operator out of business for all but the bartering of spirits between neighbors.

In the summer of 1926, Amelia Saxby was one of the most popular girls in Hastings. Her picture was painted on the side of a bright pink delivery van that transported her baked goods as far south as Wabasha and over to Prescott on the Wisconsin side of the Mississippi River. Rather than remove the wreaths from the paneled sides of the hearse, James had fashioned them into picture frames to display Amelia's likeness, holding up a three-layer cake in her outstretched hand and saying "Baked Just for You!" The inside joke was that this was an absolute truth in advertising. Amelia would take orders for all flavors of her surprise cakes and have them delivered to the doors of her customers, along with whatever accompanying version of alcoholic beverage they had requested. Her former schoolmates clambered to join her delivery staff. The tips were rumored to far exceed those collected by the milkman.

"Your pa is feeling poorly."

James poured himself a cup of coffee and stood leaning against the kitchen counter, watching Amelia cut Mason jar sized holes into the centers of round apple-nut cake layers. On the window sill, cooling in the morning breeze, were four lemon meringue pies. Tucked under the frothy egg white cloud covering each pie was a pottery flask of Minnesota 13. Not everyone liked cake, after all, and Amelia enjoyed the variety of baking a range of treats for her customers. Meringue worked well because it only required a few minutes in the oven to set, so the alcohol was safe from harm by the heat.

James absently arranged the spices on the counter so that they were lined up in alphabetical order, from allspice to nutmeg, each jar equidistant from the other. He waited for Amelia to stack the centerless cake layers, then helped her slip a jar of junkyard gin into the center of the hollowed disks before popping a solid layer on top. Amelia set to work smearing the tower with a delicate yellow cream cheese frosting.

"I know," Amelia finally replied to James' remark about her father.

"He's been off his food all week. He doesn't seem to have an appetite for anything at all."

James acknowledged this statement with a slow nod. "He needs a doctor," James advised her.

Amelia feared this was true, but she knew her father had no use for medical men. He had never forgiven them for failing Leona. "Maybe he just needs some rest, James. Maybe he'll feel better in a couple of days."

Everett did need a doctor. His belly seized up and buckled him over at the waist whenever he tried to eat anything more solid than oatmeal or custard, and his eyes had an almost greenish tint from the yellow haze that covered his once clear, whites orbs. The inside corner of his left eye was bright red from an explosion of tiny blood vessels that had leaked into the surrounding tissue. When he looked in the mirror, a sad, sick fellow stared back at him, and for the first time in a long, long time, he thought about Leona and his mother and wondered how it might feel to die. He wasn't afraid for himself. He considered any life he'd had after the catastrophe that had been Arabella Blume to be a bonus existence that he savored for its freedom from the constraints of such a tightly wound woman. And he loved her son, James, as much as he did his own children. Maybe more in a way. James was fiercely loyal to Amelia and Everett. The boy's placid surface hid torrents of strong emotional currents he simply had no way to express. He showed his love to his adopted family in every little action: helping Amelia with the baking, polishing Everett's new car, and running the garage and gas station so efficiently that Everett knew Amelia would be well-cared for financially if left in the conservatorship of James. What he didn't want to leave to his children was a hoard of problems, and bootlegging was a problem that was beginning to be more trouble than it was worth. The risks were fast outpacing the benefits. He knew of families that had been ruined when stints in prison for bootlegging convictions had drained away the only labor and resources available for survival. His own family had amassed a minor degree of wealth that he had never dreamed of having, but a single mishap could bring the wrath of the law down on their heads and everything they had worked for could be lost. Leon had told his father as much when he explained why he was going legitimate and starting an insurance agency for automobile owners.

"Don't get me wrong, Pa. I got no moral objection to the business but gangs with even less morals than me are killing the competition-- and, I mean actually killing. If they don't get ya, the law will because they're in cahoots. The gangs and the law."

Marriage had changed Leon, thought Everett. His son had never worried about risks or morals in his life, but that fiery Italian wife of his must be talking some sense into the boy.

"I mean," Leon went on, "we're still making wine up there. Two hundred gallons a year are legal and we can easily manipulate the process so that no matter how much we make, it still appears to be within the law. The syndicates aren't too worried about wine peddlers. A blind pig here or there ain't going to cut into their profits enough to bother with."

The last time Everett had been up to visit Leon in Hibbing, he had been invited by Rosella's family to a grape stomping party. Grapes hauled to northern Minnesota from California by Cesare Mondavi, an enterprising immigrant who had once been their neighbor, were placed in a large trough and the entire family would strip off their shoes, wash their feet and dance through the grapes until the juice ran freely around their purple toes. Initially reticent to remove his shoe and expose his deformed foot, Leon now relished the joyful abandon of these family events. He held the hand of his two-year-old son as the child whooped and giggled at the feel of grapes popping under his tiny feet. With his other hand, Leon clutched his baby daughter to his chest and did a little waltz with the child through the trough. Everett had helped strain and barrel the juice one rainy afternoon in Hibbing, and he was rewarded for his labors with a massive meal of osso buco made with the family's own white wine sauce and a goblet of merlot that he soon forgot had been created by the feet of his hosts.

"I've been thinking the same thing," Pa replied. Maybe time to close down. "

Everett was relieved that Leon appreciated the dangers of continuing their bootlegging pursuits, now that outsiders from Chicago and Cincinnati had infiltrated the area.

"That insurance idea sounds pretty good, son. James says he read that automobile insurance is becoming a requirement in most states."

Leon bobbed his head to acknowledge his agreement.

"Yeah. He's right. It's a business that's only going to grow. Just like you!" Leon swooped up his approaching toddler son and swung the boy around in circles through the air, a sight that delighted Everett every time he saw Leon playing with the children he'd vowed he would never have.

When he learned of his family's plans to shut down most of its moonshining activities, Raymond was relieved. As a person who had always enjoyed observing the daring feats of others more than engaging in them himself, Raymond had been increasingly uncomfortable with the personal danger involved in competing with criminal gangs for the larger liquor markets. The papers were full of articles about farmers and delivery boys being slaughtered in barns and on sidewalks for the act of encroaching on the syndicates' territories. It was decided that the Saxby's would limit their production and sales to Pasquarelli wine and the small batch hootch that so nicely complemented Amelia's pies and cakes. There was safety in this plan and still a fair amount of extra cash to cushion their needs in the years ahead. No one knew how long the Eighteenth Amendment would stand, but its long-term odds were looking less promising all the time. It was a law no one took seriously except the government, and even those agencies could be turned for the right price. The Saxbys decided to get what they could safely accumulate from a more limited alcohol business while simultaneously developing the auto insurance, auto repair and bakery enterprises into businesses that could sustain their status after prohibition was repealed, an eventuality that no one in the country doubted would happen.

* * *

As much as he hated to admit it, Raymond felt empty without Leon in his day-to-day life. Since his brother's marriage, Ray saw Leon only for brief visits when he had a soft drink delivery to Hibbing or he was invited to do a little grape stomping with Leon's new family. A life on the road, day in and day out, was beginning to lose it luster. Marriages of his peers had dwindled his opportunities for social contact. Now almost twenty-six, he was too old for the single life and too isolated by age-old sorrows to look for a woman of his own.

When he came back to his two room apartment in the evening, he had no one to share his night with, no one to laugh with over a meal, and no one to fight him for the shallow pit in the middle of the old mattress. He had no one, period. A gloom began to creep into his thoughts. He worried he would succumb to despair, like his mother before him. More and more, Raymond had to seek out the blackened ring of horse tack that he carried in his pocket to remind him of worse times in his past. Rolling the metal token of sanity and survival across his fingers only did so much to relieve his angst. He knew it was time to make a change before time changed him into an empty shadow, chasing his mother's specter into the joyless cave of depression.

"I'm coming home, Pa."

Raymond advised his father of his decision in a phone call that was remarkable for its clarity. He could hear the nuances of every word his father said, including the strangled sighs of breathlessness that softened Everett's voice to a harsh whisper.

"I can help out down in Hastings, take some of the load off of you. Maybe I can manage the gas station, like you wanted me to, remember?"

"We'll find a place for you, son. Come on back if that's what you want. Your old room will be available before long."

This statement by his father was confusing. Ray noted that his father had offered him a room but not a job. What did this say about James staying on? Maybe he was moving out but keeping the job at the garage.

"You'll have something for me to do, won't you Pa? I can do just about anything if the gas station don't need me."

Ray could hear the desperation in his own voice. He was sure his father could, too. Everett coughed into the phone and struggled to clear his throat.

"James and I have the gas station covered but we can always use help making deliveries in the van and we're thinking of getting a vehicle to tow stranded autos to the garage. I know it means you'll still be working on the road but at least you can come home each night to a good meal and a game of checkers. That's more than you got now," Everett offered. He hoped it would be enough. It would be good to get his boy back home where he belonged.

When Raymond celebrated his twenty-sixth birthday, he did so with his father, sister and James applauding him as he blew out the candles. His cake was a solid chocolate confection with a dark caramel frosting and shredded coconut sprinkled across the top. No secret center for Raymond. He really didn't enjoy the taste of alcohol enough to persevere until the effects kicked in. He had requested this cake when Amelia asked him what flavor was his favorite.

"I had a friend once. Her name was Mathilda. She used to make me cakes she called German chocolate. Because she was German, I guess," Ray told his sister.

Amelia knew that this was the sweetheart who had succumbed to the flu. She thought it a morbid choice for a celebration but honored her brother's wishes. After a little asking around, Amelia was able to find a recipe that she hoped would bring a smile to poor Raymond's face. He had seemed uncharacteristically sad to her and a little lost since he'd returned home. The good news was that he had a party to attend the next night. Not a party for him, but a party all the same. Something to bring him a bit of cheer and an evening out of the house with young fellows his own age.

The party was at a grand home in the heart of St. Paul. One of Amelia's bakery customers was a jaunty young fellow who stopped into her shop whenever he was in Hastings visiting his sister's family. He always wore a silk flying scarf around his neck to hide scars from a war injury that had burned off the skin below his chin and fused it with a web of tissue to his truncated neck. The scaring was so severe that he could barely raise his head. He had excitedly asked her if her bakery would make a special delivery to St. Paul. He wanted six cakes: each a different color, each with ten candles on top, and each with a different center beverage to delight the guest of honor who owned the house on Summit Avenue.

"He's so unhappy, you see," Norman told her. "He lives in that big house all alone since his dear mother died and if that wasn't enough, he's turning sixty! He thinks his life is over but thirty of his best friends are determined to prove otherwise to the dear old boy."

"Let me ask my brother. We don't usually make deliveries that far out but if he's willing to do it and you're willing to pay a delivery fee, maybe we can make it work," Amelia told him.

Norman brightened at the possibility of his plan coming together.

"Oh. And Amelia, dear. I've heard about your family wine. Could you just possibly send a few bottles of a nice red out, too? Our birthday boy just adores his wine!"

Amelia smiled. "I think we could arrange for that as well. Give me your card and I'll call as soon as I'm able to check with my brother."

Amelia took the card just as James walked in the door for his lunch. An excited Norman jumped up from his seat.

"Here's your brother now! Let's ask him about next Friday."

The faint smile James had arranged on his face when he saw Amelia flattened into a straight line.

"Ask me what? And I'm not her brother," James corrected the bizarre man who couldn't raise his chin high enough to look James in the eye.

"So sorry, dear boy. I had no idea that you weren't the brother in question," Norman began. "I had heard you were all related, you see. A misunderstanding on my part, I'm sure."

"I'm sure, too," James called over his back. He continued through the kitchen and into his room, where he slammed the door behind him.

"I didn't mean to upset him but I did hear that he was your brother. Please forgive me. I hope Mr. Grumpy isn't the one to decide on the fate of my order..."

Amelia could tell Norman was contrite and she felt she owed him an explanation, especially given that a discussion about the changing nature of their family dynamics had recently occured. Norman Regis wouldn't be the only one with questions.

"It's a natural assumption, Mr. Regis. James was my stepbrother for a very short time when we were quite young. He has lived as my father's ward ever since so he has been very much part of our family and he will continue to be so. You see, he and I are to be married at the end of the summer."

Norman Regis almost injured himself in his attempt to throw his head back to laugh. His chin refused to obey the demands of his mirth, and his head stayed stubbornly tilted toward his chest.

"I am so delighted for you, dear one! A wedding! I just adore weddings although I don't anticipate one in my own future."

Norman Regis let his smile slip down one side of his face when he made this last observation before he quickly regained his good humor.

"Oh. But you must invite me. I imagine the cake will be divine!"

Amelia was so touched by the positive response Mr. Regis had to her announcement that she made an executive decision and smiled brightly at her customer.

"Our wedding cake will be absolutely splendid, and, of course, you will be invited to our wedding, Mr. Regis. And you can count on Raymond to bring out your order on Friday. Just jot down the address."

She pushed the order form and a pencil in front of the giddy fellow with the strange speech and even stranger mannerisms. She had heard things about him, too. That he had been stationed in England during the war, an American volunteer for the Royal Air Force who had been injured when fire engulfed the plane he had flown over German territory. Just as her brothers had picked up some of the dialect of the Iron Range of Minnesota, she supposed Norman Regis had acquired a penchant for the King's English, with his odd endearments and effeminate inflections. She'd heard recordings over the wireless that originated in England. Sometimes, she turned the radio off because, despite the common tongue, she could not decipher what was being said. She struggled to understand folks from the South, as well. She could only conclude that language had as much to do with places as it did with words.

"Do you want any special decorations or a name on the cakes?" she asked.

Norman brightened a notch higher at the prospect of personalization. He seemed to Amelia to be a "more is more" kind of a person. He clapped his hands and closed his eyes in thought.

"Well. We have six cakes so let's have a single word on each one. Happy-Sixtieth-Birthday-Dear-Winky-Maylamb."

He wrote the words carefully on the order form and passed it back to Amelia.

"Of course, at sixty the poor dear is no longer a spring chicken, let alone a May lamb!" He snorted his delight at his own wit, and Amelia obliged him with a smile of her own.

Norman Regis left the bakery with a satisfied grin that he focused on his shoes, brown and white spectators that were polished to gleaming perfection. If he had to look down all the time due to his patriotic sacrifices, at least he was able to behold the beauty of the fine craftsmanship and spotless leather that covered his feet.

"Oh," he called back through the screen door, "you must tell your brother, the actual one, that is, that he is invited to stay for the festivities. Our little group is always anxious to meet a new fellow, especially one bearing wine, cakes and liquid happiness in Mason jars."

"I'll let him know, Mr. Regis. My brother Ray could use a night out."

"You're sure you have them all carefully packed?" asked Amelia of Raymond.

He ignored her query and swung the back door of the van closed.

"You remembered the wine?" she asked again.

Raymond was growing weary of his sister's fussiness about this delivery.

"Yes! Yes!" he told her. "Christ Almighty, Amelia. You'd think we was supplying the food for the Last Supper or something."

Amelia indulgently shrugged her shoulders at her irritated brother. "God would have us treat every supper as if our last," Amelia retorted.

She enjoyed seeing Raymond get worked up about anything these days. Even irritation was better than the flat, removed demeanor he had displayed over the last several months.

"You look nice, son," Everett wheezed to Ray. Mr. Regis had indicated that Raymond should arrive at the Summit Avenue house a little before eight and be "dressed to the nines," a term that, to Raymond, left plenty of room for interpretation. He opted for a newish tweed suit with a matching vest, brown brogues on his feet and his well-worn newsboy cap, the sight of which elicited a frown from his sister when her gaze reached his head. She snatched the cap off his slicked back hair.

"Not that hat, Ray! That's a work hat," she reminded him.

Raymond sighed in exasperation. "I thought that's what I'm supposed to be doing tonight...working!"

He grabbed the limp disc of faded wool from where she held it behind her back and plopped it back over his dark blond hair.

"If I decide to stay, I'll take it off. So you'll have no need to feel ashamed of your bumpkin brother in front of your fancy friends," he said. "See ya later, Pa."

Ray waved, started the converted hearse and headed for St. Paul, a journey of less than an hour along the highway that paralleled the Mississippi River north into the city. He planned to return as soon as he had made his delivery and secured the payment for Amelia's creations. If he hadn't been met at the door of the mansion by a creature named Violet, he would have done just that.

Standing on the honey colored flagstone steps, Raymond removed his disreputable cap and rang the brass button for the doorbell. A melodious chime announced his arrival, and he was greeted by a stunning woman in flapper attire. She extended her hand to him.

"Hello. I'm Violet and you must be Mr. Saxby."

Her short, dark hair hugged her skull; the fringed edges licked the sides of her cheeks and morphed into sleek spit curls that were so perfectly round that Raymond was tempted to touch the middle of one with his fingertip, just to see if they felt as soft as they looked. A peacock feather rose from the hairband she wore across her bangs, and it beckoned him closer to her with each motion of her head.

"Well, my, my," the woman uttered to him in a sultry, deep voice that poured through her red lips as smoothly as thirty-year-old Scotch.

"Norman said he was having a surprise delivered and aren't you just the thing?"

When she laughed and moved aside to allow him to enter the house, the thousands of tiny tassels hanging from the hem of her dress swayed to the rhythm of her slender hips. She was the living embodiment of the perfect twenties woman: sleek hair, rouged lips, adventurous smile and a slender, boyish figure held aloft by beautiful long legs, emerging from under a short skirt. Raymond gulped and did his best not to drop the cake inscribed with a deep green "Dear" on sky blue frosting. Enclosed in the center of this cake was a reasonable facsimile of rye whiskey in a quart jar.

"Please, please! Do come in!" The woman pulled him inside the foyer.

In a room to his left was a grand piano where a handsome colored fellow was on his knees before the open bench, rummaging through the compartment under the seat to find sheet music that might interest the group. Though the piano was silent, a wall of music greeted Raymond from a large Victrola placed at the foot of the magnificent staircase. When he looked into the elegant parlor to his right, he saw a room filled with mostly young men lounging about on tapestry sofas, drinks and cigarettes in manicured hands and listening with rapt attention to a mountain of a man sitting in a throne-like chair in a strategic corner where he could survey the comings and goings of the partiers. He could have been an aging Zeus, with his full beard and snowy locks gracing a face, weary and haggard, from the efforts of creating the world.

"That's our esteemed host, Winky Maylamb," the woman told Ray when she saw him looking at the massive fellow with a mane of wild white curls bouncing over his animated head.

The man seemed to spot Raymond as well, and when he smiled at Ray, it was accompanied by a sputtering squint of his right eye.

"Is that why they call him Winky?" Ray asked. "Because he winks at everyone like he just did to me?"

The woman smiled.

"Well, yes and no. You see, he certainly does wink at anyone he thinks is special in some way but it's hard to tell who meets that criteria because he has a tic that makes his eye wink all the time. It's gotten him into a whole lot of trouble over the years."

Ray nodded. He supposed a tic was not unlike the peculiar habits that James displayed, just something that made a person stand out a bit from everyone else. The woman walked into the parlor where the great man was holding court and clapped her somewhat muscular hands to get the attention of the crowd.

"Darlings! We need a little help here for our latest guest, Raymond. He's brought delights to lubricate our evening."

From somewhere on the brocade couch a voice called out, "Thank God! It's not really a party without lubrication!"

For reasons unknown to Raymond, everyone laughed uproariously. He could only surmise that most folks found liquor irresistible, which is probably why it had to be made illegal to begin with.

"Oh, here. Let me help," came a voice from the dining room just beyond the graceful parlor.

A man Raymond recognized as Mr. Regis from his occasional trips to their Hastings businesses rushed up to Ray and took the cake from his hands.

"Raymond! We're so thankful to you for coming all this way to our little soiree. Let me take that from you," he said. "Boys!" he called. "A little help here for our new friend, Raymond."

As if he were the Pied Piper, a line of well-dressed dandies marched out to the delivery van after Norman to help haul in cakes, wine and liquor. One fellow, coming into the butler's pantry with two bottles of red wine in each hand, demanded of Ray, "Is that a hearse? I heard your goods were to die for but I had no idea how accurate that description might be!"

With great precision, Norman Regis arranged the cakes across the oversized walnut table so that they spelled out the birthday greeting for Mr. Maylamb. The dozen bottles of wine each sported a big pink bow, and other gifts, wrapped in gay, bright paper, were stacked at one end of the sideboard. The rest of the hutch was covered with meats and cheeses and colorful fruits and vegetables of the sorts that rarely made an appearance in Minnesota, tropical delights that required importation from exotic locals far away.

"Turn down the volume," bellowed a deep baritone voice from the throne in the parlor. "And send that splendid young man in here to meet me," the voice ordered.

When Raymond stepped into the parlor, he was met by one of the few men who could look down on the top of his head. Winky Maylamb's six foot, six inch frame towered over Raymond, who normally took the honors for the tallest man in the room. The giant's grand head was as large as a ripe watermelon, and his benevolent smile from behind a full white beard distracted Ray from the constant flickering of his right eyelid.

"Norman has told me all about you, Raymond. Or, do you prefer Mr. Saxby? I hope you'll feel comfortable enough here to use our Christian names. May I call you Raymond?"

Ray mostly just wanted to be called "paid," but in the spirit of the evening he nodded his head and said, "Sure. Raymond or Ray, either way, Mr. Maylamb."

The big man took Ray's right hand into his soft, warm mitt and shook it up and down. "Dear boy," he said, "you must call me Winky."

There was something unsettling about the entire scene. Too many pretty men and too few of the enormously beautiful women. Too many chirpy smiles and sly digs. A bit too much of everything, including interest in himself. Ray acknowledged that he didn't feel the least bit threatened, but he did feel like he had stepped into a fantasy world. He supposed Dorothy might have felt this way when she landed in Oz. He almost fainted dead away when a little black dog scurried around the corner and Mr. Maylamb tossed the oversized tail of his shrimp cocktail to the dog and said "There you go, Toto."

The big man moved with sloth-like slowness over to the gramophone. He walked as if each inch of progress toward his destination were carefully planned out in his mind before he moved a muscle to advance his bulky frame.

"Come with me, Raymond."

He coaxed Ray over to a stack of recordings sitting on a mahogany shelf next to the Victrola.

"Do you like opera, dear boy? Please. Choose whatever you would like to hear," Winky told him.

Ray carefully sorted through the pile, not recognizing any of the music. "Do you have Black Bottom Stomp?" he asked his host.

The massive head wagged back and forth. "No, no. I only purchase recordings of the classics and opera, of course. We will have some popular tunes played a bit later by our friend, Mr. Jackson, but let me see," he shuffled the disks until he came to one that put a smile on his face. "Ah, 'La Donna e' mobile' from Rigoletto. No one can do it like Caruso. You really must hear this."

The powerful voice of the Italian virtuoso filled every corner of the cavernous house, and a look of pure rapture so overtook Mr. Maylamb that his face relaxed into a placid mask of contentment. Even his twitchy eyelid seemed to stop its constant motion in deference to the resonant sounds of the brilliant recording. When the aria came to a close, Raymond smiled at his host and had to agree with his assessment.

"Yeah. That fellow is pretty good, alright."

The big man laughed so hard that his fluffy waves of white ringlets dropped from their disheveled perch atop his rotund head and fell into his face. When he brushed them back into place, Ray could see that the wink had been reactivated. This time, it seemed to signal a genuine approval of Ray's observation of the legendary tenor.

"Close your eyes, Winky," Norman directed. "It's time to honor your journey into your seventh decade. Chop, chop, everyone!"

With that, Norman and Violet each took one of the older gent's arms and led him into the dining room. The spastic eyelid fluttered enough to give him a peek of the surprise, so Violet covered it with one of her large, smooth hands.

"No peeking, you naughty boy!" she told him.

Winky pulled her hand down to his lips and kissed her palm before he returned it to its place as a temporary blindfold. At the doorway, he was steadied in place, and the assembled guests sang out to him.

"Happy Birthday, Winky!" A chorus of male voices regaled him with the traditional birthday song before he was urged to make sixty wishes and to blow out his candles.

"I bet he puts them out in one big puff," Violet cried. "We all know that blowing is his specialty!"

A peel of laughter enveloped the room, and another voice called from the side of the table where some presents were stacked.

"And we all know you speak from experience, Vi."

Soft moans, mixed with sniggering laughter, ran through the guests. "Ooh. Meow!" someone murmured, and then a burst of applause erupted when Mr. Maylamb did, indeed, blow all sixty of his candles out with one ferocious breath.

As the evening wore on, Raymond became convinced that this was not a typical big city party. Some of these men seemed too friendly with one another to be friends as he understood ordinary male relationships. He witnessed kisses on cheeks and surreptitious pats on derrieres. He was reminded of something his father had explained to him years ago, back on the farm. They'd had a runty male lamb that had been born from old Sowbug. Instead of butting its head and bullying the other lambs in play, this little fellow followed the other males around the pen and rubbed his face across their hindquarters. As it grew, it showed no interest in the females during estrous cycles and continued to inflict affection on the males by mounting them whenever another would tolerate his attention. His father named the strange ram Lavender.

"Why's he do that, Pa?" Ray had asked his father at the time.

Everett shook his head and told his son, "I don't know why he's the way he is but I've seen it before. It happens. Even to people. Some just like their own kind, is all. Poor old Lavender. He's worthless for breeding so he's going to end up as lamb chops. Poor old fellow."

As Ray remembered it, Lavender did eventually become a tasty Easter dinner. Poor old Lavender. Served with mint and new potatoes.

These fellows at the party seemed anything but poor. By examining the clothes they wore, Raymond learned the meaning of the term "dressed to the nines." There were spats and cashmere coats with belted backs, fine silk cravats and velvet collars. Every foot was covered with the softest looking leather Raymond had ever seen. He wanted to run his finger along the insteps to feel the buttery softness but didn't dare touch anyone, lest they think he shared their tastes in intimacy. Still, they were kind and welcoming and appeared to respect that he had only a peripheral place in their world. He wondered about the women in attendance. There were only three of them, and the men seemed eager to be in their company. Ray couldn't quite figure out why, given the obvious preference of the men for other men.

"Raymond! Come, sweet thing," Violet called to him. "You must be the one to cut the cakes. We don't want to make a mess with the little hidden surprises you've brought us."

Soon the entire table, the sideboard and the counters in the butler's pantry were filled with an array of six uniquely-flavored cakes cut into uniform slices. The canning jars of counterfeit booze sat next to a large tub of ice and a shelf of sparkling crystal glassware. The party goers made a sport of combining as many different flavors of cake as they could with the varieties of liquors available. The possibilities seemed endless to Raymond, but as his sister had advised him, these were definitely "more is more" kinds of folks who couldn't get enough of a good thing.

"What can we do to add a little magic to the drink menu?" asked one fellow dressed in what looked to Ray to be silk pajamas with a brocade jacket over the top. While he asked this of no one in particular, Violet shot her attention over to Raymond and raised her eyebrows into question marks.

"Ray, dear. Any ideas?"

He thought for a moment before responding. Most folks would be happy to slosh down straight booze to get the drunk started as quickly as possible, but these fellows wanted an elegant experience before they ended up passed out in each other's arms. Ray did have an idea. In the butler's pantry he had seen some of the very soft drinks that he had spent the last seven or so years delivering for the brewery. He saw spices on the shelves above the counters and the piles of fruits and vegetables that lingered on the platters of leftover food.

"Leave it to me," he told her.

For the next three hours, Raymond followed the lead of his fanciful new friends and indulged his imagination in the creative possibilities of the moment. He mixed bathtub gin with a splash of ripped-off rum, added a squeeze of lemon, a pinch of ginger and a healthy dose of simple syrup. After a good shake in one of the empty jars he had brought from Hastings, he poured the libations into lowball glasses filled with cubes of ice and garnished them with sprigs of mint and a wedge of lime.

"Beautiful! You're an arteest!" one markedly-inebriated fellow said to Ray between sips of the drink. "Does it have a name?" the fellow asked.

Ray shook his head. "Nope. Just made it up. How's it taste?" he asked.

"Sweet, sassy and tart all at the same time. You know, I think we should call it a Cuban Queen. Because it's so beautiful and smells of rum. What do you think?"

Ray thought about it for a moment before he replied. "Sounds good to me."

The Cuban Queen was a star only until Raymond came up with his next inventive combination. Each new drink seemed to enjoy more praise than the one preceding it, but of course Ray's audience was also getting more stewed with each tantalizing sip. In the past, Leon and Ray had experimented with soft drinks as a means to hide the questionable quality of some liquor, and on this night, he used his old products to good effect. He mixed strained fruit pulp with Brewberry soda, added a counterfeit vodka and chunks of floating ice and called the blue drink Superior Spring, as an homage to the big lake he had come to love. He made drinks with barnyard bourbon, egg white, orange soda and strawberry garnishes; he mixed red wine (over a loud protest from Winky) with sparkling white grape soda and lemon juice. Like an artist painting a canvas, he floated orange slices and nasturtiums plucked from the centerpiece over the drink, and he served it in a delicate champagne glass. He became lost in his zest to make each new drink better than the last. He no longer felt like a stranger among these strange men, and the party he had so dreaded became one of the most enjoyable evenings he could remember.

There was laughter, camaraderie and good music, served up by Bijou Jackson on the grand piano. Raymond was finally able to cut a rug to the Black Bottom Stomp when the lovely Violet took him by the hand and led him to the kitchen where the linoleum made for a perfect dance floor. Ray felt his head spinning from the sampling he'd done as he mixed his inventive concoctions. He closed his eyes and shook his body with abandon and in doing so, loosened the knots of pain and despair that had burrowed into his soul from the losses in his life: his mother, Mathilda, Inka Siskanen, Kurt, and his off-and-on-again relationship with his brother. Jackson changed the pace of the evening when he saw his audience was winding down. His rendition of *Blue Skies* encouraged the dancers to embrace. Raymond swayed to the music and allowed Violet to hold him close to her body as they merged into a single being, fused together by the chemical reaction of alcohol and need. He allowed Violet to take his hand in hers and rub it up and down the side of her silvery shift. When Violet moved his hand to the front of her dress, Raymond froze in recognition of what he was feeling beneath his fingers. Violet held him tightly with the arm she had around his neck, but she released her hold on the hand she had directed to her pelvic region.

"No need for alarm, Baby Ray. I'm just showing you what you could have if you were so inclined, which I know you're not. You can still enjoy most of me. After all, I'm actually about ninety percent woman. In school, I'd get an "A" with a score like that."

She (Ray couldn't wrap his head around another pronoun at this point) laughed and kissed him on the cheek. A little bit drunk, a little bit frightened and a little bit flattered, Raymond bowed to Violet when the dance concluded.

"Thank you, madam," he said. "Whatever you are, you're one hundred percent beautiful but I think I will leave you now for some coffee."

It was after 2:00 AM when the party had wound down enough that Raymond felt comfortable making his escape. He recovered the empty jars and the platforms used to transport the cakes and stowed them in the van. As his last piece of business, he approached Winky Maylamb and handed him the bill. Norman had indicated that, while he was the planner, Winky was the payer.

"That was quite the party, Mr. Maylamb. I hope you enjoyed it and happy birthday, by the way."

"Thank you, Raymond. And thank you for staying tonight. I realize that our little group may seem strange to you but we're harmless and really, just your everyday citizens when you get right down to it. Many of these men are fathers, good husbands, or the sons of prominent people in town. It is only in very rare instances, such as tonight, that they are able to let their hair down and relax into their true identities. You understand, if word got out about these gentlemen, their lives would be ruined?"

Raymond had thought as much. He nodded to Mr. Maylamb. "I do, sir," he said.

"Good. That's a good fellow. Tonight you were a fly on the wall but remember, flies can't talk and neither should you. It's the number one quality of a good bartender and from what I observed, you could be one of the best."

Winky put his long arm around Ray's shoulders and pulled him close to give him a little peck on the top of his head. That done, he extracted his wallet from the breast pocket of his smoking jacket and handed Raymond the thickest roll of bills he'd ever held.

"For a job well-done, my boy. Keep a generous tip for yourself and be sure your sister gets a nice gift to celebrate her wedding."

Ray couldn't believe the heft of the wad in his hand.

"Thank you, Mr. Maylamb. You're very kind to give us so much more than we agreed we would charge."

Ray tucked the fat sheaf of bills into the pocket of his brown tweed trousers.

"Is there anything else I can do for you tonight?"

Winky Maylamb's eye started to twitch in tune with the thoughts in his head.

"Why, there is perhaps something you can do. Your wine was really quite nice, Raymond. Much better than most of the homemade versions I am able to procure. Could we agree that you will make a monthly delivery of a case or two?"

"Sure. I can do that. Do you want red or white?"

Winky didn't waste a second to inform Ray of his choice. "Oh. Red. Absolutely a nice Merlot or pinot noir facsimile would do. I do love the reds. They're so exquisitely--reddish."

PART IV

PIGSEYE

13

St. Paul, Minnesota 1995

I
t was May. A couple of months after the ski jaunt to Spirit
Mountain, I was able to sell my cottage in White Bear Lake and
purchase a lovely 1920s home on Arlington Avenue in St. Paul. It
was a classic old foursquare with a butter yellow stucco exterior,
burgundy shutters and a concrete gargoyle sitting like a watchdog on
the front porch. Inside, it was still 1926. With the exception of the stove
and refrigerator, the home was completely intact in its original itera-
tion. I fell in love with it even quicker than I had fallen for Dwight.
Literally, the sellers had me at "hello." The sellers had their own issues,
however.

I had been looking for a place closer to my new clinical assignment, in an area I could afford, for the last couple of weeks, when I
happened upon a shady street tucked between Payne Avenue and
Edgerton on the east side of St. Paul. Back then, this area of the city
could be kind of dicey. Even so, this particular pocket of homes, so
close to Wheelock Parkway and Lake Phalen, offered a hint of the

graceful, vintage lifestyle I had always coveted after growing up in low-slung, California ranch houses. When I saw the for-sale-by-owner sign impaled into a smallish lawn with a beautiful big pine tree in the front yard, I slammed on my brakes to get the phone number. I immediately dismissed it as something I could ever afford. It was tall and stately. It was in good condition and it had a gargoyle. Be still, my heart! What the hell, I thought to myself. Maybe I can just have a few minutes of fun, wandering through it and imagining it as my own.

Like any neighborhood that has been around awhile and has had its share of hateful weather, the old homes in many areas of Minnesota could be pretty worn down. The exceptions to this were houses in pricey areas. Summit Avenue comes to mind, as does Lake of the Isles in Minneapolis, to name a couple. Keeping an old home in decent condition through the harsh elements of extreme weather requires diligence and money. Lots and lots of money, which I never had. Still, I could dream, and that's what I had planned for the afternoon that I arranged to tour the home. I brought a new little nurse that I had hired just out of St. Kate's along with me that day. She was in the midst of a breakup with an asshole boyfriend and recently on a new medication to numb the pain. I offered her an afternoon of diversion, riding as my shotgun on the home tour.

"Well, here it is," I said, as I pulled to the curb in front of the house. "My aspirational home on Arlington Avenue."

I was already so in love with the house that nothing she could say would be able to dissuade me.

"Wow! It's bigger than I thought it would be," she told me.

She had been to my little house in White Bear, the one by the White Bear Bar, where she always thought she could get lucky if I just took her over there for a beer. She was very young and more than a little naive, despite an intellect that propelled her to be a former valedictorian of Stillwater High School. She needed a mentor, and I figured she could do worse than yours truly. As I was her boss, she had no choice but to agree, and she became my sidekick for the next few years. We each laughed when people we encountered assumed that we were a lesbian couple. We were both ragingly hetero but played along for our own entertainment.

"I love you, FiFi," she would tell me when we parted, and the neighbors would take note when I replied, "Love you, too, kiddo."

Pretty tame stuff but enough to raise the drawn-on eyebrows of my neighbors. We thought it was funny to observe how quickly people jumped to conclusions. The woman next door stopped speaking to me altogether when she saw darling Michelle leave in the morning and Dwight arrive that same evening, greeting me with a full-throttled kiss and a little roving of his hands. I'm not sure which one she thought I was cheating on, I only know she no longer chatted with me over the fence and diverted her eyes whenever she saw me in the driveway. The situation became more strained when my dog went native and killed her pet bird. It had escaped its cage and decided to land on my deck to peck at Duke's dog food, a fateful miscalculation on its part.

When I rang the doorbell at the Arlington house, Michelle and I were greeted by what I could only describe as a real dyke. She was dressed in a dirty flannel shirt, ragged combat boots and a Twins cap that was so battered that it looked like the Twins had used it as home base for batting practice. Under the cap, her hair was sheared down to a stubble on top. The only real hair she had left was a long, skinny braid that snaked down her broad back from the nape of her remarkably thick neck. I could feel my sidekick tense to my right. If we were a low decibel bark, this bitch was bite--pitbull bite.

"You guys here about the house?" the lady of the manor asked me.

"We are. I called yesterday to set up a tour," I replied, all smiles and a boundary telegraphing distance in my voice.

"OK. Come on in but lose the shoes," she ordered. I didn't even attempt to tell her that my sandals were just out of the box that morning. New from Kmart.

As soon as I shouldered our hostess to the side to get through the door, I knew the house had to be mine. I almost fell to the floor when she told me the price. I could afford it, thanks to the fact that there would be no real estate agent to bump up the fees. The tour only validated my need for its future ownership: hardwood floors, stained glass windows, glass hutch cabinets in the kitchen and a two-car garage to house the only real treasure I had ever owned, a beautiful old English sports car I had bought just out of high school. Like me, it was a little worn around the edges but still elicited an occasional second look for how well it had aged. A garage was a must for me.

At the end of the tour I said, "I'll take it."

No negotiation, no hassle. Just sign me up. My little nurse buddy was agasp.

"You didn't even think about it!" she admonished me.

"No need," I told her. "I've fantasized about owning a place like this since I was old enough to dream."

The cottage in White Bear Lake was small and old but had been spruced up considerably by its former owner, and it was in the heart of White Bear, walkable to restaurants, shops and of course, the White Bear Bar. It sold in a week and the closings on both properties were scheduled for the same day, a month out: the cottage in the morning and the St. Paul house later that afternoon. I spent the following weeks packing and hauling things over to the new house, where Ms. Gracious was kind enough to let me store things in the garage off the alley. By the eve of the closing, the only things not transferred over to the garage in St. Paul were a sleeping bag and the dog.

The closing in the morning went smoothly. An inch-thick pile of papers was signed, rubber stamps applied and money transferred from one account to another. Everything was all smiles and good coffee. The afternoon was a different story.

After a quick lunch of White Castle hamburgers that I shared with the dog, I scooped him up, rolled up my sleeping bag and left the house keys on the counter for the new owners. I had made arrangements to let Duke hang out in the fenced backyard at the Arlington house while I met with the sellers at the title company's office. I had no idea they would still be there when I opened the gate to deposit my dog on the overgrown lawn. I found out when I heard a loud crash and the sound of glass breaking. Packing must be a bit behind, I thought. The crash was followed by screaming. Thinking someone had been hurt, I cautiously knocked on the back door and called out, "Hello. Everything alright?" The answer I received may or may not have been directed at me.

"Get out!" a high-pitched voice shrieked to the rafters of the house that was almost mine.

"Oh-oh. This can't be good," I managed to think with a brain starved for blood after it had drained to my feet in fear. If this fell through, I was homeless.

I was about to back out of the yard when the seller I had previously met came bolting through the door. She was dressed out of season in full-on Vikings gear, including a Fran Tarkenton throwback jersey. Must be her business casual, I mused, until my thought was interrupted and I saw that the long braid at the back of her head was being firmly gripped in the hand of a lovely feminine creature with murder in her eyes.

"You whore!" she screamed at her partner through the tears and bubbles of snot expanding from her perfect nostrils.

"Hello, ladies," I said.

"Screw you," the petite blond replied.

I was pretty sure she was right and I was about to get screwed....out of my dream home or any home for that matter. My dog sat on a patch of sunny lawn and tipped his head at the goings-on. Even he looked worried.

It took a few minutes to get the two of them unraveled and calmed down. What I hadn't known was that the sale of this house happened as a result of the dissolution of their partnership. It was revealed to me that "Ms. Tarkenton" had continued her penchant for turning straight housewives into her love slaves, as Blondie had once been in a marriage with an IT specialist and her replacement was leaving a doctor for her partner's rustic charms. The machinations of love had always fascinated me, but on that day, they were seriously disrupting my life and I had done nothing to cause them.

"I understand that this is very emotional for you both," I offered in empathetic nurse-speak. "Do you two think you need to postpone the closing or are you still willing to go ahead?"

I did my best to keep cool and diffuse the situation to my advantage.

They looked at each other with unbridled disdain and asked for a few minutes to talk privately. I spent the time tossing a stick to Duke and hoping I could do the same thing with him in this very spot the next day. Finally, they emerged from the house and walked over to me. The dog growled and I didn't scold him. Some welcome he had received to his new digs.

"We'll meet you over there at three. Just like we planned," the rough girl announced.

She meant the title company, and I was relieved beyond words.

"Duke's okay here for now?" I asked.

They both nodded, and I left to look for a glass of wine at two o'clock in the afternoon. It wasn't to celebrate. It was to keep from falling apart from the stress.

When I saw their cars, the same ones that had been parked in front of the house, located at opposite ends of the lot that serviced the escrow office, I breathed a sigh of relief. I walked in the door and the receptionist directed me to an office where the two ladies were seated across from one another at a table headed by a smartly dressed young woman who wore a name tag stating she was called Lisa, Office Manager. We shook hands, I declined a bottle of water, and we got down to business. Things went well for about ten minutes, and then all hell broke loose. Without any provocation except whatever slights were wandering around in her troubled mind, Blondie jumped up, used her arms to scatter all the dozens of official documents to the floor, then winged a mostly full uncapped bottle of Perrier water at her former partner's head. She missed her mark when Tiffany (a name that didn't much fit the tough-customer persona) bobbed to her left like the athlete she probably was, and the water bottle landed on the disheveled pile of papers, drenching them to such a degree that the ink was pooling on the pages that were exposed and soaking stains into the pale berber rug beneath them.

My heart sank until Blondie started sobbing and begging for forgiveness. Tiffany rose from her seat and pulled the delicate woman into her ample arms, offered her a Twins Homer Hanky to dry her eyes, then rocked her back and forth. It took a bit of negotiating, and they had to agree to behave themselves and pay for the rug to be cleaned of the spots of ink, but the closing was rescheduled for the following day, first thing in the morning. That would give the office time to redraw the paperwork. I crossed my fingers and hoped for the best. In the meantime, Duke was allowed to bunk down in the garage, where his doggie bed had already been ensconced. I wasn't sure what I would do, but another glass of wine was about as far as planning could take me after the day I'd had.

I bummed around for a few hours, soothing my nerves by combing the shelves of my favorite thrift stores. In a hopeful moment, I bought a set of antique dishware that exactly matched the color of the celery green kitchen cabinets. I considered it an omen that was telling me all would be well and these would be proudly displayed behind wavy glass cabinet doors in no time. After checking in on my clinic and telling them I would also need to take off the following day, I phoned the ladies at the house to see how Duke was doing. Blondie had left, and Tiffany reported that Duke was barking non stop and I'd better come over to calm him down. Great. Another problem in a day full of them.

The little Boston terrier jumped into my arms as soon as I set foot on the lawn. He licked my face and cried when I made an effort to put him down. I wondered if Tiffany had kicked him or abused him in some way. He was normally a little fellow with a lot of bravado, but this evening he was a whiney mess. Clearly, I would need to keep him with me tonight which ruled out my plan to get a hotel room. I needed a place to stay so I called Dwight's home. It was nine-thirty by now, and I was surprised when Raymond Saxby answered after just two rings.

"Oh. Hello Mr. Saxby. It's Fiona. Sorry to call so late. How are you, tonight?" I asked. I had assumed he'd be in bed by this time of the evening.

"I'm pretty good. Just sitting here watching Law and Order. I think there's gonna be a plea bargain after the next commercial."

Not wanting to disrupt the viewing of his favorite show, I got on with my reason for calling. "Can I speak to Dwight?" I asked him.

There was a deafening silence on the other end of the phone.

"Mr. Saxby? Are you alright?" The lack of response was troubling. At his age, he could have died mid-thought.

I heard him clear his throat before he told me, "He's not here. I don't think he'll be back until tomorrow afternoon. He's with Leslie."

It had been a particularly fraught day and now this. I was going to ask Dwight if Duke and I could sleep on the couch at his house. My nerves frazzled and all hope fading, all I could think of was, "Who the hell is Leslie?"

"I see," I replied to Mr. Saxby, not seeing at all. "Can you tell him I called?"

Again, it took him a moment to respond. "Looks like there's going to be a trial," he reported.

I wanted to scream at the dear old boy. "Of course they're going to trial! There's a half hour left in the program...What do you think Sam Waterston is going to do for the next thirty minutes!" All I said was, "Goodnight, Mr. Saxby. Enjoy the rest of your show."

I was left with only one real choice. My sons were off to college and I had nowhere to go on such short notice. I couldn't even get to my tent, packed as it was in the overstuffed garage at the St. Paul house. I called Tiffany to ask her if I could sleep on my own couch in the garage. She said yes. Come on over.

It was probably about one o'clock when I felt Duke stir at my side and start to growl. A moment later, there was a soft rap at the door of the detached garage.

"Fiona? Are you awake?" It was Tiffany.

"What the hell does she want?" I thought.

"Can we talk a minute?" she asked me.

I told her okay through the door and wrapped the sheet around my shoulders before I stepped out to behold her standing before me in a sports bra and boxer-style camouflage undershorts. No way were these what I would call "panties."

"I'm so impressed by you," she told me. "You're so calm and mature. And you're so hot, Fiona. I've been lying awake, thinking about you. Have you ever been with a woman?" she asked me.

A horrible day had ended just about forty minutes earlier, and it looked to me as if the new one was shaping up to be just as bad. I did my best to stay calm. My future as a homeowner depended on it.

"That's very kind of you but also, not something I have any inclination to experience--though I do enjoy K.D. Lang. All I want from you is your signature on the papers and your house keys," I told her. "I'll see you at the office in the morning."

By noon the next day, the house was mine. When I stuck the key in the lock and walked into the lovely old house, even it seemed to let out a sigh of relief to be free of the strife the ladies had inflicted within its walls. I called Kat's Keys to come out to change the locks the following day. I could imagine one of those crazy women coming back to settle some imaginary score. Better safe than sorry.

I was busy setting up the bed when Dwight knocked on the door and called up the stairs, "Anybody home?" I could hear him bound up the steps before I saw him. He stood in the doorway to the master bedroom, a room that stretched across the entire front of the upper floor of the house. He walked over and pulled me into an embrace.

"Congratulations!" he told me before sealing the greeting with a kiss. I pushed him away. "Did your dad tell you I called last night?"

"Yeah. Sorry about that. A buddy needed help with a plumbing problem."

Right. "Leslie?" I asked.

He backed away and threw his hands in the air. "Hey. No need to get upset. Leslie ain't just a girl's name, you know."

The droll face of Leslie Nielsen in *Airplane* popped into my mind and I felt like a jealous witch. Apparently, I wasn't the only one who had dealt with a domestic problem the preceding day. I tamped down my suspicions and admonished myself for my lack of trust. After another kiss, I gave him a tour of my new house. We finished in the bedroom, back where we started, and he helped me get the big bed put together. Once that was finished, we decided to give the bed a test run, and by the time he left, I was confident that the bed had been assembled in the proper fashion.

Hastings, Minnesota 1926

It wasn't long after his encounter with Winky Maylamb that the phone calls to the Saxby residence were increasingly likely to be seeking out Raymond for his bartending services at underground drinking events, some of which were actually located underground. He was summoned to a clandestine affair at a nightclub located in converted mushroom caves not far from the Mississippi River, off Wabasha and Plato in St. Paul. There he met revelers impressed with his drink concoctions, and his subsequent weekend was also booked up with a party out on Manitou Island in White Bear Lake. Before he realized what was happening, he found his night jobs were interfering with his ability to be out of bed at the crack of dawn to tow stranded vehicles into the garage. Being a tow truck driver was messy and erratic; mixing drinks was clean and the hours certain, as long as one considered all night to be regular hours.

"There's another phone call for you, Ray." His sister hollered out the announcement, then sat the earpiece of the candlestick phone down on the counter in the kitchen.

"Who is it?" he asked his sister as he entered the kitchen, but she just shook her head and continued rolling pie crusts.

"No idea," she told him.

"Ray Saxby, here," he said into the little cup on the mouthpiece. "Oh! Hello to you, Mr. Maylamb. How have you been, sir?"

Once he left the Summit Avenue house on the night of the birthday celebration, he had never expected to hear from the big man again. In the months since the party, Enrique, Maylamb's Philipino houseboy, had been the one to accept the monthly shipments of wine. Now Maylamb was asking Ray to meet with him at one of the fancy hotels in town.

"Yes, sir. I can do that. I'll meet you in the cafe at half of six...Yes. I know where it is. Everyone knows how to find the Ryan Hotel."

"Was that Norman's friend? The one who needed all the cakes for his party?" Amelia asked her brother.

"One and the same, Sis. I got to meet him later tonight. I'll tell Pa that I won't be available for towing after supper."

Amelia sighed. "What are we going to do about Papa? He's getting too tired out to fill in for you or James anymore."

There was genuine concern in her voice and Ray was worried, too, but he also knew that his fate lay elsewhere, just as it had when he'd boarded the train for Duluth a good decade before.

Raymond was half-way down the hall to his room when he felt a tug at the back of his jacket. "Please, Ray," Amelia begged. "Can't you go early so I can come along and look for a wedding dress at the Emporium?"

Amelia and James were having a very small affair, in large part because James hated dealing with people staring at him for any reason and because the relationship he enjoyed with his adopted family was complicated. Many in town considered his fiance to be his sister, this despite the fact that they shared no blood and hadn't officially been kin for many years. It was an open secret that marriages between cousins were accepted and commonplace, but the coupling of unrelated young people who had been reared together under the same roof evoked the taboo of incest and that's all it took to set the gossip wheel spinning. Some of the biddies in town subjected James and Amelia to open scorn, tsk-tsking behind their backs at the unholy impropriety of their love. Neither of the young lovers cared a diddly-damn. They knew that the judgement of their neighbors would not interfere with their businesses. Folks needed gas and liquor and cakes and would go where they could get these commodities at the best prices, and that was Saxby Auto Repair and Bakery, as the new sign on the lawn advertised. Still, Amelia wanted one special thing for her wedding day. She would bake the cakes, arrange the flowers and cook the meal, but she wanted a wedding dress like those she'd seen in McCall's magazine: a white confection with a dropped waist and a scalloped hem that fell just below her knees. She wanted to be modern and chic, if not every day, at least on the day she wed her dear, darling James.

"Sorry, Sis," Ray told her, without much regret at all in his voice. "This is business. I thought you were gonna wear your Sunday dress. Anyway, no one cares what you wear, not even James...especially not James."

Sometimes Amelia wished for a sister. She had grown into womanhood with no one to help her navigate the feminine world. A sister would be excited to share the hunt for a wedding dress. A sister would love to wander the aisles of the Emporium looking for just the right ensemble for her special day. But here she was, her wants dismissed, as always, as trivial distractions that no one else deemed worthy of consideration. For whatever reason, making money was much more important than spending it, which made Amelia wonder why so much effort went into getting it in the first place.

* * *

"Hello, hello, dear boy." Winky Maylamb waved his handkerchief in Raymond's direction when he saw him walk through the door into the cavernous space that was the Hotel Ryan Coffee Shop. "You'll forgive me for not getting up to greet you, Raymond. Once I get settled in, I am loath to overcome the inertia involved in getting back to my feet."

Raymond reached across the table and shook the giant palm he was offered by the big man.

"Good to see you, Mr. Maylamb. Hope you're well," Ray replied, not sure if Mr. Maylamb was too infirm to rise to meet him properly or just plain too lazy. He suspected a little of both.

"You're a good man for coming all the way in this evening, Raymond. Good man, indeed."

The more Winky thanked him, the more Ray felt a niggling unease creep up his shoulders. He hoped this gentleman entertained no bent fantasies involving Raymond Saxby.

"Please sit down."

Winky waved the handkerchief at the chair across from him, and Raymond relaxed. He would be out of reach at this distance. Business must be on Maylamb's mind, not misplaced desires.

"Have you eaten, dear boy?"

Winky pushed a menu at the young man and smiled benevolently when Ray whistled at the prices.

"Get whatever you like, Raymond. I shall be delighted to treat you in gratitude for allowing me to meet with you on such short notice."

Ray smiled. "Thanks, Mr. Maylamb. My sister was annoyed that I didn't bring her with me so she could shop for a wedding dress at the department store up the street. But I told her this was a business meeting. No time for browsing around. Anyway, she didn't feed me to make her point about being left behind."

When Ray's hot beef sandwich arrived, accompanied by a heap of mashed potatoes and gravy, he tucked into the dish with gusto.

"Aren't you having anything, sir?" Ray asked.

Maylamb moved his massive head side to side in a slow expression of a negative response. "I'm not a devotee of coffee shop fare. I just happened to have business here today. But I can see that you are savoring your meal."

Ray was busy mopping the last drops of gravy from his plate with a piece of bread speared onto the end of his fork. He shook his head up and down, his mouth too full to speak in polite company. He swallowed and lay his fork down on the empty plate.

"I enjoy watching a young man indulge his appetites. Shall we have tea, Raymond?"

What Ray wanted was to get down to business, but he decided to let things progress on Winky's schedule. When finally they slurped the last drops from the delicate cups, Mr. Maylamb cleared his throat and came to the point of this rendezvous.

"I was so impressed by your creativity with alcohol during my birthday soiree that I couldn't help but sing your praises to a colleague of mine," Winky told him. "He has connections to the Commodore Hotel. Do you know it?"

Raymond had heard of it, but he'd never been there. He had no reason to go to fancy hotels unless he had been summoned for a private party where a bartender was needed. He'd been to several nice hotels in town, but the Commodore wasn't one of them. Ray shook his head.

"I've heard of it, sir. But I never been there," Ray responded.

Winky mopped his bulging brow with the linen square he held in his hand before he got to the point.

"Well, my boy, it seems they badly need a fellow with just the talents you have displayed. Your official capacity would be maitre d' in the dining room but your skills would be primarily put to use in more, shall we say, clandestined enterprises in hidden rooms throughout the hotel. It would be a steady job with good pay for a young fellow who can manage guests with high expectations. It also calls for a fellow with discretion, which you have proved yourself to be. Are you interested, Raymond?"

Ray thought about how he would handle the logistics of such a change. It would be too far to drive in from Hastings at all hours, but it also sounded like a good opportunity for him to move forward with his life, to strike out on his own again.

"That sounds like a pretty good offer, Mr. Maylamb, but I don't have any place to stay here in the city."

Winky smiled. "Well, dear fellow, if you think you can stand my company for a month or so, you can stay in my attic apartment. I assure you, I would respect your aversion to my intimate preferences. Besides, the attic room has a padlock you may utilize at any time. I suspect that within a few weeks we can secure a nice room somewhere that will meet your approval. What do you say, lad?"

Winky Maylamb and Raymond Saxby shook hands and headed out of the diner to go their separate ways. At least, for now. Before he had lumbered very far, Winky turned back to Raymond.

"Dear boy. Please bring your sister into the Emporium at your earliest convenience. When she finds whatever dress she desires, tell the clerk that it is to be charged to my account, W.M. Maylamb, Esq."

His twitching eye tapped out a Morse Code of sheer delight when he saw the smile on Raymond's face. Amelia was going to be one happy girl.

"Thank you, Mr. Maylamb. First the big tips and now this. You're too kind, sir," Ray told him.

Maylamb smiled and replied, "Nonsense, dear boy. No one can possibly be too kind."

* * *

Everett felt the two-sided vice of age and infirmity slowly crushing the life out of him. Only fifty-two, he had long expected the family legacy of unexpected death to strike him down in a moment of mundane doing. The instantaneous demise of his mother in the act of making pot roast and the quickly punched ticket to oblivion that had been handed to his grandfather in a church pew so many years ago had weighed heavily on Everett in the last few months. He didn't fear death, but he did feel that its likely sudden demand for departure might be damned inconvenient for him and especially for his family. He wanted to see the children settled before he shuffled off the mortal coil. He marveled at the unexpected domestication of Leon. He had been the one Everett thought would defy convention and lead the life of a vagabond, and now here he was, a proper businessman with a thriving insurance agency, a capable wife with an extended family that wrapped Leon in a blanket of security and support--so ingrained among the immigrants on the Range--and a third child due to be born in a few months' time. Even Leon's nightmares had receded into the past, and he woke each day with a sense of hope and determination. Everett was pleased with the direction Leon's life had taken. He would see to it that Amelia May was safely wedded to James before the summer was over, but he knew that union, while it would be as solid a pairing as any, would face scrutiny from the townsfolk until enough time passed that no one would remember them as anything other than husband and wife. That would happen, he knew. Life was nothing if not a series of episodes where the urgency of the moment drifts into the past and a new concern fills up the space that an old one had once occupied. He had learned this after his experiences with Leona and Arabella. Time eroded grief and rage until all that was left was the faint smudge of distant loss that lingered in the fabric of one's life.

Leon would be fine. Amelia would be fine. That left Raymond.

Raymond had long been the most timid of his children, the boy who followed along and watched from a distance. True, he had been heroic during the fires of 1918, but he had seemed adrift since then, never finding a girl to take the place of the German lass he had fancied and never rising above the station of a simple delivery driver, despite many years at the brewery. It puzzled Everett that Raymond should be so taken with his current situation. He couldn't imagine sleeping all day in a musky attic, with a suspected pervert just steps away, and spending the nights mixing drinks for belligerent swells, hidden away in hotel rooms that had no beds, fooling no one as to their actual purpose. Everett didn't like the scene that had captivated his boy, but he had to admit that some of the joy that had been drained away from Raymond seemed to be trickling back into his soul. He was smiling more now and excited to be living in the capital city. Maybe he should accept Raymond's situation and settle for seeing the young man content in the moment. After all, he'd heard it said that contentment was the secret to the human condition. Happiness is fleeting but, with the proper mind-set, contentment could go the distance.

Everett was pretty sure that his own moments were ticking away and he knew he had to be ready. He met with a lawyer in St. Paul, one recommended by Ray's dandy friend Winky Maylamb, Esq., and laid out a plan for the disbursement of his estate. Then he called a family meeting, the first all-inclusive family gathering since the christening of Leon's first child at the Catholic church in Hibbing.

"You boys have a decision to make," Everett told his two sons over generous slices of Amelia's famous peach pie. "I'm ready to retire and I'm writing a will. I'm leaving the Hastings business and the cottage to Amelia and James. They're the ones that built that place, the garage and the bakery, so it's only right it go to them. That leaves the farm where you boys grew up. You can take it over or you can accept the offer James has made to buy you out."

James looked up and searched the faces of his one-time brothers. He wasn't great at reading expressions, but no one looked angry so that was a good start.

Everett continued. "He's got a plan and he can get the financing to buy you two out if that's what you want."

Leon and Ray looked at one another and raised their eyebrows in surprise. James must be doing pretty good if he thought he could pull off a loan. Leon put down his fork and wiped his mouth with a linen napkin that his sister had placed at his side. That linen napkin told him that money was no longer scarce. An old piece of torn calico had been their napkins when he last lived with his father. He looked squarely at James.

"You must be doing damned well, James. What's this plan Pa talks about?"

James diverted his eyes from Leon's pointed glare. His face flushed from his neck up to his ginger hair; his freckles disappeared into a sea of hot, red skin. He had always felt like a butterfly pinned to a display board whenever anyone tried to hold his gaze for more than a second or two.

"I'm thinking of building a dealership to sell automobiles and farm equipment, tractors and the like. I talked to the bank and they were mostly interested."

James related his idea to the brothers, unsure of their reactions. Leon nodded his understanding. He had to admit, it sounded like a promising plan. Raymond focused his attention on a hangnail, and he let Leon do the talking. He raised his head and focused on the discussion at hand when Leon tapped him on the shoulder.

"What do you think, Ray? About selling out to James?" Leon asked.

Ray bit the stubborn tag of skin from his right ring finger and watched the thin trickle of blood slowly seep into the ridge between his nail and the tip of his fourth digit. Leon knew that when stressed, Raymond snacked on his fingers to focus his pain onto a spot where he could chew it away in tiny bits. Gnawing on his hands did for Raymond what cigarettes did for Leon. He watched as his brother licked the blood with his tongue until all traces of red had disappeared.

"I don't want to be a farmer so I guess I'm for selling. Depends on the terms, though."

Ray turned his attention to James, who hesitated only a moment before he pulled a folded piece of yellow paper from his breast pocket.

He smoothed it down until it lay flat against the top of the big wooden table that had once been Leona's next-to-the-last resting place. He pushed the paper in front of Ray. He studied it for a time before he pushed it on to Leon, sitting across from him. Leon whistled at the figures.

"That sounds fair. At those terms, I don't want to be a farmer, either."

Leon extended his hand over the table to grab the pen lying next to James.

"Where do we sign?" he asked.

A slow smile replaced the blush on James's face. "Right here," he said.

When Leon finished, he passed the pen to Raymond and, just like that, Ray could afford his own place to stay in St. Paul.

14

St. Paul, Minnesota 1927

When the Commodore Hotel opened its elegant doors in 1920, it was largely considered to be one of the finest accommodations in the city of St. Paul. It was located in a quiet, residential part of town, an area of aristocratic families, and just a decent stroll from the Cathedral of St. Paul. The cathedral itself was a point of pride for the large Catholic populations in the surrounding neighborhoods who needed something they could lord over their haughty neighbors in the sister city of Minneapolis. Minneapolis may have the money, but St. Paul had both the cathedral and the capital. Church and state were officially separate in St. Paul. Even so, those two institutions had imbued the city with substantial pride, and the connections of the two entities flowed into the undercurrent of city politics just as surely as the currents of the Mississippi River connected Minneapolis with St. Paul. Most of the cops in the city were Catholic, and many of the barons of the underworld joined them each Sunday for a cleansing Mass and a little confession before starting with a fresh, clean slate on Monday morning.

As a residential hotel, the Commodore offered elegant living with a home-like spirit. The public areas were among the grandest in the Twin Cities; men in formal attire and women in diaphanous gowns, the colors of every variety of spring flower, feasted on delicacies from around the world in the opulent dining room. On summer evenings, the hum of mosquitoes competed with the music of a live band on the rooftop garden. The resonant tones of a trombone, the clash of a cymbal or the haunting vibrations of viola strings took flight from the roof and floated down onto the stylishly hat-covered heads of the approaching clientele. The entire scene was a study in refinement and grace.

But not always refinement and grace. Raymond had been told of the time, years earlier, when the young writer Scott Fitzgerald and his spit-fire wife drank and fought with such ferocity in their apartment that a boy had been employed to sit near their room for the express purpose of rapping his knuckles on their door whenever the combatants' verbal assaults grew too loud to ignore. Later, after the birth of their daughter, the Fitzgeralds brought their newborn home to the Commodore, where they would have had to toss the poor babe into a drawer if not for a friend who recognized that a child might need a bed, some diapers and an item or two of clothing just to survive its first weeks of life. While her parents celebrated the child's arrival in their usual style, with a bottle of gin and whatever they could find to pour it into, this friend set up a nursery for the young parents and deposited little Scotty into a white crib, complete with a soft blanket to throw over her tiny back.

The antics of the Fitzgeralds were obvious because of the fame his books had brought upon them, but they were far from the only residents of the hotel who flaunted the strict rules of formal society. Like all good hotels almost everywhere in the United States during the 1920s, the Commodore recognized that to be competitive, it must give the customer what it wanted. And, usually, that meant alcoholic beverages. Society may well be more civil with the prohibition of spirits, but it was certainly less civilized. At least, that was the opinion of many of

Raymond's clients, and he had to agree. His hours spent supervising the waitstaff in the dining room, a space where strong coffee was about as potent a drink as one could get, were a slog of uneventful plate shuffling for Raymond. He lived for the after-hours work. He would don a fresh jacket, slick back his hair and spend the night mixing drinks for the young and adventurous movers and shakers in town. Cops backslapped with underworld kingpins, and daring girls who longed to be flappers copied the mannerisms of women more experienced in the fine arts of seduction. All the bedrocks of propriety were softened into a state of pliability by soaking them in alcohol.

In the spring of 1927, the entire state of Minnesota was ebullient at the prospect of being the home of the young man who would make the first solo flight across the Atlantic Ocean, a body of water that the vast majority of the state's residents had never seen, let alone crossed. Those who had crossed the Atlantic's depths had likely done so in the pursuit of war.

"You think that Lindbergh fellow can do it?" Leon asked his brother over the phone from his insurance agency office that he operated out of his home in Hibbing. In the background, Raymond could hear pots and pans banging in the distant kitchen and the high-pitched voices of little children berating one another over whose turn it was to use the wooden spoon on the skillet bottom.

"Give it here! Give it here!" transported Raymond back twenty years to the farm in Hastings, his mother still alive and vibrant, tapping out a patriotic beat on the metal washtub just to entertain her younger son.

"You try, Ray-Ray. Just like this. Rat-a-tat, boom, boom. Rat-a-tat, boom, boom," she sang to him as she tapped her washtub with a couple of old butter knives. Always wary of failure, Raymond shook off his mother's encouragement, then worked at the beat with two sticks in the privacy of his room until he felt secure enough to show his mother. He never forgot her smile when he displayed for her his little accomplishment. He could picture Rosella smiling now at her brood up in Hibbing. That illusion was shattered when Ray heard her scream something at them in Italian. The whines turned to cries in no time flat.

"Hold on, Ray," his brother said into the phone. "I gotta close this door."

Ray could hear the earpiece being dropped to the table in Leon's office and the scrape of a chair against the hardwood floor before the voices of the children and their ruffled mother disappeared from the background.

"That's better," Leon proclaimed when he returned to their conversation. "Rosella is about five months gone now. That's about the time she loses her patience with the children she already has. It's like she has to transfer her affection to the one that's coming in order to make it grow. But, I'm not worried. Once they get here, she treats them all the same."

Leon laughed then. A happy laugh devoid of cynicism. Rosella had been a magic balm that had neutralized the bitterness in Leon's heart. He rarely drank anything more potent than wine, and she tamed the rage that had led him to desperation. Now he sipped a nice red, smoked his usual two packs a day and took his comfort only from the beautiful, ripe body of his wife. He had also converted from atheism to Catholicism. Raymond thought that those crackers they give people at Mass must be laced with something to cause such a change in his brother. Or, maybe the Roman Church was the one true religion. It had certainly worked a miracle on Leon.

"I hope he makes it. It would be nice for Minnesota to be the center of the world for a few minutes. It would be nice to be known for the flight of something besides mosquitoes," Ray finally responded to Leon's question about the young aviator, and he could hear Leon chuckle his agreement.

"Yeah. That would be nice."

Raymond got down to the business of his long-distance call. He cleared his throat. "Listen. Leon. The reason I called is Pa's getting weaker by the day. He can't walk out to the mailbox without having to rest at the halfway point and we're just talking about a hundred feet from the house to the street. James had to set a bench on the lawn to break the trip up for him. He's yellow in the eyes and blue in the lips all the time now. I think you ought to come down to see him. Maybe say good-bye."

For a few moments neither made a sound. In the silence, Raymond visualized his brother, sitting at his desk, shirtsleeves rolled up just below his elbows, a cigarette smoldering from the first two fingers of his left hand, his right hand rubbing consternation into his handsome, brooding face. Finally, Leon spoke.

"You think he's pretty bad, huh? What's the doctor say?"

Leon had understood that his father was losing a bit of ground every day, but he had dismissed his decline as early incremental steps that would end at a point far in the distance, not just around the corner.

"What doctor?" Ray snorted. "Pa hasn't been to a doctor since old Becker closed his practice and moved out of state. He says his doctor is in Florida and that's too far to drive."

Leon laughed a weary chuckle. "Yeah. That sounds like Pa. Listen, Ray. I can't make it down right now. I don't want to leave Rosella alone with the kids and it's too far in the car to bring her with me. Just keep me posted, okay?"

Raymond considered his brother's situation. Leon had always worried that his mother's fate, brought about by the birth of Amelia, might lie dormant in his reproductive cells, infecting Rosella with a madness triggered by the fertilization of an egg. He vowed to be there always for his wife, to share the burdens of their children as equally as he could. He would not leave his new life to save anyone in his old one, and Raymond grudgingly understood. If he ever had children, he might feel the same way. Still, he knew Pa would be heartened by a visit from Leon.

"I understand you wanting to be there for Rosella but can't her folks watch out for her for a few days?" Ray asked.

He heard a lungful sigh greet him through the phone.

"Normally, that would be the plan but Rosella's grandfather had a powerful bellyache last week and by the time the doctor made it over to the house, he was on death's door. The doctor panicked, said they had to open him up right away and get out his appendix. Said he could drop dead like Houdini if they didn't operate then and there. They ended up using the kitchen table to lay him out for surgery but the old bastard weighs about three hundred pounds and he broke off the legs as soon as they got him on it. Ended up doing surgery on the floor. He's recovering but Rosella's folks have their hands full right now. Don't need three more kids and a cranky daughter to add to the mess."

Another sigh explained it all to Raymond. Leon had his hands full, too.

"Okay. I'll let you know if there's any changes with Pa. You take care and tell Rosella I said, 'Happy Easter' and all that."

Leon laughed on the other end. "The happiest thing about Easter is no more daily fish. Catholics sure have a lot of rules."

It was Saturday evening on May 21, 1927, while Raymond supervised the dining room at the luxurious Commodore Hotel, that he received a phone call from his sister. The room was in high spirits; Lindbergh, the man of the hour. In between bites of filet mignon and lobster thermidor, talk of his successful flight was on everyone's lips. Surreptitious pours of a clear, high-proof liquor spiked water glasses at nearly every table. America had something to celebrate, and Minnesota had a connection to it all. Minnesota had released its dove into the air, and it had flown all the way to France. A little whooping it up was definitely in order.

"Raymond? Is that you?" Amelia's voice was soft and subdued. Ray could tell from her affect that something was troubling her.

"What's up, Sis? I'm awful busy tonight. We're thick here with folks toasting the Lindbergh flight. Can it wait an hour or so?"

Raymond knew it couldn't wait another minute when Amelia dissolved into tears.

"Amelia! Calm down. Tell me what's wrong. Are you okay?"

Amelia seldom cried. The last time he had seen her cry was when she told him that old Brownie had died. The thought sent a chill down his spine.

"It's Pa, isn't it?"

Rather than answer her brother, Amelia let out a plaintive moan. In the middle of the sobs, Raymond heard the phone bang around before the voice of his brother-in-law James spoke.

"Raymond. Your Pa died. You better come home."

That was all the information James gave, but it was also all that Ray needed to determine what he had to do. He removed his waiter's jacket and folded it over his arm, his head full of questions about his father's death. He wondered, why hadn't they called him sooner? He walked in a daze to the manager's office and knocked softly on the closed door.

"Sir?"

He knocked again.

"Sir, it's Ray Saxby. I have to leave, sir. My pa just died."

The door opened, and a distinguished middle-aged man reached to take the jacket from Ray.

"Sorry to hear such sad news on such a happy day, Raymond. You go on and attend to your family. Call when you have an idea when you'll be back. You will be back, will you not?"

Ray nodded his head. "I'll be back, Mr. Berglund. I'll be back as soon as I can."

Only an hour had passed since Amelia's call to the Commodore when Raymond entered the bedroom where Everett had died. His father was still in his chair, a bemused look frozen on his face and his eyes closed for all but a tiny sliver through which Ray could see the hazel peeking out under his surprisingly thick lashes. He looked relaxed. Peaceful. Engaged in wherever he had gone.

Everett had been following the news of Lindbergh's impending flight for weeks. He had turned on the wireless religiously to follow the boy's progress from San Diego to Saint Louis and then to New York, from where he would begin the daring transatlantic journey all on his own. Everett marveled at what he had seen in his own lifetime. When he was a boy, if anyone were pixelated enough to dream of flying in the sky in anything other than a basket under a hot air balloon, he would have found himself the guest of a mental asylum. As a very young man, he had never entertained the idea that horses could be replaced by machines or that he would be able to tune into voices from New York on a little box like the one he had at his side right now, listening to the latest reports of the aeronautical feat. They had been exciting times, those Everett had experienced. He had witnessed mankind move from a manual to a mechanized existence, and he never once wished to return to the simpler life of hard labor and the smell of horses in the streets. His only regret was that he wouldn't be around to see what came next.

Each breath he drew was a struggle that tasked his aching ribs. Exhaling was equally tortuous. He pursed his lips to force the foul air from his lungs, and he felt the rattle deep within his chest remind him that the moments he had left were growing scant and increasingly painful. Amelia checked on him frequently. She brought him tea that he wouldn't drink and whiskey that he couldn't drink. She left fat slices of carrot cake by his side and cups of custard when he rejected the cake. It was no use. He knew he had eaten his last meal and sipped his last drops of whiskey. He sighed and settled himself into the old lounge chair next to the wireless and let his mind fly away with the boy in the plane. Over the rough seas, he soared; he flew above the clouds and into the glorious light of the finest day he had ever experienced. He was temporarily blinded by the radiance of the sun's light, and his skin was licked by fiery rays that he could feel inexplicably healing his tattered body. His breaths became easier. Into the light, a golden ladder emerged from above and he was compelled to ascend its rungs. Hand over hand and foot after foot, Everett climbed higher. The years fell away with each step until he could see his young, strong hands grasp the top of the final rung. Waiting for him in a golden mist was his dear Leona. Her face lit up when she saw her dash-fire man, climbing to her. Her smile outshone the light that surrounded her beautiful, revitalized body. Behind her, once again her hardscrabble self, was his mother, urging him to the finish line with her yellow potholders on her hands.

* * *

The tides of eternity that had swept Everett's soul into the great beyond also washed a new babe onto life's shores. Daisy Everetta Blume was born on September 16, 1928. The six-pound package of wrinkly, pink skin and boundless lung capacity entered the world on a gush of blood from a ruptured placenta that almost ended her life before it began. While her mother's pale body fought to survive its own ordeal, the newborn bellowed her complaints about the indignity of the situation loudly and frequently. The child's father, who always prided himself on his ability to fix pretty much anything, was powerless to quiet the infant or rally his spent wife. James had never been one to agonize unduly over the emotional state of anyone, himself included, but he found he was traumatized by the infant's cries. His relief was palpable whenever a nurse took the child from his stiff arms and whisked her back to the nursery.

"She seems so mad all the time," James told Amelia when she had finally recovered enough to care what anyone had to say. "Why is she so mad?"

Amelia focused a weary smile on her beloved husband.

"Oh, James. She's just telling us what her needs are. All babies fuss a lot at first. It will get better. You'll see."

She watched her husband fold the child into his arm and registered the look of love and trepidation on his face. He pushed back the blanket from the top of the baby's head and stroked her downy hair with his cupped hand.

"She looks a little like me," he said, and a faint smile rearranged his expression. "She has red hair, like me." She did, and it stayed red like her father's until a half dozen decades replaced the golden stands with the palest silver.

"But she's beautiful like you," he told his wife.

James never said much but, more often than not, his few words touched Amelia more deeply than a sonnet. When Baby Blume was at last ensconced in a yellow nursery that had been Everett's room at the cottage, she was surrounded by walls of painted daisies that echoed her name, and she slept in the little cradle that Great-Granddaddy Earl had cobbled together when Everett had been a babe. For now, all was right with her world.

* * *

Henry Ford's ubiquitous automobile dominated the burgeoning road-ways of the nineteen twenties. Grateful Minnesotans with slightly more than average means were able to escape some of the dreariest of winter weather in places as far flung as Florida or California. Even Missouri offered temporary respite if one were content with modest gains in the daily temperatures of January or February. The automobile also made escape to Minnesota, and St. Paul specifically, possible for a high-profile subset of the American population. Thanks to a unique detente between the St. Paul Police Department and the denizens of America's underworld, the saintly city became a playground of sorts for the crim-inal elements looking for a place to cool their heels when the heat became too intense in their home cities to the east. Under the O'Connor system, named for the chief of police who initiated the policy, swearing to commit no crimes within the city limits meant gang-sters were free to roam the streets of St. Paul with carefree abandon.

The corruption was not limited to police officials on the take. Local politicians, aldermen and grand juries, even prosecutors, were paid nicely to look the other way when syndicate bosses breezed into town for a little rest and relaxation from the pressures of operating their far-flung enterprises. Unofficial liaisons, criminals of a respectable sort, coordinated the agreements between the police and the violence-prone visitors. Play by the rules, and safety from harassment by the authori-ties was guaranteed.

Early in the enactment of the O'Connor system, the coordinator between authorities and the underworld was Dapper Dan Hogan. Dapper Dan was the St. Paul man. His counterpoint in Minneapolis was Big Ed Morgan, who oversaw bootlegging, gambling and prostitu-tion in the upriver metropolis. Irishmen both, they had a respectable understanding of their territories, like antagonistic brothers staying on opposite sides of the table during a contentious family gathering. Hogan acted as more than a quasi-social director for the underworld. He was also active in facilitating the laundering of cash, bonds or stolen securities that showed up in St. Paul from heists that occurred all over the country. From his Green Lantern nightclub on Wabasha Street, Hogan enforced a legal system that ignored the law. He was protected by the powers that be but not from rival gangs. Eventually his deeds resulted in a well-placed car bomb, presumed to be a payback from a disgruntled foe, that ended his life in 1928. But the system he had supported lived on in the personage of Leon Gleckman, a local underworld giant and the unofficial mayor of St. Paul. "If it ain't broke, don't fix it," Gleckman reasoned when he thought about the O'Connor arrangement, and so it continued after the demise of Dapper Dan Hogan.

This was the world that Raymond navigated nightly. He had served both men in his hospitality capacity at the Commodore Hotel. If one wanted to be seen, one celebrated at the casinos and nightclubs operated by the gangsters: among them the Green Lantern, the Hollyhocks Casino, the Castle Royal. In those establishments, the excitement ran high. Good booze and great music from the likes of Harry James and Cab Calloway made the nightclubs de rigor for a good time. If you wanted to get business done over a good steak and a quiet backroom drink, the Commodore was the place to go. More and more, the words of Winky Maylamb squirmed around in Ray's head like a song he couldn't shake. "Remember, Raymond. You're a fly on the wall. But flies can't talk and neither should you." Raymond embraced this philosophy as a survival technique. As he stood at a bar, mixing all manner of drinks for customers from all walks of life, he made it a point to disappear into the woodwork, and his efforts paid off. Deals between corrupt city officials or underworld czars were made right under Ray's nose and over the bourbon and gin he shook in his cocktail shaker. He became no more threatening to his customers than the pictures on the walls. He heard but did not listen; he looked but did not see and, in doing so, was privy to misdeeds of every kind. He witnessed bribes, adultery, and plans for illegal events that he quickly dismissed from his mind through the sieve of his compromised conscience. Had he been inclined to divulge what he knew, he had no confidence that any plans would be disrupted by his disclosures, other than his own. Who does one report to when everyone is suspect? He collected secrets the way other men collected rare coins, and he kept them safely locked away in his mind. He'd been doing that since he was a kid, and the vault was getting more crowded everyday.

"We're all going dancing at the Boulevards when we get off Wednesday evening. You should come with us."

The invitation surprised Ray. At twenty-eight, he was considered an elder statesman by the waitstaff and housekeepers employed at the Commodore. And he wasn't much for dancing. The only dancing he had done had been a few quiet waltzes around the scarred up floor in Mathilda's kitchen a full decade ago--those awkward interludes and his memorable spins with the ambiguous Violet. With the exception of the Black Bottom, he had no idea how to do the frantic moves of the current dance crazes. To him, Charleston was still a city back east someplace. But the dimpled face of Bridget, and the soft brogue of her Irish accent, reeled him in.

"You'll be there, for sure?" Ray asked.

The tiny girl with the divots in her rosy cheeks cocked her head. "Would I be asking you if I planned to stay away?"

The girl was barely nineteen, a child still in his mind but quickly approaching old maid status among her peers. Raymond Saxby looked like a lord to her in his smartly cut maitre d' jacket. And so tall! If she married such a man her children might literally rise above the familial curse of short stature. She gave him her most beckoning smile.

"Do come. Even if you don't want to dance, we can sit and watch the fun."

Raymond smiled back and nodded. "Okay. I'll do my best to make it," he told her.

When he actually showed up, tapping her on the shoulder from behind as she sat with her housekeeper friends, she looked up from her diminutive four feet, ten inches into his far-away eyes and squealed with delight. "Mr. Saxby! You came after all!"

Raymond had to fold his six foot, two inch frame nearly in half to whisper in Bridget's ear. "I'm a man of my word. If I say I'll try to make it, I try. And here I am."

He smiled down on her marcelled hair and noticed that she was wearing three-inch platform heels that topped her out over five feet tall. She looked more mature, almost an adult, in her dropped waist dress with faux pearls wrapped around her neck. Her dimples bracketed a rosebud mouth, painted cherry red. When she smiled, the dimples bounced out on her cheeks and her small white teeth glowed in happiness at him.

"Well," she said to him, "I'm really happy you came along. You're the most handsome fellow here."

Since the crushing loss of Mathilda, Ray had spent little time cultivating relationships with the fairer sex. The women he loved seemed to disappear with regularity. His mother, Inka, Mathilda...all gone. Even Grandma, but that loss was to be expected. Love, he decided, did not equate to happy ever after. In his experience, it was pain that stuck around and he'd had enough of that to last a lifetime. He had decided to attend the gathering at the dance hall not for the possibility of love, or a sexual interlude, but because he had a nagging need to be in a situation where he could genuinely interact with his fellow human beings. He wanted to be part of the action, not only an observant nonentity with no more substance than a shadow. He wanted to be served a drink as if he were somebody, too.

"Can I get you a drink, Miss Callahan?"

There were those dimples again. "Gin fizz?" she said to him.

Ray nodded. "Gin fizz coming up, miss. You stay right here and I'll be back in a flash."

At the bar, where no official liquor was provided, everything was available. Raymond ordered the gin drink for Bridget and watched the bartender prepare the drink in what Ray considered to be a slap-dash way. He noted how the man allowed drips of gin and syrup to slide down the side of the glass, something that he would never tolerate from a server under his supervision at the Commodore. For himself, he asked for a neat Scotch, and for that he was given a short glass with an amber fluid inside that promised the taste of soot from someplace far removed from the Scottish Highlands.

Bridget was waiting for him just where he had left her, a girlfriend from the Commodore staff chatting with her over the din of the dance band.

"Thank you, Mr. Saxby," Bridget told him.

He watched her rosebud lips suck a few drops of the drink into her mouth. When she swallowed, she said to him, "Do you know Martha?" indicating the girl on her right.

Ray didn't know her and didn't really care if he ever did. He resented that Martha was diverting Bridget's focus from him. Ray smiled at the girl and then smiled more brightly when a young fellow took Martha by the arm and swung her onto the dance floor.

"Come on, Marnie. Let's cut a rug," the fellow pronounced, and once again, Ray had Bridget's undivided attention.

Over so-so liquor and a great band, Ray listened to Bridget tell him the story of her life. Her parents had brought her and her three older siblings from Ireland in 1914, when she was only four. Five more children had been born since they arrived in Minnesota, and her father had somehow secured a good job with the railroad. Her older brother was a cop in Minneapolis, and one of her sisters had just welcomed twin boys whom she called Mutt and Jeff. One was actually named Jeffery and poor little Mutt had never been called by his official name of Randall since the day of his christening. Bridget's mother took in laundry to help make ends meet, and Bridget's younger siblings were in various stages of school, although one, a rangy boy of twelve, was currently learning some manners in a facility for wayward youths. The family agreed that this brother might end up being their sacrifice to a life of crime, American style.

Ray nodded along with her story. He thought it a fairly typical immigrant tale, but the endless dance of the dimples on her cheeks was mesmerizing. The broader the girl's smile, the deeper the indentations became. When she laughed, the pockets in her flesh grew into bottomless wells that Raymond imagined diving into to bathe with her in her youthful joy. Not even the tale of the naughty brother wiped the fun from her face.

"How's your drink? Ready for another?" he asked her. His attentiveness was rewarded with another big grin. She extended the empty glass to Ray.

"That would be lovely, Mr. Saxby."

Ray took her glass and started for the bar when he turned to tell her, "Now that we know all about each other, please call me Ray."

Bridget looked up at Raymond, standing tall over her, and she batted her black, smudged eyes at him. "That would be lovely, Ray."

On his way to order the drinks, Ray passed a couple of fellows he thought he had seen before at the Commodore. The men appeared to be in their thirties; the suits and shoes the men wore were signboards advertising unsavory connections. Like a uniform announcing their team, both men sported spectator shoes, off-white fedoras and gray chalk-stripe suits. The only differences were their respective sizes and the colors of grosgrain ribbons that circled the brims of their hats. And, unexplained by the temperate fall weather, both men had lightweight overcoats hanging from their shoulders. They were thugs, alright.

That was the fun of St. Paul under the O'Connor system. A night out offered a smorgasbord of edgy diversions. Few folks considered their evenings complete without a gangster story to report the next day. Dillinger was known to frequent the Boulevards of Paris. So did Dutch Schultz. Neither of the men Ray had noticed were famous or notorious. These were low-level, criminal journeymen, working their way up in the underworld hierarchy.

The bar was crowded. Ray had to wait his turn behind a line of customers. Unlike some places, there was no urgency to down drinks before the cops raided the scene. In St. Paul, the cops might be in line at the illicit bar along with everyone else. Raymond relaxed into the realization that he was having a good time. He enjoyed Bridget's company, and it buoyed his spirits to think she found him handsome. Leon had always been the handsome one. Knowing the girl felt that way about him caused Ray to hold himself taller, prouder. He asserted his presence in the room with an attitude he wore on his face. "I'm a man, not a fly," he told himself. He passed the time in line watching a couple dance, trying to memorize the steps they took. His eyes roamed over the crowd, and he noticed the two men he had spotted earlier fiddling with the grate over a floor vent. One of the men bent and banged the grate into its frame. Ray gave the displaced grate no thought other than it must have popped out of place from the vibrations of the dancers and the fellow was simply replacing it in the floor. Ray found himself staring at the men when they both looked at their watches, then back down at the grate, and finally at the nearest exit door. When the men raised their heads to survey the room, they looked directly into Raymond's observant glare and the anger that shot from their faces nearly set Ray back on his heels. They kept Raymond in their sights as they hurried to the exit. Just before backing out of the huge club, the shorter fellow pointed his finger at Raymond, signing the firing of a weapon into Ray's head. Raymond quickly concluded that the manipulation of the floor grate might not have been the work of a good Samaritan. Whatever those men were doing, the results were likely not going to be pleasant.

Raymond gave up his place in line at the bar and quickly went to the table where Bridget was laughing with her friends.

"I got a feeling we should all get out of here," he told the little group of giggling girls.

"Ooh, he wants all of us," one tipsy miss said, causing the entire table to erupt in laughter.

Another inebriated girl waved her arms and jumped up and down. "Me first!" she cried. Fortunately, Raymond was well versed in drunken behavior.

"Listen to me, ladies. I'm dead serious. A couple of obvious crooks were messing with the floor grate and casing the room. I don't like the looks of the situation. We should move on. Get out of here before something happens."

Raymond's words sobered the girls, but only by a couple of degrees. Bridget fixed Ray with the appreciative gaze of one who has met the prince who would save her from an unsavory world.

"Mr. Saxby is a man of experience," she advised her friends. "If he thinks we should go then I agree and I think you should, too."

The tipsy trio with her began to gather their things. Martha stumbled when she caught her foot on a table leg and Raymond put his hand on the small of her back to steady her. She smiled at him in a way that said she liked his touch. He met her smile with an expression of deep concern.

"Hurry up. Head for the door right now," he said to his gaggle of girls.

A saying he had encountered about herding chickens came to Ray's mind. Getting these women to move forward in a coordinated fashion was a challenge, but with some well-placed pushing on their backs, Ray had them all out the door when a brutal shove of concussive energy propelled his little group onto the courtyard outside.

Bridget dropped to her knees and cried out like the child she was.

"Oh my God, oh my God," she screamed.

Ray threw his body over hers and the weight of him quieted the distraught girl. Next to him, Martha pushed herself to a sitting position and surveyed the damage. She swiped a finger across her lower leg and raged when it came back red with blood.

"Fookin' idjots!" she railed.

Concerned, Raymond turned to appraise her injuries. "Are you okay?" he asked the young woman. He could see the blood dribbling from her calf onto the sidewalk below.

"Fookers ruined me stockings!" Martha moaned, "Ruined me brand new stockings!"

Ray figured her injuries must be minor if her stockings were her main reason for distress. He turned his attention to Bridget. She lay trembling beneath him, the way old Brownie had when the thunder of a summer storm had rattled his nerves.

"You're fine, Bridget," he assured her. "We got out in time. All your friends are okay, too. Do you think you can walk?" he asked the terrified girl.

She looked up at him and nodded. Definitely sober now, his group of young women gladly followed him to the street, where throngs of people loitered about in a daze.

"Anybody hurt bad?" inquired a man who, moments before, had been gambling with a stack of poker chips.

He reached into his pocket and clipped a policeman's badge to his lapel and assumed his public role as protector of the peace. He nodded in satisfaction when everyone he encountered denied serious injuries. When at last a final couple emerged from the building in a cloud of dust and smoke, clutching their drinks in their hands, the hoard of law enforcement personnel who had been surreptitiously present when the blast occurred declared the emergency over.

"Go on home, folks. Nothing more for you here tonight," the man with the shiny badge told the crowd.

Before the patrons could disperse, the owner of the club barged through the door at the corner of Lexington and University and hollered at the top of his lungs, "Come on back tomorrow, folks. First drink will be on the house!"

A cheer went up from the revelers. Only in St. Paul could a bombing be regarded as a precursor to a good time.

The next day, newspapers reported on the bombing at the Boulevards of Paris nightclub. The articles claimed that very little damage had been done to the building and injuries to patrons had been minor. Its owner had constructed the club from cement blocks, as if anticipating such an occurrence could happen as a natural part of doing a certain type of business. True to the owner's word, the club reopened in no time and free drinks were enjoyed by an even bigger turnout of thrill seekers than had been blown out its doors the night before.

Subsequent news reports theorized all manner of explanations for the bombing. No one knew who had planted the bomb or why. Some proposed that the act was a warning to the club's owner, John Lane, from either John Dillinger or Dutch Schultz, two crime bosses who were known to frequent the club and resented that it operated by Lane's rules, not their own. Some reported that the blast was simply the work of disgruntled partiers who had been reprimanded by Lane for their rowdy behavior. No one specific was ever accused of the crime, and the element of danger only heightened the experience of dancing at the Boulevards.

Raymond crumpled the Pioneer Press and shoved it into the trash can next to the bar. He wondered if he should call the paper, tell them what he knew. If given a chance, he bet he would be able to pick out those low-life bastards from mug shots. He had a hard time believing he was the only one whose suspicions had been roused by the behavior of the two men in the club that night. Whenever he reached for the phone, Winky's admonishment about that damn fly on the wall buzzed in his head. "Why court trouble?" he thought, placing the earpiece back in its cradle on the phone.

15

St. Paul, October 1995

I spent the blissful summer of 1995 in a flurry of nesting activities. I finally had a home that mirrored the image of the lifestyle I had always imagined for myself: a simple yet sturdy house with ample room and an original 1920s vibe. Unlike many of the houses of the era, my home was a study in unrestored grace. All the woodwork was intact in its lacquered beauty. Large oak arches stood watch over the entry to each room. When visitors would walk through the kitchen and shake their heads at the unremodeled space, asking when I planned to do "work" on the kitchen, I would laugh and tell them that I wouldn't think of changing something so perfect. The sink unit under the window to the side yard was white enameled steel. In the scattered pox of use that marred its surface, a genteel amount of rust told the stories of the families that came before. Tiffany and Stella, the unhappy couple that preceded me, had been smart enough to leave well enough alone. The clawfoot tub in the upstairs bathroom, surrounded by pink and black tile, became a nightly refuge that soothed my weary muscles after weekdays at the clinic or weekends spent wrangling small home improvement projects on my own. In one feat of engineering, I used a waterski vest as a harness to suspend myself out of the second story windows to paint the shutters outside my bedroom. I had more bravado than money or sense in those days and entertained my new neighbors with my daring work-arounds. I painted and patched, sanded and stained. When he could, Dwight would offer his help for projects beyond my expertise--things like plumbing or wiring or jobs that required more than two hands to complete. I scoured thrift stores and low-end antique malls for just the right period-appropriate furnishings and accessories to give the space the ambiance I craved. When most of my contemporaries were slapping mauve and baby blue on every surface of their homes, I favored the soft golds and muted greens of another era. By the time fall came, I was ready to hunker down for the winter in a spot that felt one hundred percent me. I was pretty damned pleased with myself and what I had achieved with almost no money or help.

"It looks great in here." Dwight wandered through the rooms giving my work an appreciative nod. "I can tell you're no carpenter, though."

He tapped his toe against an imperfectly mitred corner of base-board and gave me a look of sympathy.

"Sorry I couldn't have been around more to help you but you know how it is with dad and all."

Yes, after several years, I was well aware of Dwight's obligations. I respected his devotion to his father and his civic engagement, but I had needs, too. At least all the time I spent doing projects on my own had led me to own an impressive array of power tools. Tiffany would have been envious of my tool belt.

"I was wondering," I began. "I have things squared away now and I thought it might be nice for you to bring your dad over for dinner one night. Well, afternoon, really. I know how early he eats."

As usual, Dwight got that stricken look in his eyes that I saw when-ever I suggested anything that smacked of commitment. He rocked his head up and down and fiddled with the condensation on the outside of his glass of pop. Back in California, I had called soft drinks "soda" but had adopted the local vernacular as time went on. He used his little finger to draw arrows in the dew that developed on the glass from the humid, Indian summer day. One look at the sky told of an impending storm. Gray-green clouds accumulated on the horizon, and the air was thick with moisture. Our clothes were stuck to our bodies by a glue of sweat.

"Okay. Sure. We could probably find a time for that. It would be nice," he finally conceded.

Dwight and his father arrived at my house at 4:30 on a Friday afternoon. Since I moved to the new house, I had essentially been an empty nester as my boys had left home for college. Dwight and I had been spending our alone time christening the new rooms with an abandon that came from knowing we were free from the potential interruptions of my teenage sons. Consequently, it had been several weeks since I had seen Raymond Saxby and I was alarmed at how frail he had become in such a short time.

My house was raised from the ground by a few substantial concrete steps. It might as well have been as high as a Mayan Temple as far as Mr. Saxby was concerned. Dwight struggled to help his father up the first step, and from my perch at the door, I could see that nursing intervention was needed. I hustled down to the sidewalk to assess the situation and tried to come up with a plan to get the old gentleman into the house.

"Hey there, Mr. Saxby," I greeted him.

He fixed me with his watery blue eyes and gave me a lackluster salute with the fingers on his right hand.

"We've got to get you up to the house because I made smothered chicken with mashed potatoes for your dinner."

He smiled and held onto the railing to keep from falling down.

"Sounds good," he said to me.

I looked around frantically for some way to get him up the steps.

"I'll just pick him up," Dwight told me, but that seemed dangerous, carrying the old boy up the steps in his arms.

"No. Hang on. I have an idea," I replied.

I ran to the basement and pulled out one of the folding camp chairs my sons used for card games with their friends. I brought it up and dusted the grime from its seat.

"Let's have him sit in this and we can both lift him up the steps," I instructed.

Mr. Saxby plopped himself onto the seat, and Dwight and I had him at the kitchen table before he knew what hit him. From his nylon throne, he took in the magnificence that was my new house.

"You got a nice place here," the old fellow told me. "There was a time, years ago, when I used to come out this way, to Phalen, all the time. Me and Dolores. Long before she was in that home at the end."

A melancholy sigh escaped his lips, and he rubbed his nose with his bony hands. He looked at his son.

"Do you remember? Coming to visit Linda at Gillette?"

Dwight didn't answer right away. He finished pouring himself a Canadian Club, which he topped off with some Sprite. "No Seven-Up?" he asked me. I wagged my head no.

"I was pretty young, Dad. I just remember feeding the ducks at Lake Phalen afterwards."

In all my time with Dwight, I had heard very little mention of his younger sisters; one had died, one lived in Oregon, and one was no longer on speaking terms with her brother. I never questioned the status of these relationships because my own family had its share of awkward connections. Dwight and I had a "don't ask, don't tell" kind of unspoken agreement where family was concerned.

"She was only three," Raymond Saxby said in a voice so soft I almost missed his words. "Only three," he said again.

His eyes were always watery now; the lower lids were no longer able to recycle his tears so they flowed in little rivulets down his crinkly cheeks. It was impossible to tell if his tears were emotional markers or just spillage from the pools that formed naturally under his eyes.

"Was Linda your daughter?" I asked him. Both he and Dwight nodded.

"How long was she at Gillette?" I asked the old gentleman. He looked up at me.

"Months and months," he said. "She was in one of them iron lung things for the longest time. She had the polio. I wanted to take her to Sister Kenny but we couldn't get her a spot over there at the institute in Minneapolis. She was just three. Only a baby when she died."

A big, fat tear slowly leaked from his lower lid and snaked a trail all the way to his chest, where it was absorbed by the neckband of his dingy, gray tee shirt. I handed him a paper napkin. He mopped the moisture from his face and neck, then blew his nose with surprising force.

"Thank you," he said.

"You and Ma never let me go in to see her, remember?" Dwight asked his father. "All I remember about that time was that I couldn't do anything. Couldn't go swimming. Couldn't go to Sunday school. Couldn't go to a friend's house. Couldn't do anything but feed those damn ducks at the lake."

Raymond gave his son a tolerant smile. "Friends didn't want you around. We were a marked family for a while. Can't blame folks for trying to protect their kids. It was a terrible thing, that polio."

He looked at me as if he'd never met me before.

"How about you, young lady? You feed your kids those sugar cubes?"

I had forgotten all about the sugar cubes. My children had been immunized by injection, but rather than confuse him I told him, "You betcha. Got to keep our kids healthy."

I served dinner on the dishware I had purchased at the thrift store while I had awaited the closing on the house. The delicate green of the pattern that matched my kitchen cabinets disappeared under a load of mashed potatoes and chicken breast, smothered in onions and white gravy. A side of overcooked green beans added a bit of color and in place of a salad, I served applesauce. Everything on the plate was carefully chosen to slide right down with a minimum of chewing.

"You like it out here?" Raymond asked me. "Better than out in White Bear?"

My mouth was full so I nodded. I took a swallow of ice water to hasten the food on its journey south.

"I like that it's so close to work. If my car acts up, I can walk from here. And, I like that I can afford so much more house in this part of town," I told him.

"It's an immigrant neighborhood. That's why."

Dwight liked my house, but he wasn't crazy about the mixed ethnicity of my neighbors. I smiled at him and nodded again.

"Yep!" I said. "That's another reason why I like it. Diversity."

Dwight laughed out loud. "Diversity's just another word for rundown."

I held my temper in check. I considered my neighborhood to be a fine example of genteel shabbiness, and I liked it just the way it was. Raymond must have liked it too because he was bobbing his head up and down in agreement.

"There used to be these little cabins out here. Tents, really. Back in the twenties, I spent ten days hiding out from the mob in one of those little places. It was almost like a vacation."

Dwight and I raised our eyebrows at each other. This sounded interesting.

"Christ, Dad! You never told me that story," Dwight blurted at his father.

"You never asked me about those times," replied Mr. Saxby.

"Now you have to tell us," I encouraged him. "I think I'll make us some coffee."

I wanted to keep him awake until the end of what promised to be an intriguing tale.

St. Paul, Minnesota 1929

The articles about the explosion at the Boulevards of Paris quickly faded from the front pages of the newspapers. By the end of September, the only mention was on page thirteen, a blurb stating that no new clues had been uncovered to help pin down a suspect for the brazen act of vandalism. Raymond breathed a sigh of relief. The farther back in the paper the event migrated, the less he worried about what he had seen or if he had a duty to tell what he knew. Not that he knew anything for sure, he told himself.

Bridget, too, had recovered from the shock of that night, and the event became more catastrophic for her with each retelling.

"If Mr. Saxby hadn't been there to save us, I'm sure we'd have all been killed. Or maimed at the very least."

She told the story to her family, who promptly invited the heroic Mr. Saxby to supper to thank him for saving their daughter. She told the story to seatmates on the streetcar or to hotel guests waiting for clean sheets to be applied to their beds. She recounted the event to the neighbors in her building. She told her story to anyone who would listen. In the early tellings, she relayed a more or less accurate version of the events. But as time wore on, the story evolved. Dust became heaps of rubble and scraped skin became body parts littered about the room. Raymond Saxby hadn't just covered her body with his own to protect her from falling debris, he brought her back from the brink of death with the very breath from his lungs. She made it known to him that there wasn't anything she wouldn't do to thank him. Given the girl's penchant for exaggeration, Raymond tread very lightly in his association with Bridget. He worried that a simple "How are you?" could be construed as "Will you marry me?" Bridget was not Raymond's "Miss Right" but she could perhaps be his "Miss Right Now" if he kept his wits about him. And those dimples did captivate him.

"How about we meet at the Nankin after work for a quick meal?"

Ray had a strange schedule. He worked days in the dining hall, had a four-hour break in the afternoon, and was back in the bar by evening. He asked Bridget to help him pass some of his break time with an early supper when he passed her in the hall at the Commodore. He could hardly see her over the stacks of bedding she rolled ahead of her on a cart. Without her platform shoes, she was back to a gnome-like four feet, ten inches tall, and she looked like a child playing dress up in her mother's work clothes. Raymond noticed that she possessed a well-defined bosom, however, marking her as the woman she actually was and easing his mind about engaging with someone who seemed so childlike.

"Why Mr. Saxby," she replied. "I'd be delighted."

Located a short street car ride from Cathedral Hill to Wabasha Street in downtown St. Paul, the Nankin was one of Ray's favorite restaurants in the city. Its more well-known twin was over in Minneapolis, but he liked this place tucked into the heart of his own town. He loved the exotic ambiance of lanterns and fans and the generous helpings of chicken chow mein served with pork fried rice. He looked forward to the sweet anticipation of learning his future from a fortune cookie at the end of the meal. On one occasion, the tiny slip of paper had foretold of monetary gain and damned if Raymond hadn't stepped right on a five-dollar bill not two blocks from the restaurant. He figured the restaurant was a safe place to meet Bridget. Even if the conversation lagged, they could always just enjoy the food and laugh over the pronouncements of their fates, wrapped up in wood-hard cookie dough.

September 1929 was winding down on the afternoon of Ray's dinner date with Bridget. The humidity of summer was gone from the atmosphere, and fresh breezes of sharp, cold air swept brittle leaves into the gutters. It wasn't yet coat weather, but a jacket was reassuring when a gust of wind blew through the openings between buildings. Bridget wrapped her old-fashioned shawl around her shoulders. She liked the utility of such a garment. It could be tied around her waist when not in use, giving her black uniform a little panache with its bright blue material that matched her eyes.

"Have you been here before?" Ray asked the girl.

He thought not. She was staring open-mouthed at the decor, as if dining in a Chinese place was a new experience for her. In reality, the Nankin was about as Chinese as Bridget; the owners were merely capitalizing on the public's current fascination with all things Oriental. The Chinese food served at the restaurant was carefully prepared to appeal to the most staid of midwestern tastes, and it was a business plan that succeeded. Both the Minneapolis and St. Paul cafes were always busy but, because of the early hour, Ray and Bridget were able to grab a prime table with a view out to busy Wabasha Street.

Bridget spent several minutes studying the menu before she tossed it back onto the table. "I've not a clue what any of this food is," she declared. "And I don't care. Just order something for me."

When she laughed, her child's face radiated joy, her smile all but forcing her eyes shut in delight.

"It's you I like, me dear Mr. Saxby. If I'm lucky, I'll like the grub, too."

She looked up at him coyly from under the brim of her beige cloche hat. Already, Raymond was hoping that his fortune cookie would deliver the advice to look before he leaped, at least as far as Bridget was concerned. He worried this girl was putting the cart way before the horse. He just wanted a dining companion for the moment, and she was acting a little forward with the dear Mr. Saxby routine. He was thinking she was too much of a kid for a man of his age, but here they were, at the Nankin, and it was just a meal, after all.

"Alright, then," he told her. "Everyone loves the chicken chow mein so I'll get that for you and I'll get some egg foo yung. We can share. Oh. And some fried rice. It's my favorite. You'll like it, too."

Ray folded the menu and placed it on the table with a satisfying slap of his hand. The noise alerted their waiter, who bustled over, pulling a little tablet from his breast pocket as he came.

"You leddy?" the waiter asked them.

Bridget and Raymond looked at one another and nodded their heads. The order placed, the waiter returned a few minutes later with cups of steaming brown tea, leaves swirling at the bottom of the cups. He left a small pot of tea for the table. Ray picked up his cup and raised it to Bridget.

"To your health," he said.

She blew the steam from her cup with a suggestive kiss. "And to yours," she said.

The vapor from the tea was condensing on the window that fronted the street, a sure sign that the night promised to be a cold one. Ray enjoyed watching the activity out the window. Wabasha was a busy street where one might spy the mayor on his way back to City Hall, the latest cars from Detroit, or just a steady stream of lovely women, stopping to peer into the windows of the dress shops and jewelers across the street from the restaurant. He pulled his sleeve down and held it with the fingers on his right hand, then wiped the fog from the window next to him.

"Maybe when we're done, we can walk over to look at the jewelry in the window over there," Bridget ventured.

To Raymond, that sounded like an ambush if he ever heard one.

"Sorry," he told her. "I have to be back as soon as I can. Probably shouldn't have left the hotel to begin with. We got that big party tonight."

"What big party?" Bridget asked. "I don't remember a big party on the schedule."

Ray put his finger to his puckered lips to silence her. "Some of the biggest parties are never on the schedule. This one's very hush-hush. You know?"

Bridget considered this for a moment and nodded. "Sure, I understand."

Bridget focused her soft green eyes on Ray. His own eyes were following something happening out the window. His demeanor went from amusement to alarm in seconds. He grabbed one of the menus that had been left behind and held it to his face.

"Shit," he said and then apologized for his outburst. He heard the tinkle of the bell on the door and turned to see if his nightmare was continuing. His throat felt tight, and his heart hammered in his chest. The two men from the Boulevards of Paris, the ones he was sure had set off the bomb, were coming to a table near his own.

He knew these were the men he had seen tampering with the floor grate. They wore the same clothes as they had earlier; only this time, the overcoats were buttoned up to ward off the increasingly blustery wind blowing in from the northwest plains of Canada. It wasn't the cold that sent a shiver up Raymond's spine. His chills were from the fear of remembering one of the thugs pantomiming a gun to Raymond's head. He considered his situation. He couldn't have backed himself into a more solid corner. The only door to escape was situated beyond the men he feared, meaning his route of escape would walk him right by their table. He surmised that there had to be a door to the alley from the kitchen, but the kitchen was also located on the other side of the dining space. Either way, Ray would have to rise from his table, saunter past the gangsters and exit through one of the doors to the outside. He had to figure a way out of this situation. He couldn't hold a menu to his face for the next hour, especially now that Bridget was grabbing at it and complaining about his inattention.

"Mr. Saxby? Are you okay?" she asked him. "Are you going to order something else? You seem awful interested in the menu," she told him, a piqued look on her pretty face.

"Please, call me Ray," he told her, his face still tucked into the folder describing Chinese delicacies. The last thing he wanted was for these men to have a name to go with his face. At least a first name was somewhat anonymous.

"You're acting very strange, Ray."

Shaking her head at her date's sudden change in attitude, she poured herself another cup of tea and held her face to the steam to inhale the aroma.

Over the top of the menu, Ray observed the men. They were still distracted by their own decisions about what to order, but he saw them fold the menus and place them down on the table. One of the men picked up the chopsticks lying next to his napkin and tapped out a little rhythm on the tabletop, punctuating the sound with a crack on his water glass.

"You sound like Baby Dodds," his companion said. He picked up the glass of water and took a deep swallow. "Now try," he told the drummer.

They both laughed when the tone of the glass rang flat. "Physics," the fellow said and then laughed. "Only thing I ever learned in eighth grade." He paused for a moment. "That and what pussy feels like."

The drummer laughed and beat out a da-da-dum, then highlighted the ending with a whack on the metal teapot to simulate a cymbal.

"I skipped science that year but I got my diploma in pussy back in primary school," the drummer told his partner.

He put down the chop sticks and surveyed the restaurant, noticing the couple over by the window. He nudged his friend.

"Speaking of pussy. That's a cute little kitty over there." He cocked his head in Bridget's direction. Both men focused their attention on the couple a few feet away.

"That tall drink of water with her reminds me of someone I seen somewhere," the drummer reported to his partner.

"Yeah," the other man said. "Wish he'd put down that menu so I can see his mug but his hair and forehead are familiar." Being hitmen made them more observant than average.

Frustrated with the inattention, Bridget reached to pull the menu away from Ray's face. He stopped her hand with his own, securing hers firmly to the sticky tabletop

"Listen to me, Bridget," he began. "Keep your eyes on me and don't react. Those two fellows over there are the ones who blew up the Boulevards. If they recognize me, I'm dead."

He told her this in the softest, calmest voice he could muster under extremely trying circumstances. Bridget's eyes bulged big and round, and her mouth formed a silent"O" of alarm. She whispered to him from behind her other hand.

"What are we going to do?" she asked in a voice cracking with trepidation.

He had the girl scoot her chair next to his, and they both appeared to be canoodling behind the paper menu. Hoping to look like any young couple anxious to steal a clandestine kiss, Ray apprised Bridget of his escape plan.

The action unfolded in a slow-motion reel that lasted less than a minute. Bridget rose from the table and bent to give Ray a little peck on the cheek.

"I'll be right back, darling," she told him in a voice loud enough to hear anywhere in the restaurant.

As she jostled away from her chair, she surreptitiously knocked the teapot to the floor, spraying hot liquid everywhere. Ray bent with his napkin, mocking a clean up of the mess.

"Oh my God! I'm so sorry," Bridget roared.

Ray hoped the volume of her voice wasn't, literally, a dead give-away that something was up. The diminutive woman swung her hips with an exaggerated flair as she walked past the men and up to the counter. She rang the little bell at the desk to alert an attendant.

"Excuse me!" she sang out. "I need some help!"

In the moment that the men's attention was diverted to engaging in the appreciation of Bridget's backside, Ray leapt up and made for the door. His movements caused the men to look his way and just as he put his hand on the doorknob, the drummer fellow yelled to his companion.

"That's the guy from the Boulevards. The one who seen us!"

When they jumped to their feet, Bridget barrelled through the kitchen and made her get-away through the side entrance. She ran as fast as her tiny legs could carry her, and she darted into a pharmacy just up the street. As far as she could tell, Raymond was the only one being pursued. She busied herself reading the packaging for Lydia Pinkham's Little Liver Pills, waiting to see what would happen next. Fingering the package like a rosary, Bridget prayed for salvation and hoped for the best.

Raymond slammed the cafe door behind him and ran with more purpose than he ever had in his life. He shot up Wabasha Street and swung a left at West Seventh, the sound of running feet hot at his back. He swerved and swayed to make himself a difficult target. He assumed the men were armed; they were gangsters, after all. The farther he ran, the softer the sounds of strained breaths from the out-of-shape mobsters became. He might be able to outrun them by sheer endurance. He remembered the steep hill to Grand Avenue and huffed his way up the slope that rose above St. Paul's downtown. He could hear the men's pursuit falling away. Eventually, he found himself close to the Commodore, but he was reluctant to be seen in any place remotely public. He adjusted his course until he arrived at the doorstep of Winky Maylamb. When the door opened in response to his incessant pounding, the little Philipino, Enrique, stood staring at him with an expression of puzzlement on his face.

"Meester Saxby," he said. "We no need wine today."

* * *

"That's quite a story, dear boy," Winky remarked when Ray finished his breathless tale. "But I don't understand why you chose me as your protector?"

Raymond understood that no one welcomed a fugitive from a gangland misdeed arriving on their doorstep, looking for help. Still, in the moment, he could think of nowhere else to go. If the men who chased him ever remembered that they had seen him serving drinks at the Commodore, not even refuge in his own home would offer safety. It would be easy enough to describe the tall, blond bartender and determine who he was and where he lived. He hoped Bridget wasn't spilling the beans this very second.

"I'm awful sorry to drag you into this, Mr. Maylamb. But you seem to know just about everybody in town so I thought maybe you could help me figure out a plan. I won't stay here. I wouldn't want to bring those bastards to your door," Ray added.

"Please. Sit, dear boy." Winky heaved himself onto the big corner chair that served as his de facto throne. He motioned for Raymond to find a seat on the brocade sofa. Once settled, Winky slowly and deliberately rubbed his white beard with his massive hands and sighed.

"I do, indeed, have many carefully cultivated connections in town, among them, some in the police hierarchy. However, I don't think they will be the ones to help us in this situation."

Raymond was buoyed to hear Winky use the pronoun "we." Perhaps he would take on Ray's cause, after all. Winky sat quietly for a few moments, his hands folded over his barrel chest and his eyes closed in thought. A sly smile slowly spread over his hairy face, and when he opened his eyes, the right eyelid fluttered like a hummingbird suspended in flight.

"Do you enjoy camping, Raymond?" the big man inquired.

The last time Ray had been camping, it had been on the eve of the Cloquet fire, a time that now seemed a lifetime ago. He smiled at Winky.

"Well, sure. Everyone likes camping," Ray replied.

Winky laughed. "Not everyone," he said. "Violet hates camping. Some creatures demand a feathered nest. Our Vi is one of them."

All Ray could think was that the term "creature" seemed about right. He wasn't confident that there existed a word that described Violet with any accuracy.

"What do you have in mind, sir?" Ray asked.

"Oh. I know of a place, quite close, actually. It is sometimes used by my friends and I for a rustic gentlemen's retreat. It will be lonely this time of year but cozy and, best of all, safe."

Ray flashed a relieved smile.

"I got no problem with lonely, Mr. Maylamb. Dead is the condition I got a problem with."

A laugh proportionate to his size exploded from the giant. "Well said, Raymond. Well said. And while you are enjoying a bit of a holiday, I will use my resources to find a permanent solution to your problem. Oh, and I will smooth it over for you at the Commodore. My connections include the owner, as you may recall."

A quick rummage through the attic apartment resulted in enough discarded clothing to get Ray through a couple of days in hiding. Enrique emerged from the stairs with an armload of woolen shirts, breeches and a buffalo plaid coat that almost fit Raymond. Only the length of the sleeves was a little short. Mr. Maylamb must have hosted a lot of young men over the years, thought Ray, without a shred of judgement other than for the colors of the shirts. He preferred a more subtle palette, himself.

By early evening, Raymond was ensconced in a structure that could only be described as a tent-cabin. Some of the walls were made of white canvas and some of wood planking. The room had a plywood floor and a tin roof. An outhouse and washroom were located a short walk from the cabin's rear door. Inside, a black iron stove would keep the place warm. The cabin had rudimentary electricity, with one light hanging from the center pole and one outlet, lower on the pole, to power the occupant's needs. It was surprisingly comfortable and cheerful. Brightly colored Hudson Bay blankets covered the bed, and the broken-down sofa had tribal-patterned pillows scattered about the corners. Outside, the cabin was surrounded by several more shacks of various sizes but similar construction. It was its own little village, located in the marshes abutting Lake Phalen, and he was the only inhabitant.

"I am leaving now, Meester Saxby, but I will be back tomorrow with some more food and a fishing pole. You will like to fish in the lake, si?" Enrique asked.

"Sure. That all sounds great," Ray replied. "And, thanks for helping me, Enrique. I'll make it up to you someday."

For the remainder of the evening, Raymond rummaged through the cabin, looking for something to relieve his boredom. He wasn't used to downtime with nothing to occupy his mind or his body. He happened upon a deck of cards in a drawer next to the knives and forks and a copy of Tarzan of the Apes tucked under one of the sofa pillows. On its cover was a well-rendered picture of a nearly naked man, rippling with muscles and glowing in a sheen of sweat. Raymond supposed that to Winky's crowd, the book had been judged worthy of readership by virtue of its illustrations of savage male virility. He played a few rounds of solitaire, set the stove alight, then settled in under the harsh glare of the overhead light to read the exploits of the apeman. Soon, he saw himself as alone as Tarzan, albeit with electricity. He had no idea how long he would be marooned in this place of close-in isolation or what Mr. Maylamb might be able to do to help him put the problem behind him. For now, it was enough to be safe and enjoying an impromptu vacation. He considered that a pet chimpanzee, such as Tarzan had with him, might make the time pass more quickly. It was the last thought he had before falling asleep under a four-point red wool blanket.

Morning announced itself bright and white, the sun's rays strained through the canvas walls that made up the sides of the cabin. He awoke with a moment of disorientation until remembering where he was and why he was in this peculiar place. He made a quick trip to the outhouse before taking time to wander outside, exploring his immediate surroundings. In the distance, he could hear cars and trucks rumbling along Larpenteur Avenue, but the road seemed a million miles away.

On his walk over to the lake, he saw a red-winged blackbird perched on the top of a mass of reeds, and a short distance from the male, a female sat in a stringy nest made of cattails calling to her mate. Raymond stood with his bare feet in the sand, staring at the waters of Lake Phalen. He stripped off his shirt and eased his body into the cool water. Once in the lake, the sand under his feet gave way to a thick, viscous mud that enveloped his feet in a sensual embrace. He rinsed under his arms and ruffled the water through his hair before swimming deep enough to kick the mud from between his toes. He felt grateful to be alive but more than that, he felt more alive than he had for a very long time.

A car was parked near the cabin when Raymond returned from his swim.

"Yoohoo!" a voice cried when its driver spotted him working his way back from the lake.

Standing next to a yellow Renault CV NN, a sporty French convertible with a prow front, was someone unlikely to make the trip to the rustic camp. There stood Violet, decked out in jodhpurs, glossy black boots and a body-hugging waistcoat. On her head was a turban of artificial leopard skin. Raymond wondered if she had been the one to leave the Tarzan book behind. She was certainly dressed for the jungle.

"Raymond! Dear one!" she cried. "Come see all the goodies I've brought you."

He jogged the last few yards back to the cabin and submitted to a brief peck on the cheek.

"Hello, Violet," he said. Raymond grinned and took the bags from her arms. "You're about the last person I thought I'd see out here," he told her.

She laughed and grabbed his hand, pulling him into the cabin after her. "I know, but Enrique couldn't make it. Burrr," she shivered. "It's so cold out there. You must be freezing. You should get out of those wet clothes," she advised him.

Raymond knew she was right about that, but he had no intention of taking off his clothing in front of such a person. He was in enough trouble already.

That day Violet left him with cold fried chicken, a bag of apples just picked from an orchard in Afton, fresh baked bread, canned beef, hard cheese and some of the very wine that Raymond brought out to Winky once a month. She supplied him with a pile of current magazines, fishing gear, a flannel nightshirt and a ragg wool watch cap, a stack of books--among them Robinson Crusoe--and a half-dozen thick, fluffy towels.

Violet couldn't have been a more well-behaved gentleman. Not once did she make Raymond feel uncomfortable in her presence, and she promised to come out every other day until the situation was resolved. She assured Raymond that it would be. Winky knew everyone, and he could work magic.

As the days wore on, the weather grew colder so Violet provided thick socks and bulky sweaters to help Raymond fight off the cold. She came one time with a large crock of beef soup that Enrique had made, telling him he could just heat it on the stove. On the final trip out to the cabin, she brought him a newspaper. She unfolded the St. Paul Dispatch onto the scarred coffee table and pulled him over so he could see the article she had tagged on the third page.

"You can go home today, Raymond. Winky says those men will never bother you again."

Raymond flipped to the third page and scanned the articles. On the lower right corner were old mugshot pictures of the men who had chased him. The gangsters, he was sure, who had bombed the Boulevards. Under the picture was a caption that read: *Underworld Figures Perish In Boating Accident*. No one seemed to question why these men had been found floating next to a rowboat devoid of fishing gear, dressed in business suits, with their fedoras floating at their sides.

Violet smiled and pulled her beaver skin coat around her shoulders. "I told you Winky could work magic. Poof! Your problem has disappeared!"

16

"There's an awful lot of drinking going on today; and it's being done by folks that don't normally bother." Ray's assistant made this observation after his second trip to the cellar to fetch dusty bottles from the liquor supply shelves.

Tuesday, October 30, 1929, started like any other day until people had a chance to read the newspapers. Well-heeled patrons of the Commodore's clandestine basement bar medicated their financial anxiety with whatever promised to distract them from their pain. While the nation's economy slid south into a twelve-year ruin, Raymond Saxby's personal economy was bolstered by brisk bar orders and hefty tips, as if throwing money away on a small scale could somehow balance the massive funds lost in margin calls.

"What the hell," one customer told him when he tossed a two-dollar bill to Raymond for a thirty-five cent whiskey. "Keep the change, kid. I'd rather throw my money at a bar bill than watch it go down the drain on Wall Street."

That customer wasn't the only one to voice such a sentiment that afternoon. Though the closing days of October 1929 were devastating for the nation's financial health, they were some of Raymond's most lucrative ever. Thus far, he was a fan of the Depression, but his good fortune was not shared by everyone in the Saxby family. With each page torn from the calendar, the blazing prosperity of the twenties was doused by the collapse of the American stock market. The first two years of the new decade saw a country struggling with high unemployment and wide-spread poverty. While destitute folks still clung to liquor to soothe their despair, ensuring that Raymond could continue to eat, his brother and sister were feeling the impact of the market's decline.

"Happy New Year, everyone. Here's to a brighter 1932!"

Leon toasted the upcoming year with a sense of tenuous hope. After all, how long could such a decline last? For the last couple of years, he had watched his lucrative insurance business flounder as customers let policies lapse amid the inability to pay the premiums. He was keeping his wife and six children afloat on the proceeds from bootlegged wine, and he knew that source would soon dry up. The federal government was proposing to repeal Prohibition for the sole purpose of restocking the nation's coffers with hefty taxes on legalized hootch. It was suddenly necessary for the nation's morals to take a backseat to its flagging morale.

"No. I don't want you even thinking about that," Leon told Rosella when she proposed returning to work as a nurse. He couldn't stomach the thought of his wife wiping asses to help feed the family.

"Then what about my lasagna recipe? Maybe I can sell premade dinners or figure out a way to can it or something. Your sister has done great with her baking," she ventured to her husband.

Leon had to admit that Amelia had been a huge success. It was the bakery and the gas station that were keeping Amelia and James financially stable. The bank had called in the loan on the car dealership in Hastings, and James Blume's Quality Auto Sales had folded like the paper the loan was written on. Ever resourceful, Amelia and James doubled down on the auto repair shop and the bakery. They now had a small fleet of vintage hearses, sporting Amelia's smiling face promising "Baked Goods To Die For," making deliveries to destinations as far flung as Brainard and Rochester. The Mayo Clinic served Amelia's creations to patients and staff alike. Amelia Blume could hardly go anywhere without someone asking her, "Aren't you that cake girl?" She always repaid their inquiry with a blazing smile and a business card. "Why, yes. That's me and I hope you will call my shop if you ever need the best pastries, at the best prices, that you can imagine." Her smile was so beguiling that she could win over jealous housewives, who frequently passed off Amelia's exceptional baked goods as their own. These women reckoned that what they paid Amelia was worth the price for a contented husband, able to savor chocolate prune cake or cheese biscuits after a hard day of work.

Rosella admired her young sister-in-law's success and saw no reason why she couldn't develop a similar business of her own. To do that she would need money, and she had an idea of how to get it.

It was a warm, sticky June day when Rosella broached the subject with her husband. A war veteran of sorts herself, Rosella read extensively about the plight of the unemployed men who had served their country with honor during the Great War. In 1924, the World War Adjusted Compensation Act had awarded veterans bonus certificates for their service that were redeemable in 1945. Out of luck and out of work, the destitute men were pushing for the bonuses to be paid during their time of need, and few times were more needy than the Depression year of 1932.

"We should go to Washington with the rest of the marchers," Rosella told Leon. "We should make our voices heard. If we can get our hands on a bonus, we can set up a new business. Something like what your sister does."

"What in God's name are you yammering about? What march?"

Leon was up to his ears in cancelled insurance policies and moldy grapes, and he hadn't paid any attention at all to the so-called Bonus Army March scheduled for July in the nation's capital. He slurped down the last of his coffee, lit his cigarette and handed his wife his breakfast plate. She set it in the sink and turned to face him.

"We're both veterans, Leon," she told him with steely resolve. "We deserve to get a bonus now. That's what everyone says and the more of us to say it right to their faces, the more likely we are to get it." She took a breath and softened her approach. "And, wouldn't it be nice to show the children Washington? Have a little educational adventure with them?"

How could Leon disagree with that. Besides, the timing was right. He would have the current batch of wine bottled and shipped by the Fourth of July so why not join his brothers in arms in a bid for compensation. Hell, who even knew if he would live to 1945? Thirteen years was a long time, and like the rest of the country, he needed the money now.

It was the first long-distance trip the family had ever enjoyed. Rosella and her mother fashioned each of the children a little uniform, made of tea-stained flour sacks, and they used new brown envelopes to simulate army caps. While the women sewed, the children, all but the baby, busied themselves making signs demanding their parents' due. The family left Hibbing on July 6, 1932, five children stuffed into the backseat of a Ford touring car and the eleven-month-old girl on her mother's lap.

Chicago was fun. Leon showed the youngsters where he briefly stayed in the city after he returned from the war. He related the story of his first good suit but wisely skipped telling them how he spent his evenings while in town. The children marvelled at the skyscrapers and the sandy shores of Lake Michigan. Indiana was boring, and Ohio and Pennsylvania proved hot and unending. Frequent whines of "When are we going to get there?" were interrupted by pit stops for gas, bodily functions and picnics. By the time the family sighted the Washington Monument in the distance, the novelty of the trip had worn thin for them all. They were tired, hungry and wilted from the heat and humidity of late July in Washington, D.C.

"Where to?" Leon asked Rosella.

She directed him to the expansive lawn that spread in front of the Capitol Building.

"Look, children!" Rosella cried. "That's where our laws are made."

While the Saxby children gazed approvingly at the sites of government they had only read about in their school books, Rosella and Leon scanned the lawn for a place to set up their tent. The scene before them was almost as depressing as the war camps the veterans remembered. Plywood shanties and lean-to shacks made of cardboard, single-person pup tents, family camp tents and sleeping pallets in the beds of pickup trucks covered nearly every inch of the space. The family was eventually able to tuck themselves between two pup tents, once their owners agreed to move just enough to make space for the Saxby tent and car.

"Hey, lady? Can I take a picture of your kids?"

Reporters roamed everywhere to record the event, and this particular one thought that the Saxby children, decked out in their makeshift uniforms, would tug at the heartstrings of his readers. He posed them along the ledge of the car's running board, from smallest to tallest, and had them give their best salute. "Say money," he told them and snapped a picture that appeared in an obscure publication the next day.

Much like the trip out, the excitement of the first couple of days diminished as the heat and crowding intensified. When Rosella went to find a copy of the newspaper that carried the picture of her children, she came across other papers that warned that President Hoover had no intention of giving into the demands of the Bonus Army, and he was getting sick and tired of seeing the riffraff cluttering up his city. He threatened action and soon.

"I'm sorry. Leon. I think this has been a mistake. Coming here, I mean."

Leon had thought so all along, but he rarely challenged Rosella. He owed his ongoing sanity to her, but he also worried that the conditions in the camp would trick his mind into reliving the war through new nightmares. If she was ready to go, he was all for it.

"Do you want to go? I can have us out of here first thing tomorrow morning," he told her.

Rosella bobbed her head to answer and kissed her husband on his scruffy cheek. "At least the kids have learned something about Washington and how our government works," she said in a bid to give the scuttled trip purpose.

Early on the morning of July 28, 1932, the Saxbys picked their way off the great lawn and settled in for the long ride home. They were approaching the highway when Leon abruptly slammed on the brakes and stuck his head out of the window.

"Well, I'll be goddamned!" he exclaimed.

He was looking at a booth set up in the crowd advising folks on the benefits of family planning. "Don't have children you can't feed!" advised a sign over the booth. Leon would have known the blond beauty handing out brochures anywhere. Inka Siskanen, gorgeous as ever, was still fighting the good fight.

"It's good to see that booth out here," Rosella commented, not aware of Leon's connection to the hostess. Leon acknowledged to himself that the only two women he ever loved had a great deal in common, at least in principle. He doubted that Inka had endorsed motherhood to the degree that Rosella had.

They stayed just outside of Pittsburgh on the first night of the return trip. Leon gassed up the Ford and grabbed a paper on his way out of the station.

"Have a look at this," he told Rosella when he handed her the paper.

She unfolded the local daily and gasped at the headlines. Two veterans had been killed and the Bonus Army dispersed by Army Chief of Staff, General Douglas MacArthur, who mobilized troops and tanks to carry out the President's orders to put an end to the march. The children did, indeed, learn how their government worked.

Leon and Rosella arrived back in Hibbing on August first. The children burst from the car and ran with glee to their very own rooms, with real beds and fresh clothes. Hungry from the trip, the younger children begged for something to eat.

"Go out to the garden and see what's ready," Rosella told her brood. A few minutes later she heard laughter and cries of delight at the backdoor.

"Mama! Come look!" her six-year-old demanded. Standing at the base of the steps, three little Saxbys held their loaded shirts out by the hems, displaying piles of the most luscious tomatoes her garden had ever produced.

"Look how many and there's more. Lots more!" Anthony exclaimed. "What are we gonna do with so much, Mama?"

Rosella discovered that the bonus had been in her own backyard all along. The next day, *Bella Rosella* bottled marinara sauce began its quest to bring inexpensive and quick pasta sauce to America.

* * *

The Commodore Hotel celebrated the end of Prohibition with grand style. Not long after the national morality experiment was officially declared over on December 5, 1933, the Commodore opened a lavish art deco bar that quickly became the place to see and be seen. When Raymond walked into the splendid space, he was dazzled by the sheer beauty of the design. A hybrid of a Hollywood movie set worthy of Fred Astaire and Ginger Rogers and a modern, sleek ocean liner, the bar gave Raymond the feeling that he was presiding over a palace studded with African diamonds and Baltic amber. On the wall behind the bar counter, hundreds of bottles of genuine top-shelf liquor glowed in golden iridescence from the reflection of the mirrored shelves behind them. The sight brought back the memory of the night he had broken his leg in Duluth. He'd never forgotten the effect of the light dancing off the sparkling bottles behind the bar at the Pickworth all those years ago. The Pickworth's bar was a Cracker Jack ring compared to the opulent brilliance of the room he was surveying now.

"It's yours, Ray. You're our headman here. What do you think?"

The hotel manager was glowing almost as brightly as the illuminated mirror-covered walls. He continuously tugged at the bottom of his black suit coat in an attempt to look sharp enough to be standing in such an auspicious space. Raymond didn't share his manager's awkward gestures. This bar was the embodiment of everything such an establishment should be, and he would do whatever it took to keep it that way. He was not only the duly appointed headman of the now main-floor lounge, he was absolutely the right man for the job.

Raymond's life in the 1930s acquired a rhythm that would continue for decades to come. He would arrive at the Commodore mid-afternoon, check in with the day bartender, inventory the stocks of beverages in both the bar and the storage area, and ready himself and his charges for the onslaught of customers that appeared every evening and into the night. The end of Prohibition changed the tenor of the clientele. As bootleggers regrouped to find other lucrative criminal activities, their likes were seen less and less in the elegant digs. The seats they had occupied in the hidden lounge in the Commodore's basement were now front and center in the mirrored bar off the hotel lobby. More and more of those seats welcomed the derrieres of the city's political class. According to a prominent St. Paul crime reporter, the rakish ambiance of the Commodore as a hideout for gangsters, such as Al Capone and Ma Barker, began to deteriorate once the political class took up residence. Even so, Raymond still kept his head down and his conjectures to himself. After years of listening in on the conversations of his customers, he was well aware that there was a fine line between crime and politics. Generally speaking, politicians were less threatening, though they tended to be more tight-fisted with tips than their underworld counterparts. With steady employment in an era of rampant joblessness, Raymond had no reason to complain about a few underripe tips. At long last, he considered himself a lucky man.

Part of that luck was a girl named Dolores. She was young, tall and voluptuous, and she had a head of the most glorious honey-colored hair he had ever seen peeking from beneath her cap. He'd spotted her on her morning shift as a streetcar operator, while he stood waiting to cross St. Peter Street. There was something about the girl that drew him like a magnet. He occasionally waited for hours to catch a glimpse of her in her coach, deftly making change for customers from the mechanical coin slots she wore at her waist. Some days, he would board the car and sit as close behind her as he could, just wanting to admire the slope of her shoulders and the smile she offered new riders as they boarded her car. She was an orchid among streetcar operators, who were overwhelmingly male and the few women, hard-edged. From where Raymond sat, this girl didn't appear to have a hard edge anywhere on her. She was all soft, languid curves, topped off with a face that would have looked right as rain on the cover of Photoplay Magazine. Her voice was soft like her curves but still loud enough that Raymond was able to mostly overhear a conversation she was having with what must have been a friend. He could decipher that the two girls planned to meet at the Como Park Conservatory on the upcoming Saturday morning. What he didn't know was the time of the rendezvous, but he vowed to get there early and wait until he could intercept this enticing girl. As long as he would be able to show up on time for work in the afternoon, the rest of the day could be dedicated to making the young woman's acquaintance.

Fresh snow covered the lawns of Como Park on Saturday morning when he arrived just minutes before the conservatory was scheduled to open its doors. Since becoming a public space in 1915, the glass structure had served the city's citizens as a refuge from the dreary landscapes of winter. Under its translucent dome, fragrant blooms of color delighted the senses of those strolling the aisles, and the tropical heat of the rooms was a balm to winter-weary bones. Raymond could think of worse places to kill a few hours.

The morning passed slowly for Raymond. After two rounds through the latest conservatory exhibits of leafy tropical ferns and the riotous blooms of plant varieties that should never have been seen in the northern reaches of Minnesota, he settled in on a bench and pulled the Pioneer Press from his inside breast pocket. There, on the front page, was another lead story about the criminal circus that was ubiquitous in his fair city. The demise of the illegal liquor trade had pushed the underworld to choose from a different array of crimes on their sleazy menu. Hot items in 1936 were murder-for-hire and kidnapping. Raymond read of the convictions the previous week of Harry Sawyer and William Weaver for the kidnapping of banking magnate, Edward Bremer. He was not surprised by the outcome of the trial. The O'Connor system was breaking down. The city's law-abiding citizens were tired of reading of bodies littering the streets of their town--bodies of innocent bystanders and wealthy pawns--in addition to the collateral damage of gang-on-gang fatalities. Juries were growing as bold as the criminals and handing down verdicts that sent gangsters away to the far-off reaches of Leavenworth Prison.

After a quick glance at the sports section, Raymond refolded the paper and tucked into a crack between the slats on the bench. The morning was slipping away and with it, the time he needed to woo his prey. He fought the urge to gnaw on his cuticles by fingering the old, scorched ring of horse tack he carried in his pocket. For almost twenty years, his amulet of hope had seen him through times of anxiety. He was anxious, sitting in wait for the girl to arrive, but in a way that created an oddly pleasurable feeling. There was something about this girl that pulled him in and made the possibility of rejection an acceptable risk to his psyche.

Nervous energy propelled him to his feet, and he began the circuit around the displays once again. Then, there she was, backed up against the massive heads of red roses in full bloom while her companion from the streetcar snapped her picture with a box camera hanging from a strap around her neck.

"Too bad we won't be able to see the colors," her friend said. "The red is so divine."

The other girl threw her head back and laughed. "Doesn't matter, Marge. As long as my beauty shines through, that's what counts!"

Her friend shook her head and smiled. "Oh, Dolores. You're the bee's knees!"

Dolores. That was her name. Dolores. Ray saw his opening and like the stalker he envisioned himself to be that morning, he crept in for engagement with his target.

"Excuse me, ladies. I was wondering if you would like me to snap a photo of the two of you together. Something to remember your visit today?" He doffed his hat and smiled, hoping he appeared charming, and not creepy, to the younger women. He must have nearly twenty years on them, he thought.

The two girls looked at one another. "Should we?" Marge asked.

Dolores scooted to the side to make room for her friend. "Sure. Why not?" she said. "Give him the camera and get over here, Margie."

Once acquainted, the trio ambled through the building, capturing black and white pictures that would never reveal the kaleidoscope of colors hidden in photographic ink and shadow. At every opportunity, Dolores posed with a new flower close to her face, as if challenging the bloom to usurp her beauty. As far as Raymond was concerned, there wasn't a flower in existence on the entire planet that could compete with the stunning visage of young Dolores.

"I've got to leave for work soon," Raymond told his new friends, "but how about I get us some hot dogs before I take off?"

At a diner not far from the park, Ray and the girls enjoyed phosphates and frankfurters smeared with mustard and sauerkraut. "I had a friend once," he told them. "His ma made the best kraut ever. He died in the war...a German fighting Germans." The girls looked at one another and raised their eyebrows.

"I was born after the end of the war. I don't know much about all that," Dolores told him.

Ray did the math in his head. That would make her eighteen or nineteen to his nearly thirty-six years of age. A big gap but not unheard of in couples. Marge offered her own comment that caught Raymond off guard.

"My pa went to Germany. He's got a gas cough. You know what that is?" the girl asked him.

Ray carefully rubbed the mustard from his face and folded his paper napkin into neat squares before wiping the table clean of crumbs and shreds of fermented cabbage.

"Of course I know about the problems men got from the gas attacks. My brother told me about them. I was too young to go myself." There. He had given evidence that he wasn't as old as the girl's father. He hoped that admission would keep him in the running.

"I've got to go now," he told them, "but I hope we can run into each other again. You know," he said to Dolores, "you remind me of someone I've seen before. Do you ever go to the Commodore Hotel? That's where I work."

Dolores smiled. "You ever ride the streetcars downtown? That's where I work."

Raymond smacked himself upside the head in mock surprise. "Of course!" he exclaimed. "The morning car along St. Peter? I thought you looked familiar. Funny how different people look when they appear out of context. You know...where you aren't used to seeing them."

Dolores wagged her finger at Raymond. "Really, Mr. Saxby. I know what 'context' means. I just graduated from Wilson High."

"I'm impressed," he told her. "A high school graduate and already working your way up in a man's world."

He tossed the paper napkin into the trash and rose to leave.

"Listen, ladies," he offered. "You should come by the Commodore some evening. I'm always there and I can arrange for you to have a nice meal. On the house." On the house, in this case, meant out of Ray's pocket, but it was a sacrifice he was willing to make to lure the lovely girl into his snare.

"Why, we'd love that. Wouldn't we, Dee!" Margie replied.

The trap for Dolores' future was set. Raymond felt every bit the conquering hero when he grabbed the trolley for the ride up to Cathedral Hill. He was five minutes late for work. It was the first time he had checked in late in all his years at the hotel.

Every night for the next week, Ray kept a watchful eye on the door that led from the courtyard into the hotel lobby. He used what religious conviction he had left to pray that the stunning girl with the honey-colored hair would appear before him to redeem the free meal he had offered to her and her less-desirable friend. He was busy washing glasses for the next round of martinis that had been ordered by a table full of city officials when one of his workers tapped him on the back.

"Hey, Mr. Saxby. There's someone here to see ya." The fellow gave Raymond a wink. "How'd you get so lucky?" he asked.

It was then that Raymond knew Dolores was waiting for him in the lobby. He straightened his tie and pulled himself up to the full height of his six-foot, two and one-half inch frame and walked into the gathering space to meet his guests. Attired in what must have been her mother's dress from a few years before the Depression limited women to one or two practical dresses per year, was Dolores. What her dress lacked in current styling, it made up for with the body that filled out its shape. Dolores was a vision in emerald green satin. The collar sparkled over her clavicles from a ring of rhinestones that outlined her sweetheart neckline. On her feet were t-strap pumps that cried out "Dance with me!" The hope that had faded on Thursday and Friday, when Raymond feared that she would never accept his invitation, sprang to life. He could feel other parts of his being stirring as well.

There was little time to talk with Dolores that night. Ray was busy keeping the regulars happy, but he checked in frequently with the two young women. He learned her last name, something he had neglected to do earlier, and secured permission to call her for an official date. He did all this without the lackluster Marge becoming alerted to his intentions.

"Mr. Saxby reminds me of Jimmy Stewart," Marge mentioned over dessert. "I think he might fancy me. Wouldn't that be something?" she asked. "Me, going about town with a man like him? A real grown up and all?"

"That would be something," Dolores replied, knowing full well that it was she who would be escorted around town with Raymond's hand on her back. He was a man. They always preferred beauty over other womanly qualities. At least, that was Dolores' experience, and that trait, so ingrained in the male population, had served her well thus far. She could tell it was working its magic on Raymond Saxby.

Their first date was out to Como Park to watch ice-skating races on the frozen lake. The annual races were a feature of the St. Paul Winter Carnival, and after the races concluded, the pair rented skates for some leisurely skating of their own. Later, sipping hot cocoa and mopping the drip of thawing noses, they became better acquainted, engaging in a rigorous debate about the origins of the carnival backstory. Raymond thought it had all been made up by a reporter, hoping to sell newspapers; Dolores was sure it was based on a real Norwegian myth. When Ray pointed out that there was, by definition, no such thing as a real myth, Dolores said, "You win!" and pecked him lightly on his frozen cheek.

The next date ended with an open-mouthed kiss, and the relationship progressed into the summer. On an outing to the state fair, at the very top of the ferris wheel and in the waning heat of the dog days of summer, Raymond proposed to Dolores McBurney. She accepted, and they kissed each time the revolution of the wheel brought them back to the peak. They never bothered to look at the view of St. Paul that spread out below them in all directions. They only had eyes for each other.

After a simple wedding in late September at the Methodist Church of St. Paul, Ray and Dolores invited all their friends for a grand picnic on the lawn at Como Park. The park held special meaning for the couple. It was the site of their first official meeting, their first real date and a place they came frequently for walks through the zoo or around the lake. They had poor Marge take a picture of them in their wedding finery, standing proudly in front of the Gates Ajar. On their anniversary every year thereafter, they would return to the park and solicit a stranger to take their photograph with the famous gates in the background. As time moved forward, so did technology, and by the time the twenty-fifth picture was snapped, the photo was in color.

17

St. Paul, Minnesota 1996

Anew year had just begun, and the winter of 1996 was the first time Raymond felt old. Really and truly old. It had been a long time coming, but when he saw a reflection of himself on any surface, he had to look twice to acknowledge that it was his own face that stared back at him. Like a sock lost behind the dryer, every fiber of his being was simultaneously shrunken and saggy, and he felt as gray and listless as the dust motes that coated such a forgotten sock.

"You look kind of peaked, Dad," Dwight mentioned when he brought his father a pail of mashed potatoes with gravy from KFC.

His doctor had told Raymond that fast food was full of salt and something he should avoid, but salt was about all he could taste, and mashed potatoes, about all he could chew, so the compromise had been that he would leave the shaker in the cabinet whenever he ate from a fast food joint. Lately, that was mostly courtesy of the Colonel, thanks to the nearly predigested mashed potatoes on their menu.

"I got this cough," Ray reported to his son. "Can't hardly sleep."

Dwight looked carefully at his father's face. He scolded himself for overlooking the signs of oxygen deprivation. Plain as day, Raymond's lips were bluish under the cracked, chapped surface of the skin. "Hang on, Pop," Dwight mumbled. Raymond dismissed Dwight with an exasperated sigh.

"Hangin' on is about all I can do right now."

Dwight disappeared out the back door, and when he came back in, he was holding his open work bag. After a bit of rummaging, he pulled his stethoscope from the jumble.

"Let's have a listen to your lungs," he told his father. When he stripped the moth-eaten Faribault shirt away from Raymond's chest, he was briefly shocked by the birdlike torso beneath his hands. Every bone in the old man's chest was pushing through the dusky skin. Large, purple patches of superficial bleeding covered one side of his chest. The elbow on the same side was likewise covered with blue-black blotches.

"What happened here, Dad?"

His father brushed off the concern. "A little tumble into the table, is all."

Dwight laid the diaphragm of the stethoscope over his father's heart. He listened for irregularities and found more than a few. The old man's heart beat when it got around to it, sometimes in rapid succession and sometimes about the time Dwight was sure it had stopped altogether. When it did beat, soft whooshes of turbulence accompanied each contraction. "The old man is wearing out," he thought to himself. When he moved the instrument to examine the lungs, he heard a regular symphony of wheezes and crackles in the upper chest and deep gurgles, lower down. Dwight arrived at the conclusion that his father likely suffered from the fluid backup of congestive heart failure, or pneumonia, or both maladies together.

"What ya doin', sugar?" Dwight asked me when I answered the phone. It was late afternoon. I had been home from work for about forty minutes, and already it was pitch dark outside with an ice storm predicted on every television station. One weather person was advising viewers to throw kitty litter on their steps for better traction. I was doomed. I only had a dog.

"I'm just getting ready to warm up some soup and watch The Thin Man on the old movie station," I replied. "Why? What's up with you? Wanna come over and distract me from the television?" I asked.

Dwight didn't take the bait. "Listen. I was wondering if you could help me out. Dad's sick. I need to get him seen to but I have to go into work until I can find someone to cover. I was wondering. Could you come over and sit with him until I can make arrangements to get free?"

I collected myself and tried not to be annoyed. Getting caught out on the roads in an ice storm seemed a bit "above and beyond" to ask a nonrelative. To make matters worse, the Saxby men did not have cable. I would be stuck all night watching local news reports of pile-ups on the slick roads. By the time I would get to leave, my nerves would be frayed before I could put the key into the ignition of my ice-encrusted car.

I thought about it for a moment before I did what I always did in those days. I listened to the prodding of undeserved guilt and agreed to be there as soon as I could.

"We should probably keep him sitting up. Easier to breathe," Dwight told me.

Inside my head, I was thinking that I didn't need someone telling me how to care for a patient. Twenty-five years of experience as an RN would inform my care plan for the next few hours. But I caught myself before snarky words could be said. Dwight was a devoted son who was doing all he could to make his failing father comfortable. I couldn't fault him for being concerned. Annoyance over my interrupted evening had made me more sensitive than usual. The Thin Man was one of my favorite movies of all time, but I had a different thin man, sitting in a broken-down recliner, to attend to at the moment.

"Yep. I'll keep a good watch over him," I replied to Dwight. To Mr. Saxby, I chirped. "No worries. I'm a professional." I gave him a wink, and he responded with a weak smile from his cracked lips. He patted my hand where it rested by his arms. His old fingers were cold as ice and mottled blue at the tips.

"Do your best to get back soon, Dwight. It looks to me like he needs oxygen--at the very least. Do you think we should call an ambulance?"

Dwight shook his head. "I won't be long."

He left the living room and exited through the kitchen. When I heard his truck roar to life, I turned to Mr. Saxby and said, "Let's get you situated." I made myself busy adjusting the pillows behind his back then brushed toast crumbs from the afghan blanket that rested over his knees.

"We should find you something warmer than this. It's full of holes. Lets the cold get to you."

He clamped the crochet blanket in a bony claw and told me, "No. Leave it. Dolores made it for me. It makes me warm in other ways."

I tucked the wrap under his legs and felt the scratch of dried food stuck in the yarn. When he left to go to the doctor, I would take the blanket home for a good wash. The situation reminded me of when my older son was a baby. I had to sneak his security blanket away from his crib after he fell asleep in order to wash the sour milk smell out of the baby blue weave.

"Can I get you anything to eat?" I asked him. He brushed the question away with a swipe of his hand.

"Tea, maybe," he told me. "Just tea and someone to talk to. That's all I need just now."

I made us both cups of Earl Grey, his with a little milk to cool it down, and sat the cups on the side table next to his recliner. I scooted my own chair closer to him so I could hear his weakened voice and turned the sound on the television down with his remote.

"No need to listen to that," I told him. "We all know what we're in for tonight." Raymond carefully picked up his cup and rested it on his lap.

"This is what Dolores always did for me when I was feeling poorly. She made me tea and put this old blanket over my cold feet." He smiled at the memory.

"Tell me about your wife," I encouraged. "I'm sorry I was never able to meet her. Dwight never got around to taking me over to visit her at the home."

"Dolores was a beauty," the old man told me. "Not always easy to live with but she sure was easy on the eyes." He closed his own eyes as the memories flooded his mind.

St. Paul, Minnesota 1936

"I want to keep working on the streetcar until I'm expecting. We can save money towards a house that way."

Raymond didn't mind that she left the house for work not long after he returned from his night shift as a bartender. They always had a walk together in the late afternoon and a light supper before he left for the Commodore in the evening.

"That's a good plan," he agreed. "We can add your salary to the money from the old farm. I've hung onto it all these years, just for this reason."

Raymond was proud of the fact that his paranoia about banks had led him to keep his long-ago payout from James in a tin box hidden beneath the false bottom of an old, round-top trunk that had been his Grandma Saxby's. The bank busts of the last few years hadn't touched his stash.

What neither of the couple had anticipated was that the arrangement would go on for so long. After two years without success, Dolores no longer bothered to calculate when her bleeding would arrive. She knew that her monthly period would inevitably punctuate the end of a one-word sentence. Failure.

"It's gotta be you. You had the mumps as a kid." She accused Raymond of being the cause of her barren state. He would have liked to disprove her theory, but what could he say? He had had the mumps, but so had every other man he'd ever known, the vast majority of whom had more kids than they wanted.

"What's the doctor say?" he asked his wife.

Dolores dissolved into tears. "He says it's not me."

Raymond hated to see Dolores cry. For one thing, all the blubbering made him feel guilty and for another, it puffed up her eyes and turned her nose bright red. It took hours for the signs of her unhappiness to fade from her face. It was a tangible reminder that he was failing her, despite his best physical efforts to give her a child. Some nights, he went to work in a state of sheer exhaustion and had once prepared the wrong drink for the wrong patron--an abomination among his bartender colleagues. When he explained the reason for his lack of focus, his fellow bartenders didn't know whether to laugh or pat him on the shoulder. One fellow did both.

The years wore on, and the pile of money grew so large that Raymond eventually invested in a fireproof box to accommodate the stack of bills. With that stack, he and Dolores planned to purchase a modest home for the children who would grow up within its walls.

Another World War put its blot on history before Raymond and Dolores were able to welcome a child into their lives. Anticipating the arrival of Dwight, Raymond and Dolores bought a three-bedroom bungalow near Como Park. Shortly thereafter, three little girls joined the family. Bing, bang, bong. It hadn't been Raymond after all, the doctor told them. Sometimes a woman's desire to have a child is so strong that it shuts down the internal process. Once a baby comes, the uterus relaxes (the doctor's term) and conception occurs more easily. When his youngest daughter was born, Raymond was fifty-two years old. He hoped Dolores's uterus would tense up again. Four little children at his age was plenty.

Dolores had long admired the image of the well-dressed woman pushing a baby buggy with her older children dutifully by her side, but reality proved messier. Dwight was only five years old when her fourth child was born. For a period of seven months, Dolores had three little ones in diapers. It was all she could do to open the foul-smelling diaper pail each morning to start the never-ending chore of washing the miserable rags in the wringer machine that Raymond had insisted they purchase. "It will be cheaper than a service," he told her. On top of this task, there was the regular washing to do, the endless preparation of formula for the younger girls, and the shopping to keep them all fed.

She had prepared for motherhood by watching the likes of Greer Garson and Myrna Loy make it look so effortless. She never really noticed that the women in movies seemed to have auxiliary caretakers standing in the wings--ready and waiting to take over for a mother dressed in silk and diamonds and on her way out to some glamorous nightclub.

"I don't know how much longer I can keep this up," she lamented to her husband one evening before he left for work. "You need to hire me some help," she demanded.

Raymond looked closely at his beautiful Dolores. Her golden blond hair was greasy and fell in strings down over her nose, where she blew it out of her way with a huff. Her crystalline blue eyes were bloodshot and always on the verge of tears whenever she talked about how over-whelmed she felt by the constant needs of her children. He wanted to help her. He honestly did, but without her working, a situation now out of the question, he couldn't afford to hire help. Not even for an hour or so for a quiet dinner alone, just the two of them.

"I wish I could get you all the help you need," he told her. "But we can't afford extras right now. We're still paying off the maternity bills. But I tell you what," he said. "I did my share of cleaning diapers when my ma died and left us with Amelia, still just a baby. I'll see to those things. Maybe that would help." Dolores was skeptical, but she gave her husband a weary smile.

"Anything would help," she told him.

For the next two years, Raymond awoke earlier than usual to take on the task of keeping his little children in clean diapers. He often did other laundry as well and, slowly but surely, the children grew and the old diapers became dust rags, car buffing towels or emergency sanitary pads, until one day, about the same time that the hospital bills had been paid down to nothing, the cotton cloths disappeared from their home.

Dolores no longer complained about making formula or washing for infants. She was adept at transferring her discontent to other areas of their domestic life. In 1945, before Dwight was born and before the end of WWII brought a literal army of men home in search of housing,

Raymond and Dolores had been able to purchase their bungalow in a pleasant neighborhood near Como Park. From their home, they could walk with the children to the park and zoo or down Lexington Parkway to shops and diners. The best part of the house was that they were nearly able to pay for it outright with Dolores' savings and the nest egg Raymond had accumulated over the years.

They were a fortunate couple, but Dolores' wants created a vacuum in her soul. She badgered Raymond to update the house. If a friend purchased a new item for her household, Dolores would be heartsick until she had one, too. She acquired a Hoover upright and then demanded that the hardwood floors be covered with wall-to-wall carpeting so she could use her new machine. The wringer washer went to the dump, and an agitator washer, along with an electric dryer, went into the basement. She had to have a television, a stereo, a Mix Master and an electric turkey roaster. She needed Revereware, Corningware, Tupperware and Nordicware. She needed an electric knife. And then came the time that she needed a new color television, just to watch a couple of shows on Sunday nights; every other night of the week, the old black and white set would have been adequate. Over the next decades, the appliances in the kitchen went from white to turquoise to avocado, then back to white, and that was where Raymond put his foot down.

"If you need other colors in here, you're just gonna have to make do with new tea towels and aprons," he told her. "I can't see the point of spending so much money just to end up right back where we started."

Now and again, Dolores would grow bored with domestic competition. She sometimes lusted for a more personal victory. She decided that she would forget about the house for a while and transform herself instead. She took up sewing, telling Raymond she wanted to make dresses for the girls. She did, but for each child's dress she produced, she made two for herself. She had Butterick patterns for everything from shirtwaist dresses to evening gowns. Once she had her figure back and the proper clothes to advertise her assets, she cajoled Raymond into taking her dancing, never one of his favorite activities. On the rare occasions when Raymond could get an evening off of work, he would hire a babysitter and take Dolores out for a night on the town. While he nursed a single beer over a period of hours, he watched his lovely wife whirl and flirt her way through other women's husbands. When Raymond protested about her behavior on the dance floor, she would laugh and kiss him on the forehead.

"Yes, my darling husband. I enjoy the attention," she told him. "But you're the one who gets to take me to bed."

"It better stay that way," he replied, and Dolores just laughed again and gave his crotch a reassuring pat with her hand.

* * *

In 1955, Jonas Salk announced the success of his vaccine for polio, but his miracle came much too late for the Saxby family. Little Linda, Ray and Dolores's youngest child, awoke on a Sunday morning complaining of a sore throat and a headache. Dolores scolded Linda for trying to dodge Sunday school; Linda hated the graham crackers they were given for snacks after all the children colored pictures of Jesus enjoying himself in heaven.

"Those crackers taste like socks smell," Linda had informed her mother.

Dolores didn't care what the snacks smelled like. What she appreciated was that a church bus came to pick up all four children and she could go back to sleep for an hour before she dressed in her Sunday best and waltzed in to listen to the weekly service from the front pew. It was the perfect venue to show off her latest fashion creations. The children would rejoin their mother after the service for a slice of coffee cake in the church basement before a leisurely walk home. One morning, when the Sunday School teacher arrived in the basement to hand off her charges, she dragged Little Linda up to Dolores and demanded her attention.

"Mrs. Saxby. I think you should call your husband or maybe a cab. Linda, here, is floppy as an old wash rag and her forehead is burning up."

The limp child could barely raise her head to look up at her mother's face. "My neck hurts, Mama," Linda whined.

About the time that Raymond had plates of spaghetti on the table that evening (covered with Auntie Rosella's bottled sauce), Little Linda could no longer move her legs. By the next morning, the child was at Gillette Children's Hospital with an iron lung breathing for her.

Ray and Dolores never fully recovered from the death of their baby girl. Dolores suffered fits of anxiety whenever the children were out of her sight, and she became a dedicated germaphobe. She went through a bottle of Clorox a week, sanitizing towels, bathtubs, sinks and floors. Every towel and sheet she owned had faded to a pale ghost of its unbleached self. What she couldn't scrub out was the scar of disease that became a label on the family. "If only she had listened to the child's complaints that Sunday morning and kept her home," folks said behind her back. For not only had Linda lost her life to the polio virus, two of her Sunday School classmates had developed the disease, one of whom was left with braces on her legs. It was widely assumed that it was Linda Saxby who had infected the others. Dolores, being Dolores, refused to cower in guilt. She still showed up to church in her finery and sat in the front pew, but she no longer lingered over coffee and donuts in the basement after the service. It was Dolores' theory that Linda had been a victim of someone else's non-symptomatic germs and Sunday School was one of the few places her young child could have been exposed. "I'll be damned if I let those self-righteous hypocrites run me out," she told Raymond, not quite recognizing the irony of her vow. She continued to demand fellowship from people she couldn't stand.

For his part, Raymond did all he could to soothe Dolores's unhappiness. He supplied her with a semi-new Buick every couple of years and looked the other way when she blew money on turquoise kitchen appliances in the mid-fifties and then switched to an avocado green kitchen around 1967. He took her on trips when he could and once settled the entire family into the latest Buick for a trip out west to visit his brother Leon at his new home in central California. *Bella Rosella* brand marinara sauce had become a national staple in the latter days of the Depression. When America went to war and housewives took up jobs in factories to support the war effort, the demand for quick and inexpensive food options skyrocketed. No woman wanted to pop rivets all day and then labor over a hot sauce pot in the evening. Leon and Rosella discussed their needs for expansion with an old friend who had long supplied them with California grapes and tomatoes. It was decided that the family would relocate to Salinas, where they would be close to prime tomato growing regions and where they could also continue to produce specialty wines.

"What do you think of Leon's new place?" Ray asked his wife as they readied for bed their first night in California.

"I think that Rosella is just too pleased with herself. That's what I think," Dolores replied. "Look at these sheets!" Dolores demanded. She pulled the bright yellow topsheet up for Raymond to examine. He had no idea what she was upset about. The sheets looked fine.

"What?" he asked. "They look like sheets," he told his wife.

"They have ruffles on them, for Christ's sake. And they're ironed!" Dolores was indignant by such an affront. "And, if she bleached them like she ought to, they wouldn't be this color anymore!"

Raymond scratched his head and tried to avoid a fight over nothing. "I think Rosella wanted to give us something special. To let us know how happy she is we came all the way out here to visit them."

Dolores huffed at her husband's response. "She just wants to lord it over us, that's what these things are all about." She batted at the offensive top sheet with the back of her hand. "We'll stay two days. That's it, and that's just so the kids can burn off some energy before we start back."

Raymond nodded his head. He was used to Dolores' feelings of inadequacy. It didn't help matters that Rosella's beauty rivaled that of her much younger sister-in-law's. Beauty was Dolores' armor. She was unaccustomed to challenges from similarly equipped rivals.

"I can't stand that woman," Dolores told Raymond on the ride home. "And we're never buying her horrible tasting spaghetti sauce again."

Dwight sat in the backseat, between his warring sisters. It was his job to act as a human demilitarized zone, separating each girl from the other. At the age of twelve, he was aware of the tensions his mother exhibited during the visit with his uncle's family. He was also aware that, while his own family had less than Uncle Leon's, it didn't seem to upset anyone other than his mother. Furthermore, he thought Auntie Rosella's sauces were pretty good.

"I like her sauce," Dwight said from the back seat.

His mother reached behind her with a sweep of her arm and caught the boy on the temple with the back of her hand. "You used to like it," his mother told him. "You don't like it anymore."

Dwight knew right then that there would be no more trips to California. He added his Uncle Leon's family to the list of people his mother could not abide. The only time Dwight had been out to see his Aunt Amelia and Uncle James had been on a clandestine jaunt to Hastings with his father when the car needed some attention from his mechanical uncle. Dwight's father had sworn him to secrecy. He was never to say a word to his mother about the visit.

"Why's Mama mad at them?" Dwight asked Raymond on the ride home. Dwight was eating a batch of extra special cookies his Aunt Amelia had made, just for him.

"Finish those before we get home," Raymond said.

It saddened Raymond that he had to cut out the love of his family in order to keep the love of his wife. He wanted to tell Dwight about his mother's anxieties. The children, and Dwight in particular, had a right to know, but Raymond had been sworn to secrecy by his wife. Raymond sometimes questioned whether love galvanized by secrets was really love at all.

"Oh, your mother worries that Uncle James is too strange to be around kids," Raymond told his son.

It was really Amelia whom his mother feared. Amelia knew exactly what was what.

And so it went in the years to come. The children grew up in their insular household and eventually went their own ways: Dwight to the Marines in 1966, Debbie to California to work for Leon and Rosella (a move that cost her ten years of silence from her mother), and Janice married one of Dwight's friends from the service until divorcing him two years later to become a Minnesota flower child. She prided herself on the signs she made for the McGovern Campaign of 1972. The family seldom spoke of Little Linda. The only thing the siblings remembered about their baby sister was the swooshing sound of her iron lung. Linda had long ago entered the realm of the mythical dead. Her name was mentioned with those of Grandma Saxby, Leona, and Harland, Dolores's brother who died in battle during World War II. But mostly, in an effort to spare their mother the pain of that loss, Little Linda wasn't mentioned at all.

18

St. Paul, Minnesota 1978

When Raymond prepared himself for what always proved to be a busy afternoon and night at the Commodore, the Saturday closest to February 14th, he did so with a chuckle rumbling in his chest. He pulled the silky, boxer-style underwear from the box Dolores had given him the previous afternoon. "Happy Valentine's Day, Raymond," she'd cooed to him when he unfurled the gift from crinkly red paper.

Married for over forty years, Dolores and Ray kept the relationship alive with gifts, games and the secret looks that passed between them. When either was in the mood for love, all the proposing party had to do was turn on a light switch in the bedroom. The not-so-subtle signal alerted one or the other of what their partner had in mind, for the switch plate covering the light toggle had a picture of an old, naked man embossed on its surface. When the switch was in the down position, the toggle became a penis in repose but in the up position, there was no mistaking its intent. At seventy-seven, Raymond could only hope that he would be as reliable as the fellow on the wall.

"You can wear them tonight," Dolores had told him, "to think of me while you're at work on Valentine's Day."

Ray held out the boxer shorts, emblazoned with a large heart over the crotch, and nodded his head. "They're perfect," he told her. "But I think I'll save them for tomorrow. I'm running too late to change into them now," he said.

He carefully folded them back into the box and gave Dolores a kiss and a box of her own. She received candy, which she loved, even if it caused her once lithe figure to grow just a touch with each tiny bite. "It must be my age," she told Raymond when she lamented about her expanded menopausal waistline.

"You look as beautiful as ever to me," he always assured her. And she did. In Ray's mind, the more of Dolores he had to love, the better.

The Friday night of February 14, 1978, had been as busy in the bar as he'd expected. Love was in the frigid air, and couples held hands over Old Fashioneds and Champagne. There were marriage proposals and anniversary toasts. There were kisses on the sly and kisses that brought about stares for their displays of overt passion. In one case, an enterprising lothario booked two dinners that night. Early on, he appeared with his sullen wife for a tense meal, through which they both seemed to rush. When they departed, the wife left the wilted carnation he had given her lying on a plate of uneaten pork chops. Later that same evening, the young husband appeared again. This time, the woman on his arm wore an orchid corsage and, from the look on his face, the man was clearly looking forward to whatever sweet treat he would later get from his luscious cream puff of a mistress. As usual, Raymond mixed drinks and kept his observations to himself. He had long ago determined that folks did what they wanted and it was none of his business what those wants might entail. Decades before, he had let his opinion of a philandering husband slip out. It was the last time he concerned himself with another's morality. The fellow had snatched his tip back, right out of Ray's fingers, and told him he was lucky he didn't get shot for butting into someone else's business. From that point forward, Ray blocked the betrayals of others from his mind. He had his own life to attend to, and he couldn't do it if he got snuffed out by an angry customer.

"I'm going in early today," Raymond hollered to his wife the next day over a radio blaring the Bee Gees screeching, in their ridiculous falsettos, about staying alive, staying alive.

Ray thought that he hadn't heard such worthless music since Rudy Vallee had made it big back in the 1920s. "Young folks got no taste in music," he thought to himself. "Didn't back then and don't now." He pulled the silky Valentine's gift up over his now hairless legs and marveled at how soft they felt against his dry, old skin. He did feel sexier--at least as sexy as a seventy-seven-year-old man with a pot belly and a balding pate could probably feel.

Dolores tossed a laundry basket down on the bed next to her husband. She busied herself placing the freshly folded clothes into the dresser drawers. When she finished her task, she looked up to see Ray modeling his new boxershorts. A sly smile crept over her face and a whistle escaped her lips.

"You're an oldie but goodie," she told him. When she turned to leave the room, she nudged her husband on his arthritic hip. "Have a good shift," she said.

"I will," he responded. "It's going to be a night of nice tips. Holiday celebrations are always good that way."

Raymond could have arrived at work at his regular hour, but he generally gave himself extra time on special occasions. He wanted to be sure the evening would run smoothly. He checked for enough clean glasses; he counted bottles of wine and inspected the ice bin for cleanliness. He had once been mortified when a customer returned a drink in which a hefty chunk of black mold appeared to be embedded in an ice cube. Never again. That was never going to happen again on his watch.

"Move the chairs and be sure you mop all the way under there," Ray ordered the young bartender working with him that day. "Get that candy wrapper, too," he said. "Someone must have scarfed down the whole box of Fanny Farmer." He bowed his head to look under the bar stools. "Christ! There's more wrappers over there." Ray pointed to the pleated cups that had been swept under the bar rail. The clean-up after a holiday was always more time-consuming than usual, but he would ensure that no matter which evening a customer chose to drink at the Commodore, their experience would be top notch.

Raymond meticulously wiped the fingerprints and smudges from the mirrored walls behind the bar. He prided himself on how well the vintage space had been maintained. He had been at the Commodore for over half a century, and he made it his mission to preserve the dignity of the glorious art deco space. Even now, his old heart ticked faster when he saw himself reflected in the faceted mirrors and spotless chrome around him. He had just wiped a stubborn smudge off a bottle of VSOP when it happened.

The explosion rocked the entire building and threw Raymond halfway across the room where he landed in a crumpled heap on the black marble floor. His head was spinning, and his ears rang like church bells.

"What the hell?" he said to himself. "What the hell happened?"

He looked around and, to his immense relief the boy with him was sitting up, dusting pulverized plaster from his longish hair with white, chalky fingers.

"You okay, son?" Raymond asked his helper. The boy said nothing but nodded his head yes. With each movement of his head, a fine coating of dust fell down into his eyes. The boy's glasses had disappeared entirely, and Raymond could clearly see the fear in the boy's glazed stare.

Bells started ringing everywhere, not just in Raymond's head.

"Fire! Everybody out!"

Sirens screamed up and down Western Avenue. When Raymond tried to stand, he found that his right leg refused to obey. He called for help.

"Grab me under the arms and pull!" Ray ordered the dumbstruck youngster sitting near him.

Fortunately, the slick marble floor made sliding Raymond out on the seat of his pants an easy task. Once outside, they could see that areas of the hotel were totally collapsed and flames had erupted through the roof. No sooner had the firefighters arrived than a second, larger explosion shook not just the hotel, but entire blocks of homes around it. Raymond watched in shock as one of the newly arrived firefighters rushed into the first floor of the hotel just to see him fly back out through a window on a wave of debris. Raymond felt himself get lifted into the air on the same violent wave and, in the next instant, he found that he had been deposited against a telephone pole thirty feet away from where he had been sitting. What had been a mild ache in his leg before the second blast was now an intense pain radiating down his leg from his hip, the very hip Dolores had nudged with her own just hours before.

Raymond was transported to Ramsey County Hospital where he spent the next two weeks recovering from surgery to place a pin in his femur. The last thing he remembered before they prepared him for surgery was a cute little nurse smiling at him and saying "Nice shorts." They were until she took her tape scissors to them and cut right through the red heart that covered his crotch. She flung his Valentine's gift into a plastic garbage bag, draped an open backed gown over his shoulders and told him "Good luck."

Later that evening, with Dolores at his bedside, he watched news coverage of the blast on KSTP. Reporters stood in front of the still steaming rubble and pronounced it a miracle that no one was killed in the gas explosion, though several had been injured severely enough to require hospitalization. It was reported that, in addition to civilian casualties, forty-three firefighters sustained burns or fractures, some needing inpatient care. But the most arresting news of all, at least for Raymond, came when he saw the mayor of St. Paul, George Latimer, being interviewed for the television cameras. Latimer, a beloved character in his city, praised the first responders and spoke of heroes. Then he commented that the beautiful art deco bar had survived the dual blasts intact. Not a mirror or a bottle was broken. The martini glasses stood upright and proud, just where Raymond had left them, though they were filled with dust, causing someone to joke that the drinks would be served extra dry that evening. Latimer, his eyes sparkling, threw his arms wide and smiled for the cameras.

"I guess it goes to show that God loves a drinker," he proclaimed. George Latimer won himself plenty of new voters that night, one of them being Raymond Saxby.

With the hotel closed for the foreseeable future and laid up with a bum hip, Raymond had time to do something he seldom did. He reflected. He thought about how his own future would play out once he recovered. He'd lost his old ring of lucky horse tack when the nurses cut his clothes from his body to assess his wounds, but he felt he no longer needed it. It had come with him full circle, from one fire to another. He was nearly seventy-eight years old, still alive, if not kickin' at the moment, and jobless for the first time in sixty years. Maybe it was time to retire. Maybe it was time to use what he had left of that precious commodity to spend it with Dolores, take her out more often or enjoy something as mundane as watching reruns of Mary Tyler Moore on TV. He and Dolores had seen the house once, the one in the show. "Take a good look, Dolores," he told his wife when they drove by the huge Victorian on Kenwood Parkway. "I don't plan to drive back over to Minneapolis anytime soon."

So that's what Raymond did. He retired at what he considered the peak of his career. When all else around it collapsed, the bar...his bar...had survived. It was a personal triumph despite his having had nothing to do with that act of fate, and he took it as a sign that his work there was done.

* * *

"Mancinis or the Blue Horse?" Ray asked the party on the other end of the phone. After listening for a few seconds, Ray put the phone to his chest and called out to Dolores. "Where should we meet the gang? Mancinis or the Blue Horse? Dwayne says they got a special tomorrow at the Blue Horse but I kind of prefer Mancinis. What do you think?" he asked her again.

Since his unexpected retirement, which Raymond described as "going out with a bang," he came to realize that his entire social life had taken place at work, for what could be more social than talking with folks over alcohol and fine food. He missed those human interactions, especially since Dolores had long refused relationships with his family, and those sentiments had spilled over into her contacts with her own kin. With the children grown and gone, the Saxbys spent their evenings walking the circuit around Como Lake in the warm months or watching M*A*S*H in the winter. When Dwayne called him one day in 1980, asking if he and Dolores wanted to join a group of retired bartenders in their monthly visits to the better restaurants and bars in St. Paul, Ray jumped at the chance.

"It's just a group of fellows like me. Old barmen who go out to eat and drink and enjoy criticizing the youngsters who mix up all the newfangled cocktails. It's just once a month. It might be fun," he told his skeptical wife.

"You can't drive since the cataract thing," Dolores pointed out. "What fun will it be for me if I have to be the driver every time?"

"Well, that's the thing. They all pool their money and get a taxi or two. That way, no one has to worry about driving."

Dolores bit back her objections, and over time she came to enjoy these monthly outings. She found herself rummaging through her closet for outfits to wear on these special evenings and invested in a whole batch of good make-up from Merle Norman. Her husband might well be eighty, but she was a relatively young sixty-three. With the proper foundation wear, she could still catch a man's eye, if the lighting was right, and in the darkened bars the group favored, the lighting was usually right enough.

Raymond stood fidgeting with the phone receiver to his chest. "Well?" he asked Dolores. "Any opinion about tomorrow night?"

Dolores loved to be the contrarian. "We've been to the Blue Horse and Mancinis plenty. Let's go to the Lex. I love their bar and those pot pies they got."

When the group of eight retired drinkmasters and their wives finished their meals, they adjourned to the comfortable bar that was the main reason folks came to the Lexington. Its cozy, traditional feel allowed its patrons to down their drinks in an atmosphere that lent class to the quest for inebriation. There at the Lex, drinkers were surrounded by judges and business owners, and all the old families in town. On one occasion, Raymond looked across the room and recognized the mayor, who recognized him back. George Latimer raised his glass to Raymond in the way of men who had endured a tragedy together. Such was the comradery of drinking at the Lex.

"That young fellow thinks he's the cat's meow," Bob said to the group of old barmen. His words were beginning to slur, and it was apparent that the evening was soon to be over for the geriatric set. The retirees seldom lasted beyond ten o'clock.

Raymond watched the young bartender twirl the bottles and toss them behind his back to entertain his patrons. Those patrons were mostly attractive young women dressed in Diane Von Furstenberg wrap dresses with low-cut necklines. Dolores thought the women unseemly, but Bob and Dwayne couldn't take their eyes off the busty view. She shuddered at the crepey skin that marred her own decolletage. Dolores no longer enjoyed looking at her own chest, and it depressed her that no one else did, either.

"Show 'em how it's done, Ray." Bob and Dwayne had become emboldened by alcohol and wanted to knock the wise-ass kid down a notch or two.

"For Christ's sake. He's spraying vodka all over the place. His timing's shit," remarked Tom, another one of their group. He had spent many years at the Monte Carlo over in Minneapolis. Despite his affinity for the MiniApple, Ray's group welcomed Tom. He often picked up a round or two which allowed them to overlook his origins from the wrong side of the river.

With just enough liquor in his system and a "what the hell" attitude, Ray sauntered up to the bar and tapped the kid on the shoulder.

"You're making a mess there, son." Ray smiled when he said this, all good-natured mentor passing on tips to the next generation.

"What do you know about it, old man?" The youngster cocked his head towards the women and rolled his eyes in his handsome head.

"Allow me." Raymond took the bottle and glass from the kid's hands and smiled again at the outraged barman.

"Hey! What do you think you're doing?" he demanded of Ray. "You make a mess and you're paying for it!" the boy snarled.

Ray was unfazed. "Watch and learn, son," he told the boy.

In a performance he knew he could never repeat, Raymond tossed the bottle over his head, caught it at the perfect point in its arc and poured the liquid into the glass without an errant drop. Encouraged by his success, he picked up another bottle and then another and juggled the uncorked containers to the amazement of all watching. When he finished his display and placed the bottles carefully back down on the counter, a loud cheer and a round of applause erupted from the folks watching the show.

"Way to go, Pops!" someone yelled. The bevy of beautiful young women stood in line to kiss Raymond on his wrinkled cheek. The bartender, amazed, looked at Raymond with new respect.

"How'd ya learn to do that?" the kid asked Raymond.

Raymond smiled sheepishly and raised his shoulders in an "ahh shucks" gesture.

"I wasn't always old, you know."

That was the last such excursion for Raymond and Dolores. She was furious at him for accepting the chaste kisses from the women at the bar, and she couldn't imagine what Ray had been thinking. The incident could have gone so wrong. If he'd ended up looking like a clown, she would have looked like one, too, for not stopping him from making a fool of himself.

"But it didn't go wrong. That was the point," he told her. Regardless, Dolores told him that if he continued to be part of the group, he would have to do it on his own.

The couple went back to watching television every night of the month, and it was during a Twins game, when the home team was ahead in the fourth inning, that Ray was called to the phone. At eighty-seven, Leon had died in his sleep from emphysema. Smoking finally wore him down, but it took much longer than Ray had expected. Seventy-five years of two packs a day, to be exact.

Dolores refused to order flowers for the funeral.

"They're in California. They got flowers everywhere out there."

When his wife stepped out to go to Applebaum's, Ray picked up the phone and called a florist he'd often used to romance Dolores. He knew she would be upset with him when she got the credit card bill, but Raymond would deal with that when the time came. If he couldn't manage to get to the funeral itself, he sure as hell was sending flowers to honor his brother. Dolores could be a mighty hard woman at times, and she stayed that way until the moment she died, angry over a hairbrush.

St. Paul January 1996

"That must have been difficult for you, being shut off from your friends and family. Did she get mad about the flowers?" I asked, trying to distract him so I could concentrate on finding his ever-weaker pulse. His wrist was skin and bone and very little artery under my fingers.

Mr. Saxby looked down at the slippers on his feet.

"Oh, she got over it. You have to understand. I needed Dolores. I had to keep her happy. I had to keep her with me."

There was a plea for understanding in his milky eyes. I did understand. I had known that very need. The kind that turns your head the other way when you know you should be facing things head on.

"Tell Dwight I'm sorry. I should have done things different a long time ago. I'm sorry to you too, but when I lost Dolores, I needed Dwight."

The old man bowed his head and wiped a single tear from below his eye. Was he crying or just leaking? I had accepted Dwight's situation years ago, and I understood that his father's care would dictate the terms of our relationship. I'd wanted more but hadn't really expected to get it. Mr. Saxby had no need to ask for my forgiveness.

"I know you need Dwight to care for you. There's nothing to apologize for," I said to him, but he shook his head at the banal platitude.

"Just living makes you sorry," he told me in a strangled whisper.

His eyes drooped, and his head followed them onto his chest. His intermittent breaths became raspy, and he slumped in the chair. I shook him by the shoulder and hollered his name.

"Mr. Saxby! Are you alright?"

All those past CPR drills sent me into emergency mode. He never stirred, but his pulse and breathing continued their erratic control over his ancient body. I called 911 and then I called Dwight. The emergency operator answered right away, but I had to leave Dwight a message. I wondered if it would be his unit that would respond to my call.

After a week in the cardiac unit, Raymond Saxby was transferred to hospice care. He observed Groundhog Day 1996 in a semi-comatose state. He didn't miss much. A spate of brutal cold had settled over the upper Mississippi River valleys, bringing with it nearly a week of temperatures dropping into the negative twenties. Most of the residents of Minnesota would have prefered a coma to frostbite. Mr. Saxby's comment about having lived through almost eight years of February came to my mind. I doubted he would live through this last one, the one he needed to reach a full eight years, but I gave him credit for the entire month. I went by pension plan rules; living one day of the month granted him credit for all of February. I didn't go into the hospital to see him; he wouldn't have known me and Dwight was too distracted to care if I were there or not. He had his estranged sister and the one from out of state to manage at the hospital.

"How's your dad doing?" I asked Dwight one late afternoon when he stopped by my house for a break from hospital food. I slid a sandwich made of real turkey breast and cranberry sauce onto a plate and handed it to him. "Want a beer with that?" I asked.

He took a large bite and chewed. When he swallowed, he got up from his seat and opened the door of the refrigerator.

"What kind do you have?" he wondered. Although it embarrassed me to say so, I told him the truth.

"Just some leftover Pigseye," I said. To my surprise, he grabbed one off the shelf and popped the top.

"For a swig of swell swill," he toasted and chugged down half the can. "You know the story of Pigseye Parrant, don't you?" he asked me.

"I know he was a scoundrel from the early days of the city and that St. Paul used to be called Pigseye, named after him."

He laughed and chugged down the rest of the can, before cracking the top on another. "Well then," he said. "You know all you need to know about Pigseye. Dad thought it was a terrible name for the town beer. He favored something more elegant, whatever that might have been."

"Your dad always struck me as a rather elegant man," I replied, meaning every word. "What's going to happen now? With him not coming back and all?"

It was an accepted fact that if Mr. Saxby managed to rally, he would still need twenty-four hour care, meaning a nursing home was the only option.

"I'm going to have to get the house ready to sell. What with the money we owe the state for Mom's care and now, Dad, I can't see any other option."

"What about you? Do you want to stay with me? You can, you know?" I offered.

Dwight put his arm around my shoulder and pulled me close. He kissed me on the cheek, then released me and gave my bottom a chummy pat, like I was a football player who had just called a good play.

"We'll see what happens. It may take months to get the house ready and I don't want to leave it abandoned in the meantime." Dwight picked up his down ski jacket and headed for the door. He stopped when a thought struck him and turned to me.

"Say, I was wondering if you would be able to help me. Maybe you could go through Mom's stuff. You know, all her lady gear. Donate whatever you think is worth something and pitch the rest. My sisters don't want to be bothered. You think about it," he suggested.

I had no need to think about it. What else did I have to do with my lonely hours? It would be like rummaging through a thrift shop, only free.

"Sure," I replied. "I'd love to help out."

Shortly thereafter, I was given a key to Dwight's house, the first such gesture in our eight-year relationship. In all fairness, I hadn't given him one to my house either, but he and half the neighborhood knew where I hid mine under the cement gargoyle on my front porch steps. The one time I had been broken into, it had cost me more to fix the door than to replace what had been stolen so I had assumed a low-security stance when it came to my property. It was fine with me if you ripped me off, just don't break the door. "Use the key and help yourself" became my philosophy.

Though I had been in the Saxby house maybe a couple of dozen times over the years, I had never been in it alone. There is something magical about being alone in someone else's house. All the mysteries of domestic life are there to be discovered. Numerous liquor bottles, poured down to the dregs--a secret drinker. Risque undergarments folded perfectly and arranged with care in a drawer--a vigorous romantic life. A hundred plastic TV dinner trays, cleaned, stacked and wrapped up in grocery bags--a hoarder. I imagined some homes could boast all three conditions, but Raymond and Dwight's house fell into that last category. Then again, so did the homes of many old folks who had lived through the Depression.

Naturally, I started my foraging through the house in Dwight's room. I ran my hand over the chenille bedspread that covered the twin bed he had slept in since he was a boy. It made me sad for him that he never really got away from this little room. I glanced in his closet and smelled the Aqua Velva that he splashed on every morning. The closet was surprisingly small, smaller than the ones in my vintage house, and it was filled to the brim with outdated things I never saw Dwight wear. Where were his work clothes, I wondered? It was a mystery but only a tiny one. Maybe he did what I did. He kept them in the attic or in the storage shed in the yard. Those were inconvenient solutions but the sort of thing a clothes horse like Dwight might do when a house has inadequate closet space.

That first evening, I was able to get through all of Dolores' wardrobe. She had handmade dresses that went back to the fifties and sixties, along with cocktail wear from what must have been the eighties. Some of them had elaborate shoulder pads and a plethora of sequins trailing down the bodices or around the hems. "Those must be from the days of the retired bartender outings," I thought. I dutifully went through pockets and purses and placed whatever I found into a cardboard box I carried from room to room. There were old driver's licenses, broken watches, medical records--stuff one never quite knows what to do with. I kept those for Dwight to sort out.

Over the next few evenings, after changing from my work clothes and feeding the dog, I ventured back to continue the job. I sorted through bedroom dressers and bathroom cabinets; I cleaned out neglected laundry baskets in the creepy, dark basement. Finally, I was left with the attic and whatever Dolores had stashed up there.

Like most attics in houses built on the dawn of the electrical age, this one had a single bulb hanging down from the ceiling with a pull chain to switch on the light. When I yanked on the chain, it broke off in my hand but the light came to life and it lit up the cramped space. There were some of Dwight's things up there, but not what I had expected. On a rail held up by hooks in the rafters was a line of Dwight's old uniforms. His Marine blues had a deteriorating drycleaner's bag over them, and next to it was an outfit that had a sash that said "St. Paul Drum and Bugle Corps." Outdated paramedics shirts with "Trainee" written on a patch hung on the rail, as did a couple old softball uniforms. There was still no sign of Dwight's actual clothes, the ones I saw him in the most. A fine layer of dust covered everything in the attic, but it was warm in the room, almost cozy. Whenever I moved through the space, I disturbed dust. It whirled through the air and reflected in the light like the flecks in a snowglobe.

In the attic, I found more of the same type of thing I found elsewhere in the house, the refuse of a long life--symbols of a past that was long gone but still lingered in memory and in the tangible artifacts that lay discarded on the wooden floor. Baby buggies, old trunks, a tricycle, some spindly furniture, a few tools. Exactly what one would expect to find in an attic that no one had bothered to clean out for decades. Over in a corner, near the only window in the room, I spotted a crock, large like a butter churn, which is what it turned out to be. The top was secured onto the opening but the wooden churn handle was missing.

Maybe Dwight wouldn't mind letting me have this. It would go great in my vintage kitchen. I grabbed a rag and wiped the dust from the front of the crock. It was made by Red Wing Pottery and had been a piece to commemorate the Minnesota Centennial of 1958. That made the piece more valuable, meaning I might need to pay him for it. All the same, I was having a "finders, keepers" moment. If he didn't even know it existed, he probably wouldn't miss it. I carefully pulled it away from the wall and noticed that it was heavier than I thought it would be. When I opened the top to investigate, I found stacks of old snapshots held together by tattered ribbons.

I sat on a small stool that had once helped a child reach the sink and gave in to the desire to snoop. It was dark outside, but the overhead bulb was all I needed to learn the truth of the past.

Most of the photos were small, square, black and white snapshots with a jagged white border. For reasons I never understood, the photos of that era looked like they had been trimmed with pinking shears. I carefully pulled the ends of the ribbon apart and held the stack of snapshots in my hand. There was Dwight, sitting on the running board of a car from the late forties. He was wearing a little suit with short pants and he had a baby fedora cocked jauntily on his head. Farther down into the stack, baby girls appeared. I undid more stacks and lost track of time. I saw before me Raymond Saxby's domestic life: his wife through the years, his children changing from babies to teenagers to adults. The pictures went from the black and white squares to rectangles of color, faded to a near-sepia finish. Laughable outfits, clunky glasses and hairstyles that made me shudder. We all had photos like these hidden away somewhere in our homes. When I finished looking through the crock, I carefully replaced the items. I couldn't abscond with the receptacle of Dwight's past.

As I pushed it back to its place next to the wall, I spied a carved wooden box, about two feet square, off to the side and covered with a stack of flattened out pillows and old bedspreads. Just the edges were showing, but it looked interesting and all I had waiting for me at home were an angry terrier and a hot shower. They could both wait. I wrangled the box from beneath the bedclothes and opened its hinged lid.

More pictures, this time of Ray and Dolores posed in front of the Gates Ajar at Como Park. The pictures on top of the pile were in color and the couple wore the garb of the Disco era. Raymond looked uncomfortable in a pea green leisure suit, and Dolores sported a paisley pantsuit with exaggerated bell bottoms. They were smiling, though; his arm pulling her tightly to him. I sorted through the stack until I found what must have been their wedding photo. They were a beautiful young couple; he, tall and handsome and she with a cascade of luscious hair falling on her shoulders. Despite the black and white ink, I could tell from the highlights that she had been blond. I replaced these pictures and opened a large legal envelope that was under them. There were pictures of Raymond and Dolores' children's weddings or anniversary celebrations, all taken with the Gates Ajar in the background. Prominent among them were several of Dwight, his arm around a slender, dark-haired woman with a shy smile. In one photo, taken no more than five years ago, Dwight was wearing a shirt I had given him for his birthday. Written on the back of the oldest picture, the color sun-bleached and smeared, were the words *Dwight and Leslie-Married June 17, 1972.*

The photo dropped from my hands like a bomb about to explode. How could I have been such an idiot! How could I have overlooked all the clues! Why hadn't Mr. Saxby said something to me? I felt ill and used. I shoved the pictures back into the paper folder and slapped them back into the box, accidently ripping another tattered folder. I could see through the rip that this one held official documents. "Maybe I would find a divorce decree," I thought. I extracted the envelope and gently slipped the papers free. Among them were the elder Saxby's marriage certificate, Dolores' death certificate and birth certificates for Raymond's children. Little Linda's death certificate slept in a pink envelope that also held her birth announcement. A picture of the smiling girl was sandwiched between the two papers. Mixed in with these validations of life's beginnings and endings was another document that surprised me as much as Dwight's wedding picture.

The next evening, I mopped a couple of floors while I waited for Dwight to show up at the back door of the Saxby home. Dwight had an evening off, and he said he'd work with me, hauling out some trash.

When he called to confirm, he reported that he was bringing a pizza for our dinner. I told him I wasn't hungry. What I didn't tell him was why.

"Come and get it while it's hot!" he yelled when he came through the door.

He plopped the pizza box onto the kitchen table and busied himself getting plates from the shelf. I stuck my hand into my purse and pulled out the stack of pictures of him and his bride. I tossed them on the table. He turned a little green when he saw his wedding photo lying next to the greasy pizza.

"It's not what it seems," he said to me, trying as he talked, to take my hand into his. I pulled it away and stuffed it into the pocket of my Guess jeans.

"How could you do this to me all these years?" I cried. I was really, actually crying. "And how could you use your own feeble father as part of your sick trap?"

The reality of what he had done turned the handsome man I had loved into a pathetic, middle-aged louse, looking to undo his miserable deeds.

"You don't understand. Her and me--we don't love each other that way anymore."

He told me this as if it were an adequate explanation. I shook my head in disbelief.

"Yeah. Okay. We do live together. But I don't always sleep with her. I like sleeping with you!" he protested.

"I see," I said. "You like living with her but you like fucking with me. I think I deserve someone who wants to do both," I told him. "And what's with your dad? Why the hell did he play along with this charade for so long? I was always so nice to him!"

These last words were uttered through the slippery slime of snot bubbles.

Dwight shrugged his shoulders. "It was his bartenders' code. Never betray a secret. Besides, he needed to keep me coming around. He couldn't drive. He couldn't walk to the store anymore. He couldn't risk me being mad at him."

So that's what Mr. Saxby meant when he apologized to me. He

couldn't gamble on telling me the truth. Though, thinking back on our conversations, he had given me plenty of hints. His self-protective view of the situation was understandable, but I was too angry to forgive anyone, especially myself for ignoring all the red flags that had been waved in my face.

"We're done. I can't believe what a despicable dirtball you are!"

To punctuate the moment, I swiped the pizza box to the floor, the one I had just mopped to keep myself busy until he arrived. I wondered if he could see the smoke coming from my ears.

"Oh. Don't kid yourself," he told me through a sneer. "You had to know I didn't actually live here. Did you ever see my stuff in the bathroom?"

"I never looked!" I screamed back at him.

He hung his head and stroked at a tiny tear near the corner of his eye. A tiny crocodile tear, most likely. "Please, don't leave me. I'm sorry I haven't been the man you thought I was," he pleaded.

I felt drained and sad but also resolved to end my addiction to Dwight Saxby. I went to the living room and got my coat. Under it, lying on the chair, was the torn envelope from the wooden box. I held it out to him, and he took it in his fingers.

"I'm sorry to tell you that you aren't actually the man you thought you were, either."

I put on my coat and left Dwight standing alone with the documents in his hand.

19

Hastings, Minnesota 1944

On the cusp of her sixteenth birthday, Daisy Blume got an itch. She wasn't sure why she got it or who had given it to her, but she was pretty sure it had something to do with the shirtless boy she had seen toiling in a field near Faribault.

"They're prisoners," her father told her on an outing to deliver Amelia's baked goods to the town southwest of Hastings.

"They don't look like prisoners. They look like regular people," she replied to her father.

In Daisy's mind, they looked quite a bit better than regular people. Either the draft or enlistment had taken every good looking boy in town and all that remained were the dregs of her high school class, the ones who wore thick glasses or were pigeon-toed and tripped over their own feet.

"They're German boys. Just regular German boys brought in to tend the crops and do factory work until the war is over," James explained.

Daisy watched the young men flex their muscles as they worked and noted how their golden skin glistened in the sun. It was the first time she found sweat appealing. Instead of a smelly artifact of summer, the sheen on these boys looked like a rich, amber lacquer that had been brushed over their rippling shoulders. One particular fellow caught her eye. When he bent to gather a sheaf of wheat, a lock of ashy blond hair fell onto his forehead and he brushed it back out of his eyes. His hair was exactly the same color as her Uncle Raymond's; he could have been her cousin, but it was not a familial interest she felt in that moment. She noted a peculiar sensation in her abdomen, like the butterflies she dreaded when a math test was coming, only this was more pleasant--much more pleasant. Her body responded to the boy's mere existence in a way that was new for her. She felt herself moisten between her legs. The response both embarrassed and excited Daisy. Beneath her own solid muscle and bone, her core was liquifying from a strange desire.

"This is about sex," she rightly surmised.

She came to learn that the itch in her body could be tamed by the touch of her own hand, an enjoyable enough experience but one that left her with questions about how it would be to satisfy her needs with a flesh-and-blood man. In her fevered interludes of solo intimacy, she visualized the young man in the field. She longed to run her tongue along the salty furrows between the muscles on his belly. She wondered if it would hurt to take a man into her body, then decided that it couldn't hurt too badly or no one would ever do it more than once. And she wanted to do it more than once. She wanted to do it with the German stranger. She wanted to do it as often as she could. There was no good explanation for why she felt this way. He was, after all, the enemy.

Over the winter of 1945, Daisy followed the newsreel reports of the war that raged in both Europe and Japan, but she paid particular attention to the events occuring in the waning days of the European conflict. While her schoolmates cheered each Allied victory, Daisy secretly hoped that the war would go on and on. Or at least until she could watch the Germans working shirtless in the fields once more. She cried herself to sleep on May 8, 1945, the day the German army surrendered to Allied forces, and felt like a traitor for doing so. But she couldn't staunch her fascination with the German prisoner boys who looked so clean and bright, even covered in the dusty loam from a plow.

Each morning through May and June, Daisy was the first to grab the paper from the doorstep. She searched the pages for news of the prisoners. With the war's end, they would surely be sent home, she reasoned, but to her relief, no mention was made of returning the men until our own troops began coming home in enough numbers to provide the labor needed to work the jobs these Germans filled.

"You're awful interested in the news lately, Dais," her father said one morning. " We won, you know?"

"I know, Daddy." Daisy refolded the paper and handed it to her father. "I'm just old enough now to care about what's going on," she told him.

"She's probably looking for news that our boys are coming back so she has someone besides that Wilber Cox to date for change," Amelia remarked, hoping to get a rise out of Daisy.

The girl smirked and wrinkled her nose. "Wilber's like a coat you put on a chair to keep it vacant for later. He's keeping me from caring about all that dating stuff," Daisy replied to her mother.

Wilber's appeal was his car and his allowance, although her mother was right, in a way. She was interested in the return of the American troops because their return would trigger the exit of the German labor. Daisy finished her breakfast just as her father drank the last of his coffee. He turned to the girl and gave her a conspiratorial wink.

"I'm running down to Faribault to pick up another tow truck. I want you to ride along with me. Help me by driving this car back. Think you can do that?" James asked his newly licensed daughter.

The thought of driving through the countryside, all on her own and in her own personal reverie, filled Daisy with gleeful anticipation.

"Of course, Daddy," she said. "Give me a few minutes to get ready."

"Get ready? We're not going to a dance, Daisy," James told her.

"It's girl business, Daddy," Daisy demurred.

That stopped James in his tracks. He had no desire to inquire further about the mysterious tribulations of womankind.

"Go on then. Be quick."

James shooed Daisy into the house and waited for her to reappear. When she did, she was wearing a sundress and had pinned her hair up like Betty Grable.

"You look pretty gussied up to go pick up an old tow truck, Daisy," James told her.

"Leave her be," Amelia told her husband. To Daisy, she said, "You look lovely, sweetheart."

Daisy slumped against the side of her father's car and watched the landscape fly past the window. She and her father spoke little on the trip over to Faribault. This suited James and allowed Daisy ample time to scan the horizon for intriguing sights. She was disappointed when she arrived in Faribault having seen nothing more interesting than a horse that had fallen on its back into a deep gully in a passing field. The animal's four legs jutted straight up into the air, and it clawed at the sky like a windmill. An attendant farmer was at its side, cajoling the animal to get itself up.

"Should we stop and help?" Daisy asked her father.

James shook his head. "Leave them be. They'll figure it out. If they're still in the same fix on the way back, we'll lend a hand."

Father and daughter had a quick lunch at a local diner before James finalized the deal for the purchase of the tow truck. Finally, finally, it was time for James to hand over the car keys to Daisy. She was excited and nervous to drive so far on her own, but some of the thrill had evaporated when there had been no sighting of the prisoners on the drive over from Hastings. She had seen nothing of interest at all, other than the peculiar plight of the upturned horse.

"Be careful, Daisy Girl," James told her as he handed her the keys. "Stay behind me and stop if I stop. I don't want you getting too far behind. Understand?"

Daisy grabbed the keys and nodded her head in agreement. If this little trip went well, she could soon enjoy all the freedoms that driving could offer. She could go to the movies, dances, or maybe to St. Paul for some real shopping. The world would be hers to explore on her own time and in her own way.

As Daisy drove, she found herself focusing all her attention on the back of the tow truck. The desire to see something other than fields of corn or soybeans fell away and she concentrated on keeping a decent distance behind her father. As they approached the field where the horse had been stuck on its back like a hapless turtle, the tow truck slowed and pulled to the side. Daisy carefully pulled up behind her father and waited for him to exit the truck.

James walked up to Daisy and motioned for her to cut the engine.

"Horse is still stuck. We might as well see if we can help. I can use the truck to pull it upright," he told her.

The girl hopped out of the car and ran to the front of the big Dodge. From that vantage point, she saw the animal and three men pushing and pulling on its thrashing form. One fellow had a two-by-twelve plank wedged under the horse, trying to pry it out of the ditch.

"Hey there," James called out. "Need a hand?"

The young man with the pry board looked up and waved to James. "Ya!Ya! Gut!" he replied, and Daisy smiled to herself. This one wasn't quite as pretty as the golden boy she had seen on the previous trip, but he would do. He was tall and lean, with wiry, light brown hair and a pleasant face. The closer Daisy came to him, the more she could see that his pleasant face was smiling at her and his smile was warm and friendly. He seemed no more threatening than the town boys she knew so well and a lot more attractive than most. Especially Wilber.

A rope and a tow truck made quick work of righting the horse, and before Daisy started the car for the drive home, she and Helmut had made clandestine plans, right under the nose of her father, to meet with their respective friends on the coming Sunday for an afternoon of tubing on the Cannon River. For the next three days, Daisy did nothing but think of consorting with the enemy.

Over the waning weeks of summer, Daisy Blume used her newly minted driver's license to rendezvous with Helmut. He told her in halting English that his name meant healthy in German. And Daisy had to agree. His skin glowed in the sun-dappled shade on the Cannon River; his teeth were perfect and straight; and once they got around to it, Helmut had unending energy for copulatory adventures.

"You know those German prisoners?" Daisy ventured to her parents one evening at the dinner table. Both James and Amelia nodded. "You know they don't lock them up most the time? They can just go about their business," Daisy informed them.

James said, "Yep," but Amelia offered an insight.

"Well, where would they go? The few pennies they have might as well be spent in the towns that host them."

Daisy laughed. "Host them? You make it sound like a party."

What Daisy didn't realize was that for most of the German boys toiling in the fields and factories of Minnesota, their existence in the state was a party. Home meant deprivation and devastation. On the farms of southern Minnesota they were well fed. Many bunked with farmers whose first language mirrored their own. Few had any pressing desire to return to their vanquished homeland.

The summer of 1944 drifted into fall, and harvest season occupied more and more of Helmut's time.

"After harvest, they are sending me over to Marshall to work on a big dairy farm," Helmut told Daisy in a combination of German, English and body language. The young lovers were holding hands in the hidden poultry aisle of the feedstore, pretending to read the labels on bags of chicken scratch.

Daisy took a deep breath and reached for Helmut's other hand, turning him so they stood face to face.

"I have something to tell you, too." She dropped her eyes and stared at her shuffling feet. "I think I'm going to have a baby."

Daisy reported this distressing news in a strangled sigh, tears waiting to spill down her cheeks. When Helmut shook his head to tell her he didn't understand, she patted her belly and rocked a make-believe infant in her empty arms. A startled look filled Helmut's eyes, and then he smiled.

"Some of me stays with you, ya? Some of me in America."

Helmut kissed Daisy gently on her frowning forehead. Helmut could afford to be accepting of this situation, Daisy thought; he would be gone before the snow fell and the fatherless baby would come this spring to a teenage mother whose community would find her more despicable than the German who had sired her child. In that moment, Daisy figured she had made her bed, so why not lay in it again. She led Helmut into a maze of alfalfa hay bales, stacked seven high, and spread herself out on his denim jacket. "Harm's already been done," she rationalized.

In a few short weeks, her German boy disappeared, right along with the leaves on the autumn trees.

"I think Daisy needs a new winter coat," Amelia mentioned to James one evening in late November. "She can hardly pull it closed. Maybe we should get her one for Christmas."

Daisy did get a new coat for Christmas, along with a bus ticket to St. Cloud where her Aunt Genevieve lived. Daisy hadn't realized she had a great aunt in Minnesota, but her mother told her that Genevieve was a sister to her grandmother, Leona; that she had come to Minnesota from Illinois decades ago, along with Leona and their mother. There had been almost no contact between the families for ages but, as Amelia explained, "This is one of those times when family has to step up."

Raymond was puzzled when his little sister called him out of the blue one afternoon, suggesting they meet for a cup of coffee at Mickey's Diner. Amelia rarely made the trek into St. Paul, being content to have most of her shopping needs met by the Montgomery Ward catalog. She explained to her brother that she had a return she needed to make at the Wards on University and thought it would be nice to catch up.

"Dolores would love to see you, too. I'll ask her," Raymond told Amelia over the phone. He noted a chasm of silence assaulting him through the wire.

"Let's just meet--the two of us. I have something special I need to tell you."

Ray agreed, but the intrigue of the request nagged at him all day. Was Amelia sick? Was she leaving James? It was unlike Amelia to be mysterious. Amelia was usually a straight shooter, particularly for a woman.

At a tiny table where they could look out on the corner of Wabasha and Seventh Street, Ray and Amelia sipped coffee and caught up on each other's lives.

"How long have you and Dolores been married now, Ray? Eight, nine years?"

Raymond nodded. "'Bout that. Yeah," he replied.

"And still no babies..." Amelia commented, more than questioned. Ray just nodded again. "We don't know why. We want them, me and Dolores, but it never seems to happen for us. She thinks it's me. Maybe it is, being older and all." Ray sipped his coffee to dilute the shame of his failure.

"What if you could adopt a child? How would you and Dolores feel about that?" Amelia asked. When Ray looked up from his cup, his lips curled in an involuntary gesture of hope.

"Do you know of a baby, Amelia?" Raymond asked.

"I do," Amelia told her brother.

Over the next hour and two more cups of coffee, she told him of the predicament Daisy was in and how he could help. Raymond and his sister left the diner confident that their plan would be best for all involved. Now he would need to convince Dolores.

The name on the birth certificate was Otto Helmut Huppendorfer. Daisy had insisted that her child start life as the person he really was, even if his upcoming adoption would change him into someone else. She was never told that the adoptive parents would be her own aunt and uncle or that the baby she occasionally glimpsed with them was her own newborn son. The soft brown hair the child had at birth fell away and was replaced by a tangle of rusty curls, much as Daisy's had been in her own infancy, but she didn't notice the resemblance. The girl was relieved when she handed off her little son to the adoption authorities. She came to realize that it was the German boy she longed for, not the screeching infant in the crib. She ached to have her own physical needs met and had very little interest in meeting those of her child. Daisy had instincts, but they weren't of the maternal sort. If she suspected her own son was just a few miles and a generation away, she never let on. As long as the baby was out of her life, she didn't care who had him.

Dolores, on the other hand, had very definite plans for her long-awaited child.

'We are not calling him anything that even hints at German, do you hear me, Ray?"

Ray heard his wife, loud and clear. He wanted this happy event to bring Dolores the contentment that had eluded her all these years. He would name the child whatever she wanted.

"How about Raymond, Jr.?" he ventured, but Dolores turned up her nose.

"I don't want to spend my life explaining which Ray I'm talking about. No. How about naming him after a war hero? How about Winston or Douglas, for MacArthur?" Dolores sampled the names on her tongue. "Winston Douglas Saxby. What do you think?" she asked her husband.

"Not Douglas. That bastard ran Leon and Rosella out of Washington. I told you that story, remember? How about Dwight? For Eisenhower."

The reissued birth certificate established the child as Dwight Raymond Saxby, and for safe keeping, the papers were stored in a large wooden box the couple hid in their attic. To keep the secret of Dwight's origins from seeping out, Dolores proclaimed that Amelia's family must have no more contact with the child. Dwight was their baby now, and nothing good could come from giving Amelia the chance to moon over the lost grandchild. This was a rule Raymond bent behind Dolores' back but only on the rarest of occasions.

"What will we tell the baby when he's older?" Raymond wanted to know. "We should eventually tell him he's adopted." Raymond thought such a plan was healthy and reasonable, but reason wasn't one of Dolores' strong suits.

"All he needs to know is that he belongs to us," Dolores insisted.

Dwight felt that he belonged to Dolores only until the first in a series of baby girls took up temporary residence in his mother's womb. From then on, little Dwight wondered what he had done wrong. Maybe his mother had wanted daughters to begin with, for once his sisters arrived, Dwight was told to "run along" whenever he approached his mother's side. He never shook the subtle feeling of rejection, right up to the moment that he learned the complicated story of his birth.

Dwight discovered the truth of his identity while sitting in his father's vacant recliner in the old bungalow near Como Park, minutes after I left him standing alone with the dusty adoption documents in his hands. When he mourned for the little boy he had been, his tears were real.

EPILOGUE

I didn't attend Mr. Saxby's funeral. After what I discovered in the attic, I had a much better understanding of why my presence at Dolores' service, or anywhere else Dwight had long-standing relationships, had been discouraged. I was an outsider. I wondered if Dwight's discovery made him feel like an outsider too or if he had shared his story with his wife and sisters. I hoped he did, but I never asked. The last correspondence I had from him was the note he sent me, tucked inside the memorial pamphlet, after Raymond's burial. In the brief letter, Dwight apologized again and told me his father died peacefully, his inexplicable last words being "Take care of your teeth."

Raymond was laid to rest at Acacia Park Cemetery in Mendota Heights. Not quite St. Paul, but close enough. He was finally reunited with Dolores and true to his intentions, he hadn't been to another funeral since he'd walked off the grass at that very spot four years before. I hoped the deceased couple enjoyed their view of the Minnesota River, or that the river at least brought solace to those who visited the graves--the whole "river of life flows on" metaphor for those reflective enough to notice the beautiful dichotomy of the place where they stood.

Twenty-three years have gone now, and yet my time on the

periphery of the Saxby family stays prominent in my mind. It was a long time before I trusted again. Trusting men proved hard, but trusting myself was almost impossible. I had completely missed the forest for the dazzling sight of one glorious tree: a tree that had dry rot hidden beneath its smooth and handsome bark. I came to understand that my misjudgements in those days had more to do with my own inadequacies than those that Dwight suffered. Ultimately, he had reason for his; I was blinded by a simpler need--the need to give all of myself to another when Dwight only wanted a piece of what I offered. Perhaps that's what love in a relationship most often is. A give-and-take that's almost never equal...a delicate balance between the hunger and nourishment of ravenous souls. All I know is that it's hard to get it right, and in this late stage of my life, I think I have finally found my fulcrum. He gives as well as he gets.

I am back out in California now, retired as a nurse but still a care-taker. I'm giving what I can to someone in need and am hopeful that the balance will shift in my favor if my time for help from others comes calling. In the meantime, Raymond Saxby has given my irreverent family a new catch phrase. Instead of "Goodbye" or "See you later" when we leave each other's company, we offer a bit of important advice. We tell one another, "Take care of your teeth."

ACKNOWLEDGMENTS

Minnesota is my adopted home and like most converts, I am passionate about what I have chosen of my own free will. In my travels, I learned much about the region's history that only enhanced my devotion to my new state. I wrote this story as a way to capture some of what is unique about this place called Minnesota and the people here that I have come to love.

With thanks and love to Dick Beens. I actually listened to your stories about life on the farm and your mother's switch. Thanks, too, to my late cowboy papa. You taught me more about livestock than I even realized was possible to learn. You will always be my hero.

All the people in this tale are fictitious. If you think that you see yourself in this book, it's not you, only the lingering vapor of similar shadows, muted by time and imagination...

My thanks to my early readers: Dick Beens, Diane Beens, Linda Vukelich, Barbara Read, Cathy Haukedahl and Anne Hofmann. Your insight and support have been invaluable.

I couldn't have developed this work without historical references. Thanks to the Minnesota Historical Society; The Zenith City.com; City-History.us; GC Archives; The Great War Society; MNOPEDIA; and of course, Wikipedia and it's many contributors. Also thank you to

Christopher S. Clay, author of *Minnesota and St. Paul in Vintage Postcards;* Dave Page and John Koblas, *Fitzgerald in Minnesota - Toward the Summit;* Paul Maccabee, *John Dillinger Slept Here.* These works and resources were invaluable in crafting this tale of twentieth century Minnesota.

And a special thanks to Kathleen Helms, herself an author of note and my friend and publisher and to Sharman Bastl for her expertise in finding all my mistakes.

Elizabeth Garland

Made in the USA
Monee, IL
22 July 2023

39710218R00233